"YOUR G[...]

"I am priv[...]

knowledge of.[...]

The king st[...]

"You have [...]

Instantly the men of the Council stilled. Silence sat heavily among them, like a living wall.

"Your Grace?" Lord Laislac asked the unaskable.

"He told you that I have a son. The result of a youthful . . ." He fluttered his fingers in a dismissive gesture.

"A youthful indiscretion," the king continued. "My baseborn son has been raised in secret at the edge of the kingdom. I have acknowledged him to no one but his mother and her husband. He's nearly eighteen now, on the verge of manhood."

"There are ways to make such a child legitimate in the eyes of the law and the priests," Lord Jemmarc said after a long moment.

"Will the queen agree to legitimize the boy?" Lord Laislac asked.

"This requires much thought and consultation. I declare this meeting at an end." The king exited quickly without a backward glance.

THE
SILENT DRAGON

THE
SILENT DRAGON

Children of the Dragon Nimbus #1

IRENE
RADFORD

DAW BOOKS, INC.
DONALD A. WOLLHEIM, FOUNDER
375 Hudson Street, New York, NY 10014

ELIZABETH R. WOLLHEIM
SHEILA E. GILBERT
PUBLISHERS
http://www.dawbooks.com

This book is for Sara, Lizzy, Joyce, and Lea, who have browbeaten me into being a better writer and taught me the value of silence, when to use it and when to appreciate it in others.

Acknowledgments

A lot of time has passed since the last time the *Dragon Nimbus* flew across my computer screen. Since 2005, with THE DRAGON'S REVENGE, *The Stargods #3*, to be precise.

After ten books in this world, in three different time periods, I needed a break. There are only so many ways one can introduce the same dragon. I needed that time to grow as a writer and produce other books in other worlds under other pen names. The characters I left behind needed time to grow up as well. Eventually little details and ideas I left unfinished rose to the surface of the murk we call my brain, and those little details demanded to see the light of day. Once again I found myself in a land where dragons are real and magic works. Once again I greeted old friends and found new ones.

Welcome back to Coronnan and the Dragon Nimbus.

No book is created in a vacuum. I wrote the words, but I needed help in rearranging them so they make sense. Many thanks to Carol McCleary of the Wilshire Literary Agency for believing in my dragons and helping them to find a publishing home at DAW Books. Thanks also to Sheila Gilbert, the best editor in the business as far as I am concerned, for taking a chance on an unknown writer and helping her grow into an established fixture in her office. Carol has moved on to her own writing career. So I need to thank Mike Kabongo of the OnyxHawke Agency for pulling me out of the doldrums and working with dragons again. And then there are the friends and family who have helped me with beta reads, shoulders to cry on, and people to scream at when my characters go off on a tangent and refuse to follow my plot line. Theirs is always better but I need convincing sometimes.

And lastly, much love and thanks to Tim, who knows when to leave me alone and when to surgically remove me from the computer and whisk me away.

I couldn't do this without all of you. Come fly with me and share the wonders I have seen.

PROLOGUE

M Y HUMANS ARE such fragile creatures; they have little resilience against strange miasmas that invade their lands from foreign ports, miasmas that carry sickness and death. I have encouraged Jaylor, the chief of the human magicians, to take in refugees who are persecuted for having magic. But these same people carry the red miasma with them; they spread it across the land until many fall victim to throats so sore they cannot speak or swallow life-giving water and a fever that burns them from within until they are nothing but dried-out husks.

My humans call it an epidemic of putrid sore throat.

I have given as much magic as I can to the healers. It is not enough. They do not understand the nature of the pustules that erupt within the soft tissue of the throat. Then the healers fall ill, and cannot heal themselves. That is one of the failings of magic. I weep that I can do nothing more. I grieve at the deaths.

And then the golden boy falls ill, nigh unto death. My golden child, as much a dragon as a human, conceived in the void by two fathers, one magician and one royal, in the realm of dragons. He is the destiny of humans and dragons alike.

Frantically I search among the humans for a healer who will listen to me, who will understand, will work with me to cure my golden boy.

(Jaylor, Shayla here,) I prod my magician.

He awakens from a troubled slumber, snatched when exhaustion claimed him. With a jolt he sits up, flailing for balance and awareness. "Shayla?" He pauses to find the proper protocol. "Uh, Jaylor here. Why . . . what can I do for you?"

(You must send for Maisy. She is the healer who can save our boy.)

"Maisy? She's barely trained, a new journeyman on journey."

(She has the talent. I will work with her. Guide her through what needs to be done to banish this foreign miasma.)

"But . . . but she's a woman. Women cannot gather dragon magic."

I give him enough silence to let him know that that has not always been true and may change again. Soon, I hope.

(You must gather my magic while she draws strength from a ley line. Together you will succeed. You will cool the fever with a rebalance of the humors inside our boy while she roots out the core of the illness with herbs and talent unknown to you.)

I leave Jaylor to his own thoughts and plans while I summon Maisy.

"Thank you for speaking to me, Shayla," Maisy says politely as she gulps away tears. "What brings you to honor me so?"

I explain to her about the putrid sore throat and the child she must heal.

"I . . . I cannot leave Lord Jemmarc's household. He thinks me a mere servant when I'm really Jaylor's spy."

(You must leave, now. You no longer have a place with Lord Jemmarc.)

This brings more tears.

(I'm sorry that you love him and he thinks of you as merely a servant and an ease for his lustful urges.)

"I am ill with the milk fever," she protests.

(The fever has passed.)

"My baby . . ."

(Takes sustenance from another. Your son will be given to Jemmarc's lady as a substitute for the children she cannot bear. Your son will grow up not knowing you. He will have opportunities you cannot give him.) And then I grace her with a dragon-dream, a more real than real vision of the infant grown to toddler, laughing and exclaiming with joy at a new

game his other mother plays. That image fades and I reveal him struggling with letters and numbers, growing more and learning swordplay. And then I show a possible future she cannot foresee, her son sitting in the Council of Provinces, acting as their scribe, wearing the fine garments humans treasure.

"My son!" She reaches toward the void to hold those images close to her heart.

(Your son will thrive better here than with the meager resources at your disposal.)

"You're right, Mistress Dragon. I tried again and again while I carried him to reach his mind and open it to the possibilities of magic. He did not respond. So I tried again hours and then days after his birth. I fear that he is as mind-blind as his father."

(You have given your son life. All that you can give him. Now you must leave him here in safety. The miasma has not come here yet. You, and only you, can heal the golden child. You must heal him. The future of humans and dragons alike rests on his shoulders.)

"I will go. But I do not know the transport spell. It will take me weeks to walk to the University in the mountains. By then he will be dead."

(Never fear. I have the ability to guide you through the void safely. I am not allowed to do this except in dire need. The need is dire indeed.)

Maisy does indeed cure our golden boy. But even her ability and the power of Jaylor are not enough. His throat is scarred. Unless a miracle happens, one that I cannot foresee, he will be silent for the rest of his life.

My silent dragon needs another dragon to watch over him. I give the task to a youngling from my last litter: Indigo.

CHAPTER 1

SIXTEEN YEARS LATER.

A ND THEN THERE WERE NONE. *No dragons in Coron-nan. But that did not last long. They belong to this world of Kardia Hodos. They have been here longer than people. The magicians brought them back to Coronnan. All of them. Dragons fly the skies once again. But only a few, and rarely Shayla, the matriarch. The Council of Provinces has curbed their influence, their mystique. To invoke a dragon curse is to accuse someone of being untrustworthy. I helped the process under the guidance of my pretties.*

The dragons are the source of magic. Magic has robbed me of everything good and loving in my life. Magic must be eliminated, and so the dragons, all of the dragons, must die.

Too long have I waited. Coronnan has been at peace, has become complacent. Now turmoil brews. I see an opening, a chance to once more show these blind imbeciles the value of my guidance and the evil that is magic. My retainers already listen to me and root out all traces of magic. They fear the dragons. If the lords turn deaf ears to our wishes and bring a magician into the royal circle, the people will revolt. I shall lead them.

I have allies; they do not know who they truly follow. But soon, soon I shall reveal myself and my pretties.

Then the Dragon Crown and Dragon Throne will be mine. But I will not accept the symbolism of the dragon. I will not

rule by the grace of the dragons. I will rule by my own lead-
ership and the will of the people. New laws. New traditions.
A new monarch with true majesty.

Me.

Glenndon dashed ahead of his younger brother, out the side
door of the University. He paused in the courtyard to bow
respectfully to the circle of twelve paving stones, each with
the carving of a different sigil representing a different master
magician. Lukan's footsteps sounded heavily behind him.
Behind him, Master Marcus pounded his staff upon the
wooden steps of the building that was as much home to
Glenndon, Lukan, and their younger sisters as the cabin in
the clearing half a mile away.

"Come back here. Both of you!" Marcus called, pounding
his staff again.

Waves of magic rippled through the ground, tickling the
soles of Glenndon's boots, seeking him, trying to glue his
feet to the Kardia. Or at least slow him down.

Glenndon sent a magic probe into the dirt, melding with
the ground and soothing the magic that twisted it. Then he set
off again, casting aside his pale blue apprentice robes and
dropping them in Lukan's path. The younger boy stumbled
as the cloth tangled his feet.

"You won't get away with this, Glenndon," Marcus called
again. "You cannot trade chores with your brother just because he can speak and you won't."

I answer to Master Robb. Glenndon set his mental voice
at a shout. *Lukan is your apprentice.* With another burst of
speed he ducked into the sheltering shadows of the deep
mountain forest.

Please, shelter and hide me, he begged of a straggly Tambootie tree that seemed to rear up in the middle of the well-
worn path but was really only a vision of a rare tree that hid
deep in the towering forest.

A sense of acceptance, and possibly humor, enfolded him.

"Glenndon?" Lukan called from the University grounds.
"Where are you? I can't find you!"

Sorry, Lukan. We've been through all this before. I'm sick of it. Poor Lukan was an adequate apprentice magician. But he'd never have Glenndon's strength and imagination.

The masters recognized both their limitations and gave them tests and assignments to give Lukan power and force Glenndon to speak. Neither of them had any objection to trading those assignments.

So, once again, Glenndon fled the ire of the master magicians, leaving Lukan to face them and take his punishment. Glenndon would face his own reprimands later, when he'd had time to ease his frustrations and think up a way out.

He veered off the main path toward home and sought his favorite spot overlooking a gentle pool at the base of a small waterfall. He ripped off his confining boots that he only wore with his formal robes and dangled his feet in the warm water.

Hot springs made pockets of the glacial runoff warm enough for bathing, or just easing tired feet. Farther downstream a larger fall created a pool deep enough for swimming. But this small catch basin was his favorite for just thinking.

Sun had warmed the flattened boulder he sat upon. He shook his head to loosen his blond queue and leaned back, braced on his arms, staring at the interwoven canopy of leaves and branches.

A tingling thrill coursed through his blood. Magic! That elusive Tambootie tree grew nearby. They were becoming increasingly rare in the areas touched by humans. But here, deep in the mountain forest, some of the trees flourished. He searched for the telltale fat green leaves with pink veins. The taller and more common everblue trees blocked his view. But he felt the Tambootie. He knew one was nearby, almost singing to him.

But in all the years he'd been coming to this glade, he'd never found it.

He blanked his mind in the first stage of meditation, aided by the surge of magic from the Tambootie. Soon he'd be old enough and skilled enough for a journeyman magician's staff. Soon. If his Da ever agreed that he had mastered all of the tasks set before him. Mastered them better than his classmates who had already been promoted.

But he was Glenndon, first son of Jaylor, Senior Magician

and Chancellor of the University of Magicians. The Circle expected more of him than of the others.

Some days he hated being the son of such a powerful man, a man of duty and honor and responsibility who never relaxed his vigilance. Ever. And everyone expected Glenndon to be just like him. Without a journeyman's staff to aid his magic.

Not today, he thought. *Today I am just me, in need of a rest, in a place away from all the overanxious minds that batter at my mental walls.*

For a few moments he basked in the spring sunshine with a light breeze playing across his face. Afterimages of tall everblue trees, their spiky, blue-green needles clustered in tufts at the ends of the branches, swayed gently across his closed eyelids. He imagined white, puffy clouds drifting across the sky. One of them obscured the sun. Shadow bathed his eyelids.

His eyes flew open as he prepared to defend his momentary idleness to an irate master magician.

Or his busy mother. She understood his inability to throw words past the blockage in his throat; she comforted him when he tried to speak and failed. But she also insisted he fulfill his duties as an apprentice magician.

Shimmering light wavered in front of him, gradually coalescing into the outline of a crystal furred dragon with deep, dark blue tipping his wing veins and spinal horns marching from forehead to tail.

In this strong sunlight those veins and tips showed a hint of a purple undertone. But Indigo was a blue-tip dragon, not a rare purple-tip.

Indigo, he greeted the adolescent dragon with relief. *Glenndon here,* he added, maintaining dragon protocol.

(Indigo here,) the dragon replied. Then he plopped into the pool, sending a shock wave sloshing both banks, splashing Glenndon above his knees and dampening the boulder beneath his seat. Adolescent the dragon might be, but he was still as big as a sledge steed—the really big ones that hauled heavy trade goods around the country.

You are as clumsy as a newborn dragonet even if your fur

has grown more silvery. I can see patches of clear crystal on your wings.

Indigo preened, spreading his wings. Light shone through the translucent membranes, revealing the colored veins that gave him his name. He looked bigger and more translucent than the last time they'd met. But thinner too. Glenndon could almost count the dragon's ribs, and his horns looked dull, both in sharpness and in color.

What brings you down from the mountaintop, my friend? (I am troubled.)

Glenndon didn't know how to answer, so he gave the dragon silence in which to gather his thoughts. Or his courage.

(My three siblings do not thrive. They cry with hunger every night even though they eat plenty of fresh game. I am hungry all of the time. Our fathers hunt most efficiently to feed the nimbus.) He hung his head, slurping up some of the sulfurous water, seemingly liking the volcanic taint from the hot springs better than clean spring water.

(I feel as if half of me is missing. I think I may have had a twin, lost at birth like so many others. And yet I am not a purple-tip, and only purple-tips are born twins.)

Dragon lore insisted that there could only be one purple-tip at any time. They were always born twins. So before the second birthday, one of the two had to become . . . something else.

What do you need? What can I do to help? Glenndon asked, sitting up straighter. This was dire news. And what was that about three siblings only and none of them Indigo's twin? He thought he remembered Shayla, the matriarch of the nimbus, had produced a full twelve dragonets in her last litter. But sadly no special twin purple-tips.

And when had that litter been born? When Glenndon was still a baby. Apparently she hadn't mated since.

Unusual.

(My sire, Baamin, the bluest of blue-tips, tells me that there is no longer enough of the Tambootie to feed all of the dragons. Without the Tambootie we cannot produce magic. Without the Tambootie we die. I die.)

I won't let that happen! Glenndon scrambled to his feet, ready to bound off in any direction. Not any direction. To the east. The Tambootie tree that sang to him grew over there, on the far side of the pool and . . . and a quarter league away. He just had to search tree by tree to find it.

Indigo slurped more liquid, as if trying to fill an empty belly with . . . something, anything.

(I do not know. I do not know why the Tambootie withers before it becomes big enough to feed dragonkind.) Dragons cropped the tops of new growth as they flew.

I'll find you a tree right now, if I have to chop down half the forest to find it, so that you can sate your hunger. Then I must study this. Surely the University library contains texts . . .

(Perhaps. But this is arcane knowledge, the province of dragons, not of humans. Not many learned men have written about the way dragons, the Tambootie, and ley lines are linked.)

My Da will know. Glenndon tromped across the shallow pool and searched for a game trail through the thick under-brush.

This time Indigo answered with silence, giving Glenndon time to gather his thoughts and organize them.

Da has read much. But if not many have written about this, then perhaps the text is among the lost—the library left behind in Coronnan City, or burned during one of the purges.

(Perhaps.)

If the knowledge is written anywhere, I will find it. I will do what I can to help you, my friend. You and all of the drag-ons. Perhaps if he found the answer, the Circle would find him worthy of promotion. At the age of seventeen, nearly eighteen, he should have advanced to journeyman status a year ago. At least. *There's a tree this way.* Glenndon pointed with a finger guided by his senses. *I'll find it, and then you can fly over and grab some leaves. Or should I gather some and bring them back here?*

(Here, please. I have looked for that tree, but it has not breached the canopy for easy feeding. That is why I came to you with my troubles, though the elders say that mere hu-

mans cannot help dragonkind. If there is an answer, you, Glenndon, will find it. I trust you.)

I hope I am worthy of your trust. He'd start by talking to his Da.

(You are my friend. That is enough.)

Is it?

CHAPTER 2

"THERE, BAAMIN, THERE!" Senior Magician Jaylor screamed to the blue-tipped dragon he rode. The wind tore his words away.

He had no doubt that Baamin heard his mind, if not his words. They'd worked together a long time.

The huge beast beneath him tilted to his left, his transparent wings, veined with vivid magician blue, flapped once to guide their turn. They sped to the broad river valley deep within the craggy foothills that dropped to the sea on their right.

A blacker-than-black smudge along the silvery streak of the riverbed looked like a shadow, something to be dismissed as natural at this distance. But this shadow did not belong in the spreading fields of newly sprouted grain.

"S'murghit, that's three in the last year," Jaylor muttered with mind and voice. "Not a random egg hatched on the wrong continent. We've got to find the nest."

(Or the one who nurtures each egg with blood,) Baamin replied.

The dragon circled the rim of the valley until the sun was at their back. Then he tucked his wings and dove straight at the smudge.

Quickly, too quickly, details of the valley sprang into view. Jaylor saw narrow tracks running from a cluster of simple thatched houses to the river. Stone walls bordered the track and each field. He saw figures hastening along those field separators with spades and hoes and scythes. Useless against the black menace. Cries of distress rose faintly, almost drowned out by the wind of their rapid descent. Almost. Not quite.

Anger. Pain. Fear slammed into Jaylor stronger than the words.

He clutched Baamin's spinal horns with both hands to keep the ocean of emotions from dislodging him.

The black smudge took on form and dimension: long and undulating. Blacker than midnight on a moonless night. To be visible from one hundred feet up, it had to be huge, ten feet long and as thick as one of Jaylor's thighs.

A creature out of ancient legends. And nightmares.

"It doesn't have wings, thank the Stargods. It's male and juvenile," he muttered. If a winged matriarch wreaked havoc this close to the Great Bay, they'd have a full infestation of the monsters, not random juveniles.

"This was Krej's old province. Do you suppose he left a nest as a weapon for him to use later?"

(Too many years have passed. The eggs can go dormant in extreme cold for a time and still hatch when revived. Not fifteen years in a warm and wet land.)

"Someone new nurturing the eggs?"

Baamin didn't answer the obvious.

The snake continued to push mounds of dirt into the river, oblivious to the danger from above. It used its massive head and coils to gather loose soil from the fields, uprooting crops and rocks along the way; damming the river with more and more precious soil.

It responded only to its instincts to stop the flow of water, divert it by the shortest route into the sea, leaving the land dry and sere behind.

At fifty feet up Baamin opened his jaws and loosed a thin stream of fire, directed at the snake. Too weak a flame. Not enough Tambootie in the dragon's system. The fire singed a straight line across the massive head.

The creature reared high, red eyes blinking in surprise. Then it narrowed its focus and bared fangs as long as Jaylor's arm. From twenty-five feet away he spotted the glisten of venom on those fangs.

Fighting his own dread and the incessant pull of the land, Jaylor fumbled to open the leather sack slung upon the spinal horn in front of him. Blindly he pulled forth a single spear-head made of rare obsidian. His last one, and there would be no more until Rovers brought more volcanic glass out of Hanassa. Dragons could only guess when that would be. A spell forged in dragon fire sharpened the points to slice through magical shields as well as flesh.

He affixed the precious tip to a spear and pulled it free of its loop on the sack strap.

He had time for one deep breath to access his store of dragon magic and send it along his arm and fingers. With a thrust from strong back and shoulder muscles the spear sped on an arrow-straight and magic-true path directly into the snake's spine at the base of the skull.

The snake flinched, then rippled once, flipping the spear out of its thick hide. It abandoned its work and turned to face the dragon and the magician. Its tail slapped the first of the villagers across the chest and sent him flying into the crowd of his fellows behind him. The ox-shoulder spade the man carried spun away, digging a deep furrow in the grain as it slid along the ground.

Baamin loosed another trickle of flame. Not enough to damage a damp twig.

Jaylor didn't have time to wonder at the weakness in Baamin's primary weapon. He found four throwing stars and sent them flying toward the snake's eyes. Three went wide. The fourth cut through the magic bubble surrounding the beast that the spear tip had weakened and embedded itself deep in the left eye. A spurt of black blood shot forth. The green land withered and turned brown wherever it touched.

An unworldly screech nearly split Jaylor's eardrums.

The villagers dropped to their knees, abandoning their tools to cover their ears with their hands.

Baamin dug his hind claws deeply into the ground as he landed, running toward the snake and spreading his wings to slow his momentum.

The snake responded with a lightning fast strike to the dragon's chest. Immediately the translucent skin and crystal-clear fur darkened.

"Baamin!" Jaylor screamed.

(Surface burn only. He cannot damage me,) the dragon replied as he continued running over and past the enemy.

Jaylor swung his leg over the top of the spinal horn that held him in place and slid to the ground before the dragon came to a full halt. He dragged the sack with him. Before he'd cleared the wide wing he'd grabbed three knives, exquisitely balanced for throwing.

The snake undulated toward him, hissing and glaring with every coil and lunge. Its screeches ran up the scale almost beyond human hearing.

No time to protect his ears. Jaylor had to bring down the beast. He held the first knife by its tip in his right hand, narrowed his vision to the vulnerable open mouth, and let the blade fly.

It spun through the air and collided with the fangs, bouncing away harmlessly. The second knife sunk uselessly into body flesh.

The villagers sprang forward with tools held high. A young man, probably in his twenties, slashed at the snake's back with his scythe. An older man with a thick gray queue pounded at the tail with a hoe as if digging weeds out of it. A third man, no older than Jaylor's oldest son Glenndon, hacked with a rare metal spade at the center of a coil that undulated away from the other attacks.

Jaylor's third knife flew true, sliding between the fangs, deep into the open mouth.

Venom sprayed indiscriminately as the blade pierced the poison sack in the roof of the mouth. A few more ripples and the snake collapsed. Its black skin shriveled and the muscles fell slack.

As one, the villagers descended upon the carcass with renewed vigor, reducing the massive creature to bloody pulp.

Jaylor sagged, bracing his hands against his knees. He dragged in huge gulps of air. His heartbeat sounded loud and too rapid to his own ears. His neck pulse felt as if it would break through his bearded skin.

(I remember a time when you could throw spells for half a day without resting,) Baamin reminded him, sounding intensely weary himself.

"Neither of us is as young as we once were."

(Nor as full of vigor. I shall need to rest before we fly home.)

"Sounds good to me." Jaylor forced himself upright and stumbled over to the snake head. The dead and glazed red eye still seemed to stare at him accusingly. Jaylor stared back, and struggled to retrieve the spear tip where it was stuck between two scales. The obsidian was too precious to leave behind.

The older man with the thick gray queue—a normal three-strand braid held in place with a leather thong, unlike the four strands Jaylor wore as a symbol of his seniority in the Circle of Master Magicians—stopped taking slices out of the snake carcass and approached Jaylor and the dragon, bloody hoe still in hand. "And who might be you," he asked on a surly snarl.

"Jaylor, Senior Magician and Chancellor of the University of Magicians," he replied, straightening up. "This is Baamin, mate to Shayla, the matriarch of the dragon nimbus.

The villager looked him up and down, taking in the stained and worn blue leather traveling trews and magician blue linen shirt with disdain. "Don't look so grand," he spat.

Baamin reared up, spreading his magnificent wings. The blue in his wing veins and horns pulsed with outrage and thick smoke leaked from the sides of his mouth.

Jaylor decided to ignore the man's attitude. "Don't eat the meat of that beast. It's poison," he said matter-of-factly.

"You going to order your flying steed to help clear the river for us?"

"That is not the job of a dragon."

"Then what good is it? Just another ravening beast, like the snake." The villager turned away, hacking at the churned soil with his bloody hoe.

"Excuse me, that snake was a Krakatrice! A dragon, a mature dragon is the only thing that can take one on and hope to win. Just be glad the Krakatrice was a juvenile. In another year, it would be twice as big and three times more deadly," Jaylor fought to keep his words from growing into an angry shout.

"Good thing we killed it now instead of later. Now take

that bloody big beast away before it digs up any more of our crops."

I awake in a cold sweat, thrashing against the confines of the sheet wrapped around me . . . or is that the straw in the box for my lovely that is so confining. She feeds upon my blood and I feed upon her dreams.

One of her consorts is dead, murdered by a magician and a dragon. Our hatred of both increases. Without consorts she will never mature into the graceful matriarch she is destined to become.

But the dream is more to me. I saw not the death of a Krakatrice. I relived the moment my mother rejected me and my lovely. She ordered . . . ordered! . . . her retainers to kill my beloved. In rejecting my lovely pet she rejected me. Her love is false. Her lessons of tolerance toward magic and respect for all people—noble and peasant, magician and mindblind—are false. That was the day I arranged for my father to send her away in disgrace. But he claims he loves her, he needs time to make that decision.

We have made our decision, my lovely and I. We know that my father's wife must go. She must be disgraced.

That was the day I learned she was not my true mother, that I am baseborn of a fleeting union between my father and a servant. That mother abandoned me as well. I have only my father. He adopted me because his lady could have no children of her own. He is the only one who understands my need for the pretty pet. He is the only one who understands that when he legitimized me and took me to the capital city for the ceremony, my pet had to come with me.

In the city we find more eggs that will hatch and become consorts for her when she matures and sprouts her six batwings.

Then she and I will take revenge upon all magicians and their supporters. We will rule this land together, without interference from a weak and indecisive council. My father will be allowed to give us advice. No one else.

CHAPTER 3

"YOU DO NOT WANT to be late to this Council meeting, Your Grace," Fred, King Darville's bodyguard, said as he poked his head into the royal office.

"Yes, yes. A moment more. I need to dispatch this letter . . ." Darville signed the document with a flourish, folded it, and lifted a candle to drip wax for a seal.

"Your Grace, the twelve lords of the Council of Provinces gathered half an hour ago," Fred reminded him.

Darville sighed as he pressed the great seal into the puddle of wax. "Fine, fine. Will you take this to the courier waiting by the river gate?" He held the paper out to his longtime friend. Fred had been with him for almost twenty years. Since before his marriage. They'd fought rebelling lords, rogue magicians, and invading armies together. They had few secrets.

"Her Majesty Queen Miranda of SeLennica?" Fred raised his eyebrows. "Shouldn't this go to her ambassador?"

"Not this time." Darville didn't want to explain. The entire court would know soon enough that Coronnan's neighboring queen had asked his advice and negotiation in a betrothal between her daughter, the Princess Jaranda, and the heir to the crown of Rossemeyer—Darville's nephew by marriage.

There were only a few royal children in the newest generation who could be used as pawns in the ever-changing game of alliances and trade agreements. Many of them were too closely related by blood to marry and beget children together.

"I'll see you safely in the Council Chamber, then I will deliver this," Fred said. He turned the letter over and over, examining the seal for imperfections.

"No need. I'm safe enough in my own palace." Darville gulped the last of the beta arrack in his cup. Dregs of the barrel. He nearly spat it out, but the alcohol warmed his gut nicely. He could face the lords now . . . maybe one more cup. He reached for the decanter and found it empty.

Oh, well. He'd manage.

"The Council Chamber is on the way to the river gate."

Darville grabbed the magic-imbued glass Dragon Crown from its mount beside his desk. The Coraurlia, forged by dragon fire, designed by master magicians, twinkled in the light filtering through arrow-slit windows, sending many-hued swirls twining throughout the glass. He frowned at the heavy symbol of his authority. His head ached just thinking about placing it on his brow. He hadn't had enough to drink to dull that pain.

Fred frowned at the empty cup as deeply as Darville frowned at the crown.

He lifted it into place and felt a slight jolt of energy flow through the top of his head to the back of his eyes, a not-so-subtle reminder of the protection against magical attack that the crown gave him.

Then he buckled on his dress sword and hastened out the door, Fred close upon his heels.

A broad stone staircase led downward from the center of the landing outside his door. A narrower set of steps continued upward to the family apartments along the far wall.

The angle of the sun peeking through the narrow, eye-height windows told him that noon approached, rapidly. He was more than late. In nearly twenty years of ruling Coronnan, Darville had never missed a Council meeting. Today, if he was lucky, the twelve lords would still be there, waiting for him.

He stepped lightly down the middle of the worn staircase, not bothering with the railing on either side. Almost running, he felt as if he flew a-dragonback, the wind of his passage tugging at his queue beneath the crown.

"Your Grace, slow down," Fred panted, several steps behind the king. "I'm not as young as I used to be."

"We're the same age!" Darville called back, not slowing in the least.

"My point exactly."

Darville's light indoor shoes hit each new step firmly. Five steps, ten more to go. Six, seven . . .

His soft-soled shoe hit something slimy and slid forward. Darville flailed for balance, throwing himself sideways to grab at the banister. His other foot lost its grip.

No traction. No heft to his shoes to break through the slime.

Years of training in the arts of war had kept him fit, with an unusually acute sense of balance. He twisted so that his left knee took the brunt of his fall.

The slime on the step was deep. His long legs spread in an ungainly split, throwing his balance backward.

His head hit the step above him with an audible crack.

Pain shot from his nape, straight through to his eyes.

The Coraurlia bounced down the remaining steps, thumping loudly in the sudden stillness.

Blindingly white stars flashed before his eyes as darkness crowded him from the sides.

"Your Grace!" Fred crouched beside him, cradling his throbbing head in callused hands.

"I'll live," the king grunted. He rubbed the sore spot on the back of his head. A lump rose rapidly beneath his fingers.

"Um, Fred, don't tell the queen."

"Not worth my hide to *not* tell her. She'll find out, she always does, and then rip us both to shreds with her tongue." Already he examined the stairs with both eyes and fingers.

"I'll tell her, so she'll leave you alone. Later."

Fred raised his eyebrows at that. Or was he questioning something he'd found on the stairs. He lifted his fingertips to his nose. "Stale fruit. Amazon oil. Careless of a servant to spill some and not clean it up properly."

"Palace servants are too well trained to leave a spill. All

of them have been with my family for generations." The king sat up gingerly, noting that his ribs felt bruised but not broken. He kicked his knee straight, banishing the worst of the kink. He spotted the slick tread beside his right shoulder quite easily from this perspective.

If he hadn't been in such a damned hurry . . .

"Was someone counting on you running down these stairs, not watching where you put your big feet?" Fred asked with the familiarity of someone who'd served his king for a very long time.

"I think we need to find that out. Looks to me like the spill is even all across the stair, not an unintended slop from a serving tray. And who would be carrying Amazon oil into the family wing? It's edible but not very tasty. We use it for keeping our swords rust-free, not dressing fresh greens." He rubbed his brow, trying to hide the trembling in his hands and the fear he knew must show through his eyes.

"Other uses for it, Your Grace. But not many in this part of the palace that is dominated by your wife and daughters." Fred sounded as shaky as Darville felt.

"Investigate, Fred. You're good at that. We need to know who plays dangerous games that could easily mean my broken neck. I've got to get to the meeting." Slowly, he eased upward, using the banister to hold him. He glared at the dangerous tread wondering, figuring the timing, after servants came up and down, before his wife and daughters came down for the day. Still thinking, still wondering who had the knowledge of when to stage this "accident," he stretched cautiously, assessing a wealth of bruises.

By the time Darville and Fred stood beside each other at the bottom, the king knew he could move without betraying injury. He glared down at the Coraurlia where it had landed a-tilt against the bottom stair.

Fred bent to pick it up. Darville stayed his action with a hand on his arm. "It will burn anyone not blessed by the dragons to wear the damn thing." Fred should know that.

Fred nodded. "Your Grace, I merely though to save you the discomfort of bending over." His face flushed.

"Thank you, my friend. But this is something only I can do." Leaning heavily on Fred's shoulder, Darville bent his knees to retrieve his crown, careful not to dip his head. He felt as if it might fall off. *Stargods!* He needed a drink.

Then he stood staring at the crown in his hands. He thought about the growing knot on the back of his head. "Um . . . maybe I'll just carry it today."

"Are you certain, Your Grace? The symbolism . . ."

"The symbolism be damned. My head hurts. And . . . and I think someone just tried to kill me."

CHAPTER 4

PRINCESS ROSSELINDA DE DRACONIS slipped into her place between her two ladies-in-waiting (last month they'd been girls, now promoted to adulthood because of a royal birthday) in the dark alcove behind the Council Chamber. "Am I late?" she whispered to Miri and Chastet.

"Yes. But so is the king," Miri giggled softly, eye pressed to the tiny peephole.

"Listen," Chastet ordered.

All three girls grew silent, straining their ears toward the thin wooden wall between them and the very private chamber on the other side.

"Your Grace, we of the Council of Provinces insist that your oldest daughter marry without delay and beget a son and heir to the kingdom," Lord Andrall said in his weary voice. "Unlike the dragons who grace you, you are *not* immortal."

Rosselinda, Princess Royale of Coronnan choked on her quick inhale.

"Easy, Highness." Lady Miri, daughter to Lord Bennallt of the incredibly wealthy port city of Baria, pounded Linda's back with enthusiasm.

"Hush, they'll hear us," Lady Chastet admonished them both as she pressed her ear closer to the secret panel. Her father, Floodhenst, held the western province of Fleece, large and open and home to more sheep than people.

"How did my P'pa take that?" Linda asked, trying to peer

over Miri's shoulder and through the tiny spyhole. All she caught was a pinprick of colored light from the sun glowing through the stained-glass windows of the chamber. So much lovely and precious glass wasted on dusty old men who had nothing better to do than sit around and argue.

"My lords, do I need to remind you that Princess Rosselinda is only fourteen," King Darville ground through his teeth.

Old enough to have ladies-in-waiting and to put up my hair with jeweled combs, Linda thought. *But marriage?*

Yuck. All the boys she knew at court were pimple-faced, smelly creatures who thought only about their steeds and arms practice. She could outride and trounce most of them quite soundly in sword practice. The older courtiers were just that. Old. Almost as dusty as their even-older fathers who pushed for a marriage.

Ah, that was it: each of the nobles wanted his own son to become Linda's husband so he could rule through her.

But P'pa was still young and healthy, hardly a gray hair peeked through his blond queue. He'd rule a long time before he passed the Dragon Crown to an heir.

Unless . . .

Linda choked again.

"Let me see!" She pushed Miri aside, making Chastet take two steps back, and took possession of the spyhole. Now she could see the Council Chamber in its full glory.

Early spring sunlight glinted through the costly stained glass windows. Brilliant patches of red, green, gold, and blue sparkled against the polished black glass tabletop, making it look as if it glowed from within. All of the lords sat well back from the table, as if afraid the light might infect them with magic. Or draw them too close to their king. Their very angry king.

Linda knew from the set of his shoulders how stiffly he held himself. Rigid control. He'd drilled that into her often enough. A monarch *never* had the luxury of losing his, or her, temper.

But why couldn't she see the Coraurlia above and the high back of his demi-throne? Sitting so straight and stiff, she should be able to see almost the entire circle of precious glass.

Ah, it sat on the table by his right hand. Unusual, but understandable. She'd lifted the crown once last year and knew it weighed more than a bolt of thick brocade.

The fact that he'd touched none of the beta arrack, a very strong liquor from her mother's homeland, in the golden goblet by his right hand told her more. He would not allow the liquor to befuddle his brain or numb his reaction time in such a volatile situation.

Vacantly he rubbed the back of his head, disrupting his queue. Then he reached for the golden cup, hesitated, and withdrew his hand. Something more than a disturbing meeting was going on here.

All the other lords drank wine or ale to quench the thirst of loud arguments.

"I bet none of the lords would consider betrothals for their daughters at our age, let alone marriage and children," Miri whispered. Her own father sat across the table from the king. His face flushed red, but not from the glass reflections.

"I will not consider a marriage for Rosselinda yet," the king continued. Each word came out precise and clipped.

"Not even if we agreed to allow master magicians into the Council again as neutral advisers?" Lord Jemmarc of Saria, Lord Krej's old province, asked. He'd inherited from the exiled cousin of the royal family because his blood connection was distant, without a trace of magic in his heritage. His light baritone cut through the background noise of formal brocade robes rustling with unease.

"Magic?" Linda mouthed to her companions. "Let magic return to Coronnan?" For with magic came dragons—the source of magic.

Her heart lightened at the thought. As Princess Royale she had a right to visit the dragons, if they became legal again.

"Just last month Jemmarc had a girl stoned to death because she *might* have inherited the *sight* from her grandmother," Miri said so softly Linda had to strain to hear her. "I knew her. She brought eggs to our townhouse kitchen every morning." She bit the insides of her cheeks to disguise her trembling chin.

Linda reached out and held her friend's hand.

"As much as I wish magic and magicians to be restored to

places of honor in Coronnan, I will not compromise when it concerns my daughters," P'pa insisted, loud enough for M'ma to hear on the other side of the palace, up two stories with three courtyards between them.

Good. Linda didn't want to think about marriage and babies and stuff. She wanted to have fun, enjoy being a princess with new gowns and hair jewels and freedom from her governess and the schoolroom.

"A betrothal perhaps?" offered Lord Laislac, the voice of reason and compromise. There was scandal in his past, Linda didn't know what, only that he trod carefully and neutrally through Council meetings. His stiff brown braid never dared allow a single strand to escape containment.

Unlike the king, who shifted position just enough to show Linda that almost as much of his fine blond hair hung loose as remained restrained.

"If we could show the people a promise of a future king 'twould calm some of the unrest due to the out-of-cycle drought." Laislac tapped his fingers against the table in an uneven rhythm that set Linda's teeth on edge. "Saria is already too parched for spring planting, despite its constant sea breeze."

Linda let that last slide past her consciousness. She had more immediate things to think about. A betrothal might be all right. She could flirt with her betrothed, maybe kiss him. But after a time, if she didn't like him she'd find a way to get rid of him. M'ma knew lots of tricks for bringing people in and out of favor at court.

But what was that about unrest? She'd heard nothing. Maybe it was time for a trip to Market Isle to listen in on local gossip.

"The people be damned," P'pa exploded. "'Tis you, the lords, who sit uneasily. We have stores if the crops should fail. We prepare for droughts in cycle or out of them." He half rose from his demi-throne, the remains of his queue swinging wildly from the agitated movement, and pointed to each of the twelve men in turn. "Should I die without a male heir, each and every one of you has a claim to the throne. Do I need to remind you that the original covenant with the dragons and among the lords set up the Council with the king as first among equals? Each and every one of you would plunge us into civil war for the right to wear my heavy crown. *A magical glass crown that will burn to ashes anyone who tries to wear it without the dragons' blessing.*"

Um . . . Linda had held the crown in both her hands and other than an odd tingling had felt no heat. Did that mean . . . ?

King Darville sat back so that the carvings on the throne blocked Linda's view. She wished she could see his face, understand what he was thinking as well as what he said. She had to depend upon her interpretation of how his shoulders slumped slightly and he held his head forward. Right now that was a lot.

"Will any of you take a chance that you can win the throne before our enemies invade while we are vulnerable? Is the opportunity to sit on the Dragon Throne and wear the Dragon Crown worth losing the entire country to a foreign prince?"

"We'd have to go to the Big Continent to find an eligible *foreign* prince who isn't related by blood to the princess," Lord Andrall reminded them. "We trade with the continent, but we know little of them or their culture. We know only their ports. Our ambassadors rarely deal with kings and princes, only with generals and port officials. We don't even know if they have any princes of marriageable age, or if he'd bring an invasion army with him."

That idea boggled Linda's mind. Coronnan had been at peace for as long as she knew. Her life centered on the minor conflicts of prestige at court. But P'pa had made her read accounts of battles and journals of drought years and such.

Some of the words came back to haunt her. "No food for three days now."

"No rain in six moons. Livestock suffering terribly."

"Bitter cold. Lost five toes to frostbite."

"Sickness in the camp and the next three villages. Eight men died overnight of the fever."

"Perhaps you'd rather sit beside the throne as regent for a young princess waiting to marry," P'pa snarled. His anger drew Linda out of her haunted reverie. "Will one of you put aside your wife in order to marry Rosselinda? A child for dragons' sake!"

The king spun his crown on the black glass table with one finger. The crown had been a gift from the dragons three hundred years ago as symbol of unity, compromise, and the covenant between human and dragonkind. "If any of you have the will to take the crown from me, there it is. Who among you has the courage to wear the crown that links your mind permanently to the nimbus of dragons? Who among you will face the wrath of the dragons if you kill me?" He thrust back his throne and stood straight and tall. He caught the gaze of each man in turn. They all looked away before he did.

Only when satisfied that no man dared challenge him—yet—he picked up the heavy Dragon Crown and tucked it under his arm. Briefly he turned toward the panels and draperies behind him and winked at Linda. Then he stalked out of the Council Chamber.

"Your Grace," Lord Andrall said quietly. "As husband to your Aunt, I am privy to pieces of information the others have no knowledge of."

The king stopped, without changing his posture. He did not turn around.

Linda leaned closer trying desperately to see what could make her father change his mind. About anything.

"You have a son," Lord Andrall said quietly.

Instantly the men stilled. Silence sat heavily among them, like a living wall.

"A son? I have a brother? Why didn't I know about this?" Linda asked no one in particular, not bothering to hush her tones. Her middle grew cold and her breaths grew heavy, short, painful.

"Your Grace?" Lord Laislac asked the unaskable.

"He told you that I have a son. The result of a youthful . . ." He fluttered his fingers in a dismissive gesture.

But Linda saw a softening in his shoulders.

"A youthful indiscretion," P'pa continued. "My baseborn son has been raised in secret at the edge of the kingdom. I have acknowledged him to no one but his mother and her husband. He's nearly eighteen now, on the verge of manhood."

Linda groaned. *How could you, P'pa?*

"There are ways to make such a child legitimate in the eyes of the law and the priests," Lord Jemmarc said after a long moment. "I have gone through the rituals for my own son," Lord Jemmarc looked at his hands.

"Will the queen agree to legitimize the boy?" Lord Laislac asked.

"My wife accepted Lucjemm without hesitation when she proved infertile," Jemmarc said. "But the queen?"

Linda remembered Jemmarc's scandal three years ago; various court factions rallied around him, while others sought to shun him in support of his wife. Lady Lucinda had accepted the boy into her household as an infant. The only mother he'd known. The formal acceptance of him as heir had to wait until he was old enough to accept it with his own oath, not his father's.

What was the boy's name? Linda had danced with him two weeks ago at her Coming of Age party. She knew she must have matched blades with him, and a dozen others, in the arena, but his name eluded her, unimportant until now. She hadn't registered what Jemmarc called him. The boy didn't smell too bad, didn't trip over his own feet. She vaguely remembered that he'd fought her to a draw in their last sword match. And he had a magnificent black gelding with a smooth gait and nimble intelligence.

"This requires much thought and consultation. I declare this meeting at an end." P'pa exited quickly without turning to wink at Linda.

CHAPTER 5

DARVILLE ASSUMED a wary stance, broadsword held in both hands *en garde*. He blinked against the bright afternoon sun, wishing his head would stop hurting. A good long bout in the training arena outside the household guard barracks had always banished his hurts and settled his mood.

So far he'd sent three opponents sprawling in the sawdust or staggering against the split rail fence that separated the field from the courtyard, and anger still boiled in his gut. Now he faced his fourth and most challenging adversary.

He watched his opponent's eyes between the slats of his practice helm, only peripherally aware of the stiffness in his shoulders and shifting of feet to ease his bruised knee within the many layers of quilted padding.

If only his eyes would focus as sharply as they did twenty years ago. Or even five years ago . . .

There, a flick of a glance to the left. General Marcelle betrayed himself every time. Had for years, since Darville had first learned to control his blade. The king slashed left, right, left in a quick barrage of blows. General Marcelle retreated, barely parrying the attack.

Then, just when Darville lunged to come beneath the general's guard, his opponent caught his blade with his own and slid forward until the guards engaged and tangled.

"Slow down, Your Grace. You haven't let your temper rule your blade since my father taught us this trick when we were twelve," the general whispered when they stood helm to helm.

"My apologies, Marcelle." Darville disengaged and took three steps back before settling into his guarded stance once more.

Before Darville could assess his opponent's next move, the general bore down on him in a flurry of blows. The king parried and countered move for move. Marcelle kept coming. Darville's temper lost its grip on his mind in the face of defending himself or losing all honor in front of seasoned warriors. *His* seasoned warriors.

Then he saw the opening. Marcelle allowed his strength to overcome his control. He raised his sword for a crushing blow toward Darville's shoulder. Darville parried with renewed vigor and lunged.

His attack fell short.

Instead of a strike with the tip of his blade against Marcelle's chest, a ragged half blade stopped short of his target.

He stared at the blade, broken in half. Where was the other half?

Around him, he sensed the absolute stillness of the watchers, and of Marcelle. Something had gone terribly wrong.

Suddenly Marcelle raised his sword in salute, raised his helm and bowed deeply from the waist.

Darville straightened, raising his own helm. "*S'murghit,* what just happened?" he yelled at one and all.

Two accidents in the same day. He was having trouble convincing himself they were accidents.

"Something weakened your blade, your Grace. We will attend to it." Marcelle bowed again and took one step backward.

Not an accident. Tempered steel did not "weaken" on its own.

"I thought I'd find you here," Queen Rossemikka said from behind him. A hint of laughter colored her voice.

Slowly, Darville turned, fully aware of his sweaty body and gritty face, strands of loose hair plastered across his brow. He cast aside his broken sword, making sure it landed near his squire's feet. "Your Grace," Darville said formally, bowing. When he stood straight again, he let her smile fill his world. He responded in kind, despite the ringing anvil inside his bruised head.

"We must talk," she said simply, with less delight, brushing his face free of wayward strands of hair.

Darville looked around. All of his men had retreated a nominal step or two to grant them an illusion of privacy. An illusion only.

"What brings you out of doors, so far from your sick bed?" he asked quietly, noting how the sun glistened in her red/brown/gold hair, but not as vibrantly as it had in their youth.

"I have spent far too many weeks of my life recovering in that bed. I need fresh air, sunshine, glimpses of life instead of constant reminders of all that we have lost," she replied grimly. Her eyes strayed to the sword lying on the ground, the ragged break as dangerous as the sharpened edged or piercing point.

Darville pursed his lips. A good sword, his favorite practice weapon reserved for him and him alone, should not have broken so easily. Someone had tampered with it.

He released his sudden flare of anger, nodding toward the blade so that his squire, Jensen, a good boy of thirteen, knew to stay with the blade through General Marcelle's investigation. Marcelle hurried to the boy's side and took custody. His toe nudged the stray piece in the sawdust of the practice field.

Deliberately, the king turned his frown into the smile he reserved for his queen. He raised her hand to his lips, all the while studying her face for signs of weakness. A little pale yet, far too thin, with that hesitant forward stance of guarding her belly. A gaggle of ladies stood behind her, more concerned with keeping their skirts out of the churned mud and sawdust than with the health of their queen.

"Then come, my dear. Let us sit in the rose garden a while." He stripped off the padded tunic and breeches to reveal his own simple dark clothing beneath. Divested of the outward reminders of his weapons practice, he tucked her hand in the crook of his elbow and led her back toward a postern gate in the palace walls.

With the garden and its inviting benches in sight he dismissed the trailing ladies with a wave of his hand. Only one of them paused, a protest halted on her lips.

"I shall not need you, Lady Anya," Mikka said lightly. "I am with my husband after all."

The good lady retreated with her companions.

Mikka leaned more heavily on his arm.

"You should not have challenged your strength so soon," Darville whispered, guiding her to the nearest bench and helping her sit without collapsing into a weak puddle.

"I heard about the Council's demands, and about your slip on the stairs," she said as soon as she settled with his arm behind her back. Weakly, she leaned her head against his shoulder. "Now your broken sword," she sighed heavily. "Two accidents in one day could have been a deliberate attempt to shorten your life."

"Or perhaps just a warning that I am not immortal and need to address the question of an heir." He tried to ease her worry. He worried enough for both of them.

"I wanted to be there in the Council Chamber with you, to advise you."

"I did not want to trouble you. It has only been ten days since the miscarriage."

"Linda is *my* daughter as well as yours," Mikka insisted, some vibrancy returning to her voice with the strong emotions. "I have a right to express an opinion about the eligibility of her suitors. And I knew you would not bring your troubled temper to my bedside. You always wish to spare me." She sat straighter.

"And so I let my temper control my blade and beat up my generals until I am too tired to stand, let alone yell at the idiots who pretend to guide me." Chagrin heated his face. "That was my intent until the blade broke. I have not sent it to the blacksmith for sharpening lately. No one else would have possession of the blade long enough to use heat and rapid cooling to weaken the steel. I wonder what kind of acid would eat slowly at the metal, weakening it unnoticed until the stress of my blows finally broke it. Magic?"

"No. I would have smelled magic."

"The Council Lords are truly idiots if they think these episodes will push me to agree with them. I'm too stubborn for that. It only firms my resolve to find another solution. Or stall for time."

"They are not total idiots. They have concerns about the governance of this country."

"Their concerns are misguided. I am young and healthy. And as long as I wear the Dragon Crown, I have protection."

"But you have to have that heavy crown on your head for the magic to protect you from magic. Not even the Coraurlia can protect you from mundane tricks and tampering. You do not wear it now. You have no accepted heir should an 'accident' befall you. I cannot give you the son our people think they need to keep the government and economy stable." She turned her face into his shoulder, hiding her grief.

"This latest miscarriage took a heavy toll on your health, Mikka my love. Do not speak out of grief and weakness. We can wait a little while."

"I'm not so certain. I will never carry another child and survive. Lady Anya collected some herbs at the market yesterday. I will not conceive again as long as I take them."

"Is that safe?" Darville reared back in alarm.

"According to Brevelan, my dearest friend and your first love, the herbal combination is safer than bleeding to death next time I try to carry another life within me."

"Just herbs, not magic."

"No magic necessary."

"I—I would rather risk magic than lose you, Mikka."

She smiled up at him, not bothering to hide the tears that glistened in her lustrous brown eyes. "We must send for him, Darville."

Something twisted in his gut. Humiliation, pain, he wasn't sure, only extreme gratitude that she thought of the kingdom before her own emotional needs.

"There are reasons . . ."

"Good reasons. I know. But I am more than your wife. I am your queen. I was raised to accept compromises in politics when necessary."

"My son should be more to us than a compromise." That was his Mikka, a queen before a wife and mother. He needed her stable judgment to rise above their human disappointments and his temper.

"I know. But if Brevelan and Jaylor will give him up, I will welcome him into our household, our family. His presence will give us time. Stall the assassins who seek to take you down prematurely to further their own quests for power."

"My son will give us time for Linda to grow up a bit."

"More than just a bit. I will not see her forced into a loveless marriage before she knows why she does such a thing, why it's important. Before she knows something of the world and possibly finds the love of her life. As I did."

"Ours is not a loveless marriage." He kissed her lightly on the nose, delighted anew at how much joy she had brought to his troubled life.

"It could have been. But I am glad we found each other compatible."

"More than compatible. I hope our three girls are as lucky as we."

CHAPTER 6

"WILL YOU ACCEPT ME as your escort, Highness?" A lanky, brown-haired young man with a proper court queue, about a year older than Linda, bowed before her and her ladies. His clear brown eyes sparkled with a bit of humor and more than a bit of mischief. She found herself grinning at him.

Jensen, her father's squire, hovered behind them, not at all happy to escort *girls* shopping when he could be drilling with *men* in the practice arena. But he came alert at the sudden appearance of the almost familiar young man.

"Master Lucjemm." Linda nodded her head. At last she'd found the name of Lord Jemmarc's son floating around her memory, just out of reach until she saw him and recognized his face. "If you have the patience to examine ribbons and laces in all the stalls on Market Isle . . ."

"A small price for the right to escort you, Highness. And possibly show you some of the treasures you might not notice at first look." He bowed again, not exactly graceful or practiced, but less awkward than some seasoned courtiers.

She wondered who on the Council had sent him. His father certainly. But who were his allies?

A diversion. If she found she liked him, maybe she could dangle him before the court as a potential and eligible suitor, long enough for them to forget about bringing P'pa's *bastard* to the palace as the heir.

She should be the heir, *S'murghit!*

Linda looked to Miri and Chastet for agreement. They hid giggles and rolled eyes behind delicate handkerchiefs. They each took the opportunity to smooth their light brown hair to ensure tidiness and therefore attractiveness. Linda decided that that was agreement to include the young man in their entourage. She didn't quite have the nerve to draw attention to her own gold/brown/red locks by tucking a stray curl behind her ear. That seemed the height of vanity.

"You are welcome to join us, Master Lucjemm. Jensen, you may return to your duties with my father."

Lucjemm added his own dismissal to the young man with an anxious gesture. Then he offered Linda his arm.

Jensen scooted away without a backward glance.

Um. What was the royal protocol for this encounter? She was the Princess Royale; he was the heir to one of the great lords on the Council of Provinces. She outranked him and should therefore remain one step ahead of him. Taking his arm would keep her beside her. An intimate position due a suitor . . . Um.

Miri and Chastet were no help with their barely suppressed giggles, exchanging whispers and thinly veiled glances beneath lowered lashes.

She'd never had a suitor before. She'd never taken any man's arm, except her father's, since she had become an adult.

Not knowing what else to do, Linda slipped her hand around his proffered arm.

"I let you win that bout in the practice arena yesterday," he said quietly, looking straight ahead so that she couldn't see his expression beyond a stern control of the corner of his mouth that wanted to quirk upward.

"Oh?" She tried to arch one eyebrow like Papa did, but failed miserably. "I did not know that you, or anyone, recognized me." She wanted to frown sternly but his smile was warm and inviting. She couldn't remain stern and disapproving for long.

"We were told by General Marcelle not to recognize the anonymous 'boy' who only came to practice when the king did, and always showed up already armored and helmed with queue fully hidden, and never lingered for conversation and steed play among the other boys."

"If you did not 'recognize' me, why did you let me win?" Now she was angry that Papa and General Marcelle had not allowed her to properly judge her swordwork by honest bouts. How could she learn her faults if they always "let" her win?

"To see how you took your victory. And to learn your faults."

She nodded, accepting his strategy. "And the draw the day before?" She nibbled her lower lip nervously, not caring that it revealed her overhanging upper teeth.

"Honestly fought. You learned as much about my faults as I did yours. I applaud you for taking your lessons seriously and not accepting victory as your due."

Linda smiled genuinely this time. As they crossed the bridge onto Market Isle, she did not drop his arm at the first opportunity to examine some fine silk cloth from the big continent to the northeast of Coronnan.

While Miri and Chastet cooed over bolts of silky greens with silver brocade, she half-listened to the voices around her. The sounds blended into excited babbles and serious bartering. None of the discontent the lords had hinted at. This portion of Market Isle displayed luxury goods sold by wealthy merchants with permanent storefronts. The gossip here would revolve around the court and scandalous activities of the nobles. If she wanted the truth, she needed to go farther afield.

"What did you want to show me, Master Lucjemm?"

"On the far side of the island, closest to the Bay and farthest from the city islands," he said quietly. His glance noted how absorbed Miri and Chastet had become with the luscious fabrics. Gentle pressure of his arm guided Linda away from them.

She resisted, leaning close to Miri's ear. "Remember to listen for gossip about a drought, or unrest among the people.

Miri nodded slightly.

"You may wander off with him," Miri replied, cocking her head ever so slightly toward Lucjemm. "We will not be far behind."

"Let him think he's won a victory over you in getting you away from us," Chastet muttered, barely moving her lips.

Linda swallowed her smile.

Curiosity and a need for adventure gave Linda the courage to step away from her ladies and follow Lucjemm. She knew they'd stay out of sight but close-at-hand should Lucjemm become overly familiar.

Chatting amiably, they wandered the maze of shops and open stalls. Linda tried to memorize the path they took, but quickly abandoned the task as hopeless. Chastet would remember. But how lost could she get on an island of seven acres? All she had to do was follow the river upstream to the next bridge.

As they progressed, the aisles and alleys became narrower, the cobbles less firm with wider gaps between them. The permanent store buildings became fewer; temporary stalls and tents dominated, and they became smaller, less gaudy, more tattered. The goods they offered grew less costly, less desirable, more used and less new.

Accents varied from the sharp clatter of Southern rural reaches to the lilting singsong of foreign ports. Then one voice cut through the cacophony. "Rivers to the south running higher than normal spring runoff. But here, can hardly get a canoe through some of the island passages."

That didn't sound right. Linda craned her neck to look at the River Coronnan, the lifeblood of the continent. Too many people and buildings stood between her and the water. Later. On the way home she'd peer more closely at the water levels beneath the bridges.

Linda glanced around for traces of Miri and Chastet keeping close under the guise of fingering a frayed ribbon or gaudy painted metal cosmetics jar. There. To her right she caught a flash of green brocade, the same color as Miri's gown.

Finally, she and Lucjemm fetched up before a plain canvas tent a little larger than its neighbors, a little cleaner, but still not as fine as the ones left behind nearer the city islands and bridges.

"What could you possibly want here?" Linda asked, almost afraid to examine the lackluster gems, tarnished metal pots, and threadbare cloth.

"This," Lucjemm said, picking up a black wooden box the size of a loaf of bread. The boards looked clean and polished. The lid had been inlaid with other colors of wood, also polished to a smooth and gleaming surface. It surpassed all the other goods in a ten-tent radius in quality, and probably in price.

"I've seen others similar to it from more reputable merchants." She wrinkled her nose at the dominant smell of stale fish and drying seaweed, always prevalent this close to the Great Bay. She tugged on his arm, indicating they should retreat back the way they came. "Miri and Chastet will be wondering where we have gone."

"But those other boxes offered by wealthier merchants are usually empty and of less value," he insisted, drawing her closer to his side, and to the table holding the box.

"What does this one contain?" She had to admit that her curiosity was getting the better of her good sense.

He flipped off the hinged lid easily with one hand. They both peered into the interior, lined with layers of fluffy raw wool over a layer of dry straw. A flick of his finger removed the soft nesting fleece to reveal a black egg as big as her two clenched fists. Red lines swirled angrily around the surface.

Linda drew back, repelled. It was as if that strange egg smelled bad. But it had no smell at all. If she reached out to touch it, she knew it would burn her hand.

The black lines crawled over the red surface, twining, seeking; growing the power to enthrall . . .

Linda closed her eyes to break the connection the egg sought. A snap and whir lanced through her mind, like a taut bowstring clumsily released and scraping a burn across her arm.

Lucjemm cradled the egg easily in his two hands. His eyes glazed as if in deep prayer, or a trance, the soft brown irises darkened with hints of red lines lancing across them. "Father bought one like it for me three years ago. But it . . . This one sings to me. It needs me," he whispered in awe.

Linda turned and ran back the way they'd come, to the safety of her friends and the bright gaiety of the real market, not this slovenly and disreputable stall on the edge of the island and probably the law.

My lovely needs this egg. She says it will give us a strong male worthy of becoming her consort. I remind her that I too need a consort, my princess.

My lovely remains silent. I do not think she likes Princess Linda. She sees her as a rival for my affections. This is not so. My lovely will always be my first love. My loyalty and protection are hers to command. But I am a healthy man. I need a female of my own.

The princess will bring us political power. The three of us will rule this land together, united in a common desire to make the land and the people stronger through the changes my lovely and her consorts bring. If they thrive, the land and the people thrive. She needs only a few blood sacrifices to maintain her authority over them.

Over me . . .

My mind jerks free of the connection. Something is wrong there. I'm not sure what. But I will have my princess with or without the approval of my lovely. I will ask my father to unite me with my princess. He will see the advantages of the match, even if my lovely is jealous.

My lovely . . . my lovely loves me as my mother never could. Not my real mother who abandoned me at birth or my adopted mother who rejected me. Only my lovely truly loves me.

CHAPTER 7

*D*A! GLENNDON SUMMONED his father the moment Jaylor ducked through the shimmer in the air that marked the magical barrier protecting the family clearing. He came from the direction of the University, on the far side of the kitchen garden from the cabin, leaning heavily against his twisted staff as if tired—almost collapsed in on himself. His long auburn queue needed re-dressing, badly. Clear evidence that his day in closed session with the Circle of Master Magicians had been grueling. The staff gleamed in the afternoon sunlight, almost quivering on its own, the aftermath of the many, many spells channeled through it within the last few hours. The wood grain had twisted and braided back on itself a dozen times over in a unique pattern—Da's magical signature.

In the background, his mother's gentle and ever-present song faded to a long wistful note and her magic closed the barrier with a snap. She made magic every time she trilled a note. A simple magic reserved for women who nurtured a family. But Mama made it something more, something powerful and awesome.

Da lifted his head and smiled at her sweet song. His muscles seemed to fill out again, like dried fruit soaked in brandy resuming their natural shape. Mama did that to people. Gave them back to themselves with a song.

Da . . . da . . . ah . . . ah! Glenndon winced and covered his eyes with one hand as his telepathic hail bounced off his father's psychic barrier and back into his own brain with the force of a flaming arrow.

His grip weakened on his heavy ax as his father's grip on his staff firmed. Slowly, Glenndon placed the blade on the ground, rather than drop it and dull the edge or chop off his own foot.

"You have to say the words, with your mouth and your throat, Glenndon," Jaylor said. Again. For the twenty thousandth time. "Not every person has the power to receive or project thought as you do. Not everyone will understand you."

This is important!

So far, everyone at the University of Magicians and every visitor to the home clearing had understood Glenndon. So far, every person had received his communication, and those who could not reply the same way, spoke. He understood spoken words.

But forming them? The scars blocking his throat grew thicker every time he tried, making him feel the need to cough and hack them out. But he couldn't. They were permanently buried inside him.

He'd tried. Every day since he'd broken free of the epidemic fever. He'd tried and tried again until he spat blood. He was afraid to let the words jump from his mind to his throat and out his mouth. So much easier just to *think* his words and send them outward than risk the choking and bleeding.

"If it is important enough you will speak," Da said wearily, rubbing his eyes. "The healers tell me there is nothing wrong with you anymore." He made to move past Glenndon toward the hut and his supper.

I don't understand how to do it. Help me to understand. Glenndon nearly shouted. The blast of his mental voice made Da cringe and lean more heavily on his staff.

"I can't, Glenndon." Da gritted his teeth, still trying to rub away the pain behind his eyes. "I'm not a healer. I can't do anything more than I have." Anger turned Da's face red and his voice rose. That happened a lot lately. And not just with Glenndon. Any apprentice or journeyman magician who faltered in set tasks risked Jaylor's wrath and certain punishment;

the nastiest, dirtiest, most disgusting chore he could think up—like cleaning up after journeymen who'd celebrated a tricky achievement with far too much ale. Or sluicing out the University drains.

Glenndon backed up three paces. Not that he ever thought his father would resort to blows. But he let Da know that he feared and respected the Senior Magician and Chancellor of the University.

"The best physicians in the realm tell me there is nothing physically wrong with you, Glenndon. The scarring is fading to near nothing. Why won't you speak?"

Who wanted to hear the inarticulate and painful croaks his throat made after hearing the music and laughter in his mother's voice?

Glenndon shrugged. Finally he formed the question. "The dragons?" he mouthed. *They need our help!*

But no sound emerged.

"The dragons have spoken to me. Your conversations with a juvenile can't have as much information as Baamin, the venerable blue-tip. Learning to speak clearly is more important than anything Indigo told you."

But . . .

"But you and Lukan have traded chores again. He should be chopping wood, building up his muscles. Magic is hard work. We need strong bodies as well as strong minds and talent. And you should be working with the three newest apprentices, not him. Go to them, now. Teach them the proper use and preparation of protective circles by sunset. Two hours from now." He looked up at the position of the sun just at the top of the tree canopy surrounding the clearing. "If those three mind-blind brats can't make you speak I don't know what will." Da sighed and his shoulders slumped in defeat.

Apprentice work. I've been completing journeyman duties for two years! At least let me have a staff, Glenndon pleaded as he nodded toward his father's essential tool of magic.

"You've been doing *master work* for half a year without a staff," he said evenly, looking toward the cabin rather than at his son.

Will you make me a journeyman? Glenndon asked hopefully.

"Not until you learn to speak. You belong neither on journey nor in the Circle until you can speak out loud. Now go work with your new students. They might surprise you with what they can and cannot do, if you teach them correctly."

Glenndon raised his eyes in alarm. Not one of the newest apprentices had a scrap of talent. But their families suspected they might. Their villages persecuted them and cast them out, because they *might*. So the University took them in. As they had taken in so many these last fifteen years—including those who brought the putrid sore throat across the country and killed many. Some learned a trade and settled in new places where no one knew them or their reputation. A few, those too traumatized by the persecution and torture to live outside the protective circles of the University, stayed on, working at whatever they could.

The University grew, out here in the foothills of the Southern Mountains. The wooden buildings were now almost as large and well populated as the stone edifice had been in Coronnan City before . . .

Before the dragons flew away and took their magic with them.

The dragons had come back. But the people of Coronnan still hated and feared solitary magicians—those who couldn't gather dragon magic. In their minds all magicians were rogue.

Glenndon picked up the ax and split a log. The best way to get out of a hopeless task, like teaching the "mind-blind brats" magic, was to ignore it. Pretend he hadn't understood his father's words.

"No." Da stayed his arm with a fierce grip. Then he yanked the ax out of Glenndon's hands. No matter how tall and strong Glenndon grew, his father was taller, broader across the shoulders, and stronger, because he controlled his physical and magical strength.

"You understood me, Glenndon. I saw it in your eyes and your mind. Get yourself into a clean robe and begin teaching those boys. Let Lukan chop wood for a while. Maybe the physical work will give him an appreciation for patience."

Glenndon opened his eyes wide in question. How could Da block out his projected thoughts and yet keep his mind open enough to listen to his private ones?

"Your old man still has a few tricks." Da quirked a smile. "Now get to work. Your proper work."

An insistent thrum set all of Glenndon's senses to humming.

Someone comes.

Da raised an eyebrow. "Your mama hasn't said so . . ."

"Jaylor, Glenndon, someone is coming up the hill. I don't recognize him," Brevelan called from the doorway. The waning sun turned her red hair to the color of living flame, hiding the strands of silver nestled in the tidy knot tied at her nape with a green ribbon that matched her gown. Outlined by the doorway that Glenndon and his Da had to stoop to pass through showed just how tiny she was. Glenndon tried to remember when he'd grown a full head taller than she.

Her youngest children, Jules, age two, and Sharl, age six, clung to her skirts, peeking from behind her. Jules had his thumb firmly planted in his mouth. Brevelan showed signs of expecting another but had said nothing yet. Her seventh. A lucky number. But according to the dragon lore passed from one senior apprentice down the line to the newest, Shayla had given Brevelan a dragon-dream of only six children.

All of Glenndon's younger brothers and sisters had either their mother's bright red hair or their father's darker auburn. Except Glenndon. He was the only blond in the family. Sometimes he wondered if he truly belonged in this family any more than he did on Journey or in the Circle of Master Magicians. Maybe he was the outside seventh and the new one in Mama's belly was the sixth that belonged to the family.

Glenndon waved acknowledgment to his mother. Now if she demanded he speak, he might make more of an effort to break through the barrier between his mind and his throat. But she never asked. She accepted and loved each of her children without question or reservation, allowing each to develop naturally.

"The barrier around the clearing is tuned to your mother," Da mused. "When did you start picking up its vibrations before she did?"

The day I put a crack in it chasing a witchball you made for me when I was three, Glenndon replied.

"Well, best you go see who invades our privacy."

Everyone in the family could pass through the barrier at will. But only Brevelan and Glenndon seemed able to open the portal for others. Da used to do it. But Glenndon had patched it one too many times and now his father's magic no longer harmonized with its unique vibration.

With Da close at his heels, Glenndon walked softly toward the edge of the clearing, beyond the vegetable and herb garden into a small copse where an ancient everblue tree grew through a split boulder. The marker rock stood as tall as Glenndon's hip and as big around as a small hut. Close by he heard the creek chuckle as it rushed to tumble over a six-foot fall.

Glenndon sent out a mental query.

The image of a stocky man of middling years wearing royal green and gold, with a tight and intricately braided, four-strand court queue shocked him. His purpose in coming lay buried in a sealed letter inside his tunic next to his heart. Grim determination clouded the man's aura to all other emotions, even fatigue, after climbing the hill from the village. That magic seal fueled his determination.

Quickly Glenndon flashed the image to Da, uncertain how to react. He didn't know this man in royal livery. Yet the family counted King Darville as a friend. Mama kept in touch with Queen Rossemikka through a flame and scrying bowl. Glenndon vaguely remembered having met the king once. A long time ago.

Da smiled. He waved for Glenndon to open the portal.

Are you sure?

"We will always welcome Fred, Glenndon," Da said, the smile still on his face.

Who?

"Fred, King Darville's personal bodyguard."

Glenndon didn't like that explanation any better than not knowing the man's identity and purpose. He prepared a spell of confusion to throw at this Fred the moment he crossed the barrier. Then cautiously he hummed an agitated sequence of notes.

The faint shimmer in the air, so ever-present he barely noticed it anymore, faded. Fred leaned on the tree-split boulder, blinking in surprise.

"Oh," he said. "I'll never get used to you people not being there, then suddenly big as life in front of me."

"Welcome, Fred. Come in, come in. Can we offer you hospitality? What brings you here?" Da's deep baritone voice grew lighter with hearty good humor. He extended his arm. He and Fred clasped elbows and bowed in ritual greeting.

"I forget my manners, my Lord Jaylor, Senior Magician." Fred dropped his grip on Da's arm and stepped back a pace, swept his cap off his head and bowed formally.

Glenndon took a defensive position behind Da's left shoulder, facing slightly outward. That gave them nearly a full circle of spell throwing room.

He kept ready the confusion spell, followed by a fireball that itched for release. He didn't want to be surprised by anyone who might be hiding behind that magical glamour surrounding the letter in Fred's pocket.

Fred stepped forward, eyes darting right and left until he'd examined the entire clearing. His eyes went wide as he took in Glenndon.

"Stargods! I didn't believe it," he gasped.

Da shifted his gaze from Fred to Glenndon and back again. "Believe what you want. Then forget it entirely," Da growled like an angry saber cat.

Believe what? Glenndon asked.

His father just scowled at him, still angry over what Fred had said. Or not said.

"Yes, my lord." Fred bowed again and looked toward the simple log house at the center of the clearing. His entire face brightened with a smile when he noted Mama. He nearly ran to stand before her at the threshold.

Glenndon hummed a different sequence of notes to close the clearing barrier even as he dogged the man's footsteps.

Da ambled along in their wake. His mind projected happiness at seeing an old friend, and a bit of wariness. He seemed blind to the alien magic Fred carried in his pocket.

"Welcome, Fred," Mama said, holding her arms wide for an embrace of greeting.

"My lady." Fred bowed formally, two paces in front of Brevelan. Then he advanced those last two paces to hug her heartily.

"You are probably the only person left alive who calls me by title," Mama laughed. But her chuckles carried a musicality that invoked a protective spell.

Glenndon stopped short. Jaylor paused just behind his left shoulder.

Titles?

An old custom to ennoble the Senior Magician and his wife. From before the Leaving. Must be official king's business for him to invoke titles, Jaylor returned on a tight beam. *I don't like it.* He took a wider stance, bracing himself to face the unknown.

Fred proffered the letter with another deep bow. "My lady, King Darville sends his greetings and his apologies that he could not come on this errand himself."

Da's eyes opened wide when he spotted the shimmer of magic sparkling gold, brown, and dark red in a swirling aura about the missive.

Who? Glenndon asked.

The queen.

That surprised Glenndon. By law, none of the royal family could throw magic of any kind—even before the Leaving. If the Council of Provinces found out about this little spell to prevent anyone opening or reading the letter, other than the one to whom it was addressed, they could, by law, arrest the queen and burn her at the stake.

Glenndon didn't want to think of the chaos and war that would follow. Queen Rossemikka's brother, Rossemanuel, King of Rossemeyer—all the royals of Rossemeyer carried the prenomyn Rosse—might very well gather his huge army of mercenaries and invade Coronnan for the insult.

"No!" Mama screamed. "Never. I will never agree to this." Her hands shook and her face grew deathly pale. The fine lines around her eyes furrowed deeper. The gray strands in her sunset hair shone stark white.

Glenndon barely caught her before she crumpled to the ground in a dead faint.

The letter fluttered to the ground. The last line shone stark and menacingly bright. "I fear an assassin in my household."

An assassin targeting the queen? Or worse, the king?

CHAPTER 8

GLENNDON EASED HIS MOTHER to the beaten-dirt floor and twisted himself to kneel behind her. His blond queue dangled over his shoulder to tickle her nose. He thrust it back over his shoulder in frustration. Mama crumpled the letter in her hand and thrust it at him.

Black sigils danced and swam before Glenndon's vision without meaning. He wrestled the letter from his mother's hands and glared at it. He crossed his eyes and let the meaning of the words flow into his mind rather than fight to read it.

"Send my son Glenndon to court to assume his duties as heir to the Dragon Crown." And then the signature at the bottom. "Darville, King of Coronnan by the Grace of the Dragons." The threat at the bottom of the missive was written in a smaller hand, less formal, cloaked in a different spell, less noticeable.

Mama? He propped her higher while still cradling her head in his lap.

"Jaylor, he mustn't go," Mama said. Her voice shook as badly as her hand. "The city will destroy him."

Glenndon groaned some awful sound, *Mama, how can this be?*

"Jaylor, promise me that you will not send my boy away!"

"Sweetheart, I can promise nothing until I read the letter." Jaylor knelt beside her, shoving Glenndon aside, oblivious to everyone but his wife. Gently he took the sheet of parchment from Glenndon's hands. One look and he frowned in contempt. "I thought I taught Mikka to encode her letters more effectively."

The queen could code letters magically? Glenndon's thoughts whirled in wonder. Who knew? The urgency behind the words became clearer for her to risk discovery of magic. Illegal magic.

Da made the magic sparkle disappear from the page with a pass of his hand. Then he read the words. He shook his head in disbelief and sat back on his heels abruptly. His thoughts remained guarded and closed to Glenndon.

"Send my son Glenndon to court . . . heir to the Dragon Crown," Da whispered. He did not lower his eyes to the warning of assassination.

"He cannot go." Brevelan struggled to sit up.

Glenndon had to help her.

"Promise me you will not send my boy away, Jaylor."

"I . . . I always knew this day would come," Da said. Color drained from his face. He suddenly looked older, less vigorous.

What does this mean?

"It means, Glenndon, that our past has caught up with us," Da said. He dashed moisture away from his eyes.

And my mother? Panic boiled in Glenndon's middle. How could this be? His place in the world, everything he held dear and familiar shifted and would not settle into a pattern.

He'd never had a true place in the world. A blond outsider in the clearing, a silent magician at the University. This must be why.

He had to brace himself as he lost his lock on the southern magnetic pole. His sense of up and down, right and left, center and outward disappeared with it. Only the packed-dirt floor beneath him seemed real.

"I am your mother, dear boy. That much of your life is real." Mama twisted and hugged him.

He rested his head on her breast, breathing in her unique smell of spices and baking tubers and the sweet flowers she mixed with her soap.

Safe. As long as she held him he felt safe and grounded.

Gradually he realigned his senses upon her. She was the center of his world.

But his conversation with Indigo kept intruding on his sense of well-being. Could any magician ever be safe from the loss of dragons? Dragon magic allowed many magicians to join their powers and overcome any solitary. They could impose honesty and ethics; they could guarantee ordinary people that magicians had their best interests at heart.

He wished he'd made his father understand the urgency of the quest to help dragons thrive again before this turmoil erupted.

Were they safe from the strangeness that invaded their home the moment this Fred person arrived?

Sudden anger shot from his gut to his throat. With an inarticulate roar he launched himself upon Fred, ready to claw out the man's eyes, to shed his blood, to make it all go away.

"Glenndon!" Da's voice did not stop him.

Da throwing a magical barrier between them did.

Glenndon bounced back, landing on his butt beside the hearth, jarring his spine. Lights flashed before his eyes.

"Apologize to Fred, Glenndon," Da demanded. "He is only the messenger. He is not to blame for this. If anyone is, 'tis I."

The small windowless room seemed to close in on Glenndon. Too many people in here. Not enough air or room for all of them.

Without thinking further he shot forward and upward, catching his stride by the second step. He burst free of the dark confines of the house. Another dozen steps and he broke through the protective barrier around the clearing.

"Glenndon!" Da called after him.

His head pounded with fierce pain at each jarring step.

"Come back here. Now. We have to talk about this," his father demanded.

Not his father.

The only father he'd ever known.

Glenndon guided his feet upward without thinking. Up the mountain. Away from home. Toward . . . toward the dragons. The dragons, who were fewer each year. The dragons, who were starving for lack of something vital in the Tamboo-tie.

The dragons were his true family. He belonged with them

in their lair, fighting to help them survive and thrive, not in the clearing. And definitely not in Coronnan City at the court of the king.

His breath came in sharp, shallow pants. A stitch gnawed at his side.

Still he ran. Upward, along familiar paths known only to him and a few gray scurries. He pushed his body to the limit and beyond. Still he ran. Not thinking. Reacting blindly to the need to get away.

To escape.

At last, a root tripped him. He landed face first in soft moss, the top of his head barely a hand's breadth away from a jagged rock. He shuddered at his narrow escape from having his head split like a flusterhen egg.

For many long moments he lay there panting, hearing only his heart thudding in his ears.

Slowly he became aware of the rush of water over a cascade of rocks. He knew this place. Instinctively he'd sought the glen where he'd idled away many long hours when he needed to be alone, away from people and the pressure to speak. The glen where Indigo came to speak to him.

When his breathing returned to normal and the pinch in his side eased, he sat up and unlaced his boots. Chill air stabbed at his bare feet. The spring equinox was still a few days away.

So he wouldn't have to think about . . . about his mother and the king. His father. The king.

His parents sending him away. A great deal of urgency bled from the final cryptic note of fear of an assassin and the magic that encrypted it.

The warm water caressed his feet and relaxed his entire being. In a few moments he'd stripped off his clothes and sunk into the balm of the small plunge pool.

Resting his head against the bank, queue half in the water, he let his mind wander, open, receptive to any stray dragon thoughts. Within moments he heard the rush of wings as one of the beasts fought air and altitude to land in the creek above the fall.

Glenndon here, he informed the dragon before he looked to see which one splashed water enthusiastically.

(Indigo here,) came the reply.

Glenndon smiled. No matter what turmoil clouded his mind, Indigo remained true and loyal. Closer to him than his brother Lukan. His *half*-brother.

He turned to look at his friend. *Welcome.*

Slanted sunlight bounced off the crystalline fur of the dragon, directing his gaze elsewhere, anywhere but at the beast. And yet he couldn't look away. Fascination kept his eyes probing for the spirit behind the reflection. Only the extremely dark blue of his wing veins and tips remained visible. Because his tips were darker than most dragons, Indigo was easier to spot from a distance. In some lights he looked almost purple, the deep rich color of the mountains in winter twilight.

Indigo's size had never intimidated Glenndon. He'd known the dragon when he was still a clumsy baby no larger than a lady's pony.

They'd grown up together.

(You are welcome as well, my friend. Your mind is troubled.)

Glenndon flashed a replay of the day's events from one mind to another, without editing. He had nothing to hide from Indigo.

(Two fathers. You should be excited. The more fathers the bigger and stronger the litter.) An aura of sadness clouded his eyes. *(Shayla will not mate again until we find what is missing and thrive again.)*

But I don't know the king. I would have to move to the city.

(Your brother would jump at the chance to see the city.)

I've never wanted to see the city. I like living close to the dragons.

(I think I should like to see the city. 'Twould be different. Exciting.)

You sound like Lukan, Glenndon snorted.

(If you never go anywhere else, how do you know that this is home? If you don't fit in anywhere else, how do you know where you belong? If you never try something new, how do you know that you have found your life's work?)

In a flurry of wings and a flash of light reflecting off his fur, Indigo took to the air and disappeared. *(I hear there is a secret archives beneath the palace,)* he whispered back to Glenndon from a distance.

"Glenndon? Where are you?" his sister Lillian called.

"M'ma says you must come home now," Valeria, her twin, added. Dark shadows circled her eyes. Her skin was so thin he thought he could see her veins pulse purple beneath the surface.

His sisters thrashed about in the underbrush, calling him and making enough noise to scare away an entire nimbus of dragons.

You left me with something to think about, Indigo. But I still do not like any of this.

CHAPTER 9

*T*HE TIME HAS COME. Father is ready to cast aside his
lady wife. His eye wanders and lights upon a distant relative, young, fertile. Docile.

Barely a year older than myself, this new girl should be
my wife, but I seek someone greater, more beautiful. More
powerful. Even my lovely begins to see the wisdom of bringing royal blood into the family.

My lovely has grown enough now to sniff magic in Princess Rosselinda's blood. An even bigger incentive to over-
look my father's latest light of love. I'll have her first, just to
make sure she knows who truly rules this family.

I fear that my princess will not pass the test my lovely sets
for her. Before we can mate, my lovely must feed of her blood.
I do not think my princess will allow this. Is my princess
more important than my lovely? Ultimately yes. Princess
Rosselinda is the key to controlling Coronnan and ending the
evil of magic. My princess is more . . .

Time enough to worry about that later. My lovely has set
up an aura around the herbal sachets my father's wife scat-
ters among our clothing. Father will find the one that burns
his skin at first touch. We will inform him that only magic can
do that.

He is ready to accuse his wife of magic so he can get rid
of her. He burns for his new love. But first he must exile his
wife.

I have waited nearly three years for this day. I glory in my

*power and the power of my lovely. My lovely knows all. She
is a fountain of wisdom.*

But my princess . . .

"Good morning, M'ma." Princess Rosselinda curtsied deeply
to her mother and the five ladies who attended the queen. Two
weeks had passed since she'd overheard that awful discussion
in the Council Chamber. Two weeks and no one had mentioned anything.

Lucjemm had kept his distance as well, never mentioning
how she'd abandoned him in the market. When P'pa allowed
her into the practice arena, Lucjemm pointedly found other
bouting partners.

She hoped they'd all forgotten those events. She and her
ladies almost had. They'd found other diversion to giggle
over, like the courtier who split his too-tight trews right up
the seat when he bowed to the queen. Or the greater scandal
of Lord Jemmarc formally putting aside his wife for witchcraft so he could marry a younger, prettier, and more fertile
lady. Only the dragons knew where Lady Lucinda had gone
with but one maid and one bodyguard as escort. At least Jemmarc hadn't brought her to trial and burning for her crime. If
he had, he might have had to return her extensive dowry to
her family.

Linda didn't want to think about that. Ever.

Rumor had it that he had no evidence of witchcraft. But
he did have a new candidate for his wife. If he remarried,
would he set aside Lucjemm as his heir as well?

If he did that, she couldn't use the boy to keep her half-
brother, her *bastard* half-brother, away. She'd have to find
another suitor. Um . . .

No one came to mind. *No one.* Perhaps she should ask
Uncle Andrall to investigate likely young men of noble birth
on the Big Continent.

M'ma's ladies shifted position so that they ranged around
the queen in a protective semicircle. Linda dismissed the ladies from her focus. She could never keep the ladies straight
anyway. They rotated every few months and they all looked,
dressed, and talked alike, as if to vary one tiny morsel from

court-dictated fashions might weaken the kingdom and leave it vulnerable to invasion. Except Lady Anya, Miri's mother. She was always at M'ma's side, a friend and confidante as well as assistant.

Linda flashed her skirts at the ladies, showing a gossamer trim on her petticoat, purchased on a defiant whim after she'd abandoned Lucjemm. Beside her, Miri and Chastet practiced the same flick revealing similar, but not as grand lace on their petticoats. A game they'd cooked up together. Now that Linda had reached the mature age of fourteen and been assigned ladies of her own, she'd discovered the joy in setting her own fashion with colored ribbons and touches of lace from SeLennica.

The ladies went into a huddle, discussing whether the princess should be allowed to dictate fashion to the rest of the court. From the way they plucked at the plain pleats on their bodices, Linda guessed they'd dash to the fabric stalls on Market Island the moment they finished their duties today.

Lace had been out of fashion for a few years now—probably because it cost so much. And she thought there'd been a war with SeLennica. She hadn't paid that much attention to her modern history lessons. Ancient legends and dragon lore were much more interesting. Now there was a treaty with SeLennica, but the lack of demand had dropped the prices of lace—a point of economics P'pa had taught her.

"Princess Rosselinda." M'ma dipped her head the precise depth dictated by formal protocol.

Uh-oh. Formality before breakfast meant something awful. Had M'ma missed her pair of riding gloves that Linda had borrowed?

M'ma didn't ride anymore. And Linda didn't want to see the fine leather go to waste . . .

"Is P'pa all right?" she asked breathlessly. She advanced to kneel before her mother, crumpling her heavily brocaded skirts in both hands. Best way to deflect a reprimand was change the subject as fast as possible.

"You father fares well, my dear," M'ma chuckled. "He paces like an angry spotted saber cat, but he fares well."

"What angers him?" Linda asked warily. Had he found out that 'twas she who had stripped rosebuds from their stems after the men in the arena had so obviously let her win her bouts? Lucjemm was the only one honest enough to make her work for her victories. And yesterday he'd disappeared the moment she had arrived in the arena.

On that thought her father appeared from the inner room. He prowled from window to chair to doorway, hands locked behind his back, head thrust forward, shoulders reaching for his ears. With his golden hair lightened with touches of gray, still tightly bound in a four-strand queue from its morning dressing, he resembled the predatory cat M'ma had likened him to.

No, not precisely a spotted saber cat. More like a caged golden wolf.

For some reason known only to her parents, she wasn't allowed to mention that resemblance. Clear evidence to Linda that she had landed close to a truth. A dangerous truth.

A truth told in cautionary legends of a prince enticed away from his duties by evil sorcerers and changed into a wolf so that he'd be killed on a random hunt. But he was saved by the dragons and a mysterious red-haired woman. The prince of legend was named Darville, and plainly resembled the current king; and like all tales, it supposedly took place long ago, before times anyone living had witnessed.

Could the tale be true, a part of her father's history, and could the mysterious red-haired woman be the mother of P'pa's bastard son?

A bell rang in the great hall directly below the queen's quarters.

Linda raised her eyebrows in question when her parents did not respond to the summons to break their fast.

The ladies looked to Queen Rossemikka expectantly. Almost anxiously. Were they so eager to be first on Market Isle and conforming to the newest court fashion?

The queen dismissed the women with a wave. "Yours too, Linda," she whispered.

Linda nodded her head toward Miri and Chastet. They curtsied and backed out of the room, eyebrows raised in question.

"Later," Linda mouthed. They had no secrets. Well, not many.

When they had cleared the room, M'ma indicated that Linda should sit beside her.

"What is wrong?" Linda blurted out.

"A true diplomat dances around a problem with courtesies and niceties," King Darville reprimanded her. Very much the king and not just her beloved father.

"I'm not at a foreign court. You are my family, and I know something is wrong, terribly wrong." She lifted her chin stubbornly. She'd been told she resembled her father when she did that.

Her parents exchanged a pained glance. Some silent communication passed between them. Finally her father looked away first and heaved a sigh.

"You know that we love you and would never do anything to hurt you," he said quietly. His dominant left hand reached toward her. Then he dropped it abruptly and clasped both hands behind his back again. He stiffened his spine and looked down at her from his regal height.

"However," Linda prompted. There was always a "however." She sighed. "Something about the decision of the Council to find me a husband against your wishes, Your Grace?" If he was going to play the king, then she must act the Princess Royale.

"However, the Council of Provinces demands a male heir to the throne . . ." he paused for a gulping breath that almost controlled the high color of anger on his cheeks. "They would pressure you to bear children while you are barely more than a child . . ."

Linda bristled. She was a woman now. Her body had made the transition two years ago. Since she showed all signs of living through the worst of the change in body and emotions, M'ma had helped her put up her hair, ordered new gowns with lower hems, and appointed her two closest friends from the schoolroom to be her ladies-in-waiting.

"They . . ." her father continued, ignoring her offence. "Rather than throw you into a loveless marriage with a foreign prince, with foreign interests, we have opted to send for my son."

Linda forgot to breathe. "The boy you have not admitted to fathering!" She bit her cheeks before she shouted ugly words at him. How dare he betray M'ma? That red-haired woman was an evil seductress, as evil as the sorcerers who transformed P'pa into his totem animal: a great golden wolf.

She dredged up the rest of the conversation she wasn't supposed to have heard. "The people will not accept a bastard."

"Linda!" her mother reprimanded. "Where did you learn that word?" She looked paler than usual. For as long as Linda could remember, her mother had been ill. Only recently had she realized that five miscarriages in as many years after three pregnancies in five years had weakened her. Drained her vitality.

Now she understood the whispers among the ladies that another pregnancy would kill her.

Five potential heirs dead before birthing.

"I am as smart and as well educated as any man in the kingdom," Linda asserted. She resisted the urge to stamp her foot. "Why will they not accept me as your heir?"

"I have trained you and your two sisters to follow in my footsteps," her father said. "I had hoped that by this time the Council of Provinces would have relaxed their insistence upon a male heir. Their only compromise is to offer a joint crown to you and a husband. You are too young to marry. I have no choice but to bring my *bastard* son to court."

"But if he is illegitimate, and baseborn, then he can't rule," Linda shouted. Panic rose hot and vile in her throat. She needed to spit the acid of her jealousy and bewilderment back at her parents.

Her mother's gentle hand kept her sitting when she wanted to pace and prowl as relentlessly as her father.

"There are ways to correct the boy's illegitimacy. His mother has some royal blood in her heritage. Her grandmother was my father's cousin."

"Ways of making him legitimate include putting aside my mother, your *queen,* and marrying the mother of your *bastard?*"

"That is not an option. That has never been an option," her father said vehemently.

"Then why?"

"I had not yet met your mother. I did not yet know how

deep and abiding my love for her would be. Brevelan and Jaylor were my best friends. My only friends when Lord Krej tried to usurp the throne. We thought Jaylor had died. Brevelan and I turned to each other in our grief. Our love for each other and for him stretched out to the realm of dragons and brought Jaylor back from the brink of death. Out of that night came a beautiful baby boy."

Linda gasped in dismay at the names. She knew them as well as those of her sisters. The Senior Magician and his witch-wife were both revered and reviled. Lord Krej's name and that of his daughter Rejiia were held up as examples of the dangers of allowing a monarch to possess magic. Lord Krej was the evil sorcerer who transformed Darville into a wolf.

"The people will never accept your *magician* bastard as their king," she retorted. What else could she say? How else could she defend herself and her position at court?

"Probably not, but we have to give them the chance," M'ma said quietly. "We have to stall and give you time to finish growing up. We expect word any time now of Glenndon's imminent arrival."

Wild anger flashed through Linda's blood. It flushed her face and made her fingers tingle. Her heart beat too fast and her thoughts swirled. She grew hot then cold. And still that tingle that demanded she *do* something. Something bold and . . . destructive.

She took a deep calming breath, and then another, and another. The tingle withdrew.

"If you . . . The moment he arrives I will no longer consider myself a member of this family. Bring him here and you throw me away!" She surged up and ran, picking up her skirts to an indecent level.

She had to get away. She had to run far and fast to escape her own fear and anger and confusion.

How could M'ma be so calm about accepting P'pa's son into her household? How could her father insult M'ma by bringing the boy here?

Down the long broad corridor she ran. Deep into the oldest and least trafficked part of the keep she ran. Around this corner, under that archway. She ran until a stitch grabbed her side. She kept running until her breath came in great racking sobs that might have been tears.

"Princess Royale Rosselinda Mirilandel Kathleen de Draconis, stop right there," King Darville shouted from a shadowed alcove to her left.

"How?" she gasped. She didn't have enough breath to say more.

"I've been taking shortcuts to hidden rooms in the palace a lot longer than you." He tried to look stern, but a tiny smile twitched at the corner of his mouth.

Linda allowed herself to set her balance and deepen her breathing.

He tilted his head as if listening. Linda had seen him do that from to time.

She wished she knew who spoke to him with magic in secret.

"Yes, I agree," he whispered.

"Agree to what?" she demanded.

"Linda, please break your fast with the rest of the court in the Great Hall. Then meet me by the mounting blocks." P'pa turned away, blending into the shadows, ready to disappear again.

"Yes, Your Grace." She curtsied without looking at him.

"Don't you want to know why?"

"That is for Your Grace to inform me when he deems the time right." She parroted her governess' phrase.

"You want to know everything, right now. You do not believe in secrets. That is why you listen so closely to Council meetings. I have let you remain hidden so that you could learn something of politics. Now I wonder if I should have kept you more sheltered."

"What point in teaching me to be a king when I will never be more than the wife to one?" She set her chin in defiance.

"Because I had hoped . . . Linda, we will ride out to Battle Mound southeast of the city."

A two-hour ride, half of it negotiating the islands of the river delta and the connecting bridges that made up Coronnan City. Battle Mound, the site of the last great battle between barons and their battlemages, the last conflict before

Nimbulan created the covenant with the dragons and made magic communal and governable.

"Why? Do we go alone? Or will half the court follow?"

"You will tell no one of this excursion. No one. Especially not your ladies or your sisters. We take no servants or bodyguards. Only the groom who fetches our steeds will know of our departure."

Curiosity sent her mind spinning, dissolving her anger. A trip outside the city with P'pa. Just the two of them. Not even Fred, P'pa's bodyguard who was always within spitting distance, except these last two weeks when he'd gone home to attend a dying grandmother or something. Special. Unusual.

"The entire city will know of this venture before we set out. They always do."

P'pa almost laughed. "Undoubtedly. They always do. A contingent of soldiers and lords will follow—hopefully discreetly. And they will witness a miracle. And so shall you, my daughter. So shall you."

CHAPTER 10

LINDA DUG HER HEELS into the flanks of her favorite fleet steed, a big, opinionated, chestnut mare. The beast bunched her muscles and lengthened her stride. Together they flew across the open meadows to the east and south of the river delta islands that comprised Coronnan City.

The wind of their passage blew Linda's cloak hood back and tangled her hair. She laughed out loud and pressed the steed to gallop faster.

"Ease up, Linda!" her father called. His big black stallion moved alongside, matching stride for stride. He looked over his shoulder often, like he was afraid of pursuit.

"I want to run free," she called back to him.

"You will slow down before you fall off. Never override your steed. I thought I taught you that when you were five." He edged ahead by half a nose, forcing his steed closer to hers until he grabbed her reins and turned them in a slowing circle.

Linda's steed fought the restriction. Her father tweaked the reins back and down, until they had made two complete circles, P'pa on the inside, and stopped.

Even then he did not release the reins.

"But Belle likes to run wild," Linda protested. She knew better than to try to wrest the reins away from her father. She had to fight to keep her lower lip from sticking out in a pout. Pouts made her look ugly. And childish.

"She's had a run. Now we move at a safer pace." P'pa looked upward, tilting his head as if listening.

Listening to what?

"Why are we coming all the way out here?" Linda asked.

"You will see in a few moments."

"I don't like secrets."

"I know that. The time has come to reveal my biggest secret." He chuckled like he did when he made an amusing word play. Then he released Belle and kicked his own mount into a sedate trot.

"A bigger secret than your *bastard* son?"

"Yes. A more important secret."

She examined his words one by one and all together while she matched his pace. She couldn't find anything funny hidden in there.

"Have you heard of Amazon oil?" he asked without prelude.

"Um," she searched her memory. The product sounded familiar, exotic, but not unknown to her. "I have heard of it, but I can't remember where. Why?"

"It is a byproduct of a fruit that grows only on the big continent northeast of Coronnan."

"Across the Great Bay?"

"Beyond the Bay. Remember your geography lessons, Little Lindy. Do I have to send you back to the schoolroom?"

"No, P'pa. I can picture it on the maps now." So this was what the outing was about, drilling her on her lessons. Oh, well, best parrot off a bunch of facts to satisfy him. Then they could get on with the adventure he'd promised. "The interior of the continent is largely unexplored, at least by those known to us here in Coronnan. We trade with the coastal city-states. Each has its own ambassador to our court. They have large resources of grain, fruit, and herd beasts."

"And?" he prodded her.

"The Stargods defeated a herd of winged snakelike creatures that were destroying the land by turning it into one vast desert. What were they called?"

"Krakatrice," the king said absentmindedly.

"Krakatrice. Right. But once the Stargods defeated the Krakatrice and eliminated them from the land, they destroyed the artificial dams and restored the riverbeds. The land is fruitful once more."

"And?"

"Amazon oil!" She remembered in a flash of blinding light. Or was that something in the sky reflecting the light of the sun?

"What is it and what does it do?" her father prodded.

"It's the residue from pressing the Amazon fruit into a pulp mixed with dried meat for journey rations. The oil sinks to the bottom of the vat—it's quite heavy—and is used to keep metal free of rust." She turned a big smile on her father, happy to have dredged those facts out of the bottom of her brain. "We use it to tend our sword blades."

"Yes. Correct. But what happens if you mix Amazon oil with miner's acid?"

"Um. Something not good. Wouldn't the acid eat through the oil to damage the metal?" She chewed her lower lip.

King Darville nodded sadly.

"But it would take a while," she mused. "Amazon oil is resilient." Was that the right word?

"Yes it is, Linda." He must approve of her assumptions if he used her familial name. "After a while, a few days, or a really long and vigorous battle, or practice session, the acid would weaken the steel until it broke without warning."

"Is this about you breaking your sword two weeks ago?" she gasped.

"Yes."

"Who would do such a thing? It wouldn't have been an accident. Miner's acid is not readily available."

"It is in the Provinces that have mines," he said flatly.

"Oh."

"Think about it while we finish our ride. I need you to know who might have damaged my sword either as a warning, or an attempt upon my life."

Linda swallowed heavily. All of a sudden the day did not seem so bright and warm. She saw in her mind the lords whose land abutted the western range of mountains that separated Coronnan from SeLennica. Geoine, Lord of Sambol, Bennallt, Lord of the Port City of Baria, Miri's father and Lady Anya's husband. No she wouldn't believe *either* could be involved in an assassination plot. Better to believe the acid and the assassin came from Hanassa, the ungovernable hidden city of rogue magicians, outlaws, Rovers, and disgruntled exiles. They looked to no lord. Any one of them could be hired or bribed to perform any dastardly deed.

"Glenndon?" Valeria shifted her gaze from her toes to her brother's face and back again. He caught the glisten of tears at the corners of her eyes. "Why do you have to leave?"

I wish I knew for sure. He had trouble meeting her gaze as well.

"Is this because you can't talk?" She looked tired today. But she was always tired.

He shrugged. *Where is Lillian? You two are never apart.*

"She . . . she is combing Mama's hair."

He lifted an eyebrow in question. *This must be important to you.*

"It is. I need to know why you have to leave us. What will I do without you? You are the only one able to force Lillian to keep our secret."

He knew that when she fought her body for energy she found it easier to speak than to project telepathically. Glenndon was the opposite.

What have you and Lillian been doing that has worn you down so much you can barely stand?

"Don't change the subject, Glenndon." She plunked her bottom onto the rock beside his favorite bathing pool while he skipped stones across the quiet water.

One, two, three jumps. He used only his muscle strength and skill. If he pushed the flat stone with magic, it would skip a dozen or more times.

Answer my question. What have you done to tire yourself so much? He was the only one who ever tried to figure out what ailed his sister. She'd be sixteen this summer and only recently showed signs of maturing. Lillian had passed into womanhood two years ago.

"Not much," Valeria replied.

He glared at her, pulling the information from her faster than she could block his penetration of her mind. He saw their usual lessons in magic, reading, writing, more magic to read beneath the printed words and to write in such a way

that ordinary words took on different meanings when viewed
by magic. Valeria had also scried for contact with Queen
Rossemikka. But the queen had either been absent from her
suite, or occupied by a visitor who must never know she possessed magic.

Glenndon lingered on that memory. She made the effort
to yank it back behind a mental wall of privacy.

"You fear that someone will betray the queen," she said
flatly. "But surely there is someone else who can protect her.
Maigret perhaps? Didn't she used to spy for Da as a lady-in-
waiting?"

*Long ago. She's too old and settled at the University now.
She and Master Robb have two children.*

"Why does it have to be you?" she wailed.

*Because the king and queen asked for me, not Maigret, or
Da, or anyone else. Me. Just me.*

"There's more you aren't telling me."

His silence told her more than his thoughts ever would.

Mama is ready for us. Glenndon dropped his latest stone
and marched back through the forest toward the clearing,
ripping fuzzycurls off the tops of the saber ferns as he passed.

Valeria followed after him. He let her drink in some of his
energy to refuel all that she had spent that day. Too much.
She'd done too much without help. She'd be ill tonight and
all day tomorrow if she didn't take what he offered to keep
her on her feet.

And he wouldn't be with her to help her through the night
when she was so tired she forgot to breathe.

How would she survive without those little bursts of
strength and grounding to the Kardia beneath her feet?

*I have found my weapon. I found it in the most unlikely of
places, Market Isle. Who knew the vendors had such extensive and illegal contacts with their counterparts across the
sea. Princess Rosselinda led me right to the man who can
bring in an unlimited supply of weapons, consorts. "The
more fathers, the bigger and stronger the clutch." That's
what my lovely tells me.*

It is the opposite for humans. The more mothers, the big-

ger and stronger my army. If I promise each soldier three wives, they will produce three times the children who will follow me without question.

What an interesting concept. I shall have the princess as my primary consort, but two others . . . Father's latest light of love is a good start on my own clutch of children.

In the meantime my princess has shown me the path to destroying her father. He is the last advocate for keeping magic and magicians in Coronnan. I shall give this egg to my father, allow the hatchling to enthrall him so that he obeys my lovely and raises the army we need to follow through with the king's demise.

With him gone, the dragons will lose their reason for staying in Coronnan. They will scatter, become easy targets to the hunters within my army when separated. Each dragon will feed a village for a winter. If I give them food in the coming drought they will love me and never reject me.

I knew my patience would be rewarded. And now I have my weapon. A little more planning, a little more recruitment, and then I shall pull together all of the little pieces of my plan.

CHAPTER 11

"WE ONLY HAVE TO GO over that rise, best to let the steeds walk a bit, cool down before we rest them." P'pa's quiet words broke Linda out of her depressing circle of thoughts.

Assassination. P'pa had forced her to think about the danger that faced all monarchs, no matter how beloved of the people. There was always someone eager to take power for power's sake without weighing the responsibilities and need for compromise.

"What happens when we get over the rise?" She had to change the subject before she started crying at the whole idea that someone she knew, *anyone,* wanted to murder her father.

"Patience, Linda. Patience. We have to tether our mounts and walk a bit."

They found some sturdy saplings near a stream to tie the steeds on a long rein, giving them a chance to crop a good circle of grass while they waited. If they needed, the beasts could also reach the stream for a drink.

As they neared the next rise on foot, P'pa took Linda's hand. A big smile creased his face. He looked younger and happier than she'd seen him in a long time. All thoughts of assassins, marriage treaties, and bastard sons seemed banished for the moment.

She smiled too, happy to see him enjoying himself away from the worries and pressure of court; happy to have him all to herself. No lords demanding his ear, no Fred hovering constantly at his shoulder on the lookout for danger, no servants fussing over his appearance, no missives to write, and neither of her sisters, Manda and Josie, pestering him for attention. A bubble of pride spread through her. Today was special. *She* was special to share this secret with P'pa.

A strange sound startled her, like ten thousand birds descending in a flock, and the cackle of ten thousand fluster-hens screeching in protest at having their eggs stolen. Or . . .

And then she saw movement without substance. A hint of color here and there. More than the flash of sunlight on crystal she'd seen moments before.

And a pressure in the back of her mind.

She stopped short, tugging on her father's hand. Fear rooted her in place. At the same time her feet itched to turn and run. Run back to the fleet steeds that would carry her home to the city and safety.

P'pa firmed his grip on her hand. "What happened to your insatiable curiosity?" he asked on a chuckle.

Linda gulped. Well, she did want to know what could make such a terrible racket. Even if it did scare her.

"Look closer, Little Lindy."

A name she thought she'd outgrown. But at the moment the familiarity, and the affection behind it, reassured her.

Sidling behind, she peeked around him into the sheltered vale, a wide bowl surrounded by rolling hills covered in lush meadow grasses and small shrubs.

There at the center sat the biggest animal she'd ever seen, ever dreamed about. Taller than two sledge steeds and broader than two more, it swung its massive head around to face her. Light danced along a single horn growing from a broad forehead. Spines marched down its back, diminishing in size and sharpness. Iridescent wings and body drew her eye. All colors swirled together, but no single definable color. And yet the bright noon sunlight reflected and pushed her to look elsewhere.

The pressure in her mind increased. Not really painful, just a bit of urgency. She pressed her fingertips to her temples.

"Is . . . is that a dragon?" she whispered, afraid the animal would see her.

(Welcome, Rosselinda, daughter to our King Darville and Queen Rossemikka. Shayla here.)

The words popped into her mind. Real and yet not. The pressure eased a bit.

"Greet her, and call her by name." P'pa drew her out from behind him. "She won't hurt you. I don't think she *can* hurt one of royal blood."

"But . . ."

"Go ahead."

"What is her name, P'pa?" The dragon's greeting slipped from her memory, crowded out by amazement, confusion, fear, and . . . curiosity.

P'pa laughed long and loud. "Have you forgotten the dragon lore you read and reread to tatters until I had to have the book copied, the very tales we told you to put you to sleep in the nursery?"

"This can't be . . ."

"Yes, it is. And she will be with you forever, protect and guide you, as long as you listen."

Rosselinda gulped and somehow found a tiny bit of courage buried deep within.

"Greetings, Shayla, matriarch of the nimbus. Greetings and . . . and welcome. I think."

Shayla reared up on her hind legs, flapping her wings. She bugled an ear-splitting screech.

Linda slapped her hands over her ears.

Then she saw the source of the dragon's distress. A line of lords and soldiers ranked along the hilltop. The soldiers had all nocked their crossbows and aimed at the dragon's heart.

Linda ran to stand between the magnificent beast and the army. She stood tall and proud, as much a target as Shayla. "This is my dragon, you may not hurt her," she yelled. "I forbid it!"

Not a single bowman shifted his aim.

"I know I told you never to use this spell, Glenndon," Da, no, not his Da, *Jaylor* said. He pinched the bridge of his nose as if trying to banish the headache of fatigue.

Glenndon had to stop thinking of this man as his father.

But how could he? Jaylor had made the first witchball for him, a concoction of twigs and moss and magic that fell apart when it hit anything hard. Jaylor had showed him the magic in a spring flower first coming into bloom as well as how to gather dragon magic, or pull magical energy from a ley line deep within the Kardia. Jaylor would always be his Da, even if King Darville was his father.

"There is a sense of urgency in Mikka's letter," Mama added. "There isn't time for you and Fred to walk to Coronnan City, or even ride fleet steeds." Shadows darkened her deep blue eyes even though she held herself straight and strong and ready to battle dragons or rogue magicians, anyone who might threaten her family.

One by one, the family gathered in a circle around Glenndon and Fred, the awed, but not cowed, king's bodyguard. One by one, they hugged Glenndon tightly, then joined hands to enclose them with magic and with love.

"You know how to transport both yourself and Fred safely. This is a dangerous spell; it will drain you of energy. Never try to do it without preparation and a full stomach. Never try it without a firm destination and true sense of time. Take an image from Fred's mind. He will direct you to the best place and time to appear without alarming any mundane," Jaylor instructed.

"Use your magic cautiously and sparingly," his brother Lukan added. "I don't want to have to come and save your ass."

"Learn to speak. Please," Valeria added. She looked healthier than she had a few hours ago by the pool, her red-gold hair brighter.

Take care of yourself, little one. You know how to conserve your strength. Don't let Lillian bully you into overextending yourself, or your magic, he sent back to her. *Find your own aura. It is distinct from hers.*

She frowned a little as she took the hand of her heartier twin. So alike in face and form, yet so different within. He could see her flowing violet color of life energy reach out to join the tighter swirls of Lillian's plain blue aura—too pale to ever be called magician blue. The two auras twisted and twined about each other into a complex braid. The pale, almost colorless blue dominated and overshadowed the violet.

"Take care of yourself, Glenndon." Mama ran her fingertips along his cheek, memorizing the angle of his bones, the curve of his smile. He could barely see the color of her eyes for the tears that loomed there.

"Be careful, boy." Jaylor slapped his back and looked away, disguising his own moist eyes.

Lukan thought something rude. But then at sixteen, his body was growing faster than his mind, or his self-control.

Glenndon twisted the image and shot it back to his brother upside down. The boy laughed out loud.

One by one his family sent him a hearty message of encouragement and sadness.

Outside the protection of the clearing, he sensed the entire staff and student body of the University gathering to add their own farewells.

I shall send messages often. Whenever I safely can. He raised a hand in farewell.

Before he lost his courage and bolted from the family circle, he grabbed from Fred's mind an image of a grassy plain with rolling, windswept hills, dotted with small copses, and the city just out of sight.

The world dissolved into a jolt of sparkling light, threads and streams of various life colors folded away from him.

He brought them down between two trees in the midst of . . .

"Stand down!" Darville yelled, pulling volume out of his gut. The words bounced around the vale and lost themselves in the copses, the grasslands, the chuckling creek, and the dirt.

Not a single arrow shifted position, up down, or sideways. They all remained firmly aimed at the dragon's heart.

Magic sparkled in the air. He felt as if he had to wade through thick sludge to breathe while bright-colored dust danced around the edges of his vision.

Then suddenly his perspective tilted slightly to the left, every blade of grass and feathered helm took on sharper edges, cleaner lines. The skin of soldiers and lords alike turned opaque, almost translucent. He saw veins and arteries pumping beneath the surface covering; he watched hearts beat and lungs swell.

Dragon magic was like that.

(Protect your ears,) Shayla said calmly. Bemusement sent her thoughts chiming in a delicate tune through Darville's head.

He looked quickly at his daughter, making sure she heard the communication. Linda, eyes wide in wonder, nodded. Then she threw the hem of her cloak over the top of her hair and ducked down into a tight crouch, head between her knees. At the same time she waddled to the side.

Darville mimicked her action, pulling her back, behind the dragon as he did so.

Shayla reared up, wings spread to shield her king and his daughter. Then she loosed a mighty roar that threatened to down trees and sweep twigs and dry leaves all the way back to the city. Steeds reared, unable to remain grounded. Men bent double, fighting to keep their feet beneath them. One and all, they dropped their bows, swords, or pikes to cover their ears with their hands.

Two heartbeats later, the magnificent all color/no color dragon matriarch swept her wings downward once, took two running steps and launched into flapping, ungainly flight away from danger.

Two enterprising soldiers recovered enough to grab their crossbows and take aim at her unprotected belly.

"No!" Darville shouted. His command was lost in the ear-ringing aftermath of a dragon call.

The arrows flew straight.

Shayla rose higher.

High enough?

The aromatic scent of dragon magic doubled.

A blinding flash erupted from the copse behind the soldiers. The arrows turned to ash.

A backwash of magic knocked flat everyone still standing.

Above them, free of danger, Shayla loosed another screech, a deafening laugh of derision.

Who did that?! Who destroyed my plan? I needed to kill the matriarch of the dragons in order to remove magic and magicians from Coronnan once and for all. King Darville and his

pets played right into my hands. All was in place. I could have manipulated his death, the end of the dragons, the end of magic. Even the Princess Royale was in position to die.

But I did not want her to die. She is to be my consort when I am king.

But someone saved the dragon and the king with a blast of magic. Who? Who dares to rob me of my rights, again, with magic?

Who has that much magic in their hands when all the magicians have been banished from court, from Coronnan City, from respectable society?

I will have their head before this day is out.

And then I will be king. Only as king can I rid this land of the defilement of magic.

CHAPTER 12

GLENNDON STAGGERED as the fireball left his hand. Conjuring and throwing it had used up every last bit of energy he had after the enormous effort of transporting himself and Fred to an unknown location.

S'murghit, it all would have been easier with a staff to ground and guide his magic.

Frantically he searched the Kardia for a hint of a silvery-blue ley line. He wasn't supposed to tap rogue magic energy, but this was an emergency. Ah, he found a little one shooting straight and true beneath the copse of trees. A shift of his feet and the spindly tendril granted him a bit of reprieve. Not enough.

Fred caught him just before his knees collapsed. "Don't you think you overdid it a bit?" the bodyguard asked.

Glenndon looked up, following the line of Fred's pointing finger. A bright ball of blue and gold magic roiled across the sky, just beneath the light cloud covering. It continued south, traversing the land without anything to block it or break it apart.

If Da sees that he'll come after us and knock me senseless.

"Your father is there, just crawling upward." Fred shifted his point to a tall man with silver-tipped gold hair. He had managed to get to his hands and knees, shaking his head clear of the magic backwash. Beside him stood a dark-haired girl about the same age as the twins.

She shifted position, scouting the field of fallen soldiers

and frightened steeds trying to break free of their restraints. Her feet shuffled until they rested atop the same ley line he had tapped. Did she know she did that?

Then the sun caught new highlights of color in her hair. No two strands seemed to be the same. An aura as multicolored as her hair, in shifting shades of rust, gold, and brown encircled her. A lovely girl, graceful in every movement, confident in her carriage.

His heart flipped over as he drank in the sight of her.

Who's that? He couldn't be sure he sent that thought correctly. He was so tired the ideas slurred and blended together.

"There, beside your father, my boy, is your sister, Princess Royale Rosselinda de Draconis." Fred steadied Glenndon, making sure he could stand on his own before heading off toward the king and his daughter with long strides. "I think you've got some explaining to do," he called over his shoulder.

Did I save Shayla?

No one answered.

He took one cautious step forward, then another. His stomach growled and ached with emptiness. Chills crept up his spine from his belly, befuddling his brain. He needed food, and fast. Absently he pawed through his pack for the emergency rations all magicians carried. Throwing magic was a lot of hard work. His fingers closed around a packet of jerked meat mixed with berry pulp and some hard journey bread. One bite tasted like the best food ever concocted. The second bite eased the chill. He'd eaten half the rations by the time Fred reached his king and helped him to his feet.

Should he save the rest for the next emergency? He didn't know when he'd get the chance to eat again, and his mother wasn't here to provide for him.

His mother.

His middle ached even more at the thought of leaving her behind.

He looked at the bread and decided to save it. He needed the jerked meat to replenish his body now, or he'd never walk as far as the center of the vale to meet the king, let alone back to the city.

He was just about to begin the trek down the hillside when

the soldiers began to recover. Three of them, more richly dressed then the bulk of the men and each carrying a sword instead of a crossbow or pike, turned to face him. Angry scowls marred their faces.

He needed to get out of here, now.

He had no magical reserves. Another transport spell was far beyond his strength.

"You there! Who are you and what did you do?" a robust middle-aged man called. He kept his sword at his side, neither sheathing nor raising it.

Glenndon here. His greeting left his mind in a bright flowery image designed to assuage any fear or mistrust. He made sure the image was clearer than usual and carried the scent of fresh roses.

It careened back into his mind in a blinding flash of shattered crystals.

He winced and dropped to one knee, clutching his temples and clamping his eyes shut. That didn't help much.

What had happened? It reminded him of when Da had put up a psychic barrier to block his thoughts and force him to speak. The barrier in this man's mind was stronger. More like a blank cliff of reflective rock.

"I asked who you are and where did you come from! What's the matter with you? Are you too stupid to know what I say?" the man shouted as he stalked toward Glenndon.

Glenndon opened his mouth to reply. A weird croaking sound burned the back of his throat. He shut down the impulse to speak before his throat burned raw and bled.

"An idiot!" the man sneered and sheathed his sword. "Harmless." He returned his focus to the still dazzled soldiers. "On your feet, all of you. We need to sort this out. Did anyone wound or kill that ravening beast?"

"Shayla is not a ravening beast, Lord Jemmarc." A new voice, cold and disdainful. "You all still live. You wouldn't if Shayla wanted you dead for *any* reason, including defending herself from those who would execute her without thought or reason. Be grateful that her flame only burned the arrows shot at her."

Glenndon felt the anger rolling off the tall blond man who strode up the hill with Fred and the pretty princess in tow.

The king. His father.

But not his Da.

"Your Grace, I beg to differ . . ." The richly dressed man bobbed his head in some kind of greeting. Not the formal bow Glenndon's mother had taught him.

Something was very wrong here.

The king's eyes locked on Glenndon. A half smile tugged at his lips. "Lord Jemmarc, take your ragtag army of second sons, nephews, and younger brothers of the lords back to the city."

Jemmarc, the man who had called Glenndon an idiot, defied his king for the space of three heartbeats before issuing orders to gather the steeds.

"P'pa," the princess tugged at her father's sleeve. Then she tilted her head in Glenndon's direction.

"Leave two extra steeds for us," King Darville ordered, still not taking his eyes off Glenndon. "And those who dared shoot at a dragon under the protection of the crown will lose rank and pay. They will also walk back to the city. Their steeds will do quite well to transport my bodyguard and our guest. I am in a merciful mood today."

Finally he broke his fixed gaze upon Glenndon and transferred his attention to his daughter. The smile he gave her reminded Glenndon of the loving way Da gazed at the twins when they weren't looking.

Glenndon didn't have to read the man's thoughts to know how much he cared for her, or to know how complex his emotions were at this moment. Even through all that, the king's mind worked, calculating, assessing, thinking ahead, planning and discarding plans as rapidly as Glenndon gathered spells—when he was well-fed and rested.

"Fred, take Princess Rosselinda to the next rise and return with our steeds, please."

"Yes, Your Grace." Fred bowed properly and offered his arm to the girl with the fabulous multicolored hair.

She tossed her father a reproachful glance as she traipsed off ahead of her escort.

"Your chance will come, Little Lindy. I would meet with Glenndon privately a moment," the king called after her.

How do you know that I am Glenndon?

"You couldn't be anyone else. I can read your thoughts because even though the original treaty among the Provinces forbids a monarch from having or using magic, we all have inherited a small amount. It is how the Coraurlia and the dragons recognize us. Do not expect anyone else at court to be able to understand you, not even Fred. He's good at guessing what people think from their posture. You must speak to communicate."

Glenndon nodded, not knowing what else to do. His glance strayed briefly toward Jemmarc. So, the backlash of his communication was the reaction of a truly mind-blind man.

The newest trainees at the University looked to have more talent than any of the lords.

"Yes I know that you have not spoken aloud since you were ill at the age of three. I also know that the healers have pronounced your throat clear and clean," the king continued. "Perhaps when faced with the mind-blind day in and day out you will overcome your reluctance," the king said quietly. "I escaped the worst of the epidemic, but I was sick and I know how much it hurt to talk, how hard it was to force myself to stretch my throat back into working order. It must be one hundred times worse for you."

Glenndon's heart warmed a bit, pushing aside his resentment. At last he'd found someone who understood!

The soldiers and minor lords spread out across the hills and vales, chasing steeds that shied and pranced away from any movement toward them. None of the men appeared to be listening, or interested in the king or . . . or his guest.

"I had hoped our first meeting would be . . . more peaceful, if not private. Nothing at court is truly private." The king took one hesitant step forward, hands extended slightly, as if offering a more intimate greeting but not sure how it would be returned.

Glenndon wanted to accept the king's affection. He relived a moment of the fierce and intense hugs his parents and siblings passed around at any excuse. Valeria's slender fingers touched him most deeply because she depended upon him for so much. But this man, the king, was not family. He wanted to claim Glenndon as a son.

Glenndon was not ready to name him father, despite that moment of understanding.

This "ragtag" army answers to me. None other. Someone else pays them, but they understand me. I too am less than a legitimate first son and heir. They know my motives and agree with my plans. None of them shall suffer for shooting at the dragon. I ordered the deed. I alone shall walk back to the city. I alone shoulder the responsibility. But only as far as my army can see. No one else must know who leads here. Not yet. But soon.

CHAPTER 13

JAYLOR RAN HIS FINGER down two lists of names. Master Robb had proposed five apprentices ready for advancement. For the first time Glenndon's name appeared on the annual review of student progress. He let his finger linger on the name, should he run a line through it? Ritual required the candidate be present during the annual ceremony of giving the gifts of a medium blue robe to replace the light blue, a slightly larger piece of glass for scrying, and a journey to complete the training.

Glenndon could not appear for the ceremony. Nor had he learned to speak.

On the other list, Marcus had put Lukan's name at the top. Jaylor agreed that his second son—he could not get it out of his head that Glenndon was not his first—had accomplished enough over the last year to advance. Though not as strong or imaginative as his brother, he completed his assignments within allotted time periods. No better or worse than his classmates. Still, was it fair to advance the younger boy before his brother?

He raised his head from the list, listening to the air and touching his own Master-sized scrying glass, praying for word, from any one of half a dozen sources, that Glenndon and Fred had arrived safely at court.

Nothing.

But there was a firm step and clatter of boot heels in the corridor outside his office.

"Guess what I found!" Robb announced with glee. He strode in without knocking or asking permission. He'd always been precise in concocting a spell and in protocol. Until he and Maigret had gone adventuring on their own journey to explore the Big Continent and ports unknown. Marcus was the freewheeling, free-thinking, rely-on-his-luck magician in his youth. Then he met Vareena and settled in to be an excellent husband, father, and teacher. Best friends, Marcus' and Robb's talents and personalities complemented each other.

"It had better be good, and interesting," Jaylor growled. He had no need to worry about Glenndon. But he did, and worry always made him snappish.

"It is. Oh, it is very good." Robb plunked himself down in a chair facing the desk without invitation. Tall and lean—though not as tall as Jaylor—he was dressed in mud- and sweat-stained dark blue leathers—master blue—as if just returned from his latest outing to conquer the Krakatrice where they nested. Beneath his arm he cradled a painted wooden box. Garish red, blue, green, yellow, and purple designs flowed around the container, oblivious to the restrictions of corners and angles.

"Rover designs," Jaylor muttered, less angry with the world as he surmised the contents.

"Rover designs indeed, straight from the hands of Zolltarn, their chief. He's getting very old, by the way, and probably won't rove much longer."

"Zolltarn would rather die in his boots on the road with the wind in his face than peaceably in his bed—which would be inside one of their sledge conveyances. *Stargods!* He was older than I am now when I first met him twenty years ago. He is nearly ancient. So what did he give you?"

"Sold me. When has a Rover ever given away anything?" Robb cocked his head mischievously. "I'll ask for reimbursement, seeing as how the gold came out of my own pocket . . ."

Jaylor reached for a pouch he kept hidden behind him among a stash of scrolls and empty inkwells. Then paused. "What is in the box?" he demanded. Though he thought he knew.

"This!" Robb lifted the lid to display the contents: a dozen finely flaked spear heads in glistening obsidian, the black volcanic glass nearly glowing with remainders of the heat of its forging.

"At last," Jaylor sighed in relief. "Did you retrieve the spearhead I gave you this morning?"

"Of course. These things are too dear to let even one of them get lost. Broken maybe, but not lost."

"And did you kill the latest Krakatrice?"

"Barely. Very tricky situation."

Jaylor's spine tingled in warning.

"The villagers had decided an orphan girl of about twelve was a witch. She had no family to defend her. So they let the hatchling snake feed off her fresh blood." Both men shuddered. "Maigret is working a healing spell and smothering her with motherly love. Vareena will take her in. My house is already full with our own two boys and half a dozen girl apprentices. If anyone can banish the hideous memories, those two can."

"And did the village men . . . did they force their favorite 'cure' for witchcraft upon her before they fed her to the monster?" Jaylor didn't want to think about the cruelty of ignorant peasants who took the law into their own hands to satisfy their own lustful and violent needs.

"I thought we disproved that ancient prejudice long ago," Robb muttered. "Magicians do not lose their talent or powers if they engage in sex before achieving master Status."

"You and Marcus certainly didn't," Jaylor said on a smile. He had to look hard for anything good that might come of this situation. He had too many refugees who either had no talent or had had it abused out of them by torture. More and more, angry villagers declared evil and sorcerous any person they couldn't control, or who had no one to defend them.

"Seems like I remember you disproved the old saw long before Marcus and I did." Robb laughed, but he ended on a yawn and wince as he shrugged his tired shoulders. Clinging to a dragon and then fighting a giant snake—even a young one—was hard work. "So what's the news from Coronnan City?"

"Nothing yet. Glenndon has only been gone a few hours."

"If I remember the capital rightly, he's going to be so overwhelmed with new sights, sounds, smells, and wonders he won't even think about notifying you that he's safe."

"Let's hope. In the meantime, are you serious about advancing him to journeyman?"

"Wouldn't have put his name on the list if I weren't."

"Let me think on this a bit."

"Not too long, or you'll lose him as both a son and a magician. The same goes for Lukan." With that, Robb levered himself to his feet, stretched his back, and left without any formal or polite good-byes, yawning all the way.

Half an hour later, a huge ball of blue magic rolled across the sky above the clearing. Jaylor watched in wonder as the fire within wove threads of magic. All kinds of magic. He saw the glittery power of the dragons, all colors and yet no color at all, just like Shayla, the dragon matriarch. Ley line blue coiled around that, seeking, questing connections to each other, and trying to find a ground into the Kardia beneath his feet. And something else. Something he'd never seen before.

"What's happening?" Lillian straightened from digging weeds in the tuber patch. She shielded her eyes from the glare of magic and light with one grubby hand.

"Can't you see it?" Valeria asked her twin.

"I can't see anything beyond the sun's glare." Lillian bent back to her task.

Jaylor watched his daughter a moment as she pulled leafy greens with long roots from her own section of the garden as well as Valeria's. Lillian frequently shouldered her twin's chores to spare her strength.

Valeria raised her arms, palms flat, thumb and little finger slightly curved to gather as much of the power within the fireball as she could. A thin tendril of the magic twined and spat straight down into her hands. Her body grew taller, fuller, more vibrant with the flow of energy, like parched ground absorbing rain. Some of it spilled off and rerooted into the land, where it belonged.

Jaylor watched the purple shadows around her eyes fade and pink flush her skin as her lungs filled with air. She relaxed her knees and let her feet flex and rise in their own dance of thanksgiving. The chronic drag of fatigue vanished.

He worried about the girl. Never strong, she only flourished when in physical contact with her twin or when drinking in wild magic.

His frown deepened, as much in frustration at not knowing how to help Valeria as the weirdness in and around that massive fireball.

He turned his attention back to the ball of magic because he *might* be able to do something about that. As he watched, it began to fragment and weaken. Only then did he see other elements of power. Unnatural red fire that should be the green and lazy tendrils of something gentle and nurturing.

Did he hear music in the distance? Not unusual. Brevelan sang all the time, weaving her own nurturing magic into their lives. Stargods only knew if he'd have survived this long without her calming his erratic heartbeat and cooling his rush of temper. But this was different, a chiming melody that did not spring from a human throat. More like the Kardia and the sky exchanging a joke.

He almost recognized the tune. His mind sought and failed to find the lyrics that owned the music.

"What was that?" he roared to anyone and everyone within hearing distance and beyond.

Lillian shrugged. Valeria watched in wonder, choosing to retreat into silence, just like Glenndon.

"Just sunlight bouncing off the white cliffs," Lillian said on a yawn.

"That fireball smelled of Glenndon," Lukan said, staring in awe at the huge spell. He'd wandered over from where he practiced carrying firewood with his mind from one disorganized pile into a neat stack. "How'd he do that? I need to try it."

"No, you don't," Jaylor ordered, grabbing his son by the collar and turning him away from the magic's trajectory. "That magic also smells of desperation. Hasty and piecemeal. I hope Glenndon is all right."

Wind whipped around the tree canopy, bending the top boughs low. Shayla screeched in distress and anger above them. Her wings beat hard and fast against the air, propelling her back to the sanctuary of her nesting cave on the mountain's high slopes.

Even Lillian looked up from her chores to watch the distortion in the air that could only be a dragon.

An image of men gathering in a grassy vale flashed into Jaylor's mind.

"Oh, my. Glenndon just saved Shayla." The words spilled hastily out of Valeria's mouth.

". . . from attack by soldiers with crossbows," Lillian finished the sentence.

"Heh?" Jaylor asked. "It appears Shayla is not talking to me at the moment. She always reports to me or your mother first."

"She did not greet me," Valeria said.

"She only shared the image. Now she's gone," Lillian continued for her, for them.

"Is that the princess?" Lillian asked.

A reflection of Valeria's original image skittered across Jaylor's vision. One of the twins—who knew which one— highlighted the slim figure in an elegant riding costume with long multi-hued hair watching the arrows fly. Her mouth gaped in horror.

"Show me more clearly!" Jaylor demanded.

Valeria bounced the image from Lillian back to their father, and over to Lukan, complete with highlights.

He studied the image a moment, looking directly at Valeria. Or through her. He couldn't decide which.

"This is getting a little vague and dim with all the bouncing around, but I do believe the girl is Princess Rosselinda. She looks just like her mother."

"She's gorgeous," Lukan sighed. Then he pulled himself out of adolescent reverie. "And the tall man? The king?" Lukan asked, tilting his head in puzzlement.

Jaylor nodded, eyes slightly crossed, still examining things in his head.

"He . . . he does look a bit like Glenndon." Lukan blushed, like he was afraid to admit what they'd all avoided saying. "But the eyes are different."

"Noticed that, did you?" Jaylor said grimly.

Lillian gestured to Valeria in a private sign. Still bubbling with the magical energy she'd borrowed from the fireball, Valeria sent soothing waves of empathy around the clearing, making sure they lighted on her father and brother.

Immediately, Jaylor's shoulders relaxed and the frown

lines around his mouth and eyes eased. "Shayla only showed you what angered *her,* not what would sadden us. If anything hurt Glenndon, her anger would overshadow everything else. I'm sure we can stop worrying about Glenndon. For the moment," he said

Is that true, Shayla? Valeria and Lillian asked the disappearing distortion in the sky.

Jaylor had no problem eavesdropping on their mental conversation. So far. At least when they weren't consciously keeping him out.

(Of course,) Shayla replied.

Valeria relaxed, and so did her twin.

"Come, I believe your mother has a meal ready." Jaylor ushered them toward the cabin, still sorting out images and how strongly each of his children performed magic.

"I smelled yampion pie earlier," Lukan said eagerly. "With Glenndon gone maybe I'll get a piece big enough to ease my hunger."

Jaylor's mood darkened again and his shoulders slumped. "I hope they feed him correctly in the City."

"We all worry about him, Da." Lillian slipped her hand into his.

Valeria followed suit. "He's hungry now though."

Jaylor raised his eyebrows at her.

"A quick thought is all I need to find him."

"She's always been able to sense where he is," Lillian added.

"For as long as I can remember, almost like an instinct."

CHAPTER 14

LINDA ROUGHLY GRABBED her steed's reins from their loose tie around a sapling. Fortunately she and P'pa had tethered their mounts far enough away from the dragon that they did not spook as much as the others. With another yank, she freed P'pa's stallion.

"Easy, Your Highness," Fred said quietly, placing his gentle hand atop hers. His hand might lie lightly now, but the calluses on his palm and the muscles in his arms reminded her that he wielded weapons as casually as she did a pen. He probably juggled sword, knife, and throwing stars with more skill than she did any kind of word play. All the while his queue remained tight and controlled; a knotted leather thong with metal tips wove around the braid, making his hair another weapon if he ever removed the strip and used it as a whip or garrote.

"Fred, you have been a friend to me and my sisters for as long as I can remember."

"I try, Your Highness."

"I missed you these past two weeks. I didn't realize how naked P'pa looks without you beside him, until you came back. You are so much a part of the background, I don't think anyone notices you until you are absent."

"I missed you too, Your Highness." He reached out to tousle her hair, as he had before her coming of age. Reluctantly he returned his palm to his sword pommel, respectful of her rank.

"So, as a friend, tell me about this Glenndon." She focused on the two stiff figures atop the next knoll. Both tall and blond, both broad of shoulder and slim of waist with long legs. One elegant, confident, and poised, the other roughly clothed and hunched warily, out of place.

"He has been yanked away from his family and friends, his home, and all he holds dear. Be gentle with him, Your Highness. Do not judge too quickly." Fred took the leading rein of the stallion and began a slow return to the hilltop.

"Couldn't he have put on some better clothes? He looks like the gardener just come in from digging in the dirt."

"Those are his best clothes, Highness. Except for perhaps his formal magician's robes. But I do not think that would be acceptable at court."

Linda stopped short. Belle nudged her from behind with an imperious nose. She stumbled forward a bit from the prodding mare. "Are they so poor at this exiled college of magicians that all they can afford to wear are rags?"

"Not rags, Highness. Look closer. Roughly woven certainly, but not a ragged spot or mending patch on him. Out of style perhaps, but serviceable, durable, and unobtrusive. Perfect for traveling on the king's highways."

"But you did not come by the highway. I saw you appear out of nowhere in a cloud of sparkling dust bright enough to rival the dragon."

"Saw that did you? I thought all attention was on the dragon."

"Most, not all. I was looking directly at you. Couldn't miss it if I tried."

"Hmmm, I'll have to remember that. You aren't as mindblind as most people. Maybe you can cut through Glenndon's wall of lonely reserve."

"Lonely?"

"Think how you would feel if a stranger arrived with a letter demanding you go halfway across the continent to meet a relative you'd never met who was claiming you as heir. Glenndon knows no one here and is forbidden to use magic to contact those he loves, including his parents."

"But P'pa is his father."

"His Grace may be his sire. But Lord Jaylor, Senior

Magician and Chancellor of the University of Magicians is his Da."

"Oh." Linda slowed her steps while she thought about that. Suddenly the disreputable traveler Lord Jemmarc had declared an idiot didn't look so horrible.

"Is he an idiot?" She didn't think he could be if M'ma and P'pa had agreed to bring him to court as a possible heir to the Dragon Crown. Lord Andrall's son, Mardall, had been excluded from the line of succession because he was . . . had problems learning and growing beyond the mental capabilities of a five year old.

"Glenndon is probably smarter than you and me combined, Little Lindy. But very few people will be able to see that. Come, time we introduced you to your brother."

"My brother. My older brother." She tasted the words, wondering if they'd ever stop feeling alien.

"You do not sit that steed easily, Glenndon," Darville said. He'd wanted to call the boy "son" and didn't quite dare. Glenndon's stony silence made the king's gut roil with uncertainty.

Linda rode on Darville's right, as she always had.

Glenndon stared at him a moment from his precariously balanced seat atop the steed to the king's left. An image of looking at his own feet moving silently through the forest flashed across Darville's mind, so fast he almost didn't catch it.

"You walk everywhere at . . . at the University complex?" He'd known since the beginning that Glenndon did not talk. Why should he be surprised at the clarity of his telepathic communication? The boy had had a lot of practice.

A feeling of assent answered Darville's words.

"Have you ever ridden?"

Blankness. "I guess not. We'll remedy that soon enough. We walk about the City mostly because it is so crowded and the streets are so narrow." He tried to conjure a memory of walking across one of the numerous bridges that connected the city islands in the river delta. Then he imagined the latches on each end of every bridge. In times of invasion the inhabitants could retreat inward, removing the bridges as they went so the enemy could not follow. The tricky currents in and around the islands made approaching by small river boat inadvisable to anyone who had not grown up knowing which side stream to take and which inlet to beach a boat upon.

Glenndon graced him with a blazing smile.

"You caught those images?"

The boy nodded eagerly.

"Your Da taught me to swim when we were Linda's age," Darville added. "We were great friends, in and out of trouble, exploring every island, getting to know them all intimately."

Glenndon's face fell and he turned away, watching the grass and trees rustle at their passage. He looked more than a little pale and shaky.

Darville remembered times when Jaylor had much the same pallor and listlessness . . .

"Has your mother ever learned to eat meat?" he asked, wondering what he might have with him to offer the boy in the way of food.

Glenndon shook his head, but he swallowed a glimmer of a smile.

"Do you and your . . . Jaylor also avoid meat, since that meant an animal losing its life to feed you?"

A quick image of Jaylor, Glenndon, and another boy—a little younger, thinner, and less muscled, but the spitting image of Jaylor—eating vigorously in a long refectory filled with other blue-robed people carving thick slabs off a haunch of venison filled his mind.

Darville smile openly. "I wouldn't tell your mother about that either. Her anger would be . . . formidable."

Linda bristled at that for some teenage, female reason he couldn't fathom. Then she changed the subject most haughtily. "I can teach Glenndon how to ride, as you taught me, P'pa."

"You have lessons and exercises in diplomacy. Glenndon will join you at your spyhole behind the Council meeting chamber," Darville said. "You will help him learn court manners and protocol. I'd like the opportunity to teach him to ride and swing a sword."

A sense of angry objection radiated out from Glenndon.

"Yes, I know your mother taught you manners and protocols. I suspect what you needed for life at the University is a bit different from the court. I can't imagine life with magicians is as devious and manipulative as it is with nobles, all cloaked in exquisite politeness and double speak."

Glenndon laughed out loud, long and heartily.

"I guess not. I remember your Da using a truth spell once. It wasn't pretty."

Glenndon nodded.

"So magicians also have to learn to cloak their words in half-truths and innuendo so they don't truly lie, but also do not reveal the truth."

Linda's eyes went wide in wonder. "I must learn to spot such actions."

"Yes you must. Glenndon will teach you."

His two children surveyed each other, weighing and assessing strengths and weaknesses.

"Can Glenndon figure out who tried to kill you by weakening your sword?" Linda asked quietly.

Glenndon looked about in wild panic, shaking his head and moaning.

Darville couldn't tell if he meant that he couldn't do it, or if the thought of finding the truth behind the assassin frightened him.

Fred leaned over and grabbed the steed's reins just before Glenndon tried to bolt back toward the vale they'd left behind half an hour ago.

"Where are we, P'pa?" Linda whispered to her father as they dismounted in the courtyard of a strange stable. Glenndon nearly fell out of his saddle and spent long minutes massaging his thighs.

Long, low-roofed stone buildings stretched down opposite sides of the yard. Steeds poked their heads out from half doors along those buildings, curious to see the newcomers. The end building looked like a massive barn, also made of stone, that towered above the compound. The fourth wall, with the broad double gate, appeared to be four stories of quarters for the families who managed the steeds.

Beyond the stable, spacious pastures, also neatly fenced, spread out in three directions. She'd spotted a number of steeds grazing on the bright grass.

She thought they might be on the north shore of the Coronnan River, but couldn't be certain after the serpentine route they'd taken around the fringe of outer islands, crossing four or five bridges, some broad and arched over a wide channel, others narrow and low. They'd passed compact fields showing the first hints of new plantings and marked by neat fences. Few people lived this far out. Not many pairs of eyes to note the passage of their king and his miniscule entourage.

"Where do you think our steeds are housed? Not in the city itself where space is precious."

That made sense. "Do we walk back to Palace Isle?" She estimated the distance to be at least two miles, maybe more considering the jagged pattern of bridges. Nothing lay in a straight line through Coronnan City, to slow down invaders and avoid unstable temporary aits.

"In a way, Little Lindy," P'pa laughed.

Fred led them into the stable at the far end, where the left-hand building met the barn. He kept a wary hand on his sword, eyes searching the shadows for signs of danger.

Glenndon watched everything. His hesitant steps looked more cautious than curious. Would he be able to detect danger lurking behind the high wooden walls of the steed boxes?

His hands clenched and released at his sides, at the ready. Ready for what?

Linda drew closer to her father. She'd trained in sword and bow, more out of boredom than a need to protect herself. P'pa rested a reassuring hand on her shoulder, letting her cling just behind his right side. His left hand dominated, she knew better than to interfere with his ability to draw his sword and defend them.

History lessons of war and murderous power struggles among the lords suddenly became real, more than just stories she had to memorize.

Seemingly satisfied that they were alone, Fred moved into

a large, loose box intended for mares about to foal. Narrow
alleys for grooming tools and buckets and stools and such
separated the box from the other narrower stalls. The hay on
the floor and in the feed box was fresh, as was the water in
the trough. It looked ready for use at a moment's notice.

In the back corner, closest to the barn, Fred ran his fingers
along a stone seam. Linda heard a tiny click as Fred pressed
his hand flat against a stone about even with Linda's chest.

Glenndon watched him as closely as Linda did.

Slowly a section of wall swung inward on well-oiled pivots. Darkness, blacker than a cloudy night at the new moon,
yawned before them. It smelled damp and musty. She wondered when the door had last been opened. Recently, judging
by the care taken with the silent hinges. But it smelled of
long disuse.

"I should not need to tell either of you that this passage is
known only to the family and special retainers," P'pa said
quietly.

My parents?

Linda heard Glenndon's question almost as if he had spoken directly into her ear. But the words blossomed in the
center of her head.

Beside her, P'pa stiffened and grimaced, then made himself relax. Why?

"Your Mama and Da know that the palace and Palace Isle
are riddled with secret passages and forgotten rooms. I do not
know if they have ever been through this one," he replied.

Glenndon turned a tight circle, sniffing the air much like
a cat or dog would, learning who had passed through here.

"You are both considered my heirs. You need to learn as
many of the hidden paths as possible. I do not trust some of
the lords to value your safety above their quest for power."
With that, P'pa turned sideways and took two long steps into
the darkness. He disappeared as soon as his shoulders cleared
the opening.

A heartbeat later, a torch flared, revealing him and a steep
staircase of damp stone descending behind him.

Linda took a deep breath and followed. Fred had to push
Glenndon into the passageway before closing the door behind them. She watched carefully, learning the stone that

stood out from the others just a tiny bit. Fred pressed it hard, leaning most of his weight into it. He did not release his pressure on it until no light shone around the edges of the narrow door.

"If you ever need to reopen this door when it is mostly closed, you must wait until it closes fully, wait for the count of thirty, then press the latch again," Fred explained. "Otherwise it will jam."

The flickering torch created a small pool of light that separated them from the absolute nothingness beyond.

"Watch your steps, and learn them well. There may come a time when you have to move through here silently and without light. There are side passages that loop back, and others that end abruptly in deep pits, or narrow to the point where a grown man can become irretrievably wedged in an airless crawl space, as the roof changes height frequently and abruptly. These passages are for our safety. Make them a part of yourself and they will not betray you." P'pa began the descent as he spoke.

"P'pa, why? How . . . ?"

"In my youth, when I first accepted the Coraurlia, others thought me unfit to wear the crown or lead Coronnan. They feared the dragons and their magic as much as they loved the idea of power and wealth. I had to run for my life and fight to the death more than once."

Linda hurried after him rather than be left in darkness.

Fought to the death, more than once. She shuddered with more than chill, suddenly not so easy with the privilege of being a princess. It came with a high price.

CHAPTER 15

GLENNDON MOVED one foot forward cautiously. His boots slid on damp stone. He fought for balance. Cut off from sun and fresh air, with no landmarks, and no dragons to direct him, he lost connection with the magnetic south pole. His command of up and down, right and left deserted him. His very sense of self threatened to flee with the light they'd left behind. He needed to run back there, take off his boots and ground himself in the Kardia.

Fred grabbed his arm. "Breathe, boy."

How could people breathe down here?

Fred slapped his back, forcing him to open his mouth. Rancid air filled his lungs. Enough. He'd survive a while, if not thrive.

Another cautious step, this one not quite so slick. His balance held but his head still whirled. A third step and he knew something was different about it. More than the absence of wet. The fourth step was absolutely dry.

He cast about him for an explanation. His eyes failed him. The torch gave him enough light to guide his steps but blinded him to anything beyond.

He needed to take his boots off to widen his senses through his feet. He would not touch the walls of this narrow tunnel with their layers of green slime. Boots should only be worn in the worst of weather to protect him from frostbite and snow.

Two more steps down, not quite so steep as the first half

dozen. The light projected forward a bit further than before. He took one step down without looking at his feet. The stone dipped a bit in the center, cradling his foot. And it was warm.

In surprise he looked down, concentrating on the essence of stone. Hints of silvery blue light rimmed his foot.

A ley line? Da had taught him how to find and use the magic embedded in the land, along with lessons on how to gather dragon magic and hold it deep within him for a time. All magicians received basic lessons in both forms now. But using ley lines to power their talent took its toll on a man's strength. It also limited his power to what he could dredge up through his own body. Alone. Dragon magic gathered from the air around them and held in reserve could be combined with the strength of other magicians in physical contact with each other. The strength of each spell grew exponentially with each magician added to the circle.

Ley lines should be reserved for emergencies when he had no dragon magic left, and no other magicians to draw upon.

He'd taught Valeria how to draw physical strength as well as magic from a ley line long before her tutors had. She seemed to need the lines to survive as much as she did to fuel her magic.

Greedily he drank in the power that beckoned him. Not much. The line was weak, not much more than a tendril. It would not travel far from the larger line it had branched from. It gave him enough *sight* to sense the dressed stones constructing this tunnel. The breaths of both Rosselinda and the king rasped in his ears. But not Fred's.

(Blood link,) someone whispered. *(You feel your father and sister through your blood. The other you must learn to attune your senses to.)*

Who spoke? Surely not a dragon, though the words carried the tone and pattern of dragon thoughts. If the Kardia sapped the dragon magic he'd gathered unconsciously through the day, how could a dragon thought penetrate the depth of dirt and stone that separated him from fresh air?

(You are never far from us. You are one of us.)

He pressed onward, eyes shifting up and down, back and forth. The tiny ley line ran straight and true down the center of the tunnel, then stopped abruptly. The wall curved to the right. Ley lines could not shift direction. They only appeared to when they interested another line, or branched off of a larger one.

Ah, there, the parent line ran through the center of this new direction. But not for long. Another twist of stone and another line, then another. The stone work followed the lines.

A side tunnel branched off to their left. No line there. Secretly he smiled. Now he knew how to navigate this tunnel, and probably all the tunnels and underground passages.

Another jog onto the path of an even larger line.

Where were they all coming from?

Ley lines formed a web around all the world of Kardia Hodos, and according to legend, they ran off into the skies to guide the Stargods to and from this planet, their refuge. To cover the entire world, the lines needed space between them, intersecting rarely. In some places on the mountain he'd traveled half a mile or more to find and memorize the next line.

Here, beneath Coronnan City, traversing the multiple islands in the river delta that made up the capital, the lines seemed to converge and knot together.

(The Well of Life.) That strange voice in his head again.

The Well of Life. Ley lines, the Tambootie trees, dragons, and magic were all linked. Indigo had told him so. And there was a magically protected archives beneath the palace.

So much to think about. So much to learn.

By the time they climbed upward from bedrock beneath the river, Glenndon had so many questions he didn't have time to fear the weight of the Kardia above him, or the confrontations he knew must come when he met the king's court. And his queen. The woman who would become his substitute mother. He didn't like this at all.

Jaylor leaned heavily against a boulder on the edge of an ancient rock slide—which was rapidly becoming a mountain meadow as new grasses and low shrubs sprouted through the thick layer of gravel. Baamin had deposited him here before flying home to the dragon nest. He slid to the ground and rested his head against sun-warmed rock.

Where were the Krakatrices coming from? Everyday, magicians and dragons killed another. This one was older, more experienced, sought a damming spot on a stream higher in the mountains and away from murderous villagers. Jaylor'd had no help, or interference, this time. That didn't make the expedition any easier.

"*S'murghit,* I wish I had a Tambootie tree near," Jaylor muttered under his breath.

He wished he'd had another master magician with him to share the burden of throwing magic as well as sharp objects.

Robb had gone out this morning; Marcus tomorrow. Both young men usually returned more tired than they wanted to admit. No one else had the skills to go snake hunting.

But dragon magic was getting harder and harder to gather. Ley lines were sinking deeper into the Kardia, not releasing their power so easily.

"The magic is going away. Slowly but surely." Maybe that was why the Krakatrice infested the land.

And the Circle of Masters were either too old or unskilled to do battle with diminishing magic and mundane weapons at the same time. He wondered if any of the journeymen could be trained . . . ?

He needed to seek out old references, find out where the ancient menace originated and then suddenly appeared where it had no business living.

A rustle in the underbrush brought him out of his drowsy musing. He didn't want to face people right now. So he remained silent, hidden from the forest by the boulder.

"We have to hold hands to make this work," Lillian said. Her voice was a tone deeper than her twin's; physically more mature.

"I know that," Valeria replied, her light soprano tones squeaking a bit back into childhood range.

"But we aren't gathering dragon magic. Women can't do that. It's impossible," Lillian said, less certain then before.

"I know," Valeria added wearily. "I've listened to all of Da's lectures as well as you."

Probably better, Jaylor thought. Valeria had more interest in magic and less in cooking and managing the kitchen garden.

"We're drawing power from the Kardia. Just like Glenndon taught us," Valeria said, sounding like she was instructing her sister.

He peeked around his boulder to see the girls perched upon another sun-warmed rock between him and the chuckling creek, attention on each other, not their surroundings. *Careless,* he thought.

Lillian nodded uncertainly. They sat, crossed-legged, facing each other on the big flat rock. They joined hands, like they always did, never far from each other, always touching, two halves of a whole.

"I know we've never called a dragon before. But we really need to do this. Glenndon is in trouble," Valeria reassured her sister. "I know how to do this."

"For Glenndon," Lillian repeated. She closed her eyes and drew a tune out of the air.

Valeria picked up the music. She could follow any tune, but when it came time to begin a song she could never find one. Or those she did find were wrong for the spell.

"Listen to Mama," Lillian said. "Her music keeps her in contact with Shayla and the Kardia. All the time. For a dragon summoning song just listen to Mama."

That made sense; Jaylor chuckled to himself, learning something obvious from his own daughters.

Jaylor closed his eyes and listened. Sure enough, lilting notes danced on the wind. He couldn't imagine Brevelan without a song teasing her mouth and her eyes.

Then Lillian began singing in a voice reminiscent of her mother. Valeria picked up the words and the tune half a beat behind her sister.

> *Come to me,*
> *Indigo,*
> *Purple and blue,*
> *Both in the glow.*

Not much of a song but it would have to do. Intent was more important than the words.

The girls repeated the song, letting it fill the meadow, themselves, and Jaylor. He let himself vibrate in rhythm.

Suddenly he felt better. Still tired and hungry, but no longer discouraged and aching with bone-deep fatigue.

The ground beneath his rump vibrated as the girls coaxed power from the Kardia to climb upward through their bodies, quicken with the music and grow and grow until they could contain the music no longer.

Simultaneously she and Lillian opened their mouths to release the music and the spell.

Jaylor needed to add his baritone to their music but refrained. This was their spell. They needed to complete it on their own. He needed to stay silent and observe to make sure they made no mistakes.

The music flowed out and out in visible tendrils of purple and blue and rust and yellow-tinged green entwined, sometimes in an organized braid, partly in knotted chaos. And they sang.

Valeria pulled more and more magic from the Kardia through her body. And when her strength flagged, Lillian took up the chore, her voice rising in a magnificent soprano full of depth and lyrical lilt. Together they told the story in harmony of their need for Indigo to come to them.

Jaylor felt how Valeria strained to maintain her part of the spell. White dots began to mar the growing perfection of the colored braid of magic. But still she sang.

Wind buffeted them. Valeria sagged and wavered. She leaned closer to Lillian, using her stronger body as a windbreak to keep her from tumbling into the creek. Or away from the creek.

A last long high note that symbolized a dragon calling across the void cracked in Valeria's throat. It splintered the magic. The spell dropped back into the Kardia, bright dust, rapidly fading. Rich green saber ferns and moss along the creek absorbed it until there was no trace. It might never have been.

Tiredly, she coughed, and coughed again.

Jaylor half stood, ready to come to her aid.

Before he could move, Lillian dropped their clammy handclasp and pounded upon Valeria's back. "You did it again! You promised you wouldn't push yourself to exhaustion. How am I going to explain this to Mama?" she wailed.

So that's what happened to weaken Valeria, she actually carried the spells with her stronger talent, and Lillian gave meager support.

Something to think about.

"Did we succeed?" Valeria croaked. She rested her head on her sister's chest, breathing raggedly.

(Yes. You succeeded.) Then on a brighter note, almost as an afterthought, *(Indigo here.)*

Jaylor held his finger to his lips to signal that the dragon should not acknowledge him.

Indigo winked back, youthful humor across his face and rippling along his spines.

Jaylor knew the dragon would include him in any telepathic communication with the girls.

Sunlight bounced off his crystal fur that still held faint traces of juvenile silver. Soon, each strand of hair would reflect all light, forcing the eye of an observer to slide away, making him nearly invisible. Except for his horns, wingtips, and wing veins, so dark a blue it looked almost purple, or black, depending on the angle of the light. He shook spray from his outstretched wings and folded them neatly against his sides, hiding the outline of color. Only the horns dancing from his forehead down his spine to his barbed tail revealed his length, and therefore the breadth of chest needed to support him.

"Hello, Indigo," Lillian returned the greeting for both of them.

(Little one,) Indigo sounded concerned. He dipped his head so that his spiral head horn prodded Valeria's shoulder in query. *(I heard your first note as if you were another dragon calling me. You need not have spent so much of yourself to complete the spell.)*

"A spell must be completed and grounded. Otherwise stray magic will wander around uncontrolled seeking mischief," Valeria parroted an early lesson.

"You are right. I'm glad one of my offspring learned something about magic theory," Jaylor growled as he rose from his hiding place and approached his girls. "Good to see you, Indigo. Jaylor here." He followed formal dragon protocol and bowed as well. "But, little Valeria, you exhaust yourself because you pour all of yourself into each spell. You must learn finer control. Conserve your strength."

(Your sire is correct.) Indigo stood in the middle of the upper creek, head tilted as if listening, or surveying a puzzle.

"What is so important that you had to summon a dragon with enough power to light the entire capital city with glow balls for a year?" Jaylor knelt beside Valeria and Lillian, gently soothing backs and legs and arms with his touch. He'd done his master magician duty in finding their error. Now he needed to be their loving Da.

(I cannot find Glenndon,) Indigo answered for the girls.

"And neither can we," Lillian added.

"I can always find Glenndon with a thought. But not now," Valeria finished.

Jaylor sat back on his heels. "I can barely decide who said what. Are you all one personality?"

Indigo chuckled. Steam leaked out of his nose in his mirth. *(Closer to the truth than you imagine, Senior Magician.)*

"What is that supposed to mean?"

"Nothing, Da. Nothing. But Glenndon must have fallen into deep trouble if a dragon cannot find him," Valeria insisted.

"Especially if he has royal blood as the letter claimed. The dragons are tied by magic, love, loyalty, and tradition to the royal family," Lillian finished.

Da lifted Valeria slightly, cradling her in his own lap.

"I cannot go to Coronnan City at this time. Indigo, can you seek out my errant son?" He avoided confirmation of Valeria's statement.

(No. I may not go. Shayla has forbidden any dragon to approach the city. Soldiers shot arrows at her.)

"So that's what the fuss was all about earlier," Da mused. "Then we must find another way to contact Glenndon. I will summon a circle of masters. Together we should be able to scry him out."

(There is another way. Dangerous. I do not know if I can do this.)

Jaylor stood up, still holding Valeria close against him.

"How?" she asked, turning her head to peek at the dragon while still letting it rest on Jaylor's shoulder.

"Can we help? Give you strength or guidance?" he asked the dragon.

"I'll help too," Lillian said. She stood beside Jaylor, holding Valeria's hand.

(Trust me.)

CHAPTER 16

KING DARVILLE LEANED heavily on the last door mechanism. The stone wall moved ponderously on its pivots. He hadn't had to use this portal in nigh on twenty years. In those days, the room at the end of the tunnel had been the guest chamber for the then-visiting Princess Rossemikka of Rossemeyer, his betrothed. He pushed aside the musty tapestry that obscured the portal, a half smile on his face in delightful memory. He patted the weaving fondly. The once bright colors depicting a mythological scene of the Stargods descending on a silvery cloud of fire were reduced to shades of gray from the accumulation of dust and cobwebs.

Behind him, Linda sneezed in the cloud of dust he disturbed. Fred rubbed at his itching nose. And Glenndon . . .

Glenndon was so absorbed in watching his feet that he barely noticed they'd emerged from underground.

The torch guttered and spluttered one last flame before slinking back down to the barest glow of ember. He ground it against the tunnel wall to extinguish the last of the fire and thrust the useless handle at Fred.

"Where are we?" Linda spun in a slow circle, memorizing every detail of the abandoned room at the end of an abandoned corridor. She blinked in the reduced light sneaking past three arrow-slit windows on the eastern wall.

"Another part of the maze this palace has become over the centuries. This is the oldest part of the keep. The foundations are still solid, but some of the mortar has begun to crumble. My architects decided a decade ago that we'd all be more comfortable in newer, less drafty quarters."

And he could keep some delightful memories intact; prevent strangers from trampling them by altering any portion of this room.

"The outer walls will stand forever, some of the inner walls, floors and ceilings are less safe. Be careful if you ever decide to explore this section."

Linda nodded as she continued gathering details from the center of the room.

Fred moved silently to the door, checking for unlikely intruders or observers.

"Glenndon?" Darville tried to draw him out of his deep concentration.

The boy didn't respond. Not that Darville expected him to. He could at least acknowledge the summons by making eye contact. Instead he examined every crack in the plank flooring and the edges where they met wall panels.

"What are you looking for?"

A web of glowing blue lines appeared in his head. "Ah, you follow ley lines."

Glenndon opened his eyes wide, questioning Darville's knowledge of the esoteric magical knowledge.

"Your Da is my best friend. We had more than one adventure tracing out the forbidden knowledge. There is more for you to discover in Coronnan City. But not today. Not now. Now you must meet the queen."

Glenndon shrank against the wall, trying to disappear into another tapestry. This one memorialized a ship from the Big Continent approaching the Great Bay with a precious cargo of grain and fruit during a famine long, long ago.

"You must present yourself to my wife. Better now than later. She won't hurt you. She agreed some time ago to accept you into the court. And your Mama is her best friend."

Glenndon shook his head as his face drained of color. His sense of abandonment nearly overwhelmed Darville with loneliness. He shook it off.

"Your family has not abandoned you, Glenndon. Try to

think of us as more of your extended family. Please. We want you to feel welcome and comfortable here."

Not belong.

"I don't care if you come or not. I have wondrous things to tell M'ma. I saw a dragon today. And I touched her. And she spoke to me," Linda said. She held herself tall and proud. Excitement gleamed from her eyes.

But Darville noted a small shadow at the corner of her mouth. His daughter had also faced danger today; witnessed more magic in two heartbeats than had occurred in her protected life since before her birth.

He'd hoped to protect her a little longer before plunging her into the kinds of adventure he'd endured as a young man.

Suddenly Darville lost patience with the boy, with the politics that had forced him to drag his son away from the protected clearing and his loving family.

"Come, now!" he ordered.

Glenndon pressed himself closer to the wall.

Roughly, Darville grabbed his arm and propelled him into the antechamber and thence onto the staircase landing. He was too angry to bother with subtlety. He'd run out of time for secrets. He needed to parade them all before the court, while ignoring curious questions and inopportune demands for government decisions.

He needed to announce to the world that he had a son, no matter how flawed or defective the boy might be.

Linda ran ahead of her father and Glenndon, whom he held firmly by the arm all the way across closed courtyards, open halls, and up winding staircases. Breathlessly she burst into her mother's suite without ceremony or permission.

"Linda? Something must be terribly wrong or you owe me and Lady Anya an apology for your presumption," her mother said sternly. The queen sat on a low stool while Lady Anya dressed her thick hair. The long tresses shimmered with a new luster that had been missing during her last illness. Light reflected off the strands of gold, brown, auburn, and black like iridescent mica on the beach. Only the streaks of white radiating out from her temples absorbed light, reminding them all that the queen's health had nearly broken once and for all.

From their seats by the window, Manda and Josie held fingers in front of their mouths to partially hide their giggles. Linda frowned at them, knowing the game they played, a court game to ridicule someone behind a mask of formality.

"Your Grace," she started formally, executing a proper curtsy to her mother, but couldn't contain her excitement. Lady Anya was practically family. And her sisters were . . . her little sisters. "P'pa took me to see the dragon, Shayla, and some soldiers shot at her and Glenndon arrived with Fred in a dazzle of dragon magic, and Shayla flew away and we came back through the tunnels . . ." She had to pause for breath.

"You've had an exciting day, my dear. Now come sit and tell me and your sisters what happened. Slowly," M'ma laughed.

Her *sisters!* Manda and Josie perched primly on the edge of their chairs beneath the big stained glass window (not as big as the one in the Council Chamber, but still an enormous luxury) working embroidery samplers. Like proper young ladies.

Linda drew a deep breath and swept her riding skirts out of the way as she took a stool close to M'ma.

"Now what is this about soldiers and shooting?" M'ma asked. She sounded calm and no worry lines marred her face, but Linda saw a flash of blind panic in her eyes.

"Nothing to worry you, my love," P'pa said strolling in behind Linda and dropping a kiss on M'ma's cheek.

Glenndon followed cautiously, peering into corners as if danger lurked in every shadow. His blond queue (a common three strands) swung back and forth across his back like a cat's twitching tail. Given what had happened today, he had a right to be scared, Linda supposed. Fred took up the rear. Probably making sure Glenndon did not flee.

"Soldiers shooting outside of drills and hunting expeditions is always a concern," M'ma insisted sternly.

P'pa sighed as he sprawled in an overstuffed chair reserved for him. "May I at least introduce you to my son before we dissect the who, what, when, why, and how?"

M'ma nodded.

Manda and Josie gasped and bent their heads together in a tight, whispered conversation. They knew he was coming. They had to. They were better at eavesdropping than Linda. Then they turned bland faces toward their father, properly trained court faces without a hint of personality or concern.

But they giggled behind their fingers, *again,* when Glenndon bent from the waist in an awkward and hesitant bow. He had a lot to learn if he was going to survive at court.

"I am very pleased to have you join us, Glenndon," M'ma said regally. "Please come to me with anything you need. I will do my best to make you comfortable and welcome."

He smiled and took her hand, planting a gentle kiss on her fingers. Then he produced a bouquet of wild lilies and lace roots out of the air, presenting them to M'ma with a huge smile that stayed. A genuine one, not one of the masks courtiers usually showed.

"Nice to see your Mama taught you a few manners," P'pa grumbled. "But you have to stop using magic. At least in public. It is forbidden here. Has been for a long time." At Glenndon's frightened frown P'pa added, "For your protection, for the family's, and mine, please refrain."

Glenndon's face went blank, but he edged closer to M'ma, as if she offered him protection from the king's wrath, or the law. M'ma patted his hand reassuringly.

"Oh, Darville, leave the boy alone for today," M'ma cajoled. When she used that half laugh, she always got her way. P'pa could deny her nothing. Linda vowed in that moment to learn her mother's manner and wiles. Maybe she could cajole Lucjemm into forgiving her for abandoning him in the market.

Glenndon smiled again and gazed at the queen with gratitude and . . . and affection?

"Give Glenndon a chance to get used to us before we impose the artificial rules of court life on him. We'll present him tomorrow, or the next day. When he's ready," M'ma said, burying her nose in the simple bouquet.

Linda didn't think he'd ever be ready.

"If you insist, my love." P'pa uncurled his long form and stood tall beside Glenndon. Not so much taller. Glenndon's head was level with P'pa's cheek. "I leave you in good hands, my boy." He squeezed Glenndon's shoulder. "Her Grace will take care of you, see that you have quarters, clothes, meals— I suspect you need a substantial one now—whatever, and as much as you need. I have to track down some malcontents who dared shoot at a royal dragon."

"May I come with you, P'pa?" Linda asked. She needed to know how her father dealt with malcontents so that some day she too could do it. She had no doubt that some day she would have to.

"Not today, Little Lindy. Help your brother settle in."

"He's not *my* brother!" Heat flushed her face and made her heart race.

"Yes, he is. And for now, he is my heir. Remember that and behave." P'pa stalked out, leaving Linda staring at Glenndon, daring him to steal her position and rank. And her place beside her father.

The king must be using magic. It is the only explanation for the way he disappeared. I placed guards and spies on all of the city bridges to watch for his return. Surely I can use this to bring him down. Then I will not have to marry his head-strong daughter to position myself to take the crown and the throne. Marriage to Princess Jaranda of SeLennica will make a better alliance for Coronnan.

But my Princess Linda is so very lovely. If I can make her love me and my lovely . . . I will need help to finalize that relationship. Help from my lovely. Then I can have both princesses.

If I can prove that Darville threw magic, or he ordered someone to throw it for him, then by law he cannot be king. His entire family will die or be exiled. That is the law. The people will flock to my army with this knowledge. I will not need to use my lovely to convince all the lords and their re-

tainers to join us. They love the law more than they love my lovely.

For them I will make stronger the laws against magic with sterner punishments. Exile is too good for magicians.

The law is on my side. The de Draconis family must now prove their innocence.

CHAPTER 17

GLENNDON STARED IN DISMAY at the huge bed with four posts, a canopy, and heavy draperies tied in clumps to each of those posts. The bed frame rose off the plank floor until the top of the mattress, thick and soft enough to swallow him whole, came nearly to his chest. A portable set of two stairs rested conveniently on the side to make getting into the monster easier. He decided then and there he'd sleep on the floor by the hearth—an inefficient and decorative thing set *into* the wall and sending most of its heat up a flue while allowing cold drafts to roar downward and permanently embed themselves in the thick stone walls.

Now if the hearth and chimney extended into the room they would radiate enough heat to truly warm the place. He wondered if he had the authority to rebuild.

No. He wasn't going to be here long enough.

He shivered, longing for the cozy warmth of his mother's cabin. If he stayed here long enough to sleep, he'd probably be warmer with the thick coverlet from the bed in a small corner on the roof, if he could find a place out of the wind that blew constantly off the Great Bay.

Promise me, you'll give them a chance to love you as we do, his mother had demanded before she sent him here to meet his *father.* The king. Become his heir.

S'murghit, he didn't belong here.

He didn't belong at home anymore either. Maybe he should stay a while until he figured out where he did belong.

Glenndon had no idea what a king actually did. Was it like the meetings that occupied Da's time? Running the University to train the next generation of magicians was a lot of work. That Glenndon understood. As Senior Magician, Da needed to keep track of all of Coronnan's magicians and work to integrate them back into everyday life. That Glenndon understood.

Perhaps the king performed similar duties with the mindblind.

Thankfully the queen, the lovely and gracious queen, had left him alone for a time after feeding him generous portions of roasted beasts, fresh bread, and greens dressed in vinegar and bacon fat. When he'd satisfied his appetite and replenished his energy stores, she'd shown him his room and then taken her two younger daughters back to her suite. He might, after a time, get used to thinking of Manda and Josie as his *half*-sisters. They weren't so different from Valeria and Lillian, except they had no magic (not even the tiny trace he'd seen in the king's aura and the older princess, Linda) and talked endlessly of dresses and hairstyles and their ponies.

His sisters hadn't time for such frivolity. They worked, in Mama's garden and at their lessons. They had no one to impress with fancy garments. An apprentice's robe was impressive enough, a journeyman's or master's even more so.

Why am I here?

No answer. He was indeed alone. No dragons to hear his mental call. No magicians to stand beside him and work with him. No Lukan to make fun of him and twist his spells inside out and upside down for the joy of it.

Hot tears of loneliness burned in the back of his eyes. He wanted to throw himself onto the bed and cry, like a small child.

He couldn't even reach the bed top to throw himself upon it without carefully negotiating the rickety steps.

A sharp knock on the door startled Glenndon out of his reverie. He dashed the tears away from his eyes and turned to face the intruder.

"You did say 'come in,' didn't you? Thought so. Wouldn't presume to enter the chamber of a royal without permission, now would I. Clothed enough of you lot to know my place.

And you'd be the new heir presumptive . . ." A stout woman in a dark dress with a black apron and a mop of gray-streaked dark hair bustled in. She wore a long piece of knotted cloth around her neck, pins stuck into her apron bib, and some sort of metal tool with a circle at the end of each handle protruded from her pocket.

"*Stargods,* I didn't quite believe it when they told me, but can't be any doubt now. Look just like him, you do. Golden locks the color of snow-streaked sunshine, same broad shoulders, and hips so slim you can barely get a belt to stay up. He's got a few inches on you but you got time to grow a bit. But your eyes be different. Oh, yes, you got magician blue eyes, just like your Mama."

Glenndon backed up against the mattress as far as he could and gave this woman possession of the room. She seemed to use up all the air in her gushing conversation. She carried on both ends better than anything he could add. Glenndon felt no need to comment with mind speech or words.

"Now let's get your measure and I'll have new tunics and trews for you by the time you break your fast. Boots might take an hour or two longer." She stared at his muddy footwear with disdain.

Glenndon didn't like the boots either, but at the moment they felt like some protection from this woman.

"Oh, excuse me, forgot we hadn't met. Been around the palace so long everyone knows old Maisy, seamstress to the court. And I thought the young princesses were a bit of a chore to keep up with, what with them growing faster than Devils vine—they can be just as thorny in their demands if you ask me—and the way the Princess Royale changes fashion with every other thought so's she can keep the other ladies jumping to mimic her, but she's always ahead of them by at least two steps. You, young man, need a lot of work. I see your Mama kept you in good sturdy cloth, but that *will not* do at court. Now get them old clothes off so's I can measure you proper."

Glenndon fled. He closed his eyes and thought of nowhere except away from here. No when except not now.

Half a heartbeat later he opened his eyes in a vast nothingness. No up or down, right or left, forward or back. Just a sea of all-color, no-color tangles twining about his body, which he couldn't see or feel.

※

"I look forward to meeting your son, Your Grace," Lord Andrall said, formal as ever.

Darville allowed himself a small grin. Andrall had married his father's sister. He was family. Still, the man never, ever, presumed upon the relationship, other than to offer his complete, unshakable loyalty. His only son should be able to claim a place in the lineup of heirs to the crown. However, Mardall had been born to Andrall and Aunt Lynnetta late in life. His moon face always appeared happy, and life never disappointed him. At the age of thirty-five, he had yet to learn to read, or hold a sword, or show any interest in politics. He did have an uncanny touch with taming and gentling wild steeds and wilder children.

But then fourteen years ago a totally mad Lady Ariiell, daughter of Lord Laislac, seduced Mardall, hoping to displace Darville and rule Coronnan through her child. That child, Mikkette, appeared to be growing up normal.

No one mentioned Mikkette when discussing heirs to the crown out of fear that his parents' heritage of sorcery and madness, or a simple mind, would overtake him at any time.

"Glenndon is more, and less, than I expected, my lord," Darville replied. "You'll meet him tomorrow after we break our fast privately. He's nervous and shy as a wild colt."

"Perhaps my grandson could help ease the transition . . ."

"Not yet, uncle. Let us see how he deals with his half-sisters and the queen. They may gentle him enough to endure court."

"But will the court endure him?" Andrall asked.

"They must. For a time anyway."

A frantic movement at the small private door to the round chamber caught his attention. That entry was reserved for the king. All lords and courtiers had to use the double doors that chimed with bells above and to the side every time they opened more than a hand's breadth. The private door on the other hand made no noise, and the light in the room did not change with its use.

Darville turned his frown toward the entry, expecting a furious Linda to stomp in, skirts and curls flying in the wind of her passage. Instead, the stout household seamstress beckoned to him, panic evident in the flutter of her fingers. She wove her wrist in a complex twist that he'd almost forgotten the meaning of.

"Your Grace," she said breathlessly. "He's gone."

"Who?" though Darville had a good idea who she meant.

"I didn't mean to frighten him, honest I didn't. Chatty and welcoming, I was. I swear. I meant to remind him of his Ma, I did. Honest. But he took fright, Your Grace, was downright ready to scurry afore I got there. Never said a word. Didn't make a single peep. Didn't look happy at all, neither wanting to be alone, or bothered, if you know what I mean." She paused for breath, a rare occurrence.

"Who, Maisy? Who are you talking about?"

"The young master, Your Grace. Prince Glenndon. Though he didn't look much like a prince in them homespun clothes. I know his Ma meant well dressing him in his country best. But, Your Grace, you and I know that country best ain't nowhere near as good as what servants wear here in the palace. Couldn't have him prancing about court in those clumsy boots and rough-woven tunic and trews in them muddy colors."

"Maisy. Where has he gone?" Darville shook the woman who had been at court almost as long as he'd worn the Coraurlia.

"Don't know, Your Grace. He just winked out in a sparkle of gold dust. Took on the face of a wolf just before I lost sight of him. If that don't tell me he's your son, then that silver-tipped golden hair sure did. Looks just like you did when you was that age."

"Maisy." Darville shook her again to knock the words out of her and some sense in. "You are never to speak of this. Ever. Now take yourself off to whatever private place you call your own and send word to your master. He is the only one who can deal with this."

"Yes, Your Grace." She dipped a hasty curtsy and fled back the way she'd come.

"Sounds like he is your son, indeed," Andrall chuckled. "You know where he's run to, don't you?"

"Of course. He's gone back to the clearing and his mother. Where we all end up sooner or later. Brevelan heals all."

"Perhaps. This may be the one thing she can't cure."

"If she can't?"

"Is it time to bring my grandson Mikkette to court?"

"You know there is a taint in his ancestry. The people will fear him as badly as they do my son. For different reasons."

"I know. But once they get to know him . . ."

"I had hoped the same thing for Glenndon. Neither boy is a good candidate . . ."

"But it will give us time. Time for the Princess Royale to grow up a bit. And if the Council of Provinces and the people will still not accept *her* as reigning queen, then at least she will be old enough to choose a suitable husband. Are she and Mikkette too close in blood to wed? He is but a year older than her. Time is what we need."

"Yes. Time." Darville paused a moment, pacing round and round the magnificent black glass table, hands behind his back, head thrust forward. His "wolf" posture. If he looked closely at the colors hidden within the black glass, he could almost see his other persona, the one magic brought out of him: the great golden wolf that dragons and Brevelan had protected so ardently all those years ago.

Now he had to protect himself and his daughter. Had to secure the throne for her to succeed to. Queen Miranda ruled SeLennica without a king. He'd heard that the city-states on the Big Continent traced their leaders through the female line, a man could only be king if he married a queen. Why couldn't his lords accept that a woman could rule Coronnan?

"We will stall, uncle. Order your grandson brought to court. But not your son. And I will order my son back here. I'll have Jaylor put a geas on him if necessary so he can't flee again."

"And what of my grandson's mother? Her father, Lord Laislac, has been agitating for proof that she still lives, proof that she is still insane—as was her mother. If she has recovered any sanity at all, he wants her back. Stargods only know why."

"I haven't thought of Lady Ariiell in years. Does she still live?"

Lord Andrall heaved a weary sigh and sat down in the chair reserved for him, his crest worked into the tapestry headrest. "Yes."

"And?"

"Jaylor had to send a healing magician from the University as her primary attendant. She can soothe the worst of her tantrums, but not eliminate them. Her magic is as wild and uncontrolled as her mind."

"Then I hope she remains locked up in a remote tower with an abundance of glass in her quarters to reflect her magic back into her."

"There isn't enough glass in all of Kardia Hodos for that. And recently, a black cat and a tin-colored weasel have been spotted in the vicinity of her hospice."

Darville had to sit heavily into his demi-throne. "Rejiia and Krej? Seeking release from the ensorcellment that put them into the bodies of their personality totems?"

"I fear so."

"Stargods help us if they are ever restored to their human bodies."

CHAPTER 18

"LILLIAN, VALERIA, what are you doing here?" Jaylor whispered to the half-hidden girls beneath an everblue sapling. "It's nearly sunset."

Valeria tugged on her sister's sleeve to pull her out into the open and face their father. Only about a half mile of winding trail separated the University courtyard in front of them from their home.

Valeria and her sister had grown up running back and forth. Jaylor encouraged them to observe other apprentice lessons, even practice gathering dragon magic, though they physically couldn't do that, long before they were old enough to begin their own formal classes. Was this so different?

"How are we supposed to learn if we don't watch the masters at work?" Lillian replied, squirming back into the nest of needle litter. "Twilight, betwixt and between day and night, light and dark, here and there. It's the best time to throw tricky spells that need both energies . . ."

"I don't know . . ." Valeria said, wavering between curiosity and obedience.

Jaylor swallowed his smile. The girls were right where he expected them to be, and where he needed them. He marked the scope of the ritual courtyard. They could see and hear everything that occurred there.

"Valeria, you need to learn finer control of your magic to keep from exhausting yourself. Watching twelve master magicians work a scry/summoning spell can only help. Lillian, you need to learn more about observation of little details."

"This is supposed to be a big secret. We'll have to be masters before you actually teach us this spell," Lillian said cautiously.

"We'll never be able to use dragon magic, so we can't learn this *particular* spell. Only men can gather dragon magic. But we can learn the basic skeleton of the spell to try using our own magic," Valeria corrected her twin. She smiled at Jaylor, sharing in the conspiracy. She crouched down and wiggled beneath the lowest fluffy branch, chin on her hands, eyes watching the courtyard for anything unusual before the spell to come.

"Rest now, both of you. This is going to be a long night. I must prepare. Lukan is across the way. In the morning I'll need a report from all three of you. Aura colors, shifts in power, anything and everything you can remember about the spell."

"Yes, Da," they said together, then they leaned their heads so their foreheads touched.

He had no idea what kind of communication they shared. Girl children were a mystery. Teenagers more so. Twins? He shuddered inwardly, wondering if he'd ever understand them.

Half an hour later, Jaylor led the twelve blue-robed men in a stately march around their ritual circle. Long ago, their ritual space had been outlined in the cropped grass by paving stones. Each one had a different rune etched in the flat surface that echoed the pattern of magic weaving through the masters' staffs.

Jaylor's staff had twisted and tangled into an impenetrable knot—like his queue after a long and tiring day. The pattern on his stone was a braid entwined back on itself into a complex knot. His magic took on red and blue twined with bright sparkles when he threw a spell, colors the stones could not deploy.

When each man stood on his own stone and had anchored his staff into the Kardia on his right, Jaylor nodded to them and placed his left hand on the shoulder of Robb, who stood beside him.

The solemn joining of each man in turn around the circle continued faultlessly until Marcus (Robb's youthful companion in getting into trouble), to Jaylor's right, completed the unbroken line.

No light shone forth from inside to alert an observer of any change.

Jaylor felt a shift in the air pressure against his face and caught a whiff of an exotic spice—the Tambootie, an addictive, and therefore forbidden, drug that was supposed to boost one's magical talent. With his senses heightened by the drug he heard how the scent enticed Valeria to move closer to the circle, to inhale more deeply, partake of . . .

"Get down!" Lillian hissed. Her voice barely penetrated the fog in Jaylor's mind created by the alluring aroma. Then Lillian pinched her hard. Her fingernails penetrated deeply, almost drawing blood.

Can you smell it? Valeria asked her twin.

"Of course. It's what makes this ritual and spell so secret. Da doesn't want anyone to know that master magicians still use the forbidden drug."

Satisfied that the girls balanced each other, he turned his attention to Lukan. He cast his senses to the roof of the front building of the complex, seeking his son. His true son of his blood. Only the Tambootie in his system allowed him to discern a blank bubble beside the chimney. A casual search for anything out of the ordinary would slide right over the boy.

Nice work, he sent, then closed his mind to everything but the spell he led.

Jaylor noticed a hesitation in the line of men processing around the circle of paving stones, as if they paused to listen. Jaylor lifted his head, breaking his meditation. *S'murghit,* the girls needed to shut up. What was it about teenage girls that made them need to shout every thought that entered their heads to the world?

Then his empathic bond of blood and love shared the sensations with Valeria of ducking her head beneath her arms. Together they thought about worms crawling through the dirt, undulating slowly, stretching forward, squishing up. Stretching long and thin again, pulling back into a fat lump again.

"Da is shaking his head and continuing. You can come out now," Lillian whispered.

Why wasn't she using her mind speech?

Valeria breathed deeply. Her thoughts stretched outward and latched onto a lazy strand of magic that struggled to catch up with the others in the circle. It tasted of a fresh sea breeze heavy with salt and green. Evard, the youngest and newest master magician. Jaylor boosted this tentative strand until it latched onto his own red and blue braid of power. Together, they wove and melded their thoughts into the magic blooming into a dome around the men as they continued their slow march around and around the circle, still physically connected to each other, building the power, combining with it, pushing it to greater and greater limits until a shining, pulsing, bubble of shimmering all color/no color encased them. If Valeria had not made herself a part of that bubble before it closed, following the magical currents around and around in a wide swirl, she'd not penetrate it with sight, hearing, scent, or any magically augmented sense.

Are you seeing this? Valeria asked her sister. Jaylor sensed more than saw Lillian's nod and the increased pressure of her hand on Valeria's shoulder.

Twisting and wiggling around the dome, keeping her life energy closely entwined with Evard's, Valeria relaxed a little and allowed the spell to absorb her.

Jaylor intoned long words that almost rhymed in an ancient and nearly forgotten language. He followed a codified sequence of questions and questing. His long braid of blue and red magic shot from the top of his staff to coil at the top of the dome. An eyeblink later, all of the other staffs shot forth unique colors and configurations that mimicked the way their staff's wood grain twisted.

Valeria's lavender magic sneaked in on Evard's lazy curl of seafoam green.

Breathe, Jaylor reminded her. *Slow and steady, in and out. Breathe.*

Valeria broke a bit of her consciousness away from the spell to tend to her distant body. When she had stabilized, Jaylor directed the combined strength of all the magicians shooting forth from the dome in a long braid that stretched thin in order to retain its connection to the dome and the hearts and staffs of the master magicians.

Valeria's spirit went with them.

A single word permeated their being. *Glenndon.*

Their sole purpose in existence was to find the golden-haired boy.

Then the rope of magic broke through a barrier of time and life with an audible pop.

Atop the roof, Lukan recoiled a bit, revealing himself for half a heartbeat. Only one master, Samlan, seemed to notice. He scowled and glared at the spot that hid Lukan. Then the oldest of the masters present slipped back into the group mind, adding his considerable power to the circle.

Jaylor's mind burst into the void. He sought to make sense of the endless white as he always did. The magic raveled back into the dome and his companions. He sorted through his connections. No up or down, right or left. No Valeria, no Lillian. Only Lukan anchored him.

(Caught you!) He heard the distant gleeful shout, but it did not touch him.

Glenndon closed his eyes. Eyes that did not seem to exist. The tangle of colored umbilicals remained in full view. Nothing looked familiar. He had no landmarks to cling to. He could only drift.

(Think)

What?

(Use your mind. That's why you have one!) That voice sounded mature, feminine. Almost like his mother when she was mad at him for not following through on a chore or task she'd entrusted to him, or traded chores with Lukan.

Think. What was he supposed to think about? All he could perceive was this mass of wiggling, twining, living strands of color.

(Think!)

Wiggling, twining, living strands of color.

Living strands of color. Life energy. Each one represented a life. If that was so, then the ones closest to him should be the people closest to him.

He'd seen these colors in the auras of his family, every day. They were so much a part of his life, he rarely thought about them, barely noticed them. Now he had to think and sort and decide. *Think*

A thick golden cord pulsed right beneath his nose, or where his nose should be if he had a body.

Gold. Who did he know that was gold?

(The king. Your father.)

He is not my father!

Silence. Disapproving silence.

He may have sired me, but Jaylor, Senior Magician and Chancellor of the University is my Da.

(Agreed. Both are honorable. Both love you. In different ways.)

Glenndon decided he could live with that. He didn't like the idea that King Darville loved him. His sire needed him to fill his own agenda. Nothing more. He couldn't believe that Darville actually expected him to succeed him to the crown and throne.

The golden cord pulsed more rapidly, more vibrant than any of the other colors. Except maybe the green, many different shades of green growing things, of a more slender and fragile tendril of life. *Mama.*

But she drifted away, almost as if she'd given up on him when she gave him to the king.

The blue and red braid could only belong to Da. It twisted and coiled around itself, tying itself into knots. That was Da.

Two purple ones that shaded back and forth to lavender—actually one was purple shading lighter, the other lavender shading darker into blue—must belong to Valeria and Lillian. The paler lavender shifted away from the darker, bluer tendril. For the first time in their lives, Glenndon caught a sense that his twin sisters were more than twins, each one had a separate identity that could only separate from the other in the void . . . or while working magic.

And that vibrant gold, rust, brown, gray, with hints of green must be either his half-sister Rosselinda or her mother. Both of them had the same multicolored hair that matched the cord.

If his other half-sisters, Manda and Josie, were there, they were too faint and undeveloped for him to find.

And then there were the crystal umbilicals, looking brittle

and delicate but moving smoothly and confidently through the mass, not quite pushing aside the other colors, but ignoring them and gliding past unnoticed, unheeding.

The dragons.

They pulsed slower than the others, as if each heartbeat was a struggle.

(Correct. Choose wisely.)

I've got to choose one? Only one?

Silence again.

I need to go home.

(Choose wisely.)

Meaning he had more than one home to choose from. Well, there was the clearing with Mama's cabin. The University with its massive wooden buildings. Where else?

(Choose wisely.)

The tone of that command told him he hadn't considered something else. Something important.

Home was home. What other choices could there be?

(Consider the needs of those who love you.)

He didn't like that. He'd landed here in a desperate attempt to escape . . .

Now he couldn't remember what exactly had driven him here other than intense loneliness and homesickness. He needed to go home to Mama, and Da, and Lukan, and the twins, and the little ones. To the other students. And to his friend Indigo.

A flash of another mind crossed his own. Someone . . . someone he couldn't quite identify but knew he should.

(Caught you!)

CHAPTER 19

G LENNDON FELL, uncontrolled, to who knows where.
He flailed his arms and legs, frantic to find something,
anything to latch onto.

He had arms and legs? He had a body to flail?

(Caught you,) Indigo chortled. *(Hid from me. But I found
you.)*

Indigo. My friend.

"I've got you, Glenndon. Stop fighting me!" Da said. He
sounded angry. More angry than relieved.

Da, thank you.

"Don't thank me yet."

Glenndon opened his eyes to find himself in the middle of
the circle of master magicians at the University. Twelve stern
men glowered at him from their posts, with Da at the south,
closest to the magnetic pole.

A sense of direction steadied him. He grounded himself
toward the constant pull of the pole.

"What were you thinking fleeing into a transport spell
without a definite destination and *time* in mind?" Da demanded. His fists clenched and his jaw worked as if he
chewed his anger into smaller bits so he could swallow them.

Glenndon hung his head in dismay. He'd made a big mistake. A huge and dangerous mistake. But he wasn't the only
one.

"Look at me, Glenndon, and explain yourself."

He couldn't. That other presence he'd felt in the void just

before Indigo and Da yanked him out nagged at him. He tried flashing an image to Da.

It bounced back at him in brittle shards, worse than any mind-blind wall. He threw up an arm to shield his eyes from the ricochet.

"Now I am going to take you back to the palace and make sure you stay there," Da fumed.

But . . .

That protest made less impact than his first attempt.

Da made a ritualistic gesture. The dome of power that shielded the twelve magicians from outsiders and joined them to each other in the spell dissolved. Each of the men, except Da, rotated shoulders and necks, shrugging off the tension of holding their magic and tuning it to the whole. Hard work. Now that they'd been dismissed they'd wander inside the University in search of food and sleep to replenish their reserves.

Da stood firm, shoulders hunched, fists clenched. The right hand looked as if it might snap his venerable staff in two.

Glenndon's belly began gnawing at his backbone. He'd used a lot of energy through the course of the day. Before he could indulge in food and sleep he had to convey some urgency to his Da.

"Come along then." Da grabbed his collar and closed his eyes in preparation to transport them both.

No magic would penetrate his shields. Not now.

Glenndon closed his eyes and prepared to transport himself back into the void.

Da grabbed his dominant left hand as well as his collar to stop him. "You aren't going anywhere without me. And I say when and where."

Glenndon opened his mouth. A twisted, croaking sound emerged.

"I'm not taking 'no' for an answer, boy. Even if it is bad enough to finally force you to try to speak."

"Val . . ." He couldn't get anything more past the dry closure in the back of his throat.

"I know you were in the void . . ."

Glenndon shook his head. "Valeria," he finally managed to push the sounds out.

"What about your sister?"

"Void."

Da stopped short. He turned his head right and left, eyes flicking faster than his neck could swivel. "Lillian, where is your sister?"

Glenndon felt Lillian's sobs more than heard them.

"How did she manage that?" A morsel of pride underrode Da's concern. "I have to go find her," he sighed.

Let me. I know where I felt her last.

"No. The void is no place to wander around without direction and anchors. I had the full circle and a juvenile dragon holding tight to me while I looked for you, Glenndon."

Indigo?

(Got her. Safe with me.)

"Indigo?" Da called out.

A yawn met both their inquiries.

(Sunset. Sleep now.)

"I don't trust that dragon . . ."

This time Glenndon stopped his Da from charging off up the mountain alone. *Trust the dragons. You always taught us that. When all else fails, trust the dragons.*

"We'll see."

"Da . . ." and then Glenndon ran out of words. He wasn't sure he'd know what to say even if he had spoken all his life. So he fell back on what had always worked. He sent an image to Da. An image from his earliest memories, which he'd never forgotten, or could forget.

He took his Da back in time to the anxious hours right after the twins' birthing when everyone feared for the life of the younger and weaker twin as well as for her mother. The magician healers and midwives could do nothing for the babe as they worked hard to stop Brevelan from bleeding to death. (That was why there was almost a ten-year gap between the twins and Sharl, the next youngest.) Left in a cradle to die alone, too weak to even cry out her hunger and fear, Valeria threatened to slip out of this life, as if she never existed.

Glenndon, drawn to the tiny baby, stood over the cradle, willing her to live. He stuck the middle two fingers of his left hand in his mouth and sucked, instinctively falling back into the infant habit for security and understanding.

Into the dark corner of the cabin by the hearth stumbled two misshapen figures. He recognized the young, broad, and sturdy back of Jack, Da's apprentice who had since grown into his master status and taken up the position as Ambassador to SeLennica. He half dragged, half carried the frail form of an old man. Lyman, the oldest of the old magicians. No one knew just how old, only that life slipped away from him. He fell to his knees, pulling Jack down with him. "Witness," the old man wheezed.

"Aye," Jack agreed.

So did Glenndon, only without words, not exactly sure what he had to witness, or what "to witness" was.

Old Lyman leaned over the cradle, gnarled hands grasping the edge with white knuckles. Then he breathed into baby Valeria's face. A dark mist emerged. To Glenndon's adult mind he now recognized the shape of the mist as that of the outline of a dragon, or a winged cat.

Valeria gasped and opened her eyes. A tiny wail came from her puckered mouth. Her face took on color. The wail grew to a howl of anguish as Lyman breathed his last and collapsed across the top of the cradle.

Jack drew him away, holding his head against his chest, rocking the corpse. Tears streamed down his cheeks as he somehow rose and carried the dead magician away from the miracle of life in the cradle.

Toddler Glenndon rushed to the cradle, trying to take the baby to someone who could tend her. His three—almost four—year-old arms couldn't quite lift her.

But then a midwife arrived and relieved him of the burden of caring for a new baby, but not of the burden of what he had witnessed.

The face of the midwife seemed familiar. Then he gasped. Old Maisy. The seamstress to the royal family had helped save Mama and the baby during that time of trial. Maisy had nursed him back to health when he almost died of the putrid sore throat.

Da reeled beneath Glenndon's grasp on his arm. "That cannot be!" he gasped.

Trust Valeria to the dragons. Somehow, she is one of them. I do not know how or why.

"For now, I have to get you back where you belong. Tomorrow I will deal with my daughter and her secret."

I belong here.

"Not anymore. I thought we made that clear to you. King Darville needs you. You are near fully grown. Your duty to him as your king is your priority right now."

I am not his son.

"You can sort that out later. He needs you. You will fulfill your duty to him and to the dragons."

"Not my father."

"Keep talking, boy. We'll make a master of you yet. After you fulfill your duty to Darville and Mikka."

Mikka. The queen. The lovely queen who had been gracious and kind, not expecting anything more of him than what he was prepared to be.

"You will also find what Indigo sent you to find."

Glenndon cocked his head in question.

"You aren't the only one the dragons talk to."

CHAPTER 20

WHEN THE MAGICIANS LEFT Coronnan City—when we, the lawful citizens of this land, drove them away—they did not take everything of value. I have stumbled upon a cache of old books and scrolls. The oldest of the old writings of the Stargods forbid any but magicians and nobles from learning to read. Bah, a blatant attempt by the corrupt practitioners and their pet dragons to suppress true intelligence. A desperate measure to gather all political and economic power unto themselves.

But I have found a different scroll, an even more enlightening one. It speaks of witchsniffers, those who can detect magical power in others. I need to find one. The people of Coronnan need me to revive the honorable profession. A witchsniffer will root out the source of the king's magical appearance and disappearance within the palace. A witchsniffer will show me the way to rise above all others and become king. Without magic.

"I don't see why I can't be the heir," Linda grumbled. A book from the earliest days of the kingdom, back when Master Magician and Battlemage Nimbulan made the pact with the dragons to control magic and bring peace to a war-weary world, lay open and nearly forgotten in front of her. The words twisted into numerous interpretations until they could mean almost anything. She sought logic again in the treaty

formalizing the lord of Coronnan City as king, first among
equals, with the lord from each Province sitting in Council
with him. The only clause that made any sense and seemed
unwilling to slide into a new meaning was the one assigning
a master magician as a neutral adviser to each lord. The Senior Magician sat behind and to the left of the king in Council as conscience and learned mentor.

So why didn't the lords still have magician advisers? And
why was there only provision for a king and not a reigning
queen?

"You can't be the heir because that's the way it's always
been," Chastet said. She stood on a portable dais with Old
Maisy crouched before her, pinning new lace trim to the hem
of a favorite green gown she'd grown too tall for.

"Women are expected to organize and socialize, smooth
over ruffled feelings, discover what happens behind the
scenes . . ." Miri added. She stabbed at a piece of embroidery
with a needle too big and blunt for the delicate floral design.
Like Linda, she'd never quite mastered the subtleties of fine
needlework.

Old Maisy snorted something around a mouthful of pins.

"Speak up," Linda commanded. She pushed aside the
book she couldn't concentrate on.

"Seems to me, men are afraid of women," the old woman
said, tugging at the lace to make it hang straight.

"Afraid?" Now that was something that had never occurred to Linda. "What do they have to fear from us? They
are bigger, stronger . . ."

"Less skilled in the subtle arts of discovery," Maisy finished for her. "Look at that brother of yours; fleeing Stargods
only know where the minute he's faced with having to learn
court manners and dress. Gone two whole days now. Chop
wood he can do. Throw weapons he can do. Talk, not so
much."

"But P'pa talks all the time. He's a master of diplomacy,"
Linda protested. She agreed that Glenndon hadn't impressed
her as good for much besides diverting and burning arrows
aimed at a dragon—her dragon. A royal dragon. Like the
battlemages of old, like Nimbulan.

"But who does your P'pa talk to before entering the Council Chamber? Not Fred, his bodyguard and friend. Your M'ma, that's who. The king and queen are quite a pair, well matched. Her strengths make up for his weaknesses." Maisy mused. "Now, off with that gown, milady, and I'll have it ready for you to wear tonight at the court gathering."

"If there is a court gathering tonight. P'pa has called every dignitary in the land to the palace so he could introduce them to Glenndon. But without him, they are . . . they are stuck with me. Me. So why can't I be the heir?"

"Because men need the illusion of power and control," Miri said. She threw the embroidery down in disgust. "I say we women should do something, make ourselves important in public as well as private. We need to do more than push out babies and dress prettily."

"Yes, we do!"

"Take more than determination to bust through a thousand years and more of tradition," Maisy reminded them.

Linda chewed her lip. Maisy was right. She needed a plan. A subtle plan that would force the Council to ask her opinion and rely upon her advice. Marching in and bashing sense into their dense heads wouldn't work. M'ma was the best person in the whole world at devising plans.

Of course. M'ma truly ruled Coronnan, but from the background.

"Maisy, I need a new outfit for tonight," she said, still mulling over what she needed to do before then. "Tunic and trews befitting a prince."

"Your Highness! Surely you don't mean . . ." both Miri and Chastet squealed.

"Are you certain, Princess Rosselinda?" Maisy asked. A spark of mischief lit her eyes. She suddenly looked younger than her usual stout middle-age figure.

"Yes, I am certain. With a sword belt and cap. It is time I remind the world that I am the king's oldest child. I can wield a sword with the best of them. I can ride a steed better than most of them. I am well educated—which is more than most of the lords can say—observant, and conversant with dragons!"

And one day, when the time came, in the far future, Linda would wear the Coraurlia, just like her P'pa. She had held the crown and felt its magic but not been burned to ashes by it.

Valeria reveled in the warmth that made her muscles languid; softness cradled her back properly, removing the constant ache. Is this what most people felt when they awoke in the morning? Rested and ready to face the day?

She allowed herself to drift a few more moments in comfort, knowing it would all disappear when she rose.

She knew she rested in a bed, but not the big, downy bed where Mama and Da slept in the room behind the big room. Sometimes when she was ill, Mama let her sleep there.

She reached for Lillian as the soft light of dawn pried at her eyelids.

Her questing hand met with a wall of woven grasses and twigs.

(Welcome,) said a voice in her head. Not Mama or Lillian. Not Glenndon. Everyone else she knew used words instead of mind connections.

"Who?" She tried to open her eyes, but sleep grit held them down. Anxiously she rubbed them clear and tugged at her lashes, trying to pry them open.

At last a small glow of early golden light drifted around her, not quite filling the space, but enough to see that she reclined, not on a bed, but in a . . . in a nest?

She sat up abruptly, peering closely at the down and moss that cushioned her, the feathery boughs of everblue and sturdy lumps of hardwood woven together in a huge circle. The walls of the nest rose high, taller than she.

"Where . . . where am I?" she whispered.

(Home. Where you belong.)

"This isn't home. Home is Mama, and Da. Home is the cabin in the clearing with my friends and family." Panic made her heart flutter and her spine chill. Her breathing became fast and shallow. The woven walls around her started spinning. She lay back down, fighting for breath and consciousness.

(We are your family.)

"I want my Mama. And my Da."

(Are you certain? Are we no longer enough for you?)

"Who are you?" That was the big question. The voice

sounded like it expected her to know where she was and who she spoke to.

Nest. Big nest. Too big for any bird of prey. Too big for anything but a dragon.

A dragon.

"Shayla?"

(Yes, child.) A different voice. A softer one, less demanding. More . . . friendly.

"Why am I here in your lair?"

(Do you not remember?)

"No."

(What do you remember?) The first voice again, impatient, like a teacher admonishing a student who had not studied or practiced. Baamin, the senior male.

There was a legend that when his magician body died, the dragons honored him by allowing him to transform into a dragon body. He wore magician blue on his wing tips, veins, and horns. Hadn't he been Da's teacher at the University before the Leaving?

"I remember weaving myself into the dome of power as the master magicians formed a spell circle," Valeria mused.

(You are the only one in a human body who could do that. The only female who can utilize dragon magic,) the teacher said. *(Do you know why?)*

She felt as if the teacher's thoughts were shoved out of their mind. But not by her. By the other voice. Shayla, the matriarch and ruler of the dragon nimbus.

"I am the daughter of the Senior Magician. I can do many things others cannot."

(But at great cost to your body's ability to control your magic, your heart, your breath, your mind. You are a thing of magic with only a morsel of humanity.)

"That doesn't make sense. Can I go home now?"

Someone heaved a great sigh. The softly warm air became a breeze, circling the nest, but not penetrating lower than the loose bits at the top. Deep within the well she was protected. Warm. Comfortable.

Did she truly want to leave here?

In the back of her mind she felt her mother and her twin seeking her. Anxiety, worry. Fear.

"Please, I need to go home now."

(Alas, you are not ready to call this home. You are not yet ready to call us family.) A great deal of disappointment followed that statement, from both of the voices.

(Indigo shall take you. You will remember nothing. This will all be as a dragon-dream.)

She awoke, finding herself in Mama's bed. Down-filled comforters and quilts piled thick around her. Mama sat up in bed, singing a soft lullaby.

Valeria snuggled closer to her mother, grateful for the warmth and comfort that for once had not been a dream.

Unless it was a dragon-dream. A realer than real experience to teach her something important.

CHAPTER 21

"WILL YOU STAY?" Darville asked. He squeezed Jaylor's shoulder, his oldest friend. Perhaps his only true friend. They met as young teens before either of them understood concepts of politics, rank, privilege, and power.

"Your Grace, we both know that is dangerous. For both of us." Jaylor kept his wary glance moving throughout the king's private study. In the next room they heard the rustle of clothing and Old Maisy admonishing young Glenndon to stand straight and tall or his tunic wouldn't fit right.

"The Council offered to allow magician advisers back into Chambers if I would betroth Linda to someone, preferably one of their sons. As if I could make the very young ones grown up with the snap of my fingers, or one of the older ones young and handsome."

Jaylor chuckled and rolled his eyes. Darville wondered if his friend had concocted a spell to do just that. "Perhaps I could cast a glamour to make Lord Andrall's nephew appear less than forty?"

Darville glared at him, not finding the joke funny at all. "At the moment only my young cousin Mikkette and Jemmarc's legitimized son are of an age and nobility close to Linda," Darville said. His warring emotions roiled in his stomach: delight that the animosity toward magic and those who threw spells was fading, and rage that his fourteen-year-old daughter had become a pawn in a dangerous game.

"But since you refused the compromise, they have not

renewed the offer," Jaylor reminded him. "I'm tired, Your Grace. I serve you better at the University."

"You used to call me by name."

"Long ago, when we could go adventuring without guilt. We had no one to miss us, or care about us. No one for us to miss and worry over. What happened to us?"

"We matured into responsible men with wives and children," Darville said on a huge sigh. "I love my wife and children and do not regret my life."

"I know. But I'm tired. I need to go home," Jaylor said, pinching the bridge of his nose as if trying to banish a headache.

"I miss you. Remote and convoluted communication is not enough when I require your wise counsel. Or just a memory or joke shared between friends."

"You've managed quite well for a number of years . . ."

"I sense a new crisis looming over the question of my heir," Darville admitted.

"Who speaks loudest and longest for a betrothal?" Jaylor asked, most of his attention returning to Darville.

"Lord Jemmarc. His son is of an age with Linda and Glenndon. An old family, distantly related to Lord Krej. Wealthy from fishing and mining. 'Twould be a good match if both were older."

"Hmmm."

"What is that supposed to mean?"

"Lord Jemmarc's wife, Lady Lucinda, has taken refuge at the University. Some months ago."

"He did denounce her for a witch and offered her exile instead of burning if she left his son."

"Did she go peacefully?"

"I presume so, though Jemmarc kept her dowry since he allowed her to live. The boy is not hers. She proved infertile and Jemmarc acknowledged Lucjemm when he was but an infant. The rite to legitimize the boy and name him heir took place just a few weeks before the scandal over Lady Lucinda erupted."

"Interesting." Jaylor caressed his staff. His hand followed the twisted wood grain with easy familiarity, as if he stored memories and bits of wisdom in the knots.

"What are you thinking, my friend?"

"That the lord should be about ready to present to you a new candidate to become his lady, someone younger and more fertile than his first wife. Either that or offer his own hand in marriage to the Princess Royale."

"No!"

"Think about it."

Darville decidedly did not want to think about marrying his daughter to a man older than himself.

"Watch him closely. You said he was present when the army tried to shoot Shayla. He is the loudest voice insisting on a marriage. He is wealthy, has become used to power these past fifteen years, is probably hungry for more. If he marries Princess Rosselinda, he becomes de facto king. If he marries Lucjemm to her, he is bound tightly to the crown, does not have to allow the boy to remain his heir, and finds a new wife to provide him with a legitimate heir to his lands."

Glenndon came running through the door to the inner chamber, eyes wide, hair tousled, one boot on, the other in his hand, sword belt empty. His nose twitched as if it itched. Maisy trailed him, carrying a red cap with a rumpled white feather.

"You're sure?" Jaylor asked him as Glenndon skidded to a halt in front of them.

"What?" Darville asked, suddenly alarmed. He reached for the Coraurlia sitting squarely on its head-shaped mount beside his desk. The glass tingled in warning beneath his fingertips.

"Witchsniffers," Jaylor growled. "I haven't seen or heard of one living. Only reports in old texts from the time of Nimbulan, the first magician to make covenant with the dragons."

"Who would dare bring . . ."

Jaylor raised an eyebrow, reminding him of their interrupted conversation.

Darville kept his hand on the crown as he turned to face the outer door, the only publicly known access to his study and private dressing room. He jerked his head toward the back room, indicating that Jaylor and Glenndon should retreat, through the tunnels if necessary.

Before they could move, the door burst open from a

tremendous blow, splintering stout wood around the lock and twisting brass hinges.

Darville's left hand reached for his dress sword, scant protection from a massive assault, while his right clutched tighter on the points of the Coraurlia, a shield only against magic.

Jaylor stepped back two strides to stand beside Darville and slightly to the front. Glenndon was already slightly ahead of him on the right. They were his best defense at the moment.

Two soldiers wielding a small battering ram tipped with steel stood at the front of a pack of men. They wore the uniforms of the royal guard, but with an added black sash—they looked to the Council instead of General Marcelle or Darville for their orders. Strangely, their eyes did not focus; they looked into the far distance, unthinking, as if entranced. The rest stood with their jaws agape at the peaceful scene before them, or perhaps their audacity at invading the king's privacy.

"Explain yourselves!" Darville ordered in his loudest, most commanding voice, the one reserved for military drills and field maneuvers.

Fred appeared in the doorway to the back room, out of breath. His right hand half drew his sword. A streak of cobweb looked like a scar down his left cheek, adding to his aura of menace. His eyes took in the entire room, then settled on the offending soldiers who carried the ram.

Both of them shook themselves as if casting off a cloaking veil. Only then did they drop their gazes to the carpet while heat flushed their cheeks.

"Your Grace." Lord Bennallt and Lord Jemmarc bowed from their positions side by side, just behind the two soldiers at the point.

"We have reliable information that you were under assault by foreign magic," Laislac said from behind Jemmarc and Bennallt. He blushed and edged backward.

Jemmarc did not. Bennallt looked at his feet.

"Uncle," Darville called to Lord Andrall at the back of the pack. "Where comes this information?"

"Need you ask?" He bowed slightly to Jaylor. Then his gaze slid toward Glenndon and paused. He looked away, then back again, letting his eyes drink in the sight of the boy, tall and strong, healthy, and as blond as his sire, but sporting magician blue eyes instead of Darville's golden brown.

He ignored the man and woman standing to his side, right arms waving about, fingers clenched until their aim crossed the threshold. Then their fists opened and all fingers pointed straight into the room, but not at any one person.

"Lord Andrall, you remember Lord Jaylor, do you not?" Darville asked casually. He didn't remove his hand from the grip of his sword or his contact with the bespelled glass crown.

"I do. And welcome." Andrall bowed sketchily, as if afraid to relax too much.

"My lords," Darville called to the crowd in general. "I present to you Lord Jaylor, Senior Magician and Chancellor of the University of Magicians."

"Your Grace," Jemmarc took a step forward. "You cannot mean to break our laws by bringing a *magician* to court!" His hand tightened on his own sword. The pack of soldiers behind the battering ram did likewise. Fred stepped forward, one side shuffle from standing between the king and the lords with their soldiers.

Darville smiled inwardly. The lords had come prepared for a fight, but first they'd have to get through that doorway. One at a time. He, Jaylor, and Fred were more than a match for them. Glenndon? Glenndon just increased the odds on their side.

"The law specifically allows each lord on the Council of Provinces the attendance of a magician adviser. The Senior Magician is always assigned to the crown, the first among equals," he reminded them. His hand shifted the Coraurlia a bit, the sound of the glass sliding around the wooden mount emphasizing just who they addressed.

"But magic is illegal," Lord Laislac said. He sounded as if he parroted someone else's words, trying to keep his loyalties divided.

"It is illegal for members of the royal family to throw magic. It is not illegal for magicians to reside within Coronnan," Jaylor growled. "We withdrew from court because of the ill will of the Council, not because of any laws."

"Lord Jaylor brought my son from his country retreat," Darville added, giving excuse for their presence. "We had planned to introduce them tonight at court."

"But the magic . . ." Jemmarc protested.

"I see you brought witchsniffers—an obsolete magical talent that was banished from Coronnan three hundred years ago. May I remind you that your witchsniffers employ a form of magic themselves. Where did you find them? Or did you import them from the Big Continent?" Jaylor mused, still not relaxing his defensive stance. "And the Coraurlia contains magic, for the protection of the king. Your tools are probably sniffing that, rather than me. I have thrown no magic for them to sense."

"But . . ."

"We are finished here," Darville ordered. "Send your witchsniffers to the kitchen for a good meal. They look like they could use it. Then put them on the next boat that sails east. The rest of you are dismissed to the Grand Hall, where We will join you when We are ready. You will be assessed for the repairs to Our door. Fines for assault upon the royal palace as well as the cost of repairs." Darville fell back on the royal "We" to show some of his indignation and affront.

The men backed away, bowing abjectly. Two of the soldiers tugged at their black sashes, as if suddenly finding them uncomfortable, or heavy.

Lord Andrall lingered a bit. Finally, after all the others had removed themselves, he tipped his cap to Darville. "Our plans progress, Your Grace." Then he too departed.

Darville sagged wearily, not quite daring to release his death grip on the Coraurlia.

The law! How dare that presumptuous, that illegal magician quote the law to me! I have read every legal text. I have read all of the decisions by the Council recorded over time. Of course, the recording of those decisions has been incomplete since we sent the magicians out of Coronnan, running for their lives without bothering to pack. They left behind their hidden archives. Few who sit at the black glass table are comfortable or competent with pen and ink. No one except

the members of the Council are allowed inside the chamber once the meetings have convened. Not even the king's trusted and loyal bodyguard, Fred. And how did he get from his post at the bottom of the stairs to the back room of the king's office so quickly? I pushed him hard enough to crack his head against a stone wall. I would swear I knocked him out cold.

So no one knows for certain if magic is truly illegal or merely suspect. That will change. Tonight. Tonight I will suggest to one and all that a permanent scribe be appointed. Only one. One I trust. One who knows where his loyalty lies and will record the proceedings as I dictate.

I will own the law. Not that sneaky, manipulative, cunning, EVIL magician.

CHAPTER 22

"WITCHSNIFFERS? WHAT ARE THEY?" Linda asked incredulously as she fussed with the way the masculine clothes fit across her shoulders. The polished metal mirror made her look so *different* dressed as a boy. With her hair braided tightly into a proper court queue and the tunic unbelted, she doubted many could tell her true gender.

"Aye, witchsniffers. Nasty critters, them," Maisy confirmed. "Ain't heard of one living, but heard about them from the cradle on. Stories to scare a child into staying in bed when she was wont to explore." She stood back appraising Linda's outfit and the way it fit. "You needs a belt," she concluded.

Linda took the long length of leather Chastet handed her. Tied tightly around her waist, it showed off her modest curves, but still left her gender in doubt. Now if she were only bigger up top, no one would question it. She frowned, suddenly unsure of her decision to challenge the court and her parents.

"Explain," she ordered Maisy.

"Nasty people so hateful of magic and magicians they ignore their own magical talent, but use it to seek out the presence of magic in others and around them." Maisy suddenly sounded educated and knowledgeable beyond the gossip that slid from her tongue like a gutter shedding rain. Her face shed its mask of late middle age, then aged to an ancient crone. Which face was real? And how did she do that? Then the old woman shook from crown to toes as if ridding herself of an unwanted skin, and her face and speech returned to normal. "Holds their arms out straight in front and wave 'em in circles. When the faintest whiff o' power touches 'em, their hands open and fingers point accusingly when and where they will. Exiled they was 'cause a power-mad politician were using them to finger innocents he didn't like, or feared."

Linda nodded, understanding how a tool could turn into a fearsome weapon. "What were the witchsniffers looking for?" Linda asked.

She had to force herself to listen to Maisy's blathering rather than dwelling on her own doubts about tonight's adventure. Her father had always told her that a decision once made needed to be followed through. To waver cast doubt on her leadership. She needed to prove her leadership to secure her place as her father's heir.

"Your brother," Maisy answered. "Someone's afraid the boy will be named heir. Harder to manipulate an educated man than an untried girl. You're the pawn they wants— thinking you know less about governance than any man. Not Glenndon. Don't know Glenndon or what he knows. Don't stop to think he's been trained to be diplomat and scribe, judge and warrior—just like his Da. Only they look to govern the University and *advise* rulers instead o' being one."

Linda frowned again, still uncomfortable thinking of Glenndon as her brother. She didn't want a brother and didn't think she needed one either.

"I were in the back room, I was, helping the young master prepare for tonight. Heard every word. Seems the Council is dead set on making magic illegal for everyone. No magic or magicians anywhere in Coronnan. If you ask me, I think they even want to break the Coraurlia. Now that would be a crime, seeing as how the dragons forged that piece of glass and embedded magic into it so the wearer is protected against any magic thrown to harm him—or her."

"But the Coraurlia also burns anyone who tries to wear it that the dragons do not approve," Linda added.

"Good reason for the Council to break it if they try to take the crown and the throne away from your papa," Miri said from the doorway, where she peeked to watch the traffic in

and out of this part of the palace. She and Chastet had also
donned tunics and trews with sheathed daggers in their belts
and feathered caps in support of Linda's new fashion.

Only Linda planned on wearing a short sword (neither of
her ladies could walk with anything longer than a small dagger without tripping). She didn't think the others knew the
grip from the forte or which side of the blade was sharpest.

Maisy gestured for Linda to turn around. Linda obeyed,
almost grateful to lose sight of herself in the mirror, to forget
for half a heartbeat how *exposed* she felt without skirts. Parading herself before the men and women of the court felt
very different from venturing anonymously into the practice
arena filled with only men who were more interested in how
the masked "boy" wielded a blade than who he was—or what
he was.

These trews fit well enough, and weren't so much different from the ones she wore beneath her riding clothes. But in
those outfits her body remained hidden beneath the skirts. On
the other hand, the tunic hid more of her neck and chest than
the low-cut court gowns made popular by her mother.

If boys and men paraded about with their legs exposed to
the view of all, even if they didn't have well shaped legs like
P'pa, then she could learn to do it as well.

"If the Council brought in witchsniffers, then they are serious in their intent to remove P'pa from the throne." That
horrible idea burst out of Linda without forethought.

"Aye, Highness. They are. Or one among them is talking
loud to overcome their objections. The others don't know
their own opinion, so they parrot whoever talks the loudest
and longest," Maisy replied.

"How did P'pa deflect them?" She knew he must have or
Maisy wouldn't be here now, and the palace would be in a
greater uproar than usual just before a major gathering.

"Lord Jaylor reminded them of the law. Just 'cause the
magicians withdrew from Coronnan, doesn't make their
presence illegal."

"Lord Jaylor?" Chastet interrupted when Maisy looked to
be ready to talk more. As was her wont.

"Aye, milady. Senior Magician Lord Jaylor. Courtesy title
it might be seein' as his family is only farmers. But he's

powerful and wise, and befriended His Grace when they was both just lads. Heard tell they pulled each other out of one scrape after another until His Grace went missing and it took a dragon to find him. And Lord Jaylor. That were some adventure they went on . . ."

"Yes, I'm sure it was." Linda remembered a comment on the ride from Battle Mound when P'pa had said that Glenndon's Da had taught him how to swim when he was the boy's age. An important skill seeing as how Coronnan City was built on a chain of islands in the river delta. Water surrounded them on all sides. The Great Bay washed back up the river with every high tide and sometimes drowned the unwary working the riverbank for fish or boat repair or whatever. Why hadn't P'pa taught her to swim along with swordplay and reading, mathematics, history, and diplomacy?

"Miri, has everyone gone down to the Great Hall?" she asked, hiding a stab of disappointment.

"Yes, Your Highness," she replied. "I saw His Grace with your mother on his arm, followed by Glenndon and a broad-shouldered man in a blue robe I do not know, just a moment ago."

"That would be Lord Jaylor with Glenndon. Making sure the boy don't flee again," Maisy said.

"Time for us to join them. We will make an entrance that all will note," Linda ordered.

"They'll take note alright," Maisy grumbled. "But will they note with favor or consign you back to pigtails and a governess?"

Glenndon walked beside his Da down the long staircase toward the Great Hall. Not his Da. He cringed inside. Maybe if he started consciously thinking of him as Jaylor, Senior Magician, he'd eventually learn to accept the tall blond man in front of him as his father. Maybe. He didn't want to.

But it was becoming obvious the adults in this kingdom were not about to allow him to return to the University and his home. After that scene with the witchsniffers, he knew he was needed here more than ever.

Life was no simpler at the University with master magi-

cians vying for prestige, seniority, and power, just like the
lords here.

Da had made certain he knew that he no longer belonged
among the magicians. He'd never belong in the palace with
its maze of rooms and wings and hundreds of servants bowing and scraping to him at every turn.

He still needed to find a cure for the dragons. When was
he to have time to himself to search out the Well of Life and
the hidden archives? Every time he turned around, Maisy was
there with new clothes for him to wear to a different event.

He guessed he had to stay until he completed his tasks.

He fixed his attention on the magnificent Coraurlia atop
the king's head and tried to imagine himself wearing the all
color/no color swirls of glass that suggested a perched dragon
watching all that dared look too close, with wings just starting to unfold around the sides. The head and horns blended
into the circle, not protruding in a lifelike sculpture, but there
nonetheless, ready to extrude at any time, without warning.

"Glenndon." Da stopped them when the king paused in
the arched doorway to the Great Hall. "There is more going
on here than I expected."

Glenndon nodded agreement, almost afraid to speak mind
to mind, lest Da . . . Jaylor . . . repulse the thoughts.

"What did you see when you were in the void?"

Automatically, Glenndon shot him an image of the pulsing and twining umbilicals of life.

"Ah, yes."

Glenndon cocked his head in question.

"I have been in the void a time or two, my boy. Tell me,
did you see your own aura?"

What?

"You know what I asked." Da grabbed his shoulders and
shook him slightly, demanding attention and concentration.
"Think a moment. There should be one particular cord that
seemed to coil around you closely. It originated with you.
Did you see it?"

Glenndon closed his eyes and tried to remember everything he saw, felt, heard, and did. He couldn't keep a tight
barrier around the memory even though he knew Da would
peek.

"Focus, Glenndon. There, right in front of your mind's eye."

Gold. He watched the bright coil a moment, wondering why it clung so close to him. He thought it had to be the king's.

"Close. It is close to Darville's color. Look closer."

Around the bright gold, clinging like an echo but not truly part of the cord, he found a paler cord, almost invisible. *Rose gold,* Glenndon sighed. *Is that weak little thing me?*

Jaylor chuckled. "Not so weak if you can see it. Remember, you are not yet eighteen, an apprentice with no lessons in this arcane magic work."

Is it important?

"Yes, but I do not expect you to understand yet. Just think about it while you reside here in the palace. Think of this as your journeyman's assignment. Your duty to the University, to all magicians, is to stay here, learn everything you can, and report back to me. Directly to me and no one else. Not one of the other masters, not your sisters or Lukan, and not your mother. Definitely not your mother."

They both grinned at that. Calm, practical, organized, nurturing Brevelan tended to get more than a little excited when one of her brood stepped beyond her protective skirts.

Glenndon nodded again. He could do this. He could pretend to go along with the idea of becoming heir to the king. Pretend only. All in the name of his duty to the magicians and the dragons.

"When the time is right, I'll send you permission to row over to Sacred Isle and cut yourself a staff," Jaylor continued. "You must row, not transport yourself. That's the way it has always been done. You must spend a night there, communing with the trees and the stars and the Bay. Then in the morning, if you are worthy, the trees will give up a stout branch to you, and you alone."

"Staff?" Glenndon croaked out. The symbol of a true magician, a journeyman on his way to master. A tool to aid him in his searches!

"Not yet. But I think you are going to need it before this is over. In the meantime, keep your magic quiet, hidden as much as possible. And please, learn to speak. You've started.

That's important. Keep it up, son." Jaylor squeezed his shoulder firmly, man to man, mentor to apprentice.

Glenndon stood straighter, proud and willing to obey. Hope of returning home brightened his perspective. He surveyed with new understanding the gathered court just beyond the stone arch where the king stood. Darville allowed torchlight to strike the Coraurlia and send multicolored prisms arcing around the room.

Show off, he thought.

"Exactly. Half of leadership and diplomacy is showing the world you aren't afraid of anyone," Jaylor chuckled. "Watch and learn." Then he faded into the shadows. "And remember, you are not the only one who talks to dragons, and *he* may be your sire, but I will always be your Da."

The king waggled his fingers behind his back. Glenndon took that as a gesture beckoning him forward. He stepped up beside his king, standing nearly shoulder to shoulder with him, letting some of the magnificent rainbows bathe his face. A lot like catching a dragon blessing on a bright sunny day.

CHAPTER 23

A GASP CIRCLED THE GREAT HALL, moving from one mouth to the next without break, like the circular ripples fanning outward from a rock dropped into the river.

Linda stepped back from the archway in dismay. Miri and Chastet caught her retreat and pushed her forward once more.

"They've seen us. We have to follow through," Miri admonished her.

The laughter of derision thrives on embarrassment; Linda remembered her mother's lessons in court etiquette. *By quietly ignoring those who wish to make you look beneath them, you rob them of fuel and they have nothing left to laugh about.*

"I have to do this. I *can* do this," she said to herself. Twice. Then a third time to firm it up in her mind. Then she lifted her chin, kept her eyes level with the tapestry across the room and took her first step forward into contention for her rightful place as her father's heir.

Murmurs followed the pattern of the gasp, rippling around the room in ever increasing waves of sound.

Her parents turned to see what had caused such a stir among the nobles and their followers. M'ma raised her eyebrows and sketched a slight curtsy to her, with the right depth and inclination of head the queen should afford an honored child. No more, no less. Then she turned back to face the court with a smile on her face.

One obstacle surmounted.

P'pa, on the other hand, scowled mightily, the corners of his mouth trying to attach themselves to his shoulders; the furrow above his nose pulled his eyebrows inward and downward until they nearly met as they might on a wolf muzzle. Did his queue bristle like a wolf's tail when scenting the unknown? His keen gaze and expression gave her a deeper impression of wolf that had sighted its prey.

She tripped over the weighted toes in her low boots. Chastet caught her elbow until she steadied. To cover her stumble, Linda whisked the be-feathered cap off her head, swept it before her and bowed low over her arm, extending her right foot forward, as she had seen other young men do when approaching a higher ranking noble.

P'pa nodded for her to rise. She did so slowly, replacing the cap on her scraped-back curls. It landed slightly askew. She left it at the odd tilt to avoid fussing, like a girl.

"Not exactly how I expected you to appear when formally presenting your brother," P'pa said. His expression returned to neutral. Only the storm that darkened his golden eyes betrayed his true emotions.

Linda braced herself for orders to return to her dressing room and come back only when properly attired.

But M'ma was biting her cheeks to keep from laughing.

Linda's heart lightened as her mother beckoned her forward to stand beside Glenndon. She did so, keeping a wary eye on her father.

Glenndon, Stargods bless him, didn't seem to notice anything untoward. Girls wearing boy's clothing might be the norm out in the wilderness of the University of Magicians for all she knew.

"Be grateful we didn't order dancing tonight," M'ma said under her breath.

"That would upset ranking and protocol to no end," P'pa replied with a glimmer of easing in his scowl.

The herald standing at P'pa's right blew his long trumpet. The banner bearing the de Draconis crest of a dragon outlined in iridescent white on a light green ground—giving the impression of transparency—with a darker green and gold background proclaimed to one and all that the king had entered the room. "Lords and Ladies of Coronnan, Darville de Draconis, king by the grace of the dragons, and his lady, Queen Rossemikka, are pleased to present to the court their heir, Prince Glenndon de Draconis, and the Princess Royale, Rosselinda Kathleen Mirilandel de Draconis," he said in his stern voice that projected to the far corners of the great room, even into the musicians' balcony above them.

All the lords and ladies, their younger family members, and retainers bowed or curtsied as one as they faced the royal family, whispers and scandalized gasps swallowed.

"Princess Rosselinda, please escort Prince Glenndon to the court," M'ma said. She turned challenging eyes upon P'pa who merely nodded, once, curtly, the storm in his gaze still raging.

But this was court. Neither he nor M'ma ever, *ever* betrayed by any gesture or expression anything but what they wanted the court to know. Family arguments remained within the family.

Linda had no doubt arguments would rage later. Until then, she had a job to do.

"Brother?" she turned her most vivacious smile on the silent boy. Then she bent her head and gestured for him to accompany her around the room, side by side. He towered over her, nearly as tall as their father, but he matched her stride, step for step, neither pushing himself forward nor drifting behind. Though she thought he might prefer to do the latter.

"Lord Andrall and Lady Lynnetta, allow me to present Prince Glenndon, my father's son," she said formally. "Lady Lynetta is P'pa's aunt," she added more quietly. Glenndon should know the family tree, but she wasn't sure how much his other family had taught him.

Glenndon bowed, a bit awkwardly.

"Not so low." Linda nudged him. "You outrank them."

Glenndon straightened with a bit of a wiggle, uncertainty in his face and posture.

"Welcome to the family," Lady Lynetta said loudly. She glanced around to make sure the gathering listened. She didn't spend much time at court, leaving that chore to her husband, but when she did come, her senior status and closeness to the king meant that lower ranking ladies *always*

listened to her. Then she placed her hands gently on
Glenndon's shoulders and reached up to kiss his cheek. "I've
wanted to meet you for a long time. Soon we must sit down
and catch up. I knew your Da a long time ago. I like to think
we were friends before the unpleasantness caused the magicians to withdraw."

Leave it to Lady Lynetta to gloss over a governmental
crisis and turn it into a mere unpleasantness.

"Welcome," Lord Andrall said heartily. He too embraced
Glenndon in that brusque way that men almost hugged and
touched cheeks.

Glenndon breathed a bit easier as he looked to Linda to
lead him to the next lord in line.

According to seniority and rank that should be Lord
Laislac, a widower who had a different lady—never a wife—
on his arm at each meeting. This one was closer in age to his
fifty-plus years than most. Unfortunately they were on the far
side of the room, almost hiding behind several junior courtiers and whispering madly behind hands that effectively covered their faces. To march over to them would be . . .
awkward at least. That left Lord Jemmarc and his son
Lucjemm eagerly pressing closer.

And who was the young woman behind them, barely sixteen if a day, very close in age to Lucjemm, and almost cow-
ering, with shoulders hunched and hands wringing? She was
dressed in a rich gown of faded red and gold brocade with
multiple layers of fine lace in three different patterns at cuff,
neck, and hem that could have been worn by Rosselinda's
grandmother decades ago. It hung loosely around the girl's
waist but crammed her bustline into too tight a fit. Obviously
not new and not made for her. Someone must have dragged
it out of storage at the last minute for her to wear tonight.

Linda looked more closely at the way Lucjemm sidled
away from her, a step before his father. Jemmarc hung back
just a bit from his son, trying to include the girl in the deep
bow he offered Linda and Glenndon.

Linda kept her nod quiet and slight. By all protocols set
forth ages ago, the young woman should be presented to the
queen before anyone. By offering first introduction to herself
and Glenndon, Jemmarc did them both high honor in ac-

knowledging one or both of them as heirs. She wanted to preen at that. But . . . if she accepted the introduction she showed disrespect for her mother.

On the other hand she showed disrespect by garbing herself in male clothing.

On the other hand . . .

Lucjemm obviously did not want himself associated with the lady. His eyes lingered on Linda and flashed with admiration.

Her heart did a silly little flip. She relaxed her shoulders and stood taller, grateful for *his* approval.

"Who do we have here, my Lord Jemmarc? A new face at court is always refreshing," M'ma said coming up behind Linda and Glenndon. P'pa stood right beside her, still scowling whenever his gaze drifted to Linda.

Linda released the breath she hadn't realized she was holding.

"My niece, Your Grace. Newly come from the country," Jemmarc said on a deep bow. "My sister's stepdaughter, Graciella."

The young woman sank into a proper curtsy, never lifting her eyes above her hands.

"Welcome, child," M'ma said. "Visit me tomorrow at the third hour after noon. We shall take refreshment and discuss your role at court. You will join us, Princess Rosselinda, properly attired for the occasion." M'ma took P'pa's arm and aimed them both to the other side of the Great Hall.

Linda gestured Glenndon in the opposite direction. He lifted an eyebrow in question, a smile playing with his mouth. In that moment he looked exactly like P'pa when trying not to laugh at an inappropriate joke.

"Yes, it is always like this," Linda grumped to Glenndon. "Always a dance of politeness trying to sort out who outranks whom and who gets to say what before anyone else."

An image of a dozen blue-robed men standing in a circle yelling at each other flashed across her mind's eye.

The same, Glenndon said. Whether it was mind speech or a whisper she couldn't tell. But he smiled, banishing his perpetual anger, and turning his face and entire demeanor into that of a handsome and charming young man.

Behind them, Miri and Chastet sighed deeply, the first sign of them both falling in love.

The challenge of staying one step ahead of either or both of those two made Linda laugh. She took his arm and steered him toward Lord Bennallt, Miri's father. An interesting game to find out if he'd smile upon or forbid his daughter chasing the Crown Prince.

CHAPTER 24

GLENNDON SUPPRESSED A YAWN and scrubbed the sleepies from his eyes. Midnight. The court had finally retired, leaving him exhausted yet unable to sleep. The events of the past few days, his mission, the tension among the courtiers jockeying for place and rank, spun through his mind in endless possibilities for disaster.

And then there were the enticing flirtations with Lady Miri and Lady Chastet . . .

He needed to do something positive while his brain sorted things out behind his surface thoughts.

Ley lines and the Well of Life tugged at him. Hunting them out was something he could do. Something he *had* to do. Now was as good a time as any.

He thought through a refreshment spell, willing new energy into his aching back and tired legs. Instantly the stones of the wall behind his room tapestries jumped into new vividness. The mortar in all its discolorations took on new meaning. This line of stones matched too evenly. The white binding material seemed missing. He traced the outline of a door with his fingertip, sensing the emptiness behind it.

Further examination with his fingertips and enhanced eyesight showed him that one stone on the left, about waist-high, protruded barely a finger's width out from the others. He pressed the flat of his palm on it hard, and winced at the grinding noise as it moved on long-unused pivots and became stuck less than halfway through its rotation.

One, two, three, he counted silently, holding his breath, waiting for someone to come investigate the noise. Six more counts and all remained silent. He didn't wait any longer and slipped through the narrow opening. The stone barely brushed the tapestry that hid it. At first glance, anyone looking into his room would not notice the opening.

The moment Glenndon stepped onto the staircase landing he sensed ley lines waiting for him. A surge of energy through his feet seemed almost like a joyous greeting from a long-absent friend. He wiggled his bare toes against the stones in reply. No need for the torch that rested in its bracket beside the door, along with flint for lighting the oil-soaked rags. (Who did the king trust enough to keep the torches fresh and viable? Probably Fred and no one else.) The tendril of silvery blue at the bottom of the stairs enticed him forward, giving him more than enough light.

He skipped downward, running his hand along the wall, memorizing the texture and degrees of dampness. On the last stair before the tunnel the line led him elsewhere as his fingers caressed an imperfection. He paused, tracing the indentation. Right, down, left, cross, spikes atop a swirl into a spiral. A rune. Part of an ancient alphabet found only in the oldest of writings about magic. A rune that meant someone royal. His room was among the family apartments. A signpost to help him find his way home.

The silvery blue line wiggled impatiently. He stepped upon it and felt his magical talent blossom. His body wanted, no, needed, to throw a spell, any spell to bind him to this ley line once and forever.

Did he dare? Were the witchsniffers still about to sense the presence of magic? Would they even be able to sense a little spell this deep beneath layers and layers of stonework?

His duty as a magician was to test them, to learn how far their talent extended.

Light. A glow ball appeared in his hand. The ley line dimmed in the contrasting light. Still it shone for him, leading him onward through the maze of tunnels.

He strode forward watching for more runes. He found access to the queen's suite, and a branch from it to the king's quite readily. Of course they would have easy exits in time of trouble. Linda's room branched from his own staircase. Manda and Josie had a room shared with a governess off the same primary steps. Farther on he found a circular rune that he did not recognize. He'd explore that one another time. For now he needed to see where the widening ley line led him.

The path descended, first a gentle slope and then stairs descending deep into bedrock. The weight of the air changed as well. He thought he left Palace Isle and was now under the river.

His lungs labored to draw in air. Acres and acres of river water weighed down on him. If any of the stones and dirt gave way . . .

He scurried back the way he'd come, despite the widening and deepening of the ley line. Another time, when he was less tired, less prone to his fears. Perhaps, less alone.

"What are you up to, Jemmarc?" Darville asked the air.

The lord in question paraded around the practice yard with his "niece" Graciella clinging to his arm as if she needed his strength to stand upright. She wore another heavily brocaded gown today, this one of simpler cut without all the extra trim weighing it down. This one fit her better, but was still a design left over from a century ago. At least.

Linda's bold trews and tunic last night would have been more appropriate for the mud and sawdust of the yard enclosed by a split-rail fence. Jemmarc should have left Graciella in one of the palace rooms overlooking the yard, even if all of those rooms were occupied by servants. Ladies did not generally like being too close to the cursing, sweat, and occasional blood that spilled in this arena.

Except Linda, who seemed to thrive in the masculine atmosphere.

"It looks to me like he is setting the girl up to become his next lady," Linda muttered beside him. Today she wore normal girl clothes, a roughly woven but sturdy skirt and bodice with tight-fitting sleeves on her snowy white shirt. The loose cut of the skirt meant that, if necessary, she could loop up the length of it in one hand while she wielded a sword in the other.

If she chose. But they also broadcast her intent to leave the rough swordplay to the men today.

"You may be right, Linda. But the girl would be a more appropriate wife for his son Lucjemm," Darville mused while testing the balance and flexibility of the sword he'd chosen from the rack for a teaching session. While going through the motions of preparation, he let his gaze wander, noting every man, soldier and courtier alike who had descended upon the yard.

"Why don't you go charm the frown off of Lucjemm's face," he suggested. The look they exchanged said there was a lot more to his request than simply lightening the young man's mood.

Linda nodded—too willingly for her contrary nature—and eased her way around the outside of the fence. She made her progress look casual, greeting this person, commending that squire, pointing out features of a new armor design. Darville trusted his daughter to worm any information from the junior lord there was to have. Her mother had trained her well.

But why was she almost eager to speak with him? Darville suddenly felt as if he'd missed something vital. Something Mikka would have noticed and he should have.

Before she reached Lucjemm, the double door to the armory burst open from the inside. Glenndon stood in the arched portal blinking in the sudden sunlight. He wore an ill-fitting breastplate, gorget, and greaves, with a sword belt and empty sheath fastened around his slim hips. He looked angrier than Lucjemm.

Linda paused in her progress and furrowed her brow at the boy. Her shoulders started reaching for her ears even as her spine stiffened. She harbored a lot of resentment.

Darville would have to work with both his children. Or throw them into a dungeon cell together and let them work it out on their own.

"Good morning, Prince Glenndon," Darville called to him. "Come and select a weapon."

The boy stomped across the yard, pulling at the ill-fitting armor.

"Tell me what's wrong," Darville asked quietly.

Glenndon turned deep blue eyes up to meet his, a gaze so similar to his mother's the king wanted to step back. He could have been looking in a mirror of himself at that age, except for those eyes—keen reminder of his first love and what they had meant to each other long ago. He knew well how age lines began to tug at the corners of his own features, how comfort and good food had begun to fill in the hollows and soften the angles on his own face. And yet . . .

"Tell me what displeases you, Glenndon."

A grimace, a shrug to ease the straps of the breastplate, and a defiant chin were the only answers offered.

"Can't help you if you won't say the words." Darville turned his shoulder to his son while he ran his gaze across the line of blunted swords. Linda hadn't been this difficult to deal with, and by all covenants and conventions she should have had no interest in weapon play.

She had moved to stand beside Lucjemm.

"Doesn't say much, does he," the young lordling sneered loud enough to be heard across the entire arena.

"He doesn't need to. I understand him when he truly wants me to," she replied diffidently. "Better to observe and learn than blurt out words just to fill an awkward silence."

Darville wanted to applaud her. His heart swelled with pride at her wisdom and her defense of the newfound brother she resented and disliked.

"Come, Glenndon, here's a sword that should suit your strength and reach." He presented the grip of the sword he'd tested earlier to his son over his crooked arm. His heart swelled with pride that he finally had the chance to show off his son to the men he worked and trained with nearly every day.

Glenndon hesitated, staring at the weapon as if it were one of the legendary six-winged vipers. His eyes grew big, pupils contracted, eyebrows reaching for his hairline.

"I know this isn't a blade you are familiar with. Take it. It won't eat you, or flame you." Why was the boy so hesitant? Hadn't he ever worked with a sword before?

Off to the side, Darville glimpsed Linda stiffening as the other men in the arena all paused to watch the interplay of father and son, teacher and pupil, king and heir.

Glenndon shrugged. He did that a lot. His face relaxed into a half-grimace of resignation. Slowly he lifted his left hand and took the end knob in three stiff fingers. The weight of the thing seemed to surprise him as he dropped it into the scuffed dirt at his feet. Then he just stood there, shifting his distressed gaze from sword to king and back again.

"*S'murghit!* Pick it up, Glenndon." Darville wanted a stronger curse, would gladly have spewed one, except that Linda stood ten paces away, taking in every word and gesture.

She'd heard worse when she trained here, disguised as a boy.

Glenndon obediently bent to retrieve the sword, again holding it awkwardly with his fingers. When he stood upright, the weapon dangling dangerously over his foot, he looked at Darville with questions in his eyes.

Now what do I do?

Darville almost heard the words. Maybe he only interpreted the boy's posture and expression.

"Didn't your Da . . . Senior Magician Jaylor teach you anything about weapons in that University?" Darville's voice rose in frustration. "An opponent on the battlefield would have run you through by now."

Glenndon half-smiled and tilted his head.

"*S'murghit!* At least show him how to hold a weapon before you expect him to fight with it. You gave me the courtesy of private lessons until I could match any squire in the arena," Linda said in exasperation. She gathered her excess skirts in her left hand and tromped over to stand beside her brother. "May I show you a proper grip?" she asked Glenndon with suitable protocol.

"Never take a weapon from someone unless you intend to use it on them. Always ask," Darville quoted the rulebook of blade etiquette. "And where did you learn that word, Princess Rosselinda?" As if he didn't know. He scrunched his face in displeasure, as much at her vocabulary as being reprimanded by his own daughter in the practice yard.

She rolled her eyes at him, as only a girl just blossoming into womanhood could show disgust at an elder.

He felt useless as a parent, as a man, beneath those oh so

superior eyes. His pride had gotten in the way of good sense. Of course the boy had no need to learn swordplay. He had other weapons. Many other weapons. Some of them blades, but all small, balanced for throwing.

"You taught me how to grip a weapon the first day. Why do you presume he already knows how?" she yelled back at him, head and chin thrust forward, a mirror image of his own posture of defiance.

"He should know . . ." Darville tried to defend himself, knowing it was a hopeless gesture. The girl had learned command from her mother after all.

"Why?" She kept her gaze on Glenndon's hand, folding it correctly round the grip.

"Perhaps I'd be an acceptable tutor, Your Grace," Lucjemm offered with a crisp bow. "Though I am not nearly as experienced or talented as yourself, my memory of my first day in the armory is more recent. And I expect less from him."

"Good idea. Do it. Report progress to me often." Darville stomped off, pride in his son deflated, expectations shattered, and patience unraveling. *S'murghit,* he knew the boy had no training. Darville had to teach Jaylor rudimentary swordplay. Why should Jaylor have taught his son? S'murghit! He'd have to answer to Mikka for this, and find a way to appease his son.

CHAPTER 25

GLENNDON ROTATED his shoulders painfully. Every muscle in his back, thighs, and arms protested the movement. Years of chopping wood to feed the family hearth had built up strength and breadth. It hadn't prepared him for the more delicate and controlled movements of holding a sword with either hand before him and executing endless drills of circling, shifting, aiming, and lunging. Over and over and over for nearly three hours. Good thing he already had calluses on his hands. Even with gloves he felt the tight burn of blisters rising from the different grip.

His stomach growled in hunger. He should seek out something to eat in the Great Hall, or even in the family apartments. Could he ask a servant to help him find something in the kitchen to tide him over until the evening meal?

But first he needed quiet and privacy. A place to clear his thoughts and ease his body. So he walked slowly toward an inner courtyard he'd espied from his own room. Pretty flowers grew there, just coming into bloom in vibrant reds and pinks and yellows. Strong vines with wickedly long thorns climbed over trellises and looped around arches to offer shady bowers. The sweet and strong scent of showy flowers with no purpose but to ornament a garden felt lovely, but empty. There was something missing.

He cast about, seeking the truant element. Too sweet, his senses told him. What mitigated the honey density of the blossoms? His mother would add something spicy or salty to a recipe that cloying.

His nose found salt in the ever-present breeze off the Bay. Nothing sharper to counter the perfume.

A sharp scent. Aromatic. *Tambootie!* The garden needed Tambootie. He hadn't seen, smelled, or sensed any of the aromatic tree since leaving home. The capital remained denuded of the tree of life. No wonder the dragons shunned this part of Coronnan.

He closed his eyes, letting the sweetness cloak him. A person could hide amongst the climbing vines and dense foliage for a long time before the inevitable squire sought him out.

Since arriving at the palace he'd been alone only during the hours he tried to sleep in the too-big, too-soft bed, or wandered the maze of tunnels beneath the palace when he could not sleep. At least no one had been present to tell him he couldn't curl up in a blanket before the wall hearth. There he slept soundly for a few hours only after exploring another series of tunnels.

He caught a lilting tune on the soft spring breeze. His spirits lifted. "Mama. Home," he whispered to himself, surprised when he actually heard the words with his ears and not just his mind.

For a moment, with his eyes closed and the scent of fresh bread baking close by and the light music sung by a sweet soprano he could almost believe himself home, in the clearing, approaching the cabin, soon to be welcomed by his family. His real family of brothers and sisters, Mama and Da, cats and dogs, birds, flusterhens, and gray scurries chittering at him or twining with his legs.

He breathed deeply, his muscles relaxed. A tightness in his neck that he hadn't realized he'd been hunching around released.

Not home. No aromatic Tambootie or dragons whispering on the wind. He didn't belong here.

Then he opened his eyes.

Definitely not home. Stone walls rose around him like a canyon in the high mountains. A swath of green lay like a carpet at his feet. A glorious riot of bright flowers in artificial groupings, heavily pruned to contain their growth and train them into unnatural shapes, grew around him.

He'd found the garden he sought.

Not home. He almost turned around, certain that he belonged here no more than he did in the stifling atmosphere of formal court.

The singer raised her voice a little.

Not Mama.

Disappointment almost brought that tightness back to his neck. But the music was so lovely, a special tune that crooned love.

He needed to twine his voice with hers, mimic each sound, harmonize with it in his own deeper, masculine tones.

Before he could think about what he did, he opened his mouth and let the words of the first lullaby his mother had sung to him spill forth. The blockage in his throat loosened. Part of it dissolved and flowed outward with the song.

> *Sleep softly my little one,*
> *Sleep gently my baby,*
> *Papa keep watch,*
> *Mama hold dear.*
> *Sleep softly my little one,*
> *Sleep safely*
> *In my care.*

The singer echoed his words, one phrase behind him so that they sang in a round counterpoint. Together they brought the song to a soft ending that tapered off into silence.

"I didn't know you could sing," Linda said peering from behind a tall column of greenery that grew over a wooden arch.

A huge black cat also peeked out. Its fur absorbed the noon light, showing purplish highlights. It twitched its nose at him and ruffled long fur all the way down its spine to the fluffy tail.

A wingtip of iridescent black feathers sprang forth from a hidden flap.

Linda's mouth opened as she stared in wonder. Then her

eyes rolled up and she collapsed in a faint at Glenndon's feet.

﷽

Plop. Plop. Two drops of cool water dripped onto Linda's forehead. She knew it. She felt it. She didn't want to face it. Just before the blessed darkness had claimed her she'd seen . . . she'd seen the impossible.

(Why do you fear me?)

A gentle, childlike voice in her head. Not Glenndon. He had deeper, more mature tones to his mental voice, even if he did sing in a tentative tenor.

"I spoke to a dragon. I faced down an army trying to kill her. Why indeed did I flee from a cat with wings?" she murmured, not sure she spoke aloud until she heard her words.

A low chuckle greeted her words. "Open eyes," Glenndon said in his harsh, underused voice.

Had she heard him speak before, outside her head that is? She couldn't remember.

Linda obeyed, fluttering her lashes until she got used to the light streaming around them. Glenndon's worried frown filled her vision. Behind him, something black hovered. She presumed it was the black cat who . . . who had hidden wings. "So you can speak."

Glenndon nodded hesitantly.

"When you have to."

A more aggressive head movement.

"So, who's the cat? He speaks like a dragon."

"Fl . . . flywacket."

"Huh?"

(I was a dragon. Now I am not. Indigo here.)

"Princess Rosselinda here," she returned automatically, remembering the dragon protocol P'pa had taught her under the gaze of Shayla, the grandest dragon of all. "My friends and family call me Linda."

(Linda.) Indigo sounded as if he tasted the word.

She wondered if he was getting ready to sample her flesh. Flusterbumps broke out along her arms and spine. *Don't think like that. Dragons respected humans. They loved the royal family; were tied to it magically.* If legend and lore could be believed.

(Pretty name. Pretty Princess.)

"You didn't greet Indigo," Linda said to Glenndon as she propped herself onto her elbows trying to sit up.

"Before. Friends," Glenndon replied succinctly.

A new thought brought her upright in a hurry. "Dragons reflect light. That's how they seem invisible. But you absorb light, like . . . like . . . the deepest dungeon." She had no other image to explain a big, really, really big dragon with crystal-like fur collapsing into this oversized cat.

Reverses, Glenndon said into her mind, as if he'd run out of voice.

"If you say so. Indigo, that's a name for dark blue. Were you a blue-tipped dragon?"

(Not exactly.) Indigo sounded embarrassed.

Glenndon flashed a mental image of a juvenile dragon, about the size of Belle, her fleet steed. His body still shone with silver lights as his fur matured into the transparent crystals of an adult. Outlining his wings, and tracing along the wing veins, a deep, dark blue that was *almost* purple, but not quite, showed clearly where his body tended to fade in and out of view as the light shifted.

(No dragon twin. Not really purple.)

"Huh?"

"Purple special," Glenndon croaked. "Always twins. Can only be one. The other must become—something else."

The longest string of words she'd heard from him. Each one sounded less certain than the previous one.

"How?"

He shrugged, having run out of words again.

(Anyone can gather magic from a purple-tip dragon,) Indigo said proudly. He stretched his cat neck and rippled his fur from ears to tail. The iridescent wings peeked out from their pouch, or fold, or whatever the extra flap of skin and fur was called.

"Anyone? Even me?"

Indigo purred and bumped his head against her chin, almost knocking her flat again. She scritched between his ears.

Glenndon looked worried. *No magic. My Da and your father said never use magic at court.*

"A lot of courtiers and nobles don't like magic. They want to control everything, and they can't control a magician. But they aren't logical about it if they brought witchsniffers in trying to catch P'pa throwing magic."

"Yes," Glenndon said, surprised at her observation. "Control."

"You are learning to control your voice better with each word."

He shrugged and blushed.

"You have to practice."

He made a face, twisting one side of his mouth up and the other down, eyes scrunched and nose wrinkled.

"I don't like practicing sewing," Linda said. "We've all got something we have to learn that we don't like."

A relaxation of the ugly face.

Sing, Glenndon said mentally, his eyes brightening. *Practice speaking by singing. Mama sings all the time. She taught me that tune you sang to Indigo.*

"She did? My M'ma taught it to me. It's a lullaby."

Yes.

"What else did she sing? Something we might both know."

Again he shrugged. She was getting tired of that response.

Linda sorted through all the tunes she knew, excited by the idea that singing might release the locks on Glenndon's voice. She needed to start with a simple tune, something familiar, something that might be common in the distant exile of the University of Magicians.

Indigo's purring took on a catchy rhythm, something one might dance to.

Glenndon picked up the beat slapping his hand against his thigh and humming a phrase or two, snatches of something . . . something old. Something very old.

"Yes! Old Maisy sings that when she's sewing. She says it helps her keep her stitches even." Linda hummed along seeking words to fit the phrases, the rhythm.

The music flowed with her blood and lightened her mind.

> *Dance, dance, wherever you may dance*
> *Prance with a lilt in your feet . . .*

A smile filled Glenndon's face with light. He touched his throat tenderly, eyes nearly alight in wonder. Then he smiled again and nearly vibrated as he picked up the answering phrase.

> *Dance, dance, whenever you may dance.*
> *Twirl and jump and keep the beat.*

Together they sang the chorus and moved into the second verse. Linda picked herself up off the ground and sat on the bench, patting the place beside her. Indigo leaped to join her. Glenndon unceremoniously shoved the cat's bottom to make him move away and replaced him on the bench, never missing a beat or a word of the song they both enjoyed.

An old song out of history, dating back as far as the Stargods, binding their different childhoods and giving them common ground to build on.

CHAPTER 26

JAYLOR AMBLED ALONG a little-used path between the clearing and the University, seeking privacy to meditate and strengthen his connection to the magnetic pole. He needed to listen to the breeze and hope the Kardia spoke to him of birds and wild creatures.

Exhaustion dragged at his bones and stabbed at his eyes. He pinched the bridge of his nose, trying to ease the strain of bright sunlight stabbing him through the trees.

He couldn't keep up the search for the Krakatrice with Baamin and continue running the University and keeping the Circle of Master Magicians organized and working together compatibly much longer. Even with the assistance of Robb and Marcus working with younger dragons than Baamin, the work was too much, too exhausting, almost fruitless. For every one of the ancient menaces they killed, three more appeared. Where were they coming from! Maybe he and Baamin could train Lukan to ride and fight with a younger dragon. Maybe he should extend the training to all of the journeymen. If they had enough obsidian spear tips. If . . .

Lukan didn't focus well on any single task. He flitted from idea to idea without ever completing something unless Jaylor sat with him and forced his attention back to the primary task. Fighting a giant snake from dragonback with magic, fire, and dangerously sharp weapons required concentration.

S'murghit, if only Glenndon hadn't been called to the

capital by Darville, the boy could wipe out the enemy with a few well-placed thoughts.

But Darville had recalled his son to the palace. And Jaylor felt his absence every moment as a huge ache in his heart. It was like there was suddenly a hole in the family.

He needed quiet, to practice the trick of fading into the background and eavesdropping unnoticed while in plain sight.

Like a dragon.

What he really needed was sleep. About three days of un-interrupted sleep before his short temper would relax.

And Brevelan's quiet healing songs. She alone could soothe his temper and reduce the pressure around his heart.

But he never had enough time to just sit with her anymore.

Snatches of conversation drifted through the tufted branches of the everblues. He sighed in resignation and leaned against a boulder where he knew a ley line passed beneath. With his feet firmly planted upon the silvery blue that teased and taunted his senses but never fully showed it-self, he drew in strength and magic to heighten all of his senses and revive his tired body.

Jaylor reached out with his mind to listen, to feel the vi-brations of feet walking and the shift of tree branches as someone, two someones, pushed them aside.

The murmur in the distance was not a stray breeze playing tag with the tree canopy. It was men's voices drawing closer.

He heard the name "Glenndon," quite plainly. Alarm bells rang in his mind. He listened more avidly.

"It's not right," a deep male voice thundered across the network of paths in and around the University buildings.

"Hush," replied a lighter tenor voice. "He'll hear you. S'murghit, the entire University will hear you."

Ah, that was Master Magician Dennilley. Middle-ranked, neither senior nor junior, younger than Jaylor, but older than newer members of the Master Circle.

Jaylor anchored his staff and tilted the knobby top toward the source of the conversation. His hand tingled, absorbing information as rapidly (and perhaps more accurately) as his ears. This sounded like something he needed to know.

"The boy is still an apprentice and he's assigned to the

court. That place belongs to the Senior Magician, or one of the Master Circle!" bass voice insisted.

Master Samlan. He was older than Jaylor by a decade or more. He'd accepted Jaylor as Senior, quite reluctantly, after old Master Baamin had died. As the man who had stood next to Baamin in seniority and power, he thought he should have been made Senior instead of the much younger Jaylor.

But Samlan had closeted himself within the old University in the city so tightly that he had little or no experience in the outside world. Politics bewildered him. Change confused him. Many of the other ancients had the same problem. Well, they weren't exactly ancient, but at least old enough to know everything about everything magical. He thought of librarians and healers who never looked beyond their own talents and jobs.

"If the court is now open to magician advisers, why didn't Jaylor tell us, let us decide who should go?" Dennilley asked mildly. "*When* the court is open to us, then masters should sit behind the left shoulder of the lords in Council. But are we certain that the court is open to us again?"

"Jaylor sent his son to them. I should have gone in his stead whatever his reasons."

Jaylor ground his back teeth together trying to keep from shouting at the self-centered, pompous . . . He ran out of expletives for the man who wore blinders, seeing only what he wanted to see.

"But only his son. And the boy went directly to the king, not the Council of Provinces," Dennilley reminded him.

Jaylor sensed that the young master took a step or two backward to separate himself from Samlan. Something more drove Samlan than affronted seniority.

"What difference does that make? The boy is only a boy. He can't possibly know enough about economics and politics and diplomacy to advise the king. In Circle tonight I will demand the right to replace the boy. If Jaylor does not agree, than we must vote to remove him. We have that right!"

"We should ask Jaylor to share information rather than assume he is supplanting us with a lesser magician," Dennilley cautioned.

Jaylor stood a little straighter. So that was what Samlan

wanted. He was tired of waiting to control the power and prestige of being Senior.

Did he stop and think about the fatigue, the worry, the loneliness?

"What if the boy is there to infiltrate the court. To spy for his father?" Dennilley removed himself another two steps. Still the voice of caution. He rose in potential in Jaylor's mind for that.

"We have other spies in residence!" Samlan thundered. "What good is one more? Are you with me in the vote to depose Jaylor?" Samlan demanded. His words bounced from tree to tree, picking up echoes and menacing undertones as they traveled. An ominous portent.

"I can't let you do it, old man," Jaylor muttered to himself, keeping his voice from traveling any farther than his own ears. His face grew hot, his belly tight, and the pain behind his eyes pounded more fiercely.

"I have plans to make." Jaylor lifted his staff from its anchor in the Kardia. His anger grew cold but more intense. His mind sorted and classified options almost before he thought them through.

"Now I know why I've allowed my children to eavesdrop on conversations and spells. I will need Lukan for certain. He likes to hide in high places. The twins?" He remembered quite vividly what had happened the last time he'd urged them to observe from hiding and in silence. A niggle of worry replaced rigid calculation.

Could Valeria survive another such adventure?

"All life is risky. She's the best observer I have. I'll just have to keep her out of the void."

"He'll be mad if you tell him," Lillian whispered from the top of a nearby tree.

"Better mad than exiled from the University," Valeria replied.

Jaylor paused a moment to think about Valeria's last comment. Yes, his family would rather risk his wrath at their eavesdropping and gossiping than do nothing and risk the disgruntled masters overcoming him and exiling him and his family away from the University, away from the clearing. Away from their home.

He continued on to his private office at the University, chuckling at how well he'd trained his children. His love for them outweighed any threat from his rivals. He had plans to make and his children to thank. He never could stay mad at them for long.

With that thought the pressure behind his temples eased and heat in his face dissipated.

King Darville studied a map spread across his desk. Each of the four corners was anchored with a different object—an inkwell, a dagger, his half-full mug of beta arrack, and the Coraurlia—to keep the huge parchment from rolling up again. General Marcelle stood on the opposite side of the desk tracing the course of the Coronnan River back to its source in the Western Mountains.

"That attack on Sambol was a feint. A test of our will and preparedness," he grumbled.

"I agree. They came out of the darkness at dawn, fired a few salvos of arrows and retreated at the first sign of resistance," Darville said.

"They gave up too easily for a well armed force of two hundred mounted soldiers. And they all wore the crest of SeLennica. Why would the queen ask your assistance, Your Grace, in delicate negotiations while preparing an attack on us?"

"Perhaps they came from somewhere else and only wanted us to blame SeLennica to provoke a war," Darville mused. That's what he would do if he wanted both countries vulnerable to . . . to what?

Two assassination attempts and now this. Connected? Coincidence?

Jaylor had taught him long ago not to believe in coincidence.

"Who else is enduring a long dry spell?" he mused, not really asking anyone other than himself.

"I haven't heard of anyone but us missing the spring rains," Marcelle replied. "Those troops couldn't have come from anywhere but SeLennica by way of the main pass. The southern pass you keep tapping is closed, the slopes around it trackless and too steep for steeds. The road through the primary pass to Sambol is smooth and broad with gradual inclines for a reason."

Darville's attention followed the crest of the mountains. He couldn't forget the addition of miner's acid to the Amazon oil on his sword. Mines occurred mostly in mountains, strong doses could melt rock around mineral deposits.

"Here," he said resting his finger on the southern pass, near Lake Apor, Laislac's Province, and a base camp for a series of mines in nearby foothills. The lake was a headwater of a tributary to the mighty River Coronnan that carried the trade of his country to the Great Bay and the capital city that guarded the port. Except for a few rapids and waterfalls near the lake, the water became an easy, near silent route for small canoes and light barges to ride to the heartland of Coronnan.

He'd have to remember to step up the guards there. Who could he trust to lead them? If he were older, more experienced, or *spoke,* Glenndon would be the obvious candidate. Good training for the Crown Prince.

No one else came to mind. He needed General Marcelle *here.* He needed Glenndon's unique talents to explore the extent of the reduced rainfall.

Dare he ask Jaylor to scout the region from dragonback while he and old Baamin sought the Krakatrice?

"The raiders actually came from here." He tapped the pass again. "They circled around in the dead of night to make it look as if they had come from the primary trade route."

"Why that pass? It connects one small military outpost on the SeLennica side of the mountains to a walled trading city on our side," Marcelle said. "Even Lord Laislac doesn't live there, or keep more than a token guard. It's a long journey. Invaders would need provisions for an extra week of travel with no place to replenish across the entire mountain range. The main pass has outposts with stockpiles of journey foods, tackle, steeds, and weapons. They used the main pass this time and will again." He pointed to Sambol near the headwaters of the river, a much larger and more important trading city.

"Too obvious. We keep the end of the pass guarded and the guards alert because it is the primary pass that leads to the highest navigable waters of the River Coronnan. No, if Queen Miranda wishes to invade Coronnan, again, she'll send her troops through here," he tapped the small outpost on the lake impatiently, "because the pass is narrow and steep, often clogged with rockfall. We maintain only a token patrol there to keep out unwanted riffraff and spies. All of whom come through the pass on foot, without steeds or more supplies than they can carry on their backs." He moved his finger to the mining symbol nearby without saying anything. These days he never knew who might listen to private conversations.

"What makes you think Miranda will invade? She concentrated on rebuilding her country after the last war, consolidating her power base and unifying her people," Marcelle continued to search the markings on the detailed map for notations of other points of interest. He nodded slightly as Darville tapped the mine again.

"My last missive from Ambassador Jack indicated restlessness among the people," Darville said quietly, hoping no one overheard. "They've shifted their economy from heavy exploitation of resources to agriculture. Fifteen years of decent food and a stabilizing economy and the old nobility is restless. They have the leisure to remember old grudges and prejudices. We are foreign; therefore we are to blame for their years of privation. They want war to prove they are right."

"Is that why the queen has sent three agents to my wife to seek a possible alliance between my grandson Mikkette and her daughter Princess Jaranda?" Lord Andrall asked, entering the room, unannounced, with an armful of more scrolls— smaller but more specific maps of sections of the border.

This meeting was private. Darville had dismissed the guards and heralds hours ago.

"An alliance by marriage would take some of the thunder away from restless nobles. On the other hand, that marriage would give more ambitious lords an excuse to depose you and unite the two kingdoms under the children. I've sent word to Lady Lynetta to keep the boy home and out of view of such plotters," Andrall said on a shrug that nearly dislodged his load of scrolls.

"You know, if we had a court scribe, we wouldn't have to crawl around the archives ourselves. This is something our *servants* should be doing," Lord Laislac grumbled, carrying yet another bundle of scrolls. Cobwebs matted in his hair and tangled with his graying queue. Dust smudged his cheek, looking like a three-day growth of beard. The maternal grandfather of Mikkette, his permission was required for any marriage or alliance. He'd granted Andrall and Lynetta the right to raise his daughter's child and care for the mother, the totally insane and magically talented Ariiell.

"We haven't had a decent court scribe since we exiled all the magicians," Andrall grumbled. "They used to keep track of all these details for us."

"And we trusted them to record our meetings accurately and keep our secrets," Darville reminded them. He wanted the magicians back in the council chamber, but not at the cost of giving his daughter in marriage while still so young. Princess Jaranda of SeLennica was only three years older. The same age as Glenndon. If Queen Miranda sought a better alliance, the marriage of Jaranda and Glenndon could lead to uniting the two countries, ancient enemies.

Stargods! He didn't want to think of marriage for any of the young royals.

"I was thinking," Laislac said.

"That's unusual," Andrall muttered into his beard.

"I was *thinking* after the incident before court the other night that Lord Jaylor could have quoted any law and we would not know if he spoke the truth or not because we no longer have magician scribes to record our decisions and decrees."

"He spoke the truth," Darville said, looking each of the lords in the eye. "I remember the laws."

"But no one else does, and if anything happens to you, Your Grace, we have no *records*," Laislac continued.

"No, we don't. Shall we invite the master magicians to rejoin us in the Council of Provinces as neutral advisers and educated scribes?" Darville asked, trying to keep his voice calm. He dared not show his excitement lest they deny him the right to bring the magicians home, as the magicians had brought the dragons home.

"No, no, no, nothing quite so drastic," Laislac protested. "I was thinking of Lucjemm, Jemmarc's son. He's educated and needs to learn the ways of the Council for when he inherits. Someday. When he grows up and Jemmarc grows old."

"I too have an educated son who needs to learn the ways of the Council for when he grows up and I grow too old to act as your king," Darville said. "Or one of you assassinates me."

An uncomfortable silence rippled around the room for the space of four heartbeats.

"Or you die in battle because we aren't prepared to fight SeLennica when they march across the mountains," General Marcelle reminded them of the reason for this informal planning session.

"I'll inform Prince Glenndon that he will attend the meetings with quill and parchment at hand," Darville said.

"What of Lucjemm?" Laislac persisted. "If we have two scribes, we make certain nothing is missed or recorded with bias."

"Yes. Yes. I agree. That is why we *each* had a magician adviser sitting behind us. We shall have both Glenndon and Lucjemm attend us. The boys are becoming friends, they will work well together."

No one had mentioned that having Lucjemm learn the ways of the Council might put him in better position to marry Princess Rosselinda so she could become their queen. Of all the noble sons, he was closest to Linda in age . . . Laislac was too old, as was Andrall's nephew. Bennallt's son was too young. The two princes of Rossemeyer were too close in blood. And no one knew what kind of princes or noble sons might be found on the Big Continent. Another chore for Jaylor to send his spies on and find out.

Darville didn't want to think of that. He had a war to prevent.

"Now, my lords, we need to search these maps for clues while the other lords look for ways to find out who is whispering words of war into Queen Miranda's ears. I thought she'd grown wiser after her husband died and left the country in ruins from *his* wars."

His gaze strayed farther south on the map to the looming bulk of Hanassa. Ages ago a monstrous volcano had erupted, whose walls then collapsed down into a vast, sere caldera. A city of outlaws, desperados, rogue magicians, exiled malcontents, and dispossessed landowners clustered there, respecting no laws or any who lived by them.

Miranda's husband, the sorcerer known as The Simeon, had hailed from Hanassa. And so had Lord Krej's mother. Darville's cousin had murdered his own royal father and older brothers, debilitated then poisoned Darville's father, and ensorcelled Darville into the body of a golden wolf and left him as bait for a dragon snack.

Who would sneak out of Hanassa next to threaten the security of the continent in a quest for absolute power?

Or did the threat hail from closer to home?

CHAPTER 27

*S*O, PRISSY QUEEN MIRANDA seeks a marriage alliance with Coronnan. Most likely her disreputable Rover lover whispers into her ear during the night, words that counter the demands of her nobles. Words of peace and prosperity rather than expansion and war.

Bah. Prosperity is good. But men need war to hone their strength and cunning, to bring out their courage so that natural leaders arise and pampered layabouts lose the privilege of rank. War is a part of life, and we are too long without it.

I am ready. But are the other nobles and the army? Doubtful. Until the time is right I shall encourage this alliance. But Princess Jaranda—she is lovely by all accounts—shall be my bride. I hail from royalty, if only distantly. My distant cousin Lord Krej, through my father, was nephew to a king. My line is respected if not ancient. We have wealth and influence. And we possess no history of magic. Ever. I am the best candidate. I will have Princess Jaranda, though I'd rather have Princess Rosselinda. That is looking less likely as Darville pushes her aside in favor of the bastard Glenndon.

We shall see.

My lovely whispers a new thought to me. There are ways of gaining power and privilege through one marriage, eliminating the bride soon after the first heir is born, then taking another bride of equal or greater rank.

I shall keep a keen ear out for the most advantageous first marriage. My spies are in place. My father has raised an army for me.

Success to the bold. Death to all magic.

"Are you certain you are well enough to do this?" Darville asked Mikka as he cupped his hands to help her mount her placid steed.

"I have to do this. 'Tis been far too long since I rode through the city. The people need to see their queen." She placed her foot into his hands and hoisted herself upward.

He had to help. More than he liked. She weighed practically nothing, and her bones looked far too frail.

"If M'ma gets to ride, why can't I?" demanded Josie, the youngest of his trio of daughters. She stamped her foot and pouted, two proven behaviors to get her way with servants.

"Josie, how old are you?" Mikka asked sternly.

"I'm six!" she proclaimed.

"Six?" Darville raised his eyebrows in question. "I thought for sure you were only two."

"No, I'm six."

"Then act like it," Mikka said. "Or should we return you to the nursery with your toys and baby dresses?"

Josie bit her lower lip.

Darville could almost see her mind churning beneath her fine blonde curls, seeking a way out of the dilemma posed by her parents. Walk to Temple like a respectable girl of her age or revert to babyhood?

"Why do we have to walk?" she asked, stalling.

"Because everyone walks to Temple services on rest day," Linda replied, not quite quoting her catechism. "We are all equal and humble in the eyes of the Stargods. Only human politics ranks royalty, nobles, merchants, laborers, peasants, and magicians."

"We walk to remind ourselves and each other that no one is above the law set down by the Stargods," Manda continued the lesson.

Darville nodded approval to them both. They might not fully understand the concept, but they knew the words. A beginning to understanding.

"But M'ma rides," Josie continued her protest.

"M'ma has been very ill. She hasn't the strength to walk so far," Darville said gently. "Come hold my hand, and if you get very, very tired, falling asleep on your feet tired, you may ride upon my shoulders."

Josie brightened at that.

Linda looked at her little sister, jealousy turning her mouth down. He used to carry her to Temple when she was tiny. No more.

"Shouldn't M'ma attend services in the palace Temple?" Linda asked, her frown turning to concern.

"We have always gone to Temple in the city," M'ma replied. "We have never hidden ourselves away from the people. And we won't now." She clucked to the steed. It plodded forward, one slow step after another.

Darville caught Josie's hand in his left and Manda's in his right. Then he leaned down to speak to Linda. He didn't need to bend nearly as much as he thought he should. Linda was growing up, both physically and emotionally. Part of him was proud of her. Part of him regretted that he couldn't keep her a baby or even a *little* girl anymore.

"Watch your mother, Lindy." No more Little Lindy. "If she starts to fall, let me know so I can catch her."

"Will you always catch us when we fall, P'pa."

"Yes."

"Promise?"

"I promise by the Stargods who guide us that I will always catch you, precious daughter."

Memories of the greased step, the broken sword, and the arrows flying toward Shayla shadowed his confidence. What if he wasn't around to protect his family? Who would watch over them?

Jaylor, I think I need you here in the capital.

Then Glenndon hurried out of the palace, still buckling his belt. Silent and yet disruptive of ingrained routines.

Darville smiled at his son. He'd almost forgotten the boy

in this family tradition. He had someone to rely on if times
got tough.

When times got tough. They always did.

"Touch," Glenndon said, proud of himself that the word
came out whole without a single hesitation or stutter.

"Acknowledged," Lucjemm replied, raising his broadsword in salute. Then, almost before he'd finished his word,
let alone his gesture of respect, he shifted his two-handed
grip, twisting the blade, cutting down and around Glenndon's
blade for a slash to the side.

Glenndon dodged right and back with a hair's breadth of
room. The tip grazed his cuirass, leaving a long but shallow
scratch on the metal. He'd seen Lucjemm perform this same
maneuver before. No need of magic to anticipate him, he
signaled his intent well in advance to anyone observing with
care. While Lucjemm recovered his balance and stance,
bringing his weapon back to *en garde,* Glenndon cut under
him in a long lunge.

"Touch," he chortled.

"Match to His Highness," General Marcelle shouted for
all in the arena to hear. "You learn quickly, my boy. Soon
you'll be challenging your father, a truly fine swordsman!"

Lucjemm frowned and then brightened to a normal countenance so quickly Glenndon almost missed it. Glenndon
forced himself to smile at the gathered soldiers and nobles
while he puzzled out the meaning of that frown.

"You have taught him well, Lucjemm. Perhaps we can
find a valuable place for you schooling some of the ham-
handed recruits. Now if His Highness could just learn to ride
as quickly as he learned swordplay . . ." General Marcelle
said good-naturedly.

Lucjemm bowed slightly to the older man, seemingly
grateful for the acknowledgment.

"Now off with you both. His Grace told me this morning
not to keep you too long from your duties with the Council
of Provinces." The general shooed them back into the changing rooms.

Glenndon saluted the general and Lucjemm by raising the

flat of his blade before his face, kissing the blade lightly with a silent thanks to both the weapon and the Stargods for his hard-fought victory, than whipping it down and out so that it whistled in the wind of its passage. General Marcelle nodded his acceptance of the honor.

Lucjemm performed the same ritual. Glenndon waited to sheathe his sword until he could do it at the same time as his opponent. That was not a ritual or courtesy he'd been taught. It just made sense. *Never trust your enemy,* Da had said many times when drilling apprentices to defend themselves with spells and weapons thrown.

Lucjemm was not an enemy, he reminded himself. But Glenndon remembered his cunning, and his pushing the rules of practice matches to the limit, and his serious frown upon defeat.

"What do you suppose the Council will bore us with today?" Lucjemm asked, friendly and relaxed, as he dumped a bucket of water over his sweaty head. He shook his hair free of water, much like a dog, spluttering at the refreshing chill. "S'murghit it's hot for so early in the season. We need a good soaking rain."

Glenndon tossed him a towel and masked his silence with a shrug while he cleansed himself in the same manner.

Three out of the last five days, he and Lucjemm had sat beneath the stained-glass window to the king's right and written every word spoken in the Council Chamber. He remembered every word, from thousands of wool bales from Fleece, to tons of fish caught in the Bay, to a relaxing of patrols at Sambol and strengthening them elsewhere along the western border. The king did not say that he moved troops around Lake Apor, lest Lord Laislac object, but Glenndon had seen the maps and knew the logic.

Not one of the lords had spoken about magic or bringing magicians back to court.

A typical meeting brought endless debate: Did Fleece owe more taxes for producing their wool and mutton on the land than the coastal provinces that captured fish from the sea that belonged to all? By the same token Fleece thought they should not pay taxes at all since they shouldered most of the burden of patrolling the border. And so the discussion continued day after day without answering any questions at all, or decisions being made.

"I wish I had your talent for holding my tongue," Lucjemm continued grumbling. "Sometimes I want to strangle each and every one of the argumentative . . ."

Glenndon stuck out his tongue and grabbed hold of it.

They both burst out laughing.

A few moments later, dressed in more formal clothes, each threw an arm around the other's shoulders, and they marched back into the palace ready to sit quietly and write the words spoken by the lords. Later they would compare notes and bite their cheeks to keep from laughing at the pompous older men who ruled the country. For good or for ill.

Having a friend was almost as good as having Lukan at his side, sharing much of the same activities as at home. He'd never had a friend before, didn't need one with Lukan around.

Glenndon had observed the shifting loyalties, agreements, and disagreements. Lukan would have noticed them first and made a joke about it. Glenndon thought he knew who sided with whom, who stood by the king even if they disagreed with him, and who would never agree to anything the king said. Lukan would have known instinctively.

But were any of the conflicting loyalties strong enough to trace back to the assassination attempts upon King Darville? Would Glenndon be able to spot the next one before it happened? Because where there was one attempt, surely there would be another and another, until the murderer was either caught or successful.

S'murghit! He needed Lukan here, now, to help him observe and figure it all out.

CHAPTER 28

I WARNED MY LOVELY that this day would come. She did not listen. She likes to think she controls me. But today she agreed. We send no more eggs to the far reaches of Coronnan. We will leave one small tangle of the newly hatched at the base of the mountain pass near Lake Apor to harass the army gathering there. The others must remain close to the city with us.

The hateful magicians have murdered too many. We can no longer rely on spreading terror around the land. We had hoped to send the peasantry into a panic when the king's troops did not deliver them from this evil, and then they would flock to my army.

Instead they have begun to hope the magicians will protect them, as they have for months now. They trust the magicians to save them.

Filthy magicians. They are not trustworthy at all. Everyone should know not to trust a magician. They work in secret and follow their own plans for mastery of Coronnan, all the while bowing and smiling and letting fools think that magic and magicians are their servants.

I will change that soon. I will keep the eggs and the hatchlings close at hand to assist my army. We will change the land back to a natural sere desert later, when we have conquered the city and the nobles.

"Are you sure this is the right way?" Lucjemm asked, clinging to the rough stone wall supporting a spiral staircase.

"Yes," Linda replied, tripping lightly up the timeworn steps—a widdershins spiral, since the kings of Coronnan all the way back to the first one, Quinnault, had been left-handed. If under attack a king would have the advantage backing up the stairs with his off hand against the wall and his sword arm free to fight an opponent below. "P'pa pointed out this tower the day we came through the keep from the stables."

Now she understood why men wore trews. She found them much easier to move about in on this circuitous route. And the boots! So much better traction, warmth—even in high summer the stone walls radiated cold they'd absorbed during countless winters—and support on her feet. She needn't fear stubbing her toes when she tripped over skirts. And she would trip if she'd worn skirts.

This oldest part of the keep enticed her, even more than the belowground tunnels. Here she had just as many hidden places to explore, but above ground, and with the occasional window to peer out of to find landmarks and orientation. She paused by an arrow-slit opening halfway up the spiral. All she could see was the Bay. Lots and lots of Bay with no land between here and there. Ah, that meant they were in the East Tower, tall enough to shadow the few islands that lay between here and the port. They were on the right track. To the left, six steps up, should be an opening onto the roof of the servants' quarters—a broad flat space used in the past to call dragons.

Indigo scampered past her, not pausing as he rubbed his face against her leg. He stopped at the landing and issued something that was halfway between a normal cat's meow and the growl of a much bigger animal. She flipped the latch on the wooden door and pushed it open for him. He bounded onto the platform and lifted his head into the constant wind off the Bay. His nose worked furiously gathering every scent.

She pulled the door closed but didn't latch it.

The roof was here. That meant their destination should be only one more landing above that.

The next step up was too shallow for her foot and tilted

alarmingly to the right. She fell forward to grasp the next riser since there were no handholds anywhere; even the windowsill was shallow and too smooth for anything but bracing a longbow.

Thank you, M'ma, for agreeing that for this adventure I needed to wear boy's clothing.

Lucjemm steadied her back as she righted herself. She flashed him a grateful smile. For a moment they stood staring at each other, not much caring how much time passed.

Glenndon marched stolidly past them carrying a flickering torch. The few windows offered too little light in this enclosed space. He kept his gaze firmly on the ground, paying more attention to the stones beneath their feet than the route.

"Glenndon?" she touched his arm slightly. "What do you see?"

"No path."

A tangle of glowing blue lines appeared in her head. Then it disappeared and he replaced the image with the open top of the tower with its crenellated wall. From there he could see far and wide, seek out whatever those blue lines were. She shrugged, much as he did when at a loss for words.

In the brief vision he caressed Indigo with a casual hand, the flywacket enhancing his search.

He flashed a grin, teeth shining clean and white in the dim light. Then, he plodded on, eyes still on the ground.

"This way." She tugged on his sleeve. "We have to exit on this landing." Hardly a landing, just an extra-wide step that barely accommodated both her feet at the same time. The boys, with their bigger feet, would have to balance precariously here.

Glenndon looked puzzled, dragging his eyes away from the ground reluctantly. "No . . . door," he said.

"Not unless you know the secret." She smiled hugely, happy to know something he didn't.

"I really don't like this place," Lucjemm said behind her, still standing on the step below her. "It's enclosed, too old. The stairs twist the wrong way. Too mysterious. Who knows what kinds of poisonous spiders and lizards and things are hiding in the cracks and crevices? Perhaps we should go back for more torches. And weapons . . ."

"P'pa said it was safe. So it's safe," Linda insisted. Boys! All muscle and brave talk in the arena with a sword in their hand. But give them an adventure and they became absolute gray scurries when confronting the unknown.

She, on the other hand, was excited to explore the home of her ancestors, where they'd fought and died, loved and given birth, argued and stood fast for their beliefs.

Grabbing the torch from Glenndon, she moved it, splaying light on the seemingly blank wall. The stone walls angled inward, and the steps grew shallower yet. A quick glance over her shoulder showed Glenndon and Lucjemm with their backs pressed hard against the outside wall. A window above them cast enough golden light to put them in deep shadow, barely visible even with a lit torch.

Fading into the stones like dragons . . .

The hair on her arms and the back of her neck stood straight up. Flusterhen bumps popped out on her skin beneath her tunic sleeves.

When she turned back to face the wall, she found a thin straight line where the stones should have been staggered.

"See, it's a dead end. We need to turn back," Lucjemm said, already sliding downward, his back still against the wall. His boots fit better lengthwise on the narrow steps. But the deep indentation in the middle threw his balance off.

Linda stretched her hand toward the wall, palm out, trying desperately to keep it from shaking, and hoping she remembered the detailed instructions P'pa had given her for opening the secret door. The lords had come here not too long ago. Surely where they trod, she could follow.

"Breathe," Glenndon whispered in her ear.

"Easier said than done," she muttered. Then she pressed her palm flat against the third stone from the left of the straight line, five stones above the floor.

Nothing happened.

"Left hand," Lucjemm reminded her. "The king is left-handed."

"Right." Linda switched hands and pressed again. Something ground and groaned, moving reluctantly.

"Harder," Lucjemm sighed. "You're such a puny thing I doubt you could move a cobweb."

"Puny!" Just to show him she wasn't, Linda applied all of her weight to the stone.

The door pivoted inward. She stumbled after it, scraping her shoulder against the dressed stones that only *looked* rough and uneven.

Magical illusion?

A soft glow in the center blossomed like dawn sunlight, growing in intensity to fill all the available space of the huge room that took up nearly the entire tower interior (no wonder the stairs were so narrow). She saw little beyond row after row of freestanding stone shelves, reaching twice her height, lined up with only a narrow space between them. Books and scrolls, small caskets and large wooden boxes were jammed together in no seeming order. Except . . .

Peering down one row after another, it looked like the back of the room had more order, and more cobwebs flowing in blankets around the books. The front of the room was a mess: fewer cobwebs, but less order.

She thought she spotted a trapdoor in the ceiling, in the exact center of the circular room, but couldn't be sure. The wooden planks were light-colored wood, reflecting the glow downward so that details eluded her. She imagined another whole story with nothing but records up there. A true treasure trove of information.

Linda placed her torch into a wall bracket to the left of the door that sat solidly sideways, showing no inclination of moving again without aid. Good, they shouldn't be trapped in here.

Glenndon touched her shoulder and pointed to a path of scuffed footprints in the dust.

"I see. But the lords who came here last were looking for maps. We need records of the Council meetings."

"Won't they be near the door, the last things shoved in here?" Lucjemm asked. Curiosity seemed to have overcome his fears as he poked at stacks of scrolls resting on the nearest shelf.

"Probably." She turned her attention to examining a different set of scrolls three steps farther along than the ones Lucjemm stabbed at with a finger, as if poking a nest of desert snakes.

"Labels," Glenndon said. He picked at the edge of a shelf with his fingernail. A shower of impacted dirt fell to the floor revealing markings in the cleaner stone.

"Of course, labels." Lucjemm shook his head. "Our ancestors weren't stupid. Devious sometimes, but not stupid."

Linda picked at her own shelf until she saw numerals. "This one is from the year before the Leaving. And the shelf below is from the end of the year before. I guess they started shelving at the bottom and worked upward until they ran out of room then started over at the bottom on the next row." She looked upward. She'd need help to find anything near the top.

Lucjemm followed her gaze upward. "If you sit on my shoulders, Your Highness, you should be able to reach the top." He blushed in the golden light.

"You needn't be so formal in private! I whacked you on the bottom with the flat of my blade yesterday. Call me Linda."

"Yes, but, very well." He knelt down beside her, bracing his hands on the edge of the shelf.

She took a deep breath and swung one leg over his shoulder. Definitely not a place or time to wear skirts. Then bracing herself with her hands on the shelf she'd just examined, she swung the other leg over. When firmly settled, he heaved himself upward with a groan and a tilt.

She squealed in alarm. He righted himself and steadied her by clutching her ankles.

They both giggled in relief.

"What do you see, Your . . . High . . . er . . . Linda," he asked lightly.

"Well, I am higher than I was." She grinned at her pun.

Her fingernails tore as she unmasked more numerals. Filth encrusted her cuticles and embedded deep beneath the quick. She kept looking.

Lucjemm moved at her direction, occasionally tilting her just enough to make her grab his hair for balance. Then he yelped and righted himself. They both smiled at the game. She touched his hair gently, smoothing the strands she had displaced.

A flitter of dark movement brushed the edge of her vision.

She turned to find Indigo on the top shelf, casually inspecting her progress. He purred encouragement but offered no other help.

"Oh, here's the date." She reached up to grab a thick tome bound in red leather right beneath Indigo's extended paw.

"Found it," Glenndon said, brandishing a stack of loose pages as he peered at her over the top of the shelving unit from the other side. He reached over and extracted the red book for her. "Important too."

"How'd you get up there?" she asked in wonder.

"Climbed." His glance strayed to the possible trapdoor in the ceiling, and then downward where another might lay. They exchanged a look that promised another day they would explore those possibilities. With or without Lucjemm?

Indigo leaped to the ground on Glenndon's side of the shelves. He landed on top of the trapdoor with a hollow thud and began pawing at the boards, claws extended to scrape away accumulated dirt and reveal the outline and handle.

Glenndon disappeared down the other side of the shelves.

Linda heard his footsteps aim for the exit. Indigo followed him, not taking care to keep his paws silent on the wooden floor.

"I suppose this means I have to put you down," Lucjemm said. He sounded reluctant.

"I suppose so."

"Or I could carry you back . . ." They both closed their eyes at the thought of tumbling down that long spiral staircase.

"Put me down, please."

Slowly he crouched until his knees rested on the floor. Linda swung her legs free. Before she could steady her balance, he rose and grabbed her waist.

They stood face-to-face, close enough to share a breath. Her mouth opened to say something, anything to break the wonderful, mesmerizing moment.

He dropped his lips to hers. Gentle. Tentative.

She savored the sensation. Warmth and excitement climbed upward from her belly until she had to close her eyes to keep dizziness at bay.

Then the light around them faded and they heard the door grind on its pivot. "Leaving now," Glenndon said around a chuckle. "Come now, or never!" His footsteps retreated rapidly down the stairs.

Laughing, Lucjemm grabbed her hand, and they dashed to keep the door from closing, together.

CHAPTER 29

KING DARVILLE TOYED with aligning the parchment sheets on the black glass in front of him. He pointedly ignored the cup of beta arrack beside him. He'd fortified himself with strong liquor before coming to this meeting.

Sunlight caught and danced prisms from the magnificent stained glass window above the ceremonial table. The Coraurlia in the center of the table reflected the colors around the circular room. The crown, the table, and the window were the most precious objects in all of Kardia Hodos; the glass could only be forged by dragon fire. No other flame blazed hot enough to burn out the impurities in the sand. Every man-made attempt at making glass resulted in cloudy shards so brittle it proved useless.

Of late the dragons gave their assistance reluctantly. And then only in the presence of a trusted magician.

The men seated around the table made a point of resisting the presence of any magician in Coronnan. If any of them knew that Darville's son and heir possessed a magnificent magical talent, they ignored it. They found the stability of a confirmed male heir preferable to confronting and examining their fears.

If they knew the truth about what Glenndon had found in the archives, they'd . . . he didn't know how they'd react. Not well, to say the least. The children had found more than he'd expected, exactly what he needed. Did he dare use it?

He *had* to in order to bring disparate loyalties together.

"My lords," he opened the meeting of the Council of Provinces. "I have sent Prince Glenndon and Master Lucjemm into the archives." He nodded to the two young men who sat back from the table on stools. They faced each other over a portable table with inkwells, spare quills, and other instruments necessary to a scribe.

No need to tell the lords that the Princess Royale had accompanied them. They wouldn't understand that she was more important to him than just a daughter. He expected she watched and listened from her spyhole behind him—with or without her ladies.

"What were they searching for?" Lord Jemmarc asked casually. He leaned back, hands relaxed on the padded arms of his chair. His family crest, worked in fine needlepoint, looked brighter and newer against the time-darkened wood of his chair. He'd inherited his title and honors from Lord Krej less than twenty years before. Rather than perpetuate Krej's disgrace, Jemmarc had chosen a new crest, depicting mountains and waves rather than mountains and an impregnable castle.

Jemmarc seemed more relaxed than Darville had seen him since he'd dismissed his wife. Perhaps his sister's step-daughter had come to court to succeed Lady Lucinda. What was the girl's name? Darville was surprised Lord Jemmarc had not yet approached his king for permission to marry her.

"I sent our scribes in search of the Council proceedings from the time of the Leaving. I wanted to know for certain what had actually transpired in these chambers on the day the magicians took themselves into exile." Darville tapped the stack of loose pages before him.

"And what did you find?" Andrall asked, leaning forward. He kept his face bland, but the thrust of his neck and twitch at the corner of his right eye revealed his eagerness.

"These seven pages were each penned by a different magician, each assigned to a different lord as adviser and observer. They all record the same thing but break off at various points in the proceedings as arguments raged and indignation rose." He looked around the table, catching the gaze of each man in turn. When he had the attention of one and all he turned back to the pages. "'. . . at which point Lord Jaylor, newly appointed Senior Magician and Chancellor of the University, rose to his feet and beckoned to his comrades saying 'Gentlemen, since we are no longer trusted here, we, like the dragons, will take ourselves elsewhere until we are invited back with assurances that our counsel is needed and wanted.'"

"What else?" Lord Laislac pressed. "I remember that day. I remember the arguments. Without the controls of dragon magic imposing honor and ethics upon magicians, any one of them could go rogue . . ."

"As my cousin Krej did with his undisclosed talent," Darville reminded them. A cold knot settled in his belly. He'd been more a victim of Krej's lust for power than any of these men knew. The months he'd spent in a wolf's body still taunted him with nightmares he couldn't escape, and the desire to return to the carefree and wild existence. "My cousin, whom you all elected regent during my father's last illness, while I lay ill with magical backlash after Krej ensorcelled me into the body of a golden wolf . . ."

"None of us wants to go through that again," Andrall sighed.

Darville nodded agreement, crisp and short. "The report ends there. We have no record of further proceedings, as we relied upon those twelve magicians to keep track of what we decided."

"And now we have your son and mine to do that for us," Jemmarc said. He puffed his chest out with pride, still relaxed, a half smile of satisfaction on his face.

"Yes, we do," Darville agreed. "I trust them to keep accurate records. But, I know from experience that observations differ. Each man brings his own perspective to the issues." He looked down at the pages before him, amazed at how much the wording differed from author to author. Yet they recorded much the same when it came to each firm decision or new law. The discussion, or arguments, leading up to a decision varied widely. Just the shift of a single word or punctuation placement could change the entire meaning of the statements.

"They can check each other . . ." Jemmarc dismissed the statement with a small wave of his hand.

"I suggest a third person, someone not present who will read both and reconcile any differences." Darville tilted his head a bit toward the spyhole behind him. He wondered if Linda listened alone or with her ladies.

"Who?" Andrall asked. He too leaned back, already half in agreement.

"My daughter Princess Royale Rosselinda."

"What?" Andrall dropped forward, hands clenching the edge of the black table. The glass surface clouded from the heat of his hands, looking like grotesque distortions of his long, slender fingers.

"If the Council thinks it necessary, we can also add your grandson Mikkette to the scribes," Darville threw out, almost as casual as Jemmarc.

"What!" eleven lords shouted in unison.

"May I remind you, Your Grace, that Mikkette's father is mentally deficient and his mother insane, unstable, and a sorceress of great talent? She was once a secret member of the Coven from Hanassa and SeLennica," Laislac said coldly. His daughter.

"No need to remind me," Darville replied bitterly. "I was nearly a victim of the Coven's convoluted and secret plans to assassinate me and place Mikkette on the throne with his mother Ariiell, your daughter, his regent. But she would not have truly ruled. The Coven would have guided her every move."

He let the men absorb that bit of information. "If not for the intervention of Lord Jaylor and his magicians, I would be dead and Coronnan either ruled by cruel tyrants able to put down any opposition with magic, or our beloved land would be in ashes, with every other country in Kardia Hodos banded together to remove the Coven at any cost."

"The magicians did much for us," Lord Stennal from Ropeura, said. "I for one miss them."

"As do I," Darville admitted, surprised that someone else broached the subject he truly wanted to discuss.

He reached for the cup of liquor to the left of the pages in front of him. The others drank ale. He alone seemed to need the bracing effect of beta arrack, distilled from the giant red tubers from Mikka's homeland.

Before the cup reached his lips Glenndon's hand slapped it away. The cup clattered against the table. The liquid sizzled and bubbled against the black glass, etching it with deadly, acidic foam.

CHAPTER 30

GLENNDON GASPED FOR AIR, fighting the bone-deep burn on his hand and arm. It ran so deep in his veins he had trouble comprehending that his hand was still part of his body.

He tried to banish the fire, but his talent failed him. This was worse than the time he'd grabbed a pot boiling over onto the hearth without padded protection.

"Glenndon, are you all right? Did the acid splash you?" King Darville's words cut through the chaos in the Council Chamber and Glenndon's mind. Someone to cling to. Someone he could trust.

He watched, as if from a great distance, as some lords jumped about, shouting and brandishing their fists. Others, like Lucjemm and Jemmarc, pressed themselves against the wall. Lucjemm's eyes glazed over as if in a trance.

Sensible Andrall threw open the door and demanded guards and servants.

Fred leaped to Darville's side, dagger and sword already unsheathed. Two quick looks about and he determined that his king still stood and appeared unharmed, so he took up a defensive stance at the doorway to make certain no one entered who didn't belong in the Council Chamber.

On the other side of the paneling behind Darville's demi-throne, feminine screams and the rustling of elegant dresses retreated.

But the king, the potential victim of a painful death from poison, thought only of Glenndon. His son.

His heir, Glenndon reminded himself. *He cares only about stabilizing his kingdom with a male heir.*

The tension in Darville's fingers as he clutched at Glenndon's shoulders, and the anxious gaze he flicked over him, from the bright red patch on Glenndon's hand to his eyes and back to the acid burn on the back of his hand, told him there was more in the king's concern.

A glimmer of warmth and a sense of belonging overrode the pain of the burn, the fear from the attack, and . . . and . . .

"Are you in pain?" Darville demanded.

Some. Glenndon couldn't manage more. A lot more than *some.* He didn't know how to describe how the fire used his veins as a river to travel from one end of his body to the other.

He had to think, had to concentrate lest the fire take his mind. Forever.

General Marcelle and three senior officers barged into the room. They immediately shepherded out most of the shouting lords while the general examined the still-foaming acid etching into the glass. It crept toward the Coraurlia resting benignly in the center.

Glenndon pointed at the endangered crown.

Darville deftly grabbed it by one protrusion and lifted it clear of danger, while still keeping his other hand firmly on Glenndon's upper arm.

"What happened? How did you know the cup was poisoned?" Jemmarc demanded, now that the chaos subsided.

Color, Glenndon replied.

The lord and the general continued to look to him for an answer.

"What was wrong with the color?" Darville asked.

Glenndon looked to him with concern that the king now acknowledged mind speech between them. Darville seemed too distracted to care.

"Cup too red," Glenndon forced himself to say out loud. The effort took his mind away from the pain. For a moment. "Gold when servant brought it."

"Did you drink any of the liquor, Your Grace? How long did it sit beside you?" General Marcelle asked.

"Almost half an hour," Linda answered, squeezing through the back door. "I watched the servants set up the room before the lords arrived. And I did not see him touch the cup. He was preoccupied with the records."

"Long enough for the acid to slowly burn through the gold," Darville mused.

Glenndon pulled his arm away from the king's grip to suck on the burn. Linda stopped him, holding his wrist. "Acid," she said. "It will burn you from the inside out as well as the outside in."

Her grip seemed to contain the fiery pain to his hand, keep his weakening knees from folding. He sniffed the red splotch. At the same time he nodded to Linda, bending over the table to sniff the now diminishing acid.

"Records?" Glenndon asked. He turned hastily to see if any of the parchment pages were in the path of the acid. Somehow he knew the records were more important than just written words. Darville had not reported everything he had read in them.

When Glenndon and Lucjemm had pulled them out of the archives, a sneezing Lucjemm had been more interested in dragging them both out of the room (while holding Linda's hand quite possessively) to get away from the dust than in reading what they'd found.

"Glenndon, can you tell anything about the cup, who brought it, who may have touched it, the nature of the poison?" Darville asked. He placed his hand on Glenndon's shoulder again. His concern and anxiety leaked through his need for touch.

Glenndon reverted to his usual shrug. Fighting the blackness that crept around the edges of his vision, he bent over the table and brought his inner sight forward.

Instantly a black aura appeared around the edge of the golden cup. Not true gold, he decided as bits of gilt flaked away from a base metal inside the bowl. He pointed to the deterioration and looked to the king with his questions.

"It should be all gold," Darville confirmed. "Very expensive and reserved for the family. Gold should be less vulnerable to the acid . . ."

Glenndon caught a memory from his father: a tin weasel with flaking gilt paint, the form Lord Krej had reverted to when his rogue spell backlashed from the Coraurlia.

"No accident then," General Marcelle said.

"You expected acid dropped into *my* drink to be an accident?" Darville scoffed.

"Miner's acid," Glenndon ground out through clenched teeth. He didn't know how much longer he could hold out against the pain.

Both Linda and her father gasped at that.

"Fast acting on tin." Jemmarc paused to gulp. "But much slower on gold. This took planning to substitute the cup for a real one ahead of time. The cups are easily had on Market Isle, cheap replicas of the royal dinnerware. I suspect someone distracted the servants bringing a tray of cups here." He pointed to the silver cups placed in front of each chair. "And substituted the already-prepared poison cup for the real one."

"Whoever did this expected me to drink soon after I entered the room with the Coraurlia—it only protects me from magical attack—and not wait until I'd presented the primary business of the day," Darville added.

Glenndon began humming in the back of his throat, an agitated and angry tune. He needed to speak his warning and knew he couldn't utter anything so complicated without the assistance of music. The music also helped keep him conscious.

"I smell fear," he sang to the tune of a funeral hymn he'd heard in the village, clearer than he could have spoken. "Fear doubled by doubt. Trebled by a wish to please. Fear directed by another's anger."

"A director and the directed," General Marcelle surmised. He seemed to have the clearest head.

"A woman's fear. Her hand moving at the behest of another."

"Despicable, to use a frail woman such," Jemmarc spat. "Lucjemm." He looked around for his son, only to find the young man had joined the exodus elsewhere. "S'murghit, where is the boy? I need him to seek out the servants and question them."

"We'll see to it," Marcelle growled. He gestured to one of his officers to follow through. Another officer lifted the dissolving cup with the point of his dagger and exited with it.

"Now, young man," Marcelle rounded on Glenndon, "what else do you 'smell' in this room?"

Glenndon backed up, seeking a retreat.

"You needn't fear me, boy. Unlike some I could name," he glared out the door toward the jumbled mass of lordly tunics huddled together. "But I could use *all* of your talents in this."

"Later," King Darville intervened. "He's too pale. His eyes are glazing over. Linda, take your brother to your mother. Have her, and her alone, treat that burn," the king barked.

Glenndon shook his head. "No bother."

"Yes, bother. I need you well and alert. At the moment I don't trust anyone but my immediate family. The queen knows healing herbs and who she trusts to pick them." He glared at Glenndon, saying more with his eyes than his words.

But Glenndon could interpret the true meaning. He needed to discover who would do such a despicable thing. And why. And then Glenndon needed to put a stop to that person's actions.

To save his father.

My plan worked. Exactly as I imagined it. But Glenndon is smarter than I believed. He hides his magic well, cloaks his talent in logic and silence. He knows more than he lets others know.

I can work with that. I can give him false information and let him draw incorrect conclusions. He trusts me.

And while he leads his father and General Marcelle astray, I will be free to direct my minions to lay my traps. Before the summer has passed, Coronnan will be looking for a new king. One who has never been tainted by magic. Someone they trust.

Me.

My lovely calls to me. She watched the day's proceedings through my eyes. She tells me in my sleep what I must do. Now I do it with glee, and determination to succeed.

CHAPTER 31

L INDA SHOVED her shoulder beneath Glenndon's arm and took his weight. She sagged a bit, finding him heavier and more dependent upon her than she expected.

Lucjemm had reappeared and he jumped to Glenndon's other side, draping the uninjured arm over his shoulders and an arm around his friend's waist. Together they helped each other half-carry a stumbling and wavering Glenndon out of the Council Chamber.

The distance to M'ma's suite was thankfully short. Linda ran up and down the stairs a dozen times a day without a second thought. Now it seemed to take an hour or more to step up one riser, haul Glenndon level with them, then repeat the process. By the time they reached the top of the long formal staircase all three of them were gasping for breath and dripping sweat. Linda found her free arm bracing against Glenndon's waist, just above where Lucjemm held him. His hand brushed Linda's several times, unapologetically. Each time he smiled at her around Glenndon's back, a bit hesitant and timid, but clearly taking advantage of their proximity to remind her of that first kiss in the archives. His eyes sparkled clearly with each reminder.

She blushed in memory. His name had been one of those put forth as a possible husband for her. The idea wasn't to-tally repulsive. He certainly didn't think so, judging by his grin in response to her reddened cheeks.

That only made her flush deeper.

Then at last they approached M'ma's suite. Lady Anya threw open the door before they could knock. The handle slammed against the wall and bounced. The lady had to push it back to keep it from slamming into the beleaguered trio.

"There is more to that wound than just miner's acid," M'ma said from across the room. She reclined on her lounge, reading official-looking dispatches, as she did every afternoon while Linda and her sisters were sent off to lessons with specialized tutors.

Linda nodded and helped her brother slump onto a stool in front of the queen. Then Linda peered over her mother's shoulder as the queen and Lady Anya applied poultice after poultice to the irregular red mark on Glenndon's right hand.

Glenndon looked pale and a bit shaky, but seemed to distance himself from the pain.

"I can smell the addition, but can't quite define it," M'ma said quietly. Too quietly. Like no one but Linda should hear.

Who did she hide the truth from? They were all family and trusted retainers here in M'ma's private sitting room.

Then Linda's eyes lighted upon Lucjemm, where he stood aside from the feminine task of mixing and applying healing herbs.

"Magic," Glenndon croaked. The effort of speaking cost him another shade or two of color in his face. His skin now rivaled the lace on Linda's petticoat.

"But why? Why would a magician wish to assassinate the king? He's pushing the Council to restore them to court!" Lucjemm protested, moving three paces closer, still out of the way of Lady Anya as she scurried back and forth to the stillroom for different combinations of healing potions.

Images and ideas flashed from Glenndon's mind to Linda's. At least he could still think clearly while he fought the pain. He just didn't have enough energy left over to fight his throat for speech.

"Someone wishes to discredit the magicians and have them banned from Coronnan for all time," Linda reported. "They meant for the poison to be discovered before P'pa drank it. The Coraurlia would have negated the magic . . . but left him vulnerable to the acid . . ."

Glenndon flashed her one of his rare smiles (though he

smiled more now than when he first arrived). He was willing to allow her the credit for the idea.

M'ma nodded in agreement. "If there was magic in the cup that mixed with the acid, the Coraurlia would have negated it, glowing in the process to show it worked."

"If he'd been wearing it!" Linda gasped. "Everyone on the Council knows how he hates wearing it. It's heavy and gives him a headache."

No more of a headache than dealing with the Council, Glenndon reminded her.

"Anyone who has been at the Council with P'pa more than twice knows he'd more likely to leave the Coraurlia on the table and wear only the demi-crown," she completed her thought. "He'd be dead from both the acid and the magic. If Glenndon hadn't sensed it first." Her knees weakened, and she had to sit on the edge of the lounge next to her mother. Until that moment she hadn't realized how close she'd come to losing P'pa. How close they'd all come to losing their king.

"I'll need more help than just herbs to put this to rights," M'ma said, inspecting the wound, which seemed bigger, redder, angrier than just a few moments ago. Blisters had formed in the center of the red. Little white circles that grew as they watched.

Just then Indigo sauntered in, walking a mazelike path toward Glenndon, making sure he rubbed his face against every piece of furniture and leg he passed.

Lucjemm jumped out of the way at the cat's slightest touch. His eyes took on a strange cast as he hugged the wall by the door. Lady Anya bent and scratched Indigo's ears. He purred loudly in response. But he didn't linger. He aimed for Glenndon.

"Who is this?" M'ma asked, her voice full of caution. She held herself rigid, leaning away from the cat.

"Indigo. He's special," Linda replied.

"Aside from being big, what makes him so special?" M'ma continued, not touching the cat. She never allowed a cat into her suite and barely tolerated any in the palace. She allowed a few in the storerooms to keep the rodent population in check, but never, ever above stairs. *Ever.*

A bit of a wing poked out from beneath the extra flap of skin.

Linda noted that the wing was on the side away from Lucjemm's line of sight.

M'ma hid her quick intake of breath with a flurry of hand movements over the cat.

"Master Lucjemm, will you inform His Grace that we will be some time in figuring out what to do?" Lady Anya asked sweetly.

"May I inform his Grace and the Council of your surmise about the wound?"

"Yes," M'ma replied. "Tell them everything, including our suspicions about the reason for the attack."

Lucjemm bowed and backed out of the room. His gaze lingered on Linda a moment longer than accepted protocol.

When he'd closed the door firmly behind him and his footsteps retreated some distance, Linda remembered to breathe again.

"Now that we have privacy, we can do something about the wound," M'ma said, shifting her position so that she could hold Glenndon's arm with one hand and keep the other on the flywacket's head.

Indigo had indeed become a flywacket now, a creature of magic, mystery, and legend, with black feathered wings fully extended and raised, as if ready to catch the next breeze and launch into the skies.

Or the ceiling.

"Linda." M'ma gestured for her to kneel beside Glenndon. "You are closer to him in blood than I. Therefore you must take the lead in this, use your strength for I have not enough. You must do everything I say, precisely when I say it, without question or hesitation. I cannot do this without making myself ill again, but I know how to do it. Can you follow me without thinking?"

Linda nodded, swallowing any trace of uncertainty.

"We have not much time. Within minutes a crowd of people will burst through that door and demand explanations. Anya, stand in the hallway and stall them. Latch the door on your way out." M'ma paused to close her eyes and breathe deeply.

Linda noted that Glenndon did the same. She took a deep breath and forced the air downward until calm blossomed outward from her middle. Another breath and her limbs went lax. A third and her ears and eyes seemed to open fully for the first time.

She heard her own heartbeat, distinguished it from her mother's and her brother's. Without thinking she urged her own pulse to match Glenndon's. A moment later her mother's came into synchronization.

Linda, you need to place your left hand on Indigo and your right upon Glenndon's arm, M'ma said directly into her mind.

As she spoke, M'ma placed both her hands on Indigo's extended wing.

Linda looked to her brother. He nodded. She complied. Left hand on the flywacket's other wing, dominant right on Glenndon. Was there a reason for that? M'ma had been most specific.

A bubble of pale blue light shading into lavender and darkening around the outer edges seemed to engulf them in a protective barrier from the outside world. As details in the room dimmed, those within the bubble brightened, took on sharper definition. She saw every stitch in every seam of Glenndon's tunic and trews. The fine embroidery and lace on her mother's gown became equally distinct, as did the pores in their skin, and the way each hair lay upon their heads.

Indigo purred louder, the rhythm taking on the same cadence as a heartbeat, their joined heartbeats. The bubble of purply-blue light emanated from him.

Linda admired the silky texture of the feathers, seeing how each tiny fluff joined another and another along the spine. Really just extremely fine fur patterned in branching arrays along a thicker spine of cartilage instead of individual hairs attached to the skin.

"Now that you have made the connection to Glenndon, place your right hand above his wound. Do not touch the red, but let your spread fingertips rest on his skin around the burn."

Sharp tingles rose up her arm when she touched his bare skin. She looked closer, seeing their common blood flowing back and forth from her body to his.

Concentrate on the burn. See the edges, feel the depth of it in the skin. Now in your mind confine the burn into one solid mass. It resisted, shooting out tendrils.

She firmed her image of control, enveloping the mass, much as the bubble of light isolated the four of them. Linda felt the damaged tissue gather itself tighter, its urge to spread fading.

Now lift the mass free of your brother's hand.

Linda yanked at the blob, expecting resistance. A great tearing sound filled her mind where her mother's gentle voice had been.

Glenndon screamed. Physically and psychically. The sharp burning stab in his hand repeated itself through her blood bond with him. Fire raced from her fingertips to her shoulder and over the top of her head into her eyes. A blackness full of steel knives jabbed in and out of her mind.

She hadn't the strength to utter more than a whimpering moan.

Gently, Little Lindy. Gently. Think of snow. Think of winter chill invading every crevice in the stone wall of the inner keep. Think of the icy wind ripping across the hills as you ride Belle.

Linda obeyed her mother, as she'd promised.

The sharpness of Glenndon's pain receded inside her to a numbing ache.

There is a root in that burn. Imagine the deep, probing taproot of the great oak at Last Bridge that toppled last winter in the windstorm. See it in your mind. Now transfer that image to the burn. See the root escaping your envelope of magic. Do you see it?

"Yes," Linda murmured. And she could. A nasty black thing that had broken through the wall she'd encircled the burn with.

Pull it back.

Pain, sharp and intense flared up to her eyes and down into her legs.

Breathe with it. Synchronize your breath and heartbeat to the pulse of the root. Glenndon's mental voice came through, weak but firm. Each syllable found the rhythm of the pain. Like a good swordsman, he'd found the magic's weak point, flowed with it, understood it, and . . . and mastered it with a neat undercut and long lunge.

The root withdrew.

Linda pulled some more, found a misshapen lump further up and pulled that too. She didn't know what it was, only that it didn't belong inside her brother. Then she slapped a mental patch on the magical envelope containing the burn and its root. Her pain eased. Glenndon breathed easier. His facial muscles relaxed.

Breathe deeply, Linda, M'ma coaxed. *In, two, three, hold two, three, out two, three.*

Linda obeyed, finding her lungs eager to work again.

Again. Breathe on my count. Find your center. Breathe again, anchor yourself to the Kardia. Breathe.

Glenndon matched the count. His chest moved in and out in time with hers. Their hearts beat as one. His mind opened to her. Hers to him.

In a flash she shared all his memories, his fears, his loneliness, all his knowledge, the books he'd read, the trails he'd explored, his bond of love with his family, his friendship with Indigo. And for this brief time out of time she shared his talent.

Linda knew what to do. Gently, slowly, she inserted her mind around the encapsulated burn. It fought her. She eased back and came at it from a new angle, wiggling here, pushing there, like a worm finding its way through rocky soil.

She felt Glenndon's mental shout of triumph when she finally got underneath the thing. Together they eased it upward, sliding it free of his body.

Don't touch it! M'ma warned as the blob burst free of Glenndon's skin.

Glenndon sent her a new thought. She lifted her hand from his, still keeping her fingers cupped.

The blob followed her until it hovered several finger widths above the back of Glenndon's hand.

Quickly he snatched his hand away, cradling it beneath his opposite arm, pressing on the bleeding wound.

The blob started to drop. Linda's skirts lay in its path. She knew it would burn through the thick fabric and petticoat to her thigh. She tried to jerk free.

Indigo's long black tongue darted out and in, like a giant lizard snapping at a fly. He chomped on the magical blob and licked his lips.

"Indigo!" Linda squealed in concern.

"He's a dragon at his core, Linda. A creature of magic. It won't hurt him like it would us mere humans," M'ma said. Her face paled. Deep lines drew her mouth down. She sagged wearily.

"Cut the circle," Glenndon ordered. "You have to cut the circle so we can get her help. We've exhausted her beyond her physical strength, even though you did most of the work, Linda." The most he'd spoken in his entire life.

"Circle?" Linda asked. Her bond with her brother remained, though it faded in intensity. "Oh, the bubble of light."

He rolled his eyes at her as if she were the stupidest and rawest of apprentices. Well, she was. She'd never even seen magic worked. Never in her wildest imagination had she dreamed of performing such an intense spell.

"Does this make me a magician?"

(Anyone can gather magic from a purple dragon,) Indigo reminded her. *(But there is more to you than you know. You could have done this alone, needing only your mother's guidance. I just made it easier.)*

"Cut the circle, Linda," Glenndon demanded.

With no knife or scissors available, she stretched out her hand and stabbed the light with her fingernail. The magic shredded and dissolved as she slashed her hand downward.

Only then did she hear pounding on the door and shouts from the landing outside. "The witchsniffers have found sorcery. Black sorcery!"

Her hand hurt as Glenndon pushed aside the latch. Blood dripped to the floor from both of them.

CHAPTER 32

"MIKKA! ARE YOU ALL RIGHT?" Darville demanded as he shouldered his way through the opening door. Silent and observant, Fred followed no more than half a step behind, where he always was in time of trouble. Dimly, Darville noted that Linda and Glenndon were on their feet, but not looking well. "Lucjemm said there was magic in the wound."

His rapidly beating heart and sweating skin told him he'd had too much drink. But he needed another. Now. Without it he couldn't think clearly, calmly.

His head pounded with a sharp ache from temples to nape and back again.

Mikka lay back on her couch, calmly reading yesterday's dispatches, as if nothing untoward occurred.

"Certain herbs and poultices will counter simple magics," Old Maisy said, bustling toward them from the back room— the bedroom where another hidden entrance led to the tunnel system. Darville and Mikka had happily explored them when newly married.

Maisy carried a pile of gauze and linen. The tip of a cat's bushy black tail disappeared around the corner of the doorway as the seamstress swished her skirts.

A cat in Mikka's rooms? Strange occurrences indeed. Mikka hadn't allowed cats anywhere near her since Ambassador Jack had found a way to separate her from the cat spirit that had shared her body for years.

"And simple magic it was, hurried and unpracticed,"

Maisy whispered so that only Darville and Mikka heard. "Now, Your Highness, I need to bandage that wound, so sit yourself down on that stool and I'll be about finishing up."

Both Linda and Glenndon stared at their hands: his left, her right.

"Those look more like knife gashes than magical burns," Lord Jemmarc said, pushing his way into the room behind Darville.

"And what would you know about magical burns, my lord?" Only old Maisy could get away with such bold talk among the nobles.

Darville smothered a laugh behind a cough into his crooked arm. Laughing made his headache worse. He needed a drink to banish it.

Mikka shared an amused gaze and a half smile with him. They'd known the not-so-ancient and not-so-decrepit seamstress a long time.

"Well . . . well, only what I've read," Jemmarc blustered. "But burns don't bleed."

"And sometimes one has to lance or even cut out alien infections," Mikka said. She laid the pages on the couch between her and the back, out of sight of any who might steal a look. "Now what is so important that you felt you must break down my door and invade the queen's privacy?" She gave the men crowding behind the king a malevolent gaze.

"The witchsniffers . . ." Lucjemm began.

"I thought I sent them home," Darville snarled.

"The wound had magic in it all right," Maisy said. She shoved Glenndon upright from his exhausted slump on his stool and began fussing with bandages. Linda she ordered to remain in place beside her brother with only a tilt of her head.

Both children obeyed, instantly and without protest.

"Unreliable, them witchsniffers. Can only smell magic present, not how good, bad, or indifferent, cain't even tell who's a throwing the spell, or if it grew out of somethin' else."

Darville whirled to face the middle-aged couple with glazed eyes and right arms swinging in uncontrolled, wide circles. "Return to your homes. Today. This hour," he ordered them, his need for a drink making him angrier than he should be. "You have done your duty. I now discharge you. You are never to return to the city. Ever!"

They blinked rapidly, coming out of their trance. "Yes, Your Grace," the man said on a bow. His wife curtsied. Both held out their hands, palm up.

Lady Anya appeared out of nowhere and placed a small silver coin in each palm. Fists closed greedily about the payment. The lady kept her head high and chin bold, deliberately avoiding eye contact with her king. He had no way of knowing if she'd taken it upon herself to reward the couple or if Mikka had discussed it with her first.

Darville decided the action was wise. They obviously had been promised money upon completion of their job and wouldn't leave until they had it. But who had hired them?

His gaze rested on Jemmarc.

"Who are you trying so hard to protect by dismissing the witchsniffers, Your Grace?" Lord Jemmarc asked, matching the king stare for stare.

"Who are you trying so hard to accuse, without legal grounds?" Darville replied. "Last I heard, witchsniffers were dismissed as unreliable . . ."

"By an old servant with questionable talents beyond her skill with a needle and thread," Laislac added.

"Dismissed as unreliable by Nimbulan the greatest magician of all time, and the first to make covenant with dragons for their magic. King Quinnault agreed and made it law. Three hundred years ago," Darville informed them. For a half a moment his head cleared of pain.

"But . . ."

"Read the law for yourself," Darville spat. "Or find a priest to read it if you can't. Witchsniffers rely upon ley line or rogue magic to fuel their powers. Only dragon magic is legal in Coronnan. Reliable magic gathered by many magicians who can add their powers, one to the other. Rogue magicians cannot gather magic and add their talents one to the other. Therefore, our magicians, with the consent and blessing of the dragons, can impose ethics, honor, discipline, and the law upon any rogue who takes their power beyond acceptable limits to manipulate any other being."

He speared with his gaze each of the lords and servants who had followed him from the Council Chamber. "You are dismissed. I have no further business with you today. Possibly not for the rest of the week. Or the year!" If he got rid of everyone maybe he could take the time to drink his headache into oblivion.

Fred emphasized his words by placing a hand on each of his weapons, dagger and sword. He glared at each man in turn, making sure they knew that he was ready to follow his king's orders with his weapons. He needed only the slightest provocation.

"Your Grace, you cannot dismiss the Council of Provinces. You are the first among equals, not a dictator!" Andrall protested.

"Try me," Darville roared. "You have invaded my wife's private apartments when she is ill. You accuse me and my family of performing illegal magic when one or all of you employs illegal witchsniffers as your tools of accusation. I should have arrested them. Be grateful I do not arrest all of you. I am done with you. All of you."

Mikka shot him a quelling glance. Not good for a king to lose his temper. He pushed aside her silent advice. Sometimes a man, and a husband and father, had to lose his temper to make sure the rest of world knew how serious he was.

"I dismiss the Council and the court until further notice."

Caught you! The king fell directly into my trap. Now I will control the Council through the ones I have already manipulated. We have an army to enforce our rulings. We shall meet in secret while we gather more armed men. Within days, a week at the most, they will depose Darville, marry me to his daughter, and proclaim me king. Then I will make sure that no magic of any kind ever enters Coronnan again. I shall lead the dragon hunt myself, guided by my lovely, my true consort.

CHAPTER 33

"BREVELAN!" JAYLOR SHOUTED from across the clearing into the cabin. He watched her shift in her rocking chair, the one he'd made for her when they were first married and she carried Glenndon inside her.

"Yes, my love?" She looked over her shoulder, stilling the to and fro of her chair.

"I need the girls." He shouldered his way into the tiny room that used to be the entire cabin, but now served only as kitchen and workroom. He dropped a kiss on top of her head and gave her chair a gentle push.

"Supper will be late without their help," she replied, looking up to claim another kiss with her lips to his.

Valeria and Lillian rolled their eyes at each other again.

"Time to teach Sharl the fine art of rolling pie crust. I need Valeria and Lillian to observe and witness," Jaylor said, letting his hands linger on Brevelan's face.

"What about Lukan? Isn't it time he took over some of Glenndon's responsibilities?" Brevelan asked, stilling her chair once more.

"I trust the girls to report accurately and not embellish their account with supposition and drama. Lukan will be there as well. But he can't say much of anything without turning it into a grand saga. Sometimes I think he stole all of Glenndon's words." He retreated, shaking his head and beckoning the girls to follow.

Lillian looked reluctantly at the perfect pie crust she'd begun to roll flat. "I suppose we'd best go with you, Da."

Valeria pushed aside the mangled mess of her own attempt. "Maybe Sharl can salvage something out of . . . out of this." She slammed the hard lump of flour and oil back into the mixing bowl. "I'd rather watch master magicians at work than cook any day."

Jaylor led them uphill toward the University, careful to match his long, anxious steps to their shorter ones. Valeria clung to his hand, keeping Lillian close to her side as well. But before they'd gone half the distance her breaths came short, sharp, and shallow.

Jaylor picked her up, cradling her against his shoulder as he would a much smaller child, without breaking stride. "We have got to do something about your lungs, Val," he whispered. "I promise that when this business is done, we will consult with the dragons."

"Shayla will want me to stay with the dragons."

The image of a huge nest lined with soft fur, protecting her from the wind, flashed past from memory, to his mind, gone almost before he grabbed hold of it.

A dream?

(A dragon-dream. Remember the import of dragon-dreams, more real than real. A prediction and a warning,) Baamin whispered into the back of his mind.

"Your Mama had a dragon-dream," he said to both girls, not sure why the vivid vision given to the love of his life was important now. "Shayla showed her living quite happily in the clearing with me and six children when she was unsure if it was safe to love me."

"But now she carries a seventh child," Lillian replied softly.

"Outside the dream. Outside time and reality," Valeria picked up the thought in a chanting cadence.

"Is it safe?" Lillian finished.

"Maybe 'tis time for you to spend some time with the dragons and figure it out."

"Not without Lillian," Valeria insisted.

"Shayla has had twins in previous litters. I'm sure she'll understand why you must stay together."

Valeria drowsed, a heavy but comfortable weight in his arms. "You're safe, Val. I'll keep you safe as long as I can."

"Here is your usual hiding place." Jaylor eased Valeria to her feet, beside the everblue tree with its lower branches almost level with the ground, hiding a sunken recess next to the trunk.

"Now scuttle deep and hide yourself well. I need you to watch the other masters. All of them, even the ones you think you can trust. Lukan is across the way." He hoped. The boy had become sullen since Glenndon left and Jaylor didn't know why. "Your brother will watch too."

"What are we watching for?" Valeria asked, sliding to her knees and catching her balance on her father's knee before crawling beneath the tree.

"I need to know who is shocked when I speak, who sidles away, who leans forward a bit."

"Who is loyal to you and who is eager for power beyond their ability to use it?" Lillian asked.

"Exactly. Now keep quiet and don't let Lukan distract you. Hide your auras as well as your thoughts and your bodies."

They both nodded and sought familiar depressions in the Kardia they had scooped out during countless eavesdropping sessions. Instinct born of a lifetime together, never more than a thought apart, they joined hands and minds. Then they watched.

Half an hour later, Jaylor led the masters into the circle in the University courtyard. All the masters, not just the twelve most senior. They too joined hands, and the dome of power shot upward. A weak dome without the essence of Tambootie grounding it. Some of the masters had eaten of the tree, but the magic within the leaves had grown less potent over the years. It did little to actually increase magic within a magician's body. Thinking it did helped their minds overcome some physical limitations. But not enough.

Jaylor knew how to work around those who'd become dependent upon the drug.

Do you see that? Lillian asked. Her mind pointed toward the circle.

There are gaps! Valeria added.

Wondering how the girls spoke to him so clearly from outside the dome of power, Jaylor followed tendrils of blue lightning around and around the dome, seeking the source of the incomplete joining. The bolts of power tried to jump across open spaces, completing the protective bubble. They spluttered into shards of empty blue dust, dropping to the ground within the circle.

That's how the girls got into his mind. He kept the connection open as he watched the magic try to complete its purpose.

Two factions, Valeria warned him. *Two colors vying for dominance.*

Ah, Samlan's yellow and orange reached out and around Jaylor's blue and red. Three masters on each side of Samlan added to his control of half the circle.

They'd eaten Tambootie leaves. Jaylor knew that without magic. He could smell the aromatic spice in the air. He'd ordered the men to forgo the drug tonight. He needed a clear head for the entire spell, without the backlash headache hitting him twenty minutes into the proceedings.

He and those loyal to him didn't need the Tambootie because they trusted each other. Twelve men and women, six on each side of Jaylor, added firmer centering to the dome. Of the other eight masters, all men, their support wavered back and forth, never attaching to either side for long.

Samlan's magic and aura seemed to writhe and swirl in random patterns. *He's uncertain of the loyalty of his side,* Jaylor thought. *He trusts the Tambootie but not himself or his followers. That's his flaw.*

Can we push the wandering ones over toward you, Da? Lillian asked him.

No, we mustn't interfere even if we could influence them. I told you to watch, and watch you will, Jaylor told them firmly.

"I understand that some of you question my decision to send Glenndon to the king's court," Jaylor said. He projected his words around the circle, made them more powerful and commanding with magic.

"You've been spying on us!" Samlan protested, pounding

his staff for emphasis, nearly breaking the circle in his agitation.

"Should I have been?" Jaylor returned. His shoulders relaxed a bit and his focus narrowed to the opposition leader. Instigator.

"Who dares speak against a master?" Dennilley asked, his question neutral, deflecting anger away from the circle.

"My source of information is mine, not yours," Jaylor said. "The problem remains that a master magician questions the decision of the Senior Magician and Chancellor of this University of Magicians. Questions and subverts without bringing the questions to me."

"You sent a damaged apprentice to the king. A master should have been sent as counselor," Samlan insisted, standing firm and determined, ready to acknowledge his discontent.

"Who said the king asked for a counselor?" Jaylor quirked an eyebrow.

When he did that, he was in control. The meeting proceeded as he planned.

"Then a journeyman, tried and true . . ." Samlan retorted. "Not an apprentice who cannot speak. Even if he is your son."

Jaylor gulped. He felt Valeria reach out in comfort to him. He pushed aside her empathy. She had to observe.

We have to do something, Lillian wailed. *He's letting his grief speak for him.*

Stargods, he hated losing Glenndon to the king. Hated that the child he'd raised truly had been sired by another man, his best friend.

Jaylor drew a deep, restoring breath, banishing all his emotions.

He lifted his head, no longer bowed down by his heavy emotional burden. "I have my reasons for sending Glenndon. The king has his reasons for specifically requesting the boy by name. You need know nothing more," he said, firmly. Some of the undecided masters joined their power to his side of the circle, giving it a deeper blue and more vibrant red hue.

"That isn't good enough, Jaylor," Samlan spat. "*We* have decided 'tis time for magic to return to court."

"We? Who is we, Samlan?" Obviously Samlan had reverted to his old ways of not paying attention to much outside of the University except his own desires. Surely he should have heard by now how Darville paraded Glenndon about the city as his acknowledged son and heir.

"Those of us who know that you are too young, too involved in your family, to continue as Senior Magician."

"My family?" His words came out cold, emotionless. His head began to ache and his face flushed as he fought his temper.

A subtle shift in the colors back and forth. The sparking tendrils trying to jump the gaps flew furiously.

"True magicians forsake the joy of family for the duty to serve the land and the king," Samlan parroted sanctimoniously.

"My family?" Jaylor said a little louder, a little angrier. "What of your family, Dennilley? And yours, Robb? Marcus, is Vareena expecting your third or fourth child?"

Samlan snorted. "They are far too young to remember the days of proper magic before the Leaving."

"I remember the *myth* that a magician loses his powers if he takes a wife. Or mistress," Robb said quietly. "That is how Krej wormed his way into political power using magic. He left the University just before his promotion to journeyman. He married and begat numerous children. Everyone *presumed* he had no magic. Their ignorance nearly destroyed Coronnan when he murdered and manipulated people, as well as dragons."

"I remember the myth," Marcus added. He and Jaylor exchanged a knowing glance. "I remember the days when women of magic were dismissed as myth and legend as well. My wife would take exception to that. Seems to me, Samlan, she brewed the potion that rid you of the lung infection that hung on for six months two winters ago."

"So would mine," Robb said proudly. They grinned at each other.

"Women," Samlan spat. "They corrupt true magic. They cannot gather power from dragons."

"Times have changed, Samlan," Da broke in. "Most of us have families. As to the charge that I am too young to be Senior Magician, I shouldn't have to remind you that I was handed the job, over my protests . . ."

"You did not protest very long or hard . . ."

"I accepted when Lord Baamin, my predecessor, passed on the job to me on his death bed. The circle confirmed me before his body was cold. You were not present at the time. You were still a journeyman, even though you are older than me."

The dome of power shifted again. Samlan's half took on the deeper and darker hues of more men joining their power to his. But the numbers of those who jumped back and forth diminished to only a few. Jaylor and Samlan commanded near equal numbers of supporters, divided by age and prejudice.

"This does not settle the matter of why you sent Glenndon to court. A totally inappropriate choice of representative," Samlan insisted. "And you did not consult any of the other masters."

"The king's request took the decision out of my hands. Glenndon's presence at court has nothing to do with magicians or magical politics . . ."

"He is a magician. His presence at court, a place denied to the rest of us, has everything to do with magical politics!"

Oh, no, Lillian gasped. *Look, look at the circle. Even Marcus and Robb are now siding with Samlan.*

Da, your pride keeps you from admitting the truth. If you'd just tell them the truth behind King Darville's summons . . .

"Enough. 'Twas my decision and mine alone," Jaylor shouted, the headache more in command of him than he wanted to admit. His voice bounced against the tall wooden walls of the University and wrapped around the circle of men. He lifted his left hand from Marcus' shoulder and shook off Robb's restraining grip. The dome of power cracked and sizzled at the abrupt severing, without proper grounding or careful cutting.

Men recoiled at the flaring whips of power that had no anchor or goal. They flung hands across their eyes in protection from the snarling and snapping magic.

Lillian and Valeria sank deeper into their nest. Across the compound Lukan rose up from his own post and hastened away, ducking and slapping at stray sparks. He whimpered in pain as one slashed his cheek, drawing blood.

"I break this circle as I dismiss the Circle of Master Magicians," Da said. "We will not meet again until we can meet in harmony and unity." He turned and stalked away from the University, downhill toward the clearing, his family, and his home.

CHAPTER 34

"STARGODS, I NEED A DRINK." King Darville sank onto the lounge beside the queen, pinching the bridge of his nose.

Da does the same thing when troubled, Glenndon thought.

"I have broken every rule that reason and experience have taught me!" the king's words drifted toward Glenndon as if from a great distance. They echoed inside his mind as if someone else said the same thing at precisely the same moment and he heard them both. He shook his head to clear it of the echo, to bring him firmly back to this room, this present.

Stargods! he was tired. And hungry. Should he eat first or sleep before banishing his hunger with solid food?

"'Twas necessary, my love," the queen said firmly. She might have been reclining on her couch, suggesting a casual interest, but somehow she made the position and the comfortable furniture a commanding throne, her presence requiring the attention of all within her sphere.

"Never before, not since the creation of the Council of Provinces united beside a king, has Coronnan been without . . ." King Darville buried his face in his hands. "More than three hundred years of stable and peaceful government destroyed in one fit of temper." He looked up at the nearly empty room. "Where's my cup and the beta arrack?"

"Not now," the queen said firmly, as if speaking to a toddler about to throw a temper tantrum.

"The Council was formed with the advice and consent of

the master magicians," Glenndon reminded him. His legs
were like damp bread from weakness and his hand ached all
the way to his shoulder blades and over the top of his head,
but a huge constriction seemed to have dissolved from his
chest and throat. *How had Linda managed that?*

The king and queen looked at him in surprise. Linda just
smiled and nodded in acknowledgment. Something amazing
had happened during that intense healing spell. Beyond the
binding of their blood through their common parent, their
minds and souls had linked for one brief blinding moment.

He could speak.

"Coronnan has been without a fully functioning government since the Leaving, limping along, only pretending to do
the work of leading the country. You, Father, merely completed the process," Glenndon continued without effort. The
words were just there, ready to spit out whenever he wanted.
He wondered, briefly, if his link to Linda meant she provided
him with the words upon command, or if she had merely
unblocked something in his mind.

"Stargods preserve us," Old Maisy gasped, throwing her
hands in the air. "Your Da will never believe this. A miracle.
And all it took . . . well, I don't know what it took, but took
it did and now we have a prince in the family."

"Not a word of this to anyone, Maisy!" Queen Rossemikka
commanded. "Glenndon will inform Jaylor himself, when
the time is right."

"I think the time is now. I need Jaylor here at my side,
now more than ever," the king said. He fixed his gaze upon
Glenndon.

Glenndon did not back down. "Is it safe?" he asked instead of the myriad things he wanted to know.

"Probably *S'murghin'* not," Darville said wryly.

Linda smothered a giggle. She didn't hear her father curse
very often. Glenndon knew that without thinking or surmis-
ing or watching her posture.

"If ever there is a time for foul words, it's now." Mikka
stroked her husband's back. "We are all family here at the
moment." Her gaze swept the room, including Lady Anya
and Old Maisy in the grouping. "We need to make some de-

cisions, quickly, before the lords recover from their shock and come up with some of their own."

"Without the Council, they could decide to break into factions and begin warring against each other . . . or us," Darville said. He bounced to his feet and began pacing, hands behind his back, head and shoulders thrust forward. His blond hair, with a few traces of silver at his temples, flew behind him in the wind created by his forceful passage around the room. His queue had dispersed some time ago.

"Father, did you know that the aura of a golden wolf follows you?" Glenndon asked, surprised at his boldness.

"Yes, I do. And you'd best learn to curb your tongue now that you've found it. The less the mind-blind nobles know of that the better." The king did not slow his pacing as he issued his reprimand.

The words cut at Glenndon. He chose not to speak of the stories passed around the hearth on dark and dreary winter evenings. Stories told by his mother and his father of how they met, how they saved a golden wolf from the prison of enscorcellment, how a princess and a cat had exchanged bodies, and then both inhabited the human body. A little brindled cat with fur in many iridescent shades of brown, red, and gold—the colors of autumn, like the queen's hair, and her daughter's.

"We have to make plans," the queen said. She dropped her feet to the floor and sat tall, seemingly recovered from the exhaustion of guiding the spell. "We have to be ready when the Council come to their senses."

"Glenndon, can you summon Jaylor?" Darville asked. "Linda, while he is doing that, I will need you to write many letters for me. Maisy, I trust no one else to listen in on the lords' discussions. They will not notice you."

"Yes, Your Grace. I'll just take myself off to the servants' quarters. Best I use the back ways, the bleak and narrow ways that no respectable man knows about but us servants use all the time . . . Now where did I put my pins and that bit of trim Princess Josie wants mended for her hair ribbon? Oh, I'll find it soon enough. Soon enough." She wandered into the queen's bedroom, appearing absentminded, simple-minded, and unremarkable because she was always under-foot.

"I will need a candle flame and a scrying bowl," Glenndon said through chattering teeth. A chill invaded his bones, he knew not from where. His hands shook as he hugged himself to ward off the sudden ailment.

Linda mimicked him.

"Shock," Mikka said. She looked sharply at Linda. "Lady Anya, blankets and hot broth for both of them."

"They should be in bed," Darville added, suddenly stopping his restless prowl. He stood over Glenndon, placing a firm but comforting hand on his shoulder.

"No." Glenndon forced himself not to stutter. "I can manage. I just need the flame and the bowl."

"They both threw a tremendous spell to remove the magic from Glenndon's wound. They had to join mind and body," Mikka said. "They need food more than anything. And rest. But I trust no one outside of this room. I'll not risk them going off to their own rooms alone."

"Agreed," Darville said.

"P'pa, M'ma, could we sit on your couch with our feet up on the table?" Linda asked through her own chattering teeth. She reached her uninjured left hand for Glenndon's. The moment they touched, his shoulders eased and a tiny bit of warmth crept up his arm. This must be what the twins felt like when they had been separated for a while and joined back up again. Neither one complete without the other.

"Stargods, I need a drink." Jaylor said, standing in the middle of the big room of the family home. He pinched the bridge of his nose. "I have broken every rule that reason and experience have taught me!" His hands trembled as he scrubbed his face with them. More like burying his face in them so he didn't have to face Brevelan.

Valeria and Lillian cringed behind him. Lukan had taken himself off up the mountain rather than deal with the aftermath of what he had witnessed. So like Lukan. When he knew that Glenndon would be on the receiving end of anyone's temper, the younger brother watched gleefully. When he became involved, he disappeared, like a dragon in sunlight, there but not visible.

"A circle that does not involve trust is as broken as . . . as you have unmade it," Brevelan said quietly. She actually put down the bit of sewing that had occupied her when they all burst into the room. Three yampion pies baked in their covered iron pots beneath coals in the hearth. Jule and Sharl sat at her feet, suddenly quiet, all eyes and ears. Jule's thumb crept into his mouth as he clung to his mother's leg.

"Since the time of Nimbulan, the University has always had a Circle of Masters working together for the good of the kingdom," Jaylor said flatly. The enormity of his actions sent chills coursing through his entire body, making his knees shake as badly as his hands. "Now I have broken the circle."

"Samlan broke the circle when he allowed his jealousy to come between him and his trust of you. Over the centuries many magicians have removed themselves from the University. Declare him rogue, exile him from Coronnan, and continue without him." Brevelan resumed her rocking and her sewing, lifting the shirt she mended enough so that Jule could climb into her lap. She continued sewing around him.

"A smaller circle is better than no circle at all. But I'm no longer certain who I can trust." Jaylor sat on the dirt floor in the place just vacated by Jule. Sharl climbed into his lap. He smoothed her dark auburn curls that nearly matched his own in color and thickness.

The twins sat beside him, nearly joined at the shoulder, and Valeria placed her hand on his knee. The empathic reassurance from his three daughters brought the pressure in his head down to normal levels and pushed his blood through his whole body, warming him and giving him better control of his shudders as well as his thoughts.

He wondered briefly if both or only one of them was a strong empath with healing talents.

"We know who you can trust," Lillian whispered.

"We watched, as you told us to," Valeria continued.

"We saw whose auras joined with yours."

"Who strayed away from you."

"Who wavered."

"And who came back to your side of the circle . . ."

"Only after you broke with Samlan."

Jaylor watched them carefully, concentrating on their eyes, as if he needed to see the truth within them. "I knew I set you two to watch for more reasons than I thought at the time." He smiled and draped his free hand around both of them. His family. The best part of his life; as essential to him as his magic.

"Lukan, you can join us now," Mama called.

He poked his head out from the opening into the sleeping loft. So, he hadn't sought refuge with the dragons after all.

Jaylor wondered if the entire family thought of the lair high up on the mountain face, nearly at the timberline, as the best place to find sanctuary.

"We have decisions to make," Jaylor said when Lukan perched on a stool, back to the hearth. "I need your observations on each of the masters. We'll start with Marcus, he stood immediately to my left."

A thrum of noise, like a cat's purr but louder and more demanding pulsed within Jaylor's robes.

"Stargods, who would dare summon me now?" He patted his pockets until he found and withdrew a small circle of glass.

Valeria's eyes grew large as the image of a candle flame burst into life within the depths of the precious object. "Soon, Val, soon you and Lillian will be advanced enough to be found worthy of a sliver of glass for summoning spells," he reassured the twins.

"Lillian, Valeria, a bowl of water and a candle. Now," Mama ordered.

They obeyed without hesitation. The girls had watched him speak to other magicians, journeymen on journey for the most part. Rarely did they get to see someone summon him.

"Glenndon? What's wrong?" Jaylor demanded as he floated the glass in the water and touched it briefly with the candle. He still held the taper of beeswax rather than setting it across the bowl of water so that the flame reflected in the glass.

Lillian placed her open palm on the side of the bowl. Valeria did the same. Their fingertips touched. Bound together and to the bowl, they should hear Glenndon's words even if his image was only a blurry outline within the depths of the bowl.

"My father has dismissed the Council of Provinces and closed the court," Glenndon said. He sounded tired, slurring his words.

Jaylor's own actions echoed in his memories. He and Darville had always been close. Friends since their early teens. Bound together by magic as well as love. Their lives had taken parallel paths.

Now this?

"Why?" Jaylor demanded. Summoning spells took a lot of energy. Glenndon already looked exhausted, face drawn and pale, dark circles around his eyes, hair in disarray. No time for idle chatter.

He's speaking! Valeria told them all.

Real words, not just mind speech, Lillian added.

Something wonderful! Brevelan nearly cried with joy.

Something dreadful as well, Jaylor finished for them.

"Our enemy tried to poison the king in the Council Chamber. Hallowed ground. He imbued a small amount of weak and hasty magic in the cup to cast suspicion on the magicians." Glenndon breathed heavily.

"And? Why are you so weak? Your spell fades."

"Acid laced with magic splashed my hand. The queen and her daughter helped remove it."

"Nasty," Jaylor spat the word that rested on all of their tongues. The pressure began to rebuild in his head. He had to do something. Now.

What could he do from a distance of eight hundred miles?

"You must come home now, Glenndon. Coronnan City, court, it's too dangerous," he said, knowing it was not enough. He had to protect more than just his boy, his family.

"The acid splashed me because I knocked the cup from the king's hand before he could drink from it. Imagine what would have happened had I not interfered. I am needed here now, more than ever. My father requests you come. Quickly. We need you. Now."

The image dissolved in a ripple of water lapping over the glass. The constant thrum of the spell fell silent.

Desperate to maintain contact and know that Glenndon

remained alive and unhurt, Jaylor reached a hand to the scrying bowl, trying to hang on to the spell and . . . his son.

His shoulders slumped in defeat and his blood pounded in his ears once more.

"S'murghit! I can't go now. I'm needed here, to rebuild the circle."

CHAPTER 35

"HURRY, LINDA," Glenndon hissed at her.

She hopped and stumbled trying to pull on her boots. Her boy's clothing made the process easier than working around long skirts, but she felt stupid with sleep and her tummy still growled with hunger. "Do we have to go now?" she whispered, afraid of waking the family.

"Yes, now. While our guards doze," Glenndon insisted. "You want to learn more about magic and how it works. This is the only time we have free to find the things I need to teach you."

For half a heartbeat Linda wished for a return of the silent Glenndon who spoke only a word or two when he absolutely had to.

"Lucjemm will want to come too. He's always interested in exploring . . ."

"He's mind-blind. Anything we discover will mean nothing to him."

"But I like having him around. He makes me laugh." She would not tell her brother how special Lucjemm made her feel, especially when he kissed her. All warm and tingly.

"Not tonight." Glenndon leaned on the wall of her room at the inside corner. The stones groaned as they scraped against each other. "No one has used this entrance in a long while," he said, leaning harder against the reluctant opening. "We may need to rub some Amazon oil on the joints and pivots."

"Is there an entrance to the tunnels from every room?" Linda asked, coming up behind him. She had the boots on, but it felt as if her stocking had twisted around the toes. If she had to walk a great distance she'd have a blister and not be able to wear proper shoes tomorrow.

"Mostly in the royal apartments. Escape routes in case of trouble." The wall had shifted enough to allow them to squeeze through. Glenndon grabbed her hand and pulled her beyond the comfortable security of her own room. Good thing M'ma had told Miri and Chastet to sleep elsewhere tonight. Her two friends had already protested how much more time she spent with Glenndon and Lucjemm than with them.

At the top of the stairs, Glenndon stopped short. Linda ran into his back, having expected him to continue on. "What?" she demanded.

"Close your eyes and count to three."

"Then what." She wasn't about to close her eyes on the fat spider that repaired a web across the doorway. They'd split it in two when they opened the stone portal. It sped back and forth from lintel to lintel. Linda swore the beast shot them poisonous stares. "Are you going to light a torch?" A thick mat of spiderweb covered the one with a tinder kit she'd come to expect beside the door, ready for use. She didn't think the spider would welcome further disruption of its home.

"I need you to look carefully at the pathway. It will light our way. I have to know what you see. But you can't see it until you center yourself and ground your awareness in the land."

Where did all those words come from? Glenndon rattled them off as easily as Linda did. Maybe a lifetime of silence had bottled them up and they needed to come out all at once before he settled down to . . . to whatever was natural for him.

"Close your eyes. Breathe deeply. Think about the land beneath your feet."

"I'm standing on twenty feet of dressed stone."

"Where did the stone come from? It was once deeply embedded in the Kardia, part of a mountain, pieces of the whole planet." He droned on and on about how every stone was connected to every grain of dirt, to every worm and mole and tree root and . . .

Linda closed her eyes, shutting out the actual words, listening more to the soothing rhythm, thinking about his hand cupped around hers, how she was connected to him and he to the Kardia and together they had magic.

Her eyes fluttered open when his words wound down to a whisper and then silence. Deep abiding silence. Not a lack of words, just no need to speak.

A dim path opened before her, leading downward into the dark. "Blue," she gasped. "Silvery blue. A path of sorts," she said quietly, awestruck, afraid of disturbing the wonderful vision of a magical path dancing ahead of her, sometimes on the floor, sometimes along the walls or the ceiling, but always ahead of her.

"That is a ley line," Glenndon said with reverence. "They crisscross all the land."

"What do they do?"

"They are energy. Power. A source of magic."

"But I thought the dragons . . ."

"An alternative. Not always available. This is older, more primitive. Not everyone can gather dragon magic. Not everyone can tap a ley line. Few can do both."

"Can you do both?" She wanted to look into his eyes and watch the truth of his words. But she dared not take her gaze away from the wondrous path of silvery blue light.

"Yes, I can. And so can my Da. Women can't gather dragon magic. If they have any talent at all, they can use the energy in a ley line to fuel their spells."

"Why can't women gather dragon magic?" She thought about Shayla and how her big body shimmered in the sunlight, not always truly visible but still *there.* Very much there and tuned to royal blood. If any woman could gather dragon magic, Linda thought she should be able to do it.

Except that members of the royal family were forbidden magic. Except that they all had some magic or the dragons and the Coraurlia couldn't protect them. Except that the Council, all the Councils going back to the first one, needed to separate magicians from nobles and kings. Except that . . .

"This is confusing."

"Only because you are overthinking it," Glenndon said gently.

"That's part of my role in life as P'pa's heir. I need to look at an issue from all sides before acting."

"For now we have to trace this line back to its source. We need to know the source of this magic. There is a Well of Power. I can feel it singing in my blood and my brain. But I can also feel the numbness, the darkness drawing closer. Something is wrong with the Source."

Indigo appeared at her side. He half-purred, half-meowed an agreement as he rubbed his face on her leg. His eyes never left the fat spider with the broken web.

"The Well of Life no longer feeds the Tambootie trees properly," Glenndon continued, bending slightly to scratch Indigo between the ears. "Indigo says that without a proper Tambootie crop the dragons do not thrive. Shayla cannot breed again until the balance is restored. Dragon numbers decrease. I have to find answers. Will you help me, sister? Linda, my friend."

"Yes." She couldn't say or do anything else. She'd follow him anywhere. Do anything for him. After the binding during the spell to heal his hand, she knew they were more closely allied by blood than she'd thought.

"Linda? Where are you?" M'ma called from the other side of the door. "Linda!" Her voice rose in panic. "Stargods help us. Darville! Darville, come quickly. They have kidnapped our daughter."

Her mother's pain stabbed Linda in the middle. Reluctantly she dropped Glenndon's hand and turned back to reality. "Here, M'ma. I'm here. I . . . I needed to explore this entrance to the tunnels in case I ever need to escape."

Glenndon slipped away without her, leaving her alone, incomplete, and nearly blind without his magical vision to open her inner eye and guide her.

I have followed Glenndon through the tunnels often enough to know how to eavesdrop without him seeing or sensing me.

My lovely tells me how to mask my presence behind stone, and still listen.

But these tunnels are too damp for her. I must walk them alone, make my own judgments, and report back to her. I learn more without her thoughts clouding my own.

I know that Glenndon is my enemy, but . . . he has become a friend.

My lovely yanks my thoughts back to her purpose. I did not know she could do that from such a distance.

What is this Well of Power? I have found nothing about it in the archives. Curse the magicians. They have stolen every book about magic and taken them away. Knowledge is power. Without knowledge of this well, this source of power, it will remain intact, a way for the magicians to always work magic even after I destroy the dragons.

My lovely insists that the dragons are the true curse to this land and must be eliminated first. Who knew such a cute little creature could be so wise. Its voracious appetite bodes well for good growth into a formidable weapon. I will need it when we face down the dragons.

First things first. Bring the dragons down, and that will force the magicians to seek the Well to continue their cruel domination of normal humans. I shall follow them and that will be their undoing. A well is easily poisoned. Easier than poisoning the king. That did not go as planned. The well is secret and therefore unguarded. All I have to do is watch and wait.

After I take my army to the dragon trap. What to use as bait? Rather, who to use as bait?

My lovely tells me that we must sacrifice someone important. I do not like . . . My lovely will not be denied.

Jaylor bent over the double cot where Valeria and Lillian slept. Gently he kissed Val's brow. "Time to get up, little one."

"Why? It's still dark." Valeria rolled over and draped an arm around her twin without opening her eyes.

"I need you both to come with me as my extra eyes."

"Call Indigo. And you have Glenndon in the city already. Someone has to stay here and take care of Mama and watch the masters," Lillian finished the thought.

"Marcus and Robb will take care of the University. They are better able to mend breaches with those who waver in their loyalty. Lukan can take care of Mama and the little ones. He thirsts for responsibility. Let him prove himself now and earn his staff when I return. Now hurry, we haven't much time." He prodded both girls with a shake of the shoulders and a stab into their minds.

"I don't want to go," Valeria shook off his heavy hand and absorbed his mental probe like a knife through butter, in one side and out the other. He blocked it from returning to him, not willing to endure another headache.

"Think about it while you eat." Jaylor prodded them both again, more vigorously.

What if I stay here until after Da leaves? Valeria asked her sister. She was so sleepy she didn't bother guarding her thoughts from her father.

"You have to be ready to transport when he's ready or he'll leave us behind." Lillian grabbed Val's arm and dragged her out of the bed. She continued to hold onto her twin as she turned her around to face the pitcher and ewer beside the clothes press.

"That's what I thought I said. I want to get left behind," Val protested.

"Val, this is important," Jaylor said firmly.

"If Da wants us to go to the city with him, then we have to go," Lillian insisted. "Think how exciting it will be to actually see the city, stone buildings, bridges, ordinary people. Markets!"

"If you are so excited about going, then go. I want to stay here. I never want to leave this mountain. There are no dragons in the city." She turned back toward the bed.

"We'll get to see Glenndon again," Jaylor reminded them. Sometimes he had to work around his daughter's stubbornness (so like his own) like water seeking a leak in the roof, entering one place, wiggling around and appearing elsewhere.

That made Valeria pause. "I truly and surely miss Glenndon."

"If you won't go, then I *can't* go." Lillian pouted. She tossed her sunlit blonde and red braid over her shoulder and turned her back on her twin.

"Why not?"

"You know why."

Jaylor raised his eyebrows in question. Both girls clamped their mouths and minds shut, barring him from entrance.

Perhaps Brevelan understood the secrets of teenage girls better than he did.

An hour later, having made sure the girls ate as much honey-laced porridge as they could swallow, Jaylor led them to the center of the clearing, where Brevelan awaited them.

Brevelan. He hated leaving her. Hated it every time he flew off on Baamin's back to battle more Krakatrices. Though there hadn't been another sighting for several weeks now. His heart ached worse than usual. He pulled his wife into his arms, burying his face in her hair, drinking in her unique scent.

"If I ever get lost, I need only think of bread baking, flowers growing, and your sparkling blue eyes to pull me home," he said, then kissed her soundly.

"Do you have everything?" She gestured to a pile of satchels and bags scattered at their feet.

He cupped her face with both of his hands. "I don't have you following behind me, my love." His only love.

"My adventuring days are over." She glanced at Jule and Sharl playing with a tame gray scurry, its bushy tail curling upward and tiny front paws holding a nut the children had given it. A curious flusterhen squawked and pecked at the seeds lumped into Sharl's apron. She was supposed to be feeding the flock, not playing with a wild pest.

"We had some interesting times when we journeyed together." Jaylor smiled.

"Go, dearest Jaylor," Brevelan said. "Take the girls and teach them something of civilized behavior while you are there."

She turned away from him and gathered both girls into her

arms, clinging to them as desperately as she had Jaylor. Sometime in the last few months the twins had grown taller than their mother (Valeria not quite so much as her sister, but still taller), and she had to stretch to enfold them into her embrace. "I shall miss you both," she whispered, kissing each girl on the cheek, then holding them tight again.

Jaylor chuckled. "I wonder if the princesses will teach them manners or if our twins will show the prim little girls how to run wild and steal onions on Market Isle."

"As you did for a young prince sorely in need of a friend?" They both laughed. Brevelan stepped away from her girls and pushed them gently toward Jaylor.

"What are they talking about?" Lillian whispered.

"I don't know, but I think they are sharing a part of their past they don't want us to know about."

"Oh." Lillian sounded disappointed. "They never kept much from us before."

"Except that bit about King Darville being Glenndon's father."

"I wonder how that happened."

"You won't find out by whispering behind our backs," Brevelan said. She speared them with a reprimanding gaze. Then she clasped her arms around Jaylor's waist and gave him one last fierce squeeze. "Take care of yourself and our girls. Don't make me come after you."

"I'll do my best. But I might just go looking for trouble so you *will* come after me." He kissed her nose and stepped away, slinging a pack over one shoulder and slipping his other arm through the straps of another. "Grab your bags, girls, and hold on to me tight. One on each side."

Valeria and Lillian stepped into the circle he'd drawn in the grass with pebbles long ago. Brevelan backed away.

Jaylor opened his mind to Valeria and Lillian, showing them an image of a dark storeroom. Barrels and boxes were stacked neatly around the sides, leaving the middle of the room open. "See the empty space, girls. Fix it in your mind. Firmly. Don't let your thoughts wander from that spot. Lillian? See the room."

"I can't, Da. It's all fuzzy."

Valeria sighed and reached around in front of him. Lillian's hand grabbed her so that they made a circle. *Now can you see it?*

Lillian nodded.

"Good. Now hang on tight and don't let that room move so much as a feather's width from your vision." Jaylor counted slowly, evenly, timing his breathing to his count. Valeria matched him. Lillian joined in, after a quick mental prod. "Here we go," he said when their hearts and lungs and minds fell into identical rhythms, matching the pulse of the Kardia beneath their feet and the song of the wind in the tree canopy.

Darkness swirled around them. Jaylor caught a brief glimpse of the bright tangled cords of life tying them together. Then more darkness that spun around and around them in ever tightening spirals until . . .

CHAPTER 36

INDIGO BRUSHED HIS FACE against Glenndon's calf,
nearly knocking him over.

"What?" Glenndon froze in place as soon as he regained
his balance. He wished Linda had ignored her mother's panic
and come with him. But they couldn't leave Mikka raising an
alarm and hurting so deeply over the possible loss of her
daughter.

They just couldn't. He'd have gone back to Mama in a
similar situation.

The flywacket chirruped like a normal cat, not using his
intelligent mental voice.

"We know that the official archives are in the East Tower.
They aren't the magical archives left behind at the Leaving.
Do you know where we need to look next?"

(Down.)

"That's what I was afraid of." Glenndon shuddered at the
thought of the weight of the river and tons of dirt and rock
pressing upon the tunnel. He knew the river sought an opening, any opening, to collapse the stones on top of him . . .

Indigo chirruped again, sounding very much like laughter.
(Dig deeper.)

"That's not much help. We'll start with the Well." He
plodded down the steps and along the main passage.

(Down,) Indigo repeated.

"Not tonight. We'll look for the archives another time. We
only have a few hours to explore tonight."

(Down.) Indigo scampered ahead of him. The light beneath his feet seemed to dim.

Glenndon continued on, following the ley lines, looking for patterns in the joining and separation of the lines, noting now-familiar landmark runes as he turned this way and that.

Indigo stopped and turned a full circle, nose working rapidly.

Glenndon gathered a glow ball into his palm.

A flitter of movement down a side passage, where the lines did not wander, captured his attention. Not Indigo. The flywacket had pranced ahead along the main passage, his bushy tail gathering dust and cobwebs. This other movement, here and gone in less than a heartbeat belonged to someone else. An eavesdropper? Or some other denizen of the deep?

He should have sensed a presence. But he'd been so engrossed with the ley lines that the Kardia could have quaked and shaken the wall stones loose and he'd not have noticed.

Who? he asked Indigo.

A mental shrug akin to his own silent responses to questions. *(No smell.)*

Everyone has a smell.

(Masked.)

He caught a whiff of acrid smoke, a common odor close to hearth fires that were quenched with water when they grew too hot. An odor strong enough to hide behind, but not so strong or alien as to alert Glenndon. Someone stalked him. At a distance. Or someone who knew the oversized black cat would be with him set and doused a fire deliberately to produce masking smoke. Someone who knew that Indigo's sense of smell would alert him to the stalker.

Glenndon gazed longingly at the tangle of ley lines that merged and grew fat, lush with power at the junction just ahead, the junction that plunged downward into the bedrock beneath the river. He was close to the Well. He knew it.

His stalker must not be allowed to find it. Anyone who couldn't find it on their own didn't have enough talent to know what to do with the source of power.

The one who followed in secrecy could not be allowed to suspect how close they were to the Well.

Are you thinking what I'm thinking, Indigo?

(Games?)
Yes!

Glenndon made a show of turning in a circle, holding up his glow ball. He examined a number of cracks and crevices, the floor, the ceiling. He sent a spider scuttling to safety away from the center of its web. A mouse squeaked as it fled into a tiny hidey-hole. A tiny lumpy black snake slithered rapidly away, avoiding the puddles. After several minutes of appearing lost, Glenndon turned resolutely back the way he'd come and then darted along a wide passage with a dwindling ley line sliding along the wall at about knee level.

The rune at the beginning of this tunnel looked like a loaf of bread. He headed toward the kitchens.

Indigo scampered off in the opposite direction, mewling and chirruping as if he chased prey.

He'd never get lost down here.

Hm. What would it take to push his pursuer into wandering down a looping dead end for a very long time before stumbling on a way out?

Glenndon could discover the stalker's identity by counting heads at court and seeing who was missing. Only his father had dismissed the court and the Council. The lords and their retainers had departed for their own lands, or residences in the city. Many were missing.

The smell of yeast and flour enticed him forward. The cooks had set the day's bread to rise. His stomach growled in response. He still hadn't replenished his energy reserves since working that healing spell with Linda the previous afternoon. He had the perfect excuse to slip into the storeroom and thence into the larder for some fruit and cheese. He'd even welcome some stale, day-old bread or jerked meat.

A new sound made him stop short in the act of opening the trapdoor that would allow him access to a small clear spot created by an odd stacking of storage barrels. From inside the room, no one would suspect this empty space. Had it been created by a spy?

The air thrummed with power. He tasted the aromatic spice of Tambootie. The delicate new leaves at the tops of the trees rather than the fat, oil-rich, succulent leaves lower down.

He tensed and watched as the air in the center of the room glowed and sparkled. Only one person would dare use a transport spell into the bowels of the palace.

From between two barrels he peered at the shifting light. Three forms coalesced out of the shimmer. The magical light faded quickly replaced by a glow ball in the palm of the central figure. Tall, broad-shouldered, barrel-chested, with dark auburn hair and a tightly braided formal queue.

"Da!" Glenndon stood up and vaulted over the precariously balanced barrels. He hurried to hug Jaylor in relief. The sight of the twins stopped him. "Why?" he pointed at the girls, suddenly tongue-tied. He couldn't see their faces very well in the dim light.

"We've come to help," Lillian said. "Haven't we, Val. Val?" she repeated herself when her twin failed to speak up.

The smaller of the two girls wilted. Glenndon just barely caught her before she slumped to the floor. "What did you do, Valeria? Manage the entire transport spell yourself?"

"She couldn't do that!" Da insisted. "Shouldn't be able to. She has no training, nor does she know the secret. The life-saving secret."

Glenndon knew better.

"Now what?" Darville yelled at whoever pounded on the door to his suite at this horrible hour before dawn. Not even the birds that cheeped at the first glow of sunlight on the horizon were awake yet. The only sign of life in the palace, in the city, was the smell of new bread rising.

He sat in a large, padded chair by the hearth, hair unbound, sleep shirt and robe rumpled, sleepless with worry. What was he going to do about a divided and angry Council? A Council he'd dismissed.

He looked into the empty goblet that dangled from his fingers. No, he dared not drink more. Especially now that dawn approached. He needed to be awake and aware, not dulled and sluggish.

Mikka stirred in the big bed, moaning slightly at the disturbance but not coming fully awake. She needed rest. More than she was willing to give herself.

The pounding renewed itself with increased vigor.

Darville stalked to the door. If the pounding hadn't awakened Mikka, his own footsteps wouldn't. He opened the door a crack to peer into the long corridor reserved for royal family quarters.

"Father," Glenndon whispered, trying hard to keep his wide smile from splitting his face.

"This had better be good news," Darville growled.

"Come," Glenndon said and beckoned him to follow toward his own room. His smile never faltered.

Darville stepped into the corridor, closing the door silently behind him. "What?" he whispered to his son. Mikka might sleep through a kardiaquake. The servants and retainers in the wing wouldn't.

Glenndon just urged him forward with an imperious wave of the hand he could have learned only from Linda.

An enormous black cat brushed its face against Darville's leg. He nearly jumped with fright. He hadn't seen a cat in the palace since . . . Ambassador Jack had banished the cat spirit from Mikka's body fifteen years ago. The cat chirruped and nearly attached itself to Glenndon's heels, tail high and fluffy, ears twitching with normal awareness but no alarm.

Then with great ceremony Glenndon opened his own door and bowed as nicely as any practiced courtier, for Darville to precede him.

"You've been working hard on your technique," Darville complimented him, not relaxing his wariness.

"Linda," Glenndon replied.

The cat agreed with him with a purr and more face rubbing. Absently Glenndon reached down and scratched between its fuzzy ears. It had tufts growing out of them and more whiskers than any cat had a right to.

Darville resisted the urge to add his own caress. Somehow it seemed like betrayal of Mikka to accept the cat.

"You needn't fear Indigo, Your Grace, he's actually a flywacket," Jaylor said from the center of the room.

The cat ran to him as if greeting a long absent friend. Jaylor obliged him with scratches under the chin.

But the two little girls, who should have been delighted by the presence of the animal, did not respond. They huddled together in one of the big chars by the hearth, arms about each other, foreheads touching, gazes locked together as tightly as their red-blonde curls tangled into one mop of hair.

"Jaylor," Darville greeted his old friend with relief and an outstretched arm. They grabbed elbows and slapped upper arms in affectionate, masculine greeting. "You came."

The heavy weight of kingship sloughed off his shoulders. A little.

"You summoned. I obeyed." Jaylor released him, turning his attention back to the little girls. Glenndon knelt before them, stroking their hair and mumbling soothing words.

Darville cocked his head in their direction in silent question.

"I need their observation skills."

"But . . . ?"

"Valeria has never been strong."

"What do you need?"

"We need a healer," Glenndon said, rising from his crouch.

"She has always recovered after a hearty meal and a night's rest," Jaylor said hesitantly.

"The hearty meal I can provide," Darville said. He turned to the bell pull to summon a servant.

Glenndon shook his head before he grasped the decorative rope. "She needs more than food this time. Her body is shutting down. As it did when . . . before. Before . . ." He looked to Jaylor for permission to complete his sentence.

Jaylor shook his head.

"What are you keeping from your king?"

"Magician's business."

"Magician's business should be my business," Darville affirmed.

"Not this time. You are my oldest friend. My one true friend. But in this matter, it is best you do not carry this information at all."

"Do you fear my indiscretion?" Anger and hurt twisted in Darville's gut.

"No, dear friend. Never that. I fear rogue magicians hired by your Council to read your mind and bring you down."

"My Council?" Darville laughed, without humor. "Magic and magicians frighten them more than Simurgh himself!"

"What of Simurgh's black offspring?"

Something in the set of Jaylor's shoulders scared Darville. "Not sure I ever heard any legends about *our* dragons allowing the bloodthirsty demon to live long enough to spawn."

"In the last year Baamin and I have fought six Krakatrice. Marcus and Robb an equal number—each. None of them were the matriarchal black snakes with six wings, thank the Stargods. Only juvenile males. My spies tell me they are returning to the Big Continent and someone is smuggling their eggs into Coronnan City."

"Are they as immediate a problem as your very ill daughter, or five of my lords gathering armies outside the city?"

"That depends."

"On what?"

"If the lords are going to attack each other or join forces to attack you."

CHAPTER 37

*M*Y FATHER HAS BETRAYED ME. *He has taken Lady Graciella to wife. To wife, S'murghit. She is already pregnant, having lived in his household less than a moon. I am no longer good enough for him as his heir. I am still only the bastard son made legitimate as a stopgap, a temporary solution. He is so smug he does not even camp with the army we have gathered for the other lords to join forces with us against the king.*

I shall show him the folly of his ways. Graciella may produce only a female. She may miscarry. There are ways to make certain that happens. My lovely tells me of herbs and poisons that I can add to Graciella's wine, as Graciella added the poison to the king's beta arrack.

Graciella switched the king's cup for me. She used her small, untrained magic at my direction. She did it to please me, I had her first. She hoped to marry me, the heir. She begged me to let her help me in my mission to gain the throne. The child might not even be my father's. Little does she know that my true quest is to rid Coronnan of the corruption of magic. The throne is just a means to an end.

First I will make certain there is no child. Then I will ensure that my father is no longer lord. As the new lord, I will be in a much better position to marry my little princess. Especially if I loan the king my army. First I become his ally, then his son. When all is in place I will turn my little pet against him. The big weapons I will save for the dragons.

"P'pa?" Linda hesitated in the doorway. Her face and hands felt icy cold while her stomach twisted into a fiery knot.

"Linda, you should be in bed," her father said, not unkindly, but with enough sternness that she knew he meant for her to leave immediately.

She couldn't. Not now.

"I think I have seen one of those Krakatrice eggs," she told him more boldly.

The broad man, who could only be Senior Magician Jaylor, stepped around P'pa and approached her with haste and determination. He sketched a curt bow to her by way of introduction then speared her with his gaze.

She couldn't move, couldn't lie, couldn't do much of anything but let him examine her soul.

"Describe what you saw," he ordered.

"Da, you didn't even introduce yourself," Glenndon protested from his place beside his sisters. They didn't look well at all. The more slender of the two looked so pale her veins showed through her thin, almost translucent skin like a light purple tracery. The deep hollows around her eyes were a darker shade of the same color.

A part of Linda needed to sit beside them, hold them close and let them heal, much as she did when something frightened Manda and Josie.

Or was that Glenndon's memory of holding the twins? So much had passed between them while joined during the magic spell, she no longer was certain which memories were hers, and which his.

"She knows who I am, and I know her, she looks just like her mother with some of her father's keen disregard for personal safety."

P'pa snorted something rude.

Linda half smiled at the accurate description of the king.

"Now describe the egg," Jaylor ordered.

"On Market Isle. I saw it. All blood red with black lines of magic writhing around it."

"Stargods! Who could be so stupid as to nurture the evil thing? And sell it?"

"The stall was at the end of the island, beyond the cobblestones, the farthest from the bridge to the city proper, closest to the port."

"A most disreputable part of the market," P'pa growled. "What in Simurgh's name were you doing there? Did Miri and Chastet go with you?"

"Sort of, P'pa." Linda hung her head, not at all sure how to explain her actions.

One word at a time, Glenndon urged her. She caught a glimpse of watching Lucjemm fondle the egg, enthralled by it. Glenndon must have access to her memories as she did his.

"Your Grace, I must take full responsibility." Lucjemm appeared in the doorway as if Linda's memories had summoned him. He looked damp, weary, and had a smudge of something dark and shiny streaking his left cheek. The skin beneath the stain looked raw, like he'd fallen on his face into a puddle of something disgusting.

"Explain yourself, young man," P'pa ordered.

"I escorted Her Highness through the market that day. I found the egg. The egg my father ordered imported from the Big Continent. He has the hatchling from it and from the previous one he bought three years ago. I have left his household and offer myself totally into your service. I will not tolerate his hypocrisy any longer. I will not sit back and watch him use magical creatures to destroy all of Coronnan because he hates magic and wants to end your reign and all possibility of magicians returning."

"Um . . ." Linda didn't remember the incident in the market in quite the same way.

Enthrallment, Glenndon reminded her. *Someone manipulates him.*

How much of what he says can we trust?

Glenndon shrugged. *As long as the snake is not with him, he's thinking on his own.*

"Let us retire to my office and order food," P'pa said. His gaze drifted over to the two little girls.

"P'pa, may I stay with the girls? I think I know what to do to help Valeria," Linda said softly.

"How do you know?" the king asked. Very much the king,

standing straight and tall with an air of authority in his voice
and the set of his shoulders.

"I . . ." She tilted her shoulders slightly toward Lucjemm.

What? Jaylor asked directly into her mind, like Glenndon
used to do before he learned to speak. Learned from her.

She thought very hard, concentrating on getting her words
into Jaylor's mind.

Nothing happened.

*Since the spell to remove the magically poisoned acid from
me, we share many memories,* Glenndon inserted for her.

Then why doesn't he know what to do? Jaylor swung his
attention back and forth, keeping everyone in the room in
view and within reach.

"Because they are his memories and have been with him
so long he doesn't know what is significant and what is not.
They are new to me. Things stand out as either being part of
a larger pattern or outside the pattern." She hoped that was
the right wording.

"What needs to be done?" Jaylor asked, sharply. His love
for the little girl bled through his posture and tone.

The flywacket, Linda sent, hoping she'd learned enough
from Glenndon's last sending to repeat it.

Both Jaylor's and P'pa's eyebrows reached for their
scalps.

"Lucjemm, please await us in my office. I will be with you
shortly," P'pa said, in his formal court voice.

Eyes wide with wonder, Lucjemm bowed sharply and exited. Linda thought she heard him move toward the staircase.
But she couldn't be sure.

"Fred!" P'pa stuck his head out the door as he called for
his bodyguard.

Rapid steps pounded down the narrow staircase from a
higher level in the family tower. "Yes, Your Grace?" Fred
asked, breathing heavily.

"Keep an eye on Master Lucjemm in the office until I get
there. Then you will guard this room. My son and daughter,
and Lord Jaylor's daughters need *complete privacy.*"

"Yes, Your Grace." Fred hurried off again.

Jaylor gestured with a flat hand, pushing downward. Keep
the words quiet so they wouldn't travel beyond the room.

"Indigo was born a dragon. A dragon spirit animates Valeria's life force," Linda said.

"So?" Jaylor asked. He had to know some of this to remain so calm.

"Valeria needs to become a flywacket. For a time."

Then she spotted Indigo poking his fuzzy head out of the nest he'd made of the girls' laps.

"Am I right, Indigo?"

He purred loud enough for everyone in the room to hear. Then he meowed something in a questioning tone.

"What?" Glenndon asked him, using words to make sure both fathers were involved in the conversation.

"Glenndon, talk to your mother before you do anything. My Lord Jaylor, come with me." And the room emptied of the tall and masterful presences of the king and his magician counselor.

"Are you sure, Linda?" Glenndon asked.

Linda looked at the tangle of two little girls, so very alike, and yet different. She couldn't put her finger on the reason for the difference, just that she knew instantly which was Lillian, the strong and capable one, and which was Valeria, the fragile and wise one.

"I'm not sure of anything," Linda confessed. "I don't know how to do this. I don't know if it will work or will kill her once and for all, as she nearly died at birth. It just seemed like the only answer."

Glenndon gave her a curt nod. *Letting her die will kill Lillian as well. They are two halves of a whole,* he added on a tight line to her, keeping the communication away from the twins. As if they had any attention or energy for doing anything other than holding themselves close to each other.

"Then let's do this. Indigo, where do we start?"

"Glenndon, wait. Shouldn't you summon your mother; the girls' mother, before you do anything." Linda grabbed his arm and forced him to look at her and tell her the truth.

"Mama will only panic and abandon the little ones to come here. She won't be thinking clearly for some time. She'll try every herb and healing spell she knows before letting us do what needs to be done. She'll also leave Lukan in charge. He's not very focused."

Linda had to think about that. How would her own mother, Queen Rossemikka, handle this kind of news if Manda or Josie, or even Linda herself, were in such dire straits? Would M'ma remain calm and direct the spell, as she had with Glenndon's healing. Or would she run about like a flusterhen trying to do everything at once, shouting orders, and accomplishing nothing?

"We'll summon her when it's all over," Glenndon reassured her.

"Is this going to hurt?" the stronger twin asked.

Linda sank to her knees in front of the girls. She imagined what it would be like if Manda and Josie were sitting there, her sisters, not Glenndon's. And couldn't. The two younger girls were so full of life and mischief and vitality that she could not picture either of them sick and weak unto death.

She didn't want to think about that. In that moment she knew to the core of her being that she had to try this. For Glenndon.

She noted that the girls had each grabbed hold of Indigo's neck ruff. The flywacket purred mightily, soothing them all, lulling them all into matching their breaths and their heartbeats.

"I don't know, sweetie. I don't know if it will work at all, but we have to try. And if it works, it will be worth whatever pain."

"Promise?"

"I promise."

"She's a princess, she has to follow up on her promises," Glenndon reminded them all.

Success or failure now rested upon Linda's shoulders, just like the success or failure of breaking the Council rested on her father's.

At this moment she could almost feel the weight of the Coraurlia encircling her head, stabbing her with guilt.

And responsibility.

Did her father's enemies have any idea what accompanied their lust for power?

CHAPTER 38

DARVILLE SETTLED behind his desk. With the massive piece of furniture between him and Lucjemm he resumed control of the interview. The vulnerability suggested by his unbound hair and sleep clothes vanished.

"Tell me about the eggs," Jaylor demanded, leaning against the closed door, a solid barrier between the boy and escape.

"The eggs? Oh, yes, my father's toys." Lucjemm nearly spat the last word.

Was that a moment of calculated hesitation at the beginning, or had recent events jangled his nerves?

Darville's nerves were certainly raw. "Go on," he urged, forcing himself to keep his voice neutral and calm. The way Jaylor kept looking in the direction of Glenndon's room where a different drama played out, he figured he'd have to conduct this interview without input or help.

"Well, ah, three years ago, Father brought home this curiosity. That's what he called it. A curiosity."

"Home? Home is where? Your castle in Saria or the manse here in Coronnan City," Darville prodded.

"At the time . . . Mother—Lady Lucinda, the only mother I have ever known—and I were in Saria. Father brought the egg home when the Council disbanded for the winter holidays."

Darville forced himself to remember when he'd last seen Lady Lucinda, before Jemmarc had exiled her. He couldn't.

She was such a vague, wispy personality, he doubted he'd remember her if he saw her face-to-face.

Three years ago? That was just before Jemmarc brought Lucjemm to the capital and arranged the boy's rite of legitimacy. They'd thrown a big party afterward at the manse. Had Lady Lucinda been there even then?

He couldn't remember. Mikka had been ill at the time, and he'd made only a token appearance at the party.

"What happened when the egg hatched?" Jaylor asked from his post at the door. So he was listening, with at least half his attention.

If one of Darville's daughters faced the trial little Valeria did, the king knew he wouldn't be attending to political business at all.

"I don't know for certain. Father and I were in the city for my Rite of Legitimacy when the egg hatched." Lucjemm suddenly found his muddy boots fascinating.

"Tell us what you know," Darville coaxed.

"Father remained in the city and sent me home right after the party. I was only thirteen, not old enough to train with the soldiers, too old for a tutor. He . . . he seemed distracted, like he didn't know what to do with me since he didn't have to hide me anymore."

"And when you got home, what happened to the hatchling?"

"Mother kept it in her room. In a nest of dry straw and fed it raw meat." Lucjemm still did not lift his gaze from his boots.

Jaylor shook his head slightly. He detected something wrong with the story.

"What else?" Darville pressed. If Lucjemm lied, surely Jaylor would detect it. Eventually. They had to keep him talking.

If for no other reason than keeping Jaylor occupied while Glenndon and Linda did whatever they needed to do.

"And . . . ?" Jaylor asked.

"And?" Lucjemm flung his head back. His queue loosened from the violence of his movement, sending stray tendrils across his face. His eyes darted right and left, not quite fixing on either Darville or Jaylor.

"What else did the hatchling eat?" Jaylor asked.

Interesting phrasing.

Lucjemm's right arm bent to rest behind his back. "Mother allowed the ugly snake to bite her finger and drink blood." Lucjemm's gaze dropped again. Not to his boots this time, but to the pattern of planks on the floor and maybe to the edge of rich rug that the desk rested upon.

"Did you ever have the Krakatrice draw blood from you?" Jaylor stepped forward. His hand flashed out and grabbed the boy's left arm so fast Lucjemm couldn't hold back. In the same gesture Jaylor pushed up the boy's sleeve.

Old white scars shone stark against his skin. Each a pair of round dots, evenly spaced.

"These scars are years old, he hasn't given blood to a beast recently," Jaylor announced. He dropped the arm as if tainted.

Lucjemm shoved his sleeve down, a blush of embarrassment coloring his cheeks all the way to his ears.

"What happened to the hatchling when your mother . . . left?" Darville asked soothingly. This boy needed his protection as much as Glenndon and Linda and the little girls.

"I . . . I don't know. I didn't see it for a long time. Then . . . then yesterday after you broke the Council, Father brought out this huge snake from his rooms at the manse, a . . . a Krakatrice and took it outside the city. He crooned to it like a lover. It coiled around his arm and neck and flicked its forked tongue like it was . . . it was tasting the air, seeking new victims to feed off of." The last came out in a rush as if he was afraid to speak his thoughts and had to get them all out at once before they choked him.

Jaylor rested his hand on the boy's shoulder and squeezed gently, reassuringly. "Your father must be using the Krakatrice to enthrall his troops. Will he rise against his king now that the Council is recessed?"

Recessed. Good word. It lacked the sense of permanence of "broken." It gave Darville hope that he could find a compromise to bring the government back together. Legally, without the Council, Darville only had authority over the city islands and small strips of land bordering the river on either side. He and his citizens were dependent upon the network

of trade with the other provinces for grain and meat, for cloth
and leather, and myriad other things to support life and civi-
lization.

"I think so. He has taken Lady Graciella to wife. I
think . . . I think she is a sorceress. I think they poisoned your
cup, Your Grace."

"Why would Jemmarc denounce one wife for working
magic and then take another and use her magical talent?"
Darville asked. Something about the entire tale bothered
him. It had no logic.

Lucjemm shrugged; a gesture so reminiscent of Glenndon
that Darville wanted to enfold him into the family. "Father
didn't really care if she worked magic or not. What he wants
is another son. As if I am no longer good enough for him.
He's willing to use Graciella's magic to further his plans."

"Could the Krakatrice be manipulating Lord Jemmarc's
mind?" Jaylor asked. He started to run his hands through his
tightly bound hair, encountered resistance and thought better
of it. Brevelan must have worked the four-strand plait and
ordered him not to disturb it.

Before he'd calmed his hands, his head snapped sharply
to his left and his eyes grew wide. "Valeria," he whispered.
He slammed out of the room without pause or apology for
waking the household when the door slammed, bounced, and
reverberated against the wall.

"Your Grace, may I ask what is going on?" Lucjemm
sounded bewildered and incredibly young.

"You can ask. But you probably won't get an answer. Satisfy yourself that you are my alibi. I am not working magic.
My wife and daughters are not working magic. I am not even
in the same room with my Senior Magician and his very talented children. And you are not either, so you cannot be witness to anything but our discussion." Darville scrubbed his
face with his hands, acutely aware of his fine, golden hair
spilling around his hands. There were more strands of silver
in it than he'd noted just a few weeks ago.

Stargods, he was tired. And he wanted a drink, but knew
better than to fill his cup now.

"And the Princess Rosselinda?" Lucjemm asked.

"Is sleeping three rooms away. You never saw her."

"Yes, Your Grace."

The scent of fresh bread had shifted from rising to baking while they talked. They'd be called to break their fast within moments.

"Master Lucjemm, consider yourself under my protection. I thank you for your warnings of your father's aberrant behavior. For now, I shall have Jensen, my squire, escort you to guest quarters where you may clean up before food arrives. You will join us in the family parlor when the bell rings." Darville stood, ending the interview.

Lucjemm either didn't understand the signal or needed to prolong this bizarre meeting for some reason known only to him.

"What?" Darville asked curtly when the boy made no move to leave.

"Your Grace, the Princess Rosselinda?"

"What about my daughter?"

"Will she be all right with the . . . the magicians?"

"I trust Lord Jaylor with my life and my soul. In fact I have done so on many occasions. Glenndon is my son, raised by Lord Jaylor and his wife. The girls are Lord Jaylor's daughters, much beloved. I assure you no harm will come to either my daughter or my son this day."

"This day?"

"I have no control over tomorrow. We face civil war if your father gathers enough troops to move against me. I can guarantee no one's safety if that happens. All I can do is my best to protect my family and the people under my care. And my country."

"What is best for the country, Your Grace?" Lucjemm took on an oddly mature expression in both face and eyes.

"I believe that restoration of the government as defined by the original covenant is best for all concerned. I will do what I have to, to achieve that."

"And that includes the magicians."

"Most definitely."

The king has just condemned himself. I cannot allow him to continue as monarch since he relies so heavily on magicians.

All magic must be removed from Coronnan for the safety of all those who have no so-called "talent." Magicians are as filthy and unreliable as the Rovers that also roam our sacred land.

I regret that my friend Prince Glenndon must be eliminated as well as the king. I've never had a friend before . . .

But the princess? My beautiful princess I regret most of all. I may find a way to redeem her, since she showed no talent and no interest in magic before her half-brother entered their household. I believe what she does this day is directed by Glenndon and Lord Jaylor. Any talent she may have now is only borrowed. For their convenience, not for the good of Coronnan.

I will save her if I can. But if she dies in the coming battle to destroy the dragons, then I must accept her passing. Her two younger sisters are too young—not yet transitioned into womanhood—and too frivolous for my purpose. The people, even the power-mad Council, would take offense if I took a girl so immature to wife. I will look to SeLennica to provide me with a royal bride if I must. But my princess is so very beautiful, smart, and . . . and I think I love her.

Wait, my lovely says that is not possible.

She cannot know. It is not in her nature to love. But Linda, my Linda loves me as I love her. She has to. I cannot continue this mission if my princess does not love me.

At all cost, I will save her. She is not available for sacrifice, but her father the king and her mother the queen are.

CHAPTER 39

VALERIA LISTENED to the discussion about her as if from a great distance. She seemed to view the entire room from somewhere around the high ceiling—such a waste of space, a loft up there could sleep three. Her brother's words, and those of the girl she presumed was the princess, had an echoey quality to them that distorted the few that were loud enough to reach her.

Lillian's arm about her physical body was the only thing that kept her from drifting away like a bit of dandelion fluff on a summer breeze. She couldn't leave Lillian alone. Not ever. They belonged to each other. If she thought about it hard enough—which seemed easier now than when her ailing body weighed her down—she could almost remember when they were one soul, one personality, all contained within one egg inside Mama.

"Valeria, wake up, sweetie," the princess said, shaking Valeria's body. "We need you to do something. Something special that will help heal you."

With a disappointing rush and whoosh of wind pushing her, Valeria dropped back into her body and regretted it instantly. Her blood and bones ached with a chill she didn't think even Mama's down comforter and a big fire in the hearth could banish.

Did she truly remember a dragon nest where she'd been warm and free of pain?

"Wake up, Val!" Glenndon ordered her.

With supreme effort she shook her head and tried to escape her body again.

"Not yet, Valeria!" Glenndon continued. "You have to help us help you."

Lillian's soft weeping pulled her back to physical form.

Then Indigo nudged her hand until it rested atop his head. His rhythmic purrs, working in time with his breathing, soothed her enough to open her eyes.

"That's a good girl," the princess said, smoothing Valeria's tangled hair, separating the long strands from Lillian's matching curls.

(Dawn, the time of transition,) Indigo said. But his voice was full, awesome in the way it penetrated her mind and body, as if he spoke with the authority and the company of all dragons.

"We have to do this now," Glenndon said. He looked to the princess with questions in his eyes.

"I don't know how," she said. "Your blood is linked to hers. Mine is not. I can't lead this spell."

"Wh . . . what spell?" Valeria croaked out.

"Val, you have to change," Lillian sobbed. "You have to become a flywacket like Indigo. You have to let the dragon spirit within you take control. You can't be my twin anymore." Tears choked her and her chest heaved with crying.

I will always be your twin. I will always be with you, Lily. Even if we are separated. My mind is only a thought away. Easier to speak with her mind than her mouth. Like Glenndon. His throat used to hurt horribly when he spoke. The effort to speak made her entire body ache.

(Circle,) Indigo said. He sounded uncertain.

"A ritual circle, or should we join in a circle, all touching you?" the princess asked. She seemed the only one capable of thinking clearly at this moment.

(Both.)

That sounded right. They needed to contain the spell within a circle drawn and then work the spell with them all involved, all touching Indigo's soft fur. So soft. So comforting. So easy to fall asleep with her face nestled in the thick luxury of his black coat . . .

(Awake, my child,) Indigo ordered. His thoughts pierced her mind like a sharp knife.

She came alert with all of the pain and chill in her body that she wanted to escape.

"All will be well in just a few moments, sweetie," the princess soothed. "I know you hurt, but if you can endure just a few more moments you will feel a lot better."

Promise?

"I promise."

Glenndon chanted something. His voice rose and fell, drifted away, and came close again. When he settled in front of her, she sensed more than saw a bubble of magic around them all. Mostly blue and gold, it had lots of purple lines dancing around, weaving patterns of light and dark, adding to the power of the circle.

Valeria wondered if every dragon alive in all of Kardia Hodos was present in that bubble.

She didn't have long to think about it. Indigo swelled beneath her cheek. First his fur bristled; each hair within his coat doubled in size and trapped air between the tips and his skin— his very pale, almost transparent skin. He extended his wings so that they formed a tent over her and Lillian. The black feathers thinned and spread, looking more like the membranes of a dragon's wings, transparent except for the indigo-colored veins and tips.

But he didn't go all the way to full dragon size. He couldn't fit inside the room if he did. Not even as big a room as this was with the useless extra height to the ceiling.

"Watch Indigo, Val," Glenndon ordered. He had one hand on the flywacket's head and the other on Valeria.

She noted that both the princess and Lillian each touched some part of Indigo and herself.

(Anyone can gather magic from a purple-tip,) Indigo chuckled.

"Watch how Indigo collapses himself, drawing all of the light his pale fur and wings reflect back inside himself," Glenndon said in that strange chanting voice, almost as if he sang the words to an old dance tune she'd heard in the village.

"Watch," Lillian added her command to their brother's.

"Watch and copy, sweetie," the princess said, her voice penetrating the fog of Val's mind better than the others. "Copy what he does. No, don't think about it. Just do it!" She sounded so much like Da when he taught her how to reach deep into the Kardia and draw forth the energy of a ley line, Valeria had no choice but to obey.

Without thinking too hard, she sent her magic deep, deeper, deeper yet through all the levels of stone and thick plank flooring into the dirt and native rock beneath, then outward, seeking a silvery blue line that pulsed with power. She rejoiced at the abundant lines, fat and luscious and eager to bleed off a little of what they were. If she took all she could absorb and then some, she barely touched the amount of energy they offered. She had no fear of exhausting the lines, didn't have to take a dab here and a drip there, never enough to sustain her or feed the dragon spirit within her. It all came to her with a jolt and a heady rush.

Dizzy with excitement she found Indigo's mind, saw how he transformed, even this partial change within the confines of an artificial building. Easy to mimic his actions. The simplest thing in the world now that she knew how and had all the ley lines in the world converging into one vast pool to feed her.

She didn't even mind the grinding and crunching sensation in her bones as they distorted and changed angles. She wanted to laugh at the tickles from sprouting fur.

And then she allowed the dragon spirit to surge forth and let her own mind drift in the background. For a time she'd let the dragon have dominance. But only for a little while, until she healed.

Her throat rumbled with new tones as she drifted to sleep, deeper tones, more authoritative.

Indigo spoke, *(The balance of twins is restored. Now, I need a strong dose of Tambootie.)* Then he disappeared in a cloud of sparkling light.

CHAPTER 40

"STARGODS! I HAD NO IDEA old Lyman was such a strong personality," Glenndon sighed as he plunked down on the floor, his legs no longer capable of holding him up, even kneeling. The cold planks seeped a chill into his butt and down his thighs that felt almost good.

The protective bubble of magic shredded, the purple lines of power remained visible longest. Eventually even they crumbled to dust and fell to the floor. A glittery sheen remained. It too faded quickly, leaving no trace of the magic except . . . expect Valeria was gone and a new black flywacket lifted its head from being tucked between curved front paws. It blinked sleepily and peered back at him with bewildered magician blue eyes.

Lillian held tight to the ball of black fur, crying copiously. Glenndon had no idea where Indigo had gone.

(The balance of twins is restored. There can only be one flywacket at a time, just as there can only be one purple-tip at a time. I can remain the purple-tipped dragon now.) He sounded quite proud of himself as his voice moved farther and farther away.

(I will not desert you, my brother. I am only a thought away from you. Always.)

"Lyman? Who is that?" Linda asked. She looked almost as tired as Glenndon felt, and she had not carried the weight of the spell. Or had she? Their bond was strong. They'd been linked to each other and to Indigo since he'd drawn the spell circle.

"He was the oldest of the old magicians. I surmise, from what I've seen and heard over the years, that he was born a purple dragon, long, long ago. He was the twin who chose to become something else at the age of two."

"He took over the body of a dying child," Linda whispered. "He saved a loving couple the grief of losing a child."

Glenndon had to gulp at that, knowing how many children Linda's parents had lost before they were born. He shared her sadness for a moment.

"But it was Valeria's body that was weak, not her spirit," Glenndon said on a deeply indrawn breath. "I think one of the reasons she was always so sickly and fragile was because of her constant battle to dominate the dragon spirit within her. She didn't have much left over to ever let her body rest and heal."

"If I hadn't just witnessed what I did, and heard Lyman's voice in my head, I don't think I could believe such a strange tale," Linda admitted. She listed a bit as she joined him on the floor. They leaned against each other, perfectly companionable in the silence.

"Glenndon! Where's Val?" Da demanded bursting into the room. The door bounced against the wall and nearly slammed back into him on the rebound. He thrust it aside again and stormed into the room with long strides and deep fear creasing his face. He'd managed to loosen his queue enough to relieve the stark uplift of his eyebrows. Mama always plaited his queue too tightly.

Mama.

"My Lord Jaylor," Linda said, not moving from her post beside him. "Indigo is gone back to the dragons. Valeria is now the flywacket, Lillian's boon companion for as long as needed." She related the necessary information without embellishment or apology.

"Your mother let you go through with this?" Da demanded.

Mama.

"We decided we did not have time for her to respond. Valeria's body was nearly dead. We brought her back in the nick of time. In such a dangerous situation, we thought it best to tell Lady Brevelan after the fact," Linda interceded again.

Da *harrumphed* and grumbled under his breath. "We'd best get that painful chore over with." He stumbled forward, one hand reaching for Lillian, the other to rest upon Valeria's head.

The flywacket sat up and preened, leaning its face into his hand, demanding chin scritches. How many times had they seen Mama's pets do the same?

But this was no pet. This was his sister, Valeria. Already a brightness that had been missing since she was born infused her eyes.

How much of that was Valeria healing and Lyman assuming dominance in their dual spirit?

(Where is the nearest Tambootie tree?) Lyman demanded.

"Um . . . Indigo told me that the Tambootie is no longer filled with nutrients essential to the dragons," Glenndon said apologetically.

"He told you that?" Da asked. His voice finally fell below the level of a roar.

"Indigo tells me many things," Glenndon defended himself. He still didn't have the strength to stand and face his father—his Da—as he should.

"And what do you intend to do about it?" Da asked, new respect in the way he surveyed Glenndon. Then he shifted his gaze to Lillian and Valeria. His countenance softened. "I never would have thought of this as a solution."

"It is only temporary. Make sure Mama knows that," Glenndon pleaded. "We have not robbed her of Val, one of her children. Just . . . I'm not certain how to describe it, but we're sure, that as soon as Val rests in body and mind, she will surge forth and demand her body back."

"If Lyman lets her," Linda said very softly. Glenndon wasn't sure Da had heard her.

He underestimated the Senior Magician.

"Is that what the problem has been all along? Val fighting Lyman for dominance?" Da roared again. High color stained his cheeks.

Glenndon was sure he'd roused the entire palace with that question.

The flywacket pressed itself deeper into the chair, almost hiding behind Lillian, who still cried abundantly into its fur.

"Lyman?" Da asked in that tone of voice that made apprentices quail and master magicians look for places to be elsewhere.

(Er, um, I may have caused the girl a little distress.)

"What's it going to take for you to give up and finally allow yourself to die?" Da reached to grab the flywacket by the scruff of its neck, but Lillian threw herself over the top of the animal.

(This time, I promise I will finally join my ancestors in the void when Valeria is ready to kick me out.) He sounded repentant. Maybe. Not really *(Unless there is another child in need of the breath of life from an old dragon. I've been around so long I am weary of life. But it is a habit that is hard to break.)*

Linda prodded Glenndon's shoulder. *That doesn't ring true. But Lord Jaylor needs to think it is.*

You think he's lying? He sent back to her on a tight and private beam.

She shrugged, mimicking his own gesture. *Everyone lies, some more than others.*

Why did Lucjemm's face flash from his memory to hers?

"I'd like to hear from Valeria," Da said, back to roaring. His eyes narrowed in pain. "Lillian needs to know that her twin still lives."

(Here, Da. Tired. Hungry. Here always. I promised Lily.) The mental voice was very much Valeria, just weak and distant. Distracted.

Da grunted something approaching approval.

(About that Tambootie?) Lyman asked, mentally clearing his throat.

"Not much anywhere near Coronnan City, even if it were still viable," Da said. His eyes narrowed like he didn't trust the old man either.

(Then I need to visit the Well of Life. I shall draw sustenance there for a time.)

Glenndon's attention perked at the mention of his personal quest.

"If you can find it, you are welcome to drink from it, long and deep," Da said. A bite of sarcasm edged his words.

(Come, boy, I'll show you where to look.) The flywacket edged away from Lillian and poised to jump down from the chair. But Lillian threw herself across his back in a new spate of tears.

"You don't move without Lillian," Da ordered. "She and Valeria are inseparable. You will cater to her needs as long as you are here."

"I think we all need to wait on that quest until we've eaten," Linda said, very much in control of herself and taking command of the situation. "My Lord Jaylor, feel free to do what you must to inform Valeria's mother of the state of things while the rest of us prepare to face the day, and what's left of the court. I shouldn't need to remind you that my mother should hear nothing of the night's alarms and dramas from anyone but her husband." She crawled upright, using Glenndon's shoulder as a brace, but nearly sagged with fatigue when she got there.

I'm proud of you, little sister.
Likewise, big brother.

"What exactly are we looking for?" Lucjemm asked.

Linda tried to loosen her clasp of his arm, but his free hand lay atop hers quite possessively.

"If we knew what we were looking for we wouldn't have to look," she returned snappishly. She was tired and uncertain of many things. As much as she wanted to think of Lucjemm as a friend and potential suitor, the memory of him staring blankly while reciting the story of how the ugly snake eggs came into his household kept sliding over more friendly images.

Everyone lies, she reminded herself. *Was that story a lie, a memory, or someone, or* something, *manipulating him?*

Parading about the city with Glenndon, Lord Jaylor, Lillian, and Valeria/Lyman required that she appear as Princess Royale Rosselinda. She had to wear a gown in the latest fashion that she had dictated, two fewer petticoats and a straighter line to the skirt. The yards of fabric snaking around her legs annoyed her almost as much as the way Lucjemm seemed to stake a claim on her.

She just wanted to be left alone so she could sleep.

What had he and P'pa agreed to last night in their private meeting?

And why had P'pa allowed Lucjemm to accompany them on magician business? The king had not allowed her any private time to ask her questions. He seemed more preoccupied than usual.

"I grew up here. Old Baamin, my other tutors, and my classmates became my family," Lord Jaylor muttered. "Now this childhood home is occupied by soldiers." He scanned the protective wall encircling the building. They had walked all the way around the perimeter on the narrow path that separated it from the river.

The old but sturdy plank bridge from Palace Isle to University Isle that they'd crossed an hour ago rose in front of them again.

Glenndon kept his eyes on the ground during the entire trek. The flywacket sniffed everything, more like a dog than a cat. Its ears cocked and rotated every few seconds. Lillian, still weepy and slumped, had no interest in anything but keeping the flywacket in sight, preferably with her hand on some part of it. Thankfully, it kept its wings safely hidden.

Then Lucjemm smiled at her. "Thank you for trusting me with this expedition. I know it involves magic, but since the Council no longer dictates or ignores our laws on a whim, I can fully and openly support your father in this search." He licked his lips, reminding her of the times they had kissed.

She couldn't help licking her own lips in anticipation of the next kiss. Linda relaxed. This was Lucjemm, the real Lucjemm, not the enthralled personality of last night. Then she got lost in his warm, brown eyes. She saw nothing beyond his need to be with her, for whatever purpose, whenever she needed him.

"Da!" Glenndon interrupted them with an imperious shout.

Linda had to shake herself out of her daydream of love and companionship.

"What have you found?" Lord Jaylor stepped from the base of the thick wall to Glenndon's post a few yards ahead, closer to the steep river embankment.

Linda shifted her vision from Lucjemm to what Glenndon saw. Not so difficult a task now as it was yesterday.

Practice makes perfect, little sister.

An entire river of silver blue sprang before her eyes. She'd expected some of the thin webbing he'd shown her earlier, not this massive accumulation. *The Well?* she thought back at him with more than a hint of breathless awe.

We are close. Very close. His gaze turned to the massive wall. "Da, we have to get inside."

Lord Jaylor nodded curtly.

"How?" Lucjemm asked. "The army does not accept visitors lightly." He sounded petulant, as if he'd tried and been rejected.

Hmmmmm. Why would he want to enter the private quarters of P'pa's army, other than to join them? Considering his rank, and his father's influence, he didn't have to join the army. He could raise his own troops (or his father's) and command them himself.

Who did have command of the army gathering at Battle Mound? Jemmarc? Or someone else?

Every time she convinced herself that she wanted to love this young man, be his friend at least, he did or said something that made her think twice about him and his actions.

She separated from him to stand a little closer to her brother.

"We can't just waltz in," Lucjemm said glumly.

Linda and Glenndon looked to each other with a single thought. "Rank has its privileges," they said at the same time.

Lord Jaylor raised his eyebrows. "Of course, the Crown Prince and the Princess Royale may go where they will. Even General Marcelle would not deny either of you entrance." He bowed with a sweeping gesture toward the narrow pedestrian gate—only wide enough for one person to enter or exit at a time—beside the central entrance that was broad enough to admit four mounted soldiers riding side by side, or two sledge steeds pulling a full load of supplies.

Glenndon offered his arm to Linda. She took it. Part of

her regretted leaving Lucjemm's side. The other part of her sighed in relief that he no longer monopolized her attention.

Lucjemm scowled so deeply that a chill stabbed her heart. Only Glenndon holding her hand tightly on his arm kept her from returning to Lucjemm's side.

CHAPTER 41

GLENNDON TRIED on the bland superior countenance his father, the king, achieved so easily. He shouldn't have been surprised that the expression, plus a rather glib Princess Rosselinda talking a blue streak, gave them ready access to the interior of the ancient compound.

Da's face went wistful with memories. Then anger hardened his features. He'd studied here from the age of twelve into his twenties. He should have ruled here when he became Senior Magician and Chancellor of the University; not in the wilderness in wooden buildings thrown together out of necessity to offer shelter to any who fled persecution for the crime of working magic.

Glenndon noted the recently whitewashed stone walls, the steps swept clear of leaf litter, and the pristine iron rails on the mounts to the parapet. The accumulation of dirt in the flagstone mortar around the iron flagpole where the colors of the royal Guard snapped in the light wind seemed out of place. It looked as if no one had set foot in that area for weeks. Or decades.

A mental prod from Da jolted Glenndon out of his musings. "It should be here. Right here!" he insisted, stamping the paved courtyard. "All of the records say over and over again that Nimbulan built this University around the Well," he whispered. "I can see a thickening of the lines but nothing to indicate a center."

Linda suddenly found the pattern of lace on her sleeve

hems fascinating. Glenndon touched her arm to draw her attention back to the problem at hand. "A web with a center. A circle. All webs begin with a circle and grow outward from there." She held up for his inspection the delicate fabric that was more air than thread. It did look akin to a spiderweb.

Circles within circles with cross ribs. Indeed Lyman/Valeria (they really needed to decide what to call the flywacket) walked a circle around the courtyard, Lillian tracing its steps cautiously.

Linda smiled. "A circle."

"What?" Da asked, finally realizing that she knew something.

"Find the circle." Her right toe swished back and forth along a line in the paving stones. A curved line!

Glenndon allowed his eye to follow it around to complete a circle. The stones had been cunningly set into a decorative pattern around a flagpole so that one had to look hard to figure out when they started curving away from the offset rectangles of the primary stones.

"I don't see anything untoward, except perhaps that the king's standard looks a little ragged on the edges," Lucjemm said, peering upward toward the flag that snapped in the hot wind blowing from the western plains toward the Great Bay.

The air smelled of dry dirt, stale smoke, and city waste, without the caress of spring green; a reminder that the crops needed a good storm from the east to soak the land and clear the air.

If Lord Jemmarc truly had a Krakatrice, could they have already begun transforming the land into desert? According to Lucjemm the big ugly snakes were still young. And there were only two.

Or had he lied about the number and their age?

He looked to his Da.

Jaylor lifted his head and sniffed the air. *I have fought and killed half a dozen of the beasts, just this year. Robb and Marcus an equal number—each. Lucjemm may have seen only two very young snakes, but there are more. Many more. They have already begun to change the weather.*

Lillian and Valeria completed their circuit of the courtyard. "Valeria says that something smells wrong," Lillian whispered to Glenndon. Her eyes were still red from crying, but her voice was sound.

"It looks wrong too," Da said. He began walking a spiral inward to the flagpole, making sure he stepped squarely in the center of each paving stone, avoiding the small spacer pieces that allowed the curve in the pattern.

"What is different from your student days?" Glenndon asked.

"Everything and nothing." Da wrenched around to face him. "I need to find a way to fix this." He pointed down, at the center of the circle pierced with the flagpole.

"What, Da?"

"Look. Really look at what lies beneath your feet, boy. I thought I taught you better than to be satisfied with the surface explanation."

"I don't see anything," Lucjemm said, leaning against the flagpole. But he did shift his feet constantly, like the paving scorched him through his elegant courtly boots.

"You can't see what we see," Glenndon muttered. "You wouldn't look even if you knew how."

Linda stepped away from him and closer to Lucjemm. She frowned.

Glenndon didn't have time or attention to deal with her adolescent emotions that shifted and swirled with every thought. He had to figure out what—

"Stargods! Is the flagpole iron?"

"Of course it is," Lucjemm sneered. "Highest grade steel from the palace foundry to withstand exposure to salt air for a long, long time. I believe polishing the pole is a reward rather than punishment among the soldiers."

"No wonder," Glenndon didn't dare finish the statement aloud. Too many mind-blind soldiers loitered around the courtyard and leaned out of windows inspecting the spectacle of the Crown Prince and his sister inspecting the flagpole.

That cursed flagpole. "How long has it stood there?" Glenndon asked.

"It was erected after the Leaving," Da said. He set his steps to spiral outward again, still carefully laying each foot flat in the center of each stone, turning the decorative paving into a ritual maze, not unlike the one at the University next to their home.

"What do you see?" Linda asked, finally controlling her thoughts and focusing.

"Ground and center yourself. Close your eyes. Steady your breathing," he coaxed. She might share everything he knew, and he everything she knew, but she didn't always know what to do with the information.

She obeyed, easily falling into the first stages of a trance.

"Stargods!" She flashed him an image of a churning mass of blue. *Worse than any maelstrom I've ever heard about. Deeper too. Deeper than the surface lines you showed me. No wonder the Tambootie trees aren't thriving. Their roots don't grow deep enough to tap the essential energy. What a mess!*

A mess that's getting ready to blow, Glenndon sent back. "The only thing keeping it from erupting like a volcano is that iron pole. Somewhere on the other side of Kardia Hodos, raw, untamed, wild magic will explode and destroy all in its path," Da whispered as he completed his spiral walk back to the main paving stones.

A smirk of satisfaction crossed Lucjemm's face so quickly Glenndon wasn't sure he'd seen it. A quick glance toward Linda and he knew she hadn't. Maybe he only imagined it. Maybe . . .

He didn't know what to think, only that they needed to retreat to the palace and plan. They needed the collective wisdom of the Circle.

But Da had broken the Circle, just as Father had broken the Council.

They were on their own with this crisis.

And so the beginning of the end of magic is here, beneath my feet. I cannot see this well as Glenndon and my Princess do. I do not want to see it. And yet I sense that something is different beneath the paving stones in this mysterious circle. It is almost as if they roll and shift over wet sand. Unstable.

Whatever is here, whatever is wrong here has upset the

dragons and the magicians. I must make sure their unease continues.

This is where I will bait my trap. This is where I will stage the final battle.

I alone will bring about the end of the domination of mankind by the dragons and their evil minions, the magicians.

I shall miss my friend Glenndon, though my lovely tells me I need no friends but her and her consorts. And Glenndon is a magician through and through. I cannot leave him alive to challenge me for the throne.

And Linda . . . ? My beloved Linda. I must find a way to keep her safe.

CHAPTER 42

GLENNDON LOOKED HASTILY over his shoulder to make sure Linda had not followed as Da led him deep into the tunnels in search of the archives of magical texts. For once in her spoiled life she had obeyed the strict admonition to remain safely in her room and keep Lillian with her. She had obeyed, under vehement protest, only because she had an important task at hand.

Da needed the flywacket to help him with something once they found the hidden room. Lillian would remain separated from her twin for only a short time. Where they journeyed tonight presented danger, a danger Da would not subject Lillian to.

And if Linda stayed behind, then Lucjemm would too. As much as Glenndon liked Lucjemm, thought of him as a friend, he was mind-blind. This chore did not belong to or involve him.

When Glenndon turned his attention back to following Da, keeping his eyes on the small circle of illumination provided by the magical glow ball in Da's hand, Lyman joined them from a side tunnel. He chirruped a greeting and trotted easily ahead of them, nose twitching from side to side, tail up but only half bristled, ears flicking back and forth. Not much would get past his senses unnoticed.

"Not far now," Da said quietly. He followed a faint ley line. This close to the Well it should be thicker and fatter.

The abundance of lines did not mean they gained potency or size.

For a moment Glenndon despaired that they would ever restore magic to its rightful place in Coronnan.

Then he remembered that Da had led him beneath the river and he couldn't breathe. The thought of all that water above them seemed to crush his lungs.

Surely Da would not allow that to happen. He was the most powerful magician in all of Kardia Hodos. He could keep the walls from collapsing. If Glenndon helped him. Could any amount of magic keep the crumbling stones intact? They didn't have enough magic; not with the ley lines running so deep and the Tambootie trees losing potency and the dragons failing to thrive and breed . . .

"Stop stalling, Glenndon. These tunnels have stood for almost a thousand years. They won't collapse now," Da said angrily.

"A . . . a thousand years? What keeps the mortar intact?"

"Old-fashioned technology from the times of the Stargods. Keep up now, we're almost there. Old Baamin showed this place to me once, before he died. The turnings are complicated and hard to find. I'll get lost trying to find you if you don't keep up."

Lyman let out a squeak that could have been suppressed laughter.

Glenndon forced himself to memorize the maze Da entered. Right, right, left, left, ignore six side tunnels which all carried a rune of no exit, then left again and two quick rights that took them almost into a complete circle. His sense of direction faltered. This deep belowground his contact with the magnetic pole dimmed to unreliability.

"Ah, here it is," Da said on a note of triumph.

Lyman pushed his nose against one of the ubiquitous ragged cracks that outlined a door. He snuffed in an affronted manner. He should be able to open the thing.

Da laughed at his indignation. "When you come back to us as your true self, you will be able to open this door, Valeria."

Black fur bristled. Whoever was in that body didn't quite believe him.

Da placed his right hand on the proper stone and pushed. This entrance was meant for magicians with dominant right hands, not kings who preferred the left.

The door creaked and groaned as it swung on its pivot. Glenndon had become used to the noise and the motion. Indeed, if it had been silent, he'd have questioned its placement and the recent lubrication of its hinges. Lyman darted into the room as soon as the opening was sufficient to allow his body to pass, nose twitching wildly.

"Lyman knows what we need. He'll lead Valeria to it quicker than I could find it," Da said. "I hope she remembers when she becomes human again."

Glenndon peeked through the opening in amazement. Da stood near the door, glow ball extended to ignite some form of illumination in the ceiling. The archives in the palace tower were big, three stories of books on shelves around the wall and on freestanding shelves.

This room dwarfed that collection by a factor of four. The shelves stretched inward for half a mile, at least, farther than he could see in the dim light. And it smelled dry. Dry as dust. Not a bit of mold anywhere.

"How are they preserved?" he asked, pushing past Jaylor to scan the titles on the first available shelf to the left of the door.

"Magic, what else?" Da cocked his head and raised an eyebrow with mischief sparkling in his eyes. "We took as much as we could at the Leaving, but that is only a fraction of what remains. Many more texts were lost in the Burning during Nimbulan's last years. The head of the University at the time decided all references to solitary, rogue magic had to be eliminated. A clever journeyman who went rogue rather than follow the man of limited vision hid books before the fire started and stole many others right out of the flames. He added more books over the years as he found them. I believe he put the stasis spell on them. The books waited, and waited, until they were needed again. Old Baamin discovered the place. He and Ambassador Jack renewed the spells. I added my own bit of preservation when Old

Baamin died." Da hung his head in respect for a beloved mentor and friend.

"Strangely, the original rogue magician had a red and blue braid as his signature too. He might have been an ancestor of mine."

"I think Lyman found something," Glenndon alerted Jaylor.

"So he has. I think Lyman may have added texts over the centuries as well. What I want is a letter written long, long ago by Kimmer, a scribe of the South. It meant little or nothing to me at the time. Now it might give us some clues about the Well of Life." Da reached down to take a thin scroll tied with blue ribbon from Lyman's mouth, much like from a dog returning a fetched stick.

"I am entrusting this place to you now, Glenndon. You must make sure its existence remains secret and renew the spells as necessary."

Glenndon gulped in awe of the huge responsibility the Senior Magician and Chancellor of the University, his Da, entrusted to him.

"What does it say?" he croaked around the lump in his throat.

"The light is too dim and the ink faded. I think we need to find some place above, but private, to read it." Da rubbed his eyes like they hurt or were greatly fatigued.

"Let me see if I can make sense of it, since you won't admit that your eyes are aging." Glenndon held out his hand for the scroll. At the same time he conjured a glow ball of his own, bigger and brighter than the one Jaylor held. "We can't get more private than this place."

Da gave it to him without protest, almost with relief that they might be able to decipher it here, where it was protected and they had no audience.

Glenndon unrolled the first bit and scanned the writing. It looked perfectly clear to him, even if the script was old-fashioned. He cleared his throat and began reading the words of a man who had lived in the time of the Stargods. Some believed he might have been one of the three divine brothers. Others dismissed such a blasphemous notion. He was only named for the youngest of the three.

My dearest brothers,

    I have safely returned to my beloved Coronnan and to the clearing.

Glenndon skimmed a long bit about family, love, and travels to places he'd never heard of. Then a phrase caught his attention.

    As for the devastation caused by Hanassa and her delusions of dragonhood . . . The river valley recovers slowly from the raw magical energy poured upon it through the iron pipe. Years, nay, decades must past before the area in and around the delta returns to its former lush productivity.

    I have noted depletion of the ley lines. I do not know if the lines will recover or not. The dragons do not know either. They grieve at the destruction of so many Tambootie trees. They retreat to their mountain lairs, refusing to breed until the trees return to feed them. I believe the element contained within the Tambootie that is essential to the dragons is unknown to modern science.

    Adieu,

    Your loving brother,

    Kimmer

    P.S. the baby does indeed have the O'Hara blue eyes. Tell Mother that her first grandchild looks just like her.

"Da, does—does this me—mean what I think it means?" Glenndon asked. His ability to speak complete sentences deserted him with his disbelief in what he read. It couldn't be. And yet here were the words written by . . .

"I think it does, Glenndon. Kimmer, the simple scribe of the South was one of the Stargods, and they devised the clearing with its protective barrier opened by a song." He sounded shaken.

"And the blue eyes? Many magicians have midnight blue eyes, they seem dominant among us. Does that mean we are all descended from the Stargods?"

"That would seem to be the implication. None of it made sense when I was twenty. Now I'm afraid the rest of the letter tells us the dangers we face. We have to get that iron pole out of the Well. Quickly. But carefully. Who knows what kind of firestorm will erupt with the removal."

"May we sit for a moment?" Glenndon pushed his Da toward a stone bench against a wall between two stacks of shelves. It looked as if it was meant for a casual reader to peruse documents.

Jaylor heaved a sigh of relief as he rested his back and knees. "I don't know if quickly is fast enough to get that pole out. But with all of the energy coursing through it, you and I will not be enough to contain it and push it back where it belongs."

Lyman rubbed his face against his leg and purred. Idly Jaylor reached down and scratched between fuzzy ears. "Yes, I know that Lyman has much knowledge to help. It's raw muscle and joined talents we need."

"You must bring the Circle of Master Magicians here to Coronnan City. Now. As fast as we can summon them and they can transport," Glenndon said.

"I cannot trust all of them. I fear Samlan has taken many of our best and most learned members . . . and set up a rival circle elsewhere. He might sabotage our efforts for sake of revenge."

"Are there journeymen you can promote to master? We need numbers and loyalty more than skill."

Da's eyes lighted. Some of the weariness passed away. "Yes. And the first promotion will be yours. Tonight you must row over to Sacred Isle and in the morning find your journeyman's staff."

Excitement leaped through Glenndon. His hands started shaking the rolled parchment until it rattled. "You know, Da, if I am a journeyman magician, I cannot become king."

"Do you want to become king?" Da arched one eyebrow again.

"No. I never did. I came to my father out of duty."

"I know, son." Da clasped his shoulder with deep affection. "But your presence here will give the king and his daughter time. That is all we truly wanted from you. Time.

Besides, you and I need be the only ones who know of your status."

"But I will be a true journeyman?"

"Yes. And I give you that promotion with pride. You have earned it. And this sojourn in Coronnan will be your journey. Now let's get back to the palace. We have much to do." He rose from the bench. The lights dimmed.

"The letter, Da?" Glenndon asked.

"We leave it here. One more secret among many that magicians must carry in their hearts."

CHAPTER 43

DARVILLE SEEMINGLY STROLLED around the palace grounds. General Marcelle impatiently matched his strides to the king's. "We must maintain the appearance of calm," Darville said out of the side of his mouth. "We are prepared. No need to transfer our concerns to the others."

Fred, Darville's silent bodyguard, moved easily two steps behind and to the right, leaving the king's dominant left hand free to wield the broadsword he wore easily. They were all well armed since the sightings of rebel troops massing on the mainland near Battle Mound. An army that reportedly grew by the hour with peasants who feared magic more than death and retainers ordered to arm and march whether they wanted to or not.

Fred kept one hand on his sword grip, the other fingering a wicked-looking dagger. A dozen throwing stars bristled from his leather jerkin. Darville was willing to bet he wore mail beneath the fine linen of his shirt. He knew the leather thong entwined with his three-strand queue was well knotted and tipped with metal weights to become another weapon.

"I found no trace of the shop with the eggs at the back of Market Isle," Fred said quietly. "I left two men in civilian dress to watch for a return of the owner. In case he departed in a hurry at first whisper of royal Guards on the island."

Darville nodded acknowledgment.

"I have ten squads patrolling the city. They are checking and oiling the latches on every bridge, even the rarely used

ones that look as if they have fallen into disrepair but
haven't," Marcelle replied. His gaze flicked right and left,
taking in details, noting shadows out of place and malinger-
ers.

Darville noted them too as he surveyed the massive gates
at the primary entrance to the royal household.

Fred saw more, he had no doubt. The bodyguard had
trained for nearly two decades to see what others dismissed.

"I want archers in and atop every one of the towers. Keen
observers along with them who can also maintain firepots."

"Yes, Your Grace. I've already ordered firepots taken to
every observation point."

"And summon the FarSeers from the port." He knew the
port authorities secretly kept a team on hand.

"Done, Your Grace, though I haven't heard back from the
Port Master. He may insist on an actual order from you to
admit he has men and women who use magic to see beyond
the horizon."

Their path took them around the training arena. The enclosed courtyard was full of men drilling while waiting their
turn to bout. They honed sword edges, adjusted the balance
of throwing axes, or lifted and thrust spears into bales of hay.
Some practiced throwing battle stars into a target; from either
hand, sideways, even backward.

"I don't see Lucjemm," Darville said. Disquiet made the
space between his shoulder blades itch.

"He requested permission to accompany Her Highness
into the city. I made certain he was well armed," Fred replied.

"Why has Linda gone shopping? I thought she'd want to
be here, training to defend her mother and sisters if we are
attacked." Darville paused, staring at the sword fights without really seeing them.

"Are you certain she is shopping?" Marcelle asked.

"Knowing Her Highness, I suspect she is patrolling in her
own way, checking the state of the city, looking for possible
weaknesses," Fred added. He'd escorted the royal daughters
into the markets often enough to know their routines.

"Of course. She has grown up so much this year I sometimes forget that she has a mind of her own. Miri and Chastet

have become little more than decorations that mask her true purpose."

"Her Highness is more than a girl. A young woman now, a beautiful young woman with thoughts of romance and her own destiny troubling her." Fred looked uncomfortable with that admission.

"Every time she saunters off on her own mission, I wish for my obedient little girl again. She is worrisome."

Fred snorted. "She has never been obedient, except when it suits her purpose."

"And Prince Glenndon? He should be here too," Marcelle added. He looked uncomfortable discussing the princess so intimately.

"I sent my son on an errand." Darville replied.

Marcelle opened his mouth ready with new questions.

"A private errand that does not concern you." At least that was how Jaylor had explained their secret foray into the tunnels deep beneath the city.

"You'll like Market Isle," Linda said gently to Lillian. She kept a firm grip on the other girl's hand as they walked briskly toward the bridge that separated Palace Isle from Ambassador's Isle. Miri and Chastet lingered slightly behind them. Linda pushed aside the guilt that crept toward her heart. She'd neglected her two friends badly these past few weeks, spending most of her time adventuring with Glenndon and Lucjemm.

Her ladies just weren't as interesting as the two young men. Especially Glenndon, who had become closer to her than her sisters since their minds had blended during the magic spell. Lucjemm offered her a chance at settling her eligibility to inherit the crown. If only she could be sure he'd rule beside her and not try to take the crown away from her.

"How do you keep from getting lost?" Lillian asked, trying to turn around and around to get her bearings. A spark of interest flashed across her eyes, the first time they'd brightened since her twin had become a flywacket.

"Easy. The palace is at the center of the islands, the largest of them," Miri said haughtily, as if the question were stupid.

"Market Isle is to the east, closest to the ports on the Bay," Chastet added, equally dismissive of their young charge in a simple homespun dress.

There are no stupid questions, only stupid people who refuse to ask when they need to know something. Papa's words came back to Linda from a long-ago lesson in politics.

"We grew up here." Linda tried to soften Miri's haughty attitude. "We learned the arrangement of the city bit by bit as we explored in wider and wider circles. I bet you can find your way through the forests at your home where we would be totally lost." She glared at her two ladies, ready to send them packing if they continued with this . . . this jealousy.

That stung her. She had neglected them sadly. And now that she needed their help, she wondered if she had the right to ask. Friendship carried a responsibility just like royal blood and loyalty to the principles of fair and honest government.

At the moment she didn't know which responsibility was greater. She leaned toward her friends, hoping their love for each other would carry them into adulthood and through additional responsibilities together.

"I really need your help," she whispered to them. "You are the only ones I can truly trust with this quest."

Miri and Chastet smiled and nodded, seemingly satisfied—for the moment.

They continued on their way, exchanging only idle chatter. Linda ran her fingers around each bridge latch on either end of the span. So far they'd all been recently oiled. She also caught signs of random boards weakened or split. If a heavy troop of soldiers managed to get onto the bridges before they were destroyed by a retreating populace, they'd probably break those boards and get stuck, or fall into the muddy river.

The water looked shallow and sluggish. Shouldn't it be running fast and clear with spring rain and snowmelt?

Before she had time to figure out that question they crossed onto the island that bustled with brightly colored merchant stalls. As usual the permanent storefronts with rich fabric and lace, custom-made boots and shoes, and jewelry lined the cobbled street closest to the bridge leading to the homes of the wealthy nobles, ambassadors, and royals.

Miri and Chastet lingered in front of a display of fine silk damask in rich jewel tones. Another day Linda would have been tempted as well.

"We need to find the eggs," Linda whispered to her ladies and Lillian.

"The produce stalls are that way," Chastet said, waving toward the west, the embankment closest to the boats bringing food from the interior of the continent. It was empty today. The few stalls left open had only a few wilted vegetables and no breads. Most of the merchants had closed up shop hours ago. A number of them looked dismantled.

Further evidence that something was wrong with the farms and the river.

"Not the kind of eggs you can eat!" Linda protested, reluctantly returning her gaze to the ladies and Lillian. "These are special eggs, magical eggs, about so big." She put her two fists together, one atop the other. Briefly she described the red and black monstrosity Lucjemm had showed her.

Miri's and Chastet's eyes went wide with wonder and fear. Did Linda see a glimmer of pride in their expressions as well? Pride that she trusted them with this important mission.

"We need to spread out and look in each and every stall, especially toward the ports. The eggs come from the east, by ship."

Her ladies hesitated before they nodded agreement. Lillian studied the cobbles.

"Whatever you do, do not touch the egg if you find one. Come find me instead."

"H . . . how will we find you?" Miri asked. Her voice was so low Linda had to strain to hear her.

Linda hadn't thought about that. She'd gotten so used to *knowing* where Glenndon was, that she assumed everyone could find anyone just thinking about it.

Think! she told herself. *Think like P'pa. Or Glenndon.*

Drawing a deep breath for courage she looked at all three of her companions, except Lillian, who still refused to meet her gaze. "Miri, you take Lillian. She has a magical talent so she can seek me, mind to mind. Chastet, you come with me. I can find Lillian's mind. If worst comes to worst, we'll meet back here when the Temple bells ring for afternoon prayer."

Lillian shook her head. "Don't leave me, Highness," she pleaded, eyes still firmly on the ground.

"We have to do it this way. We don't have time to search the entire island if we stay together. We have to finish this today and report back to the king."

"I'll take care of you, Lillian. I promise." Miri took the girl's hand gently. "And when we get back, I'll let you try on some of my gowns. We're almost of a size, I'm sure we can find something that fits you that you can wear to court." She fixed Linda with a telling gaze and turned away, toward the lesser stalls on the way to the exotic portside establishments. "Does anyone call you Lily? You're so pretty and fair, I think that fits you better than Lillian."

"I like Lily. My twin calls me that. But no one else does. Do you have old gowns you aren't wearing anymore in lavender and pale green? Val likes darker purple, and no other shades, but I like to mix . . ."

"Looks like we've been dismissed," Chastet muttered.

"Looks to me like she's taking better care of our troubled guest than I ever did," Linda muttered with regret. "Come. We have to find those eggs before afternoon prayer."

Two hours later Linda and Chastet stood before the same gaudy tent Lucjemm had taken her to. They'd approached from the south, having found nothing resembling the red and black egg. Miri and Lillian came into view two alleys north. Miri shook her head in disappointment.

They all looked and acted tired, dusty, and much in need of rest and refreshment.

"We saw some porcelain and jeweled decorations in blues and greens and white," Miri reported. "Nothing like what you described."

"I smelled no magic in the eggs we saw," Lillian added, but she refused to look up. She was hiding something.

Now was not the time to ask. Too many people jostled them. Any one of them could be paid to eavesdrop. Had she seen that short pudgy man in shades of clashing yellow and orange before?

Linda frowned as she scanned the jumble of odd wall hangings, ornaments, bits and pieces of metal, beautifully sculpted but of little, or at least little discernible, use. The wooden casket with soft lambswool lining was nowhere in evidence. Neither was the merchant who offered the diverse collection for sale.

"Excuse me," Linda called, hoping someone, anyone, hid behind a black and red tapestry at the back of the tent. "Is anyone here? Do you have any exotic eggs for sale?"

"Sold 'em all," came a quavering and elderly voice. "Young lord bought all three. Every time I have one of those cursed eggs for sale, he buys 'em. Pays more than they're worth."

Linda grew cold all the way past her bones to her stomach and heart.

CHAPTER 44

"**D**A, WHAT AILS YOU?"

Jaylor roused from the miasma of fatigue to focus on Glenndon. He stumbled on the last step before the landing at Glenndon's room. "I'm missing something," he mumbled.

"Besides Mama?" A wry chuckle escaped Glenndon as he held Jaylor's arm with one hand and opened the pivoting door with the other.

Jaylor didn't want to admit how tired he was, or how grateful for Glenndon's supporting arm. "I always miss your mother, even when she's only a half mile away." He leaned heavily against the wall while Glenndon closed the door and straightened the tapestry over it.

"So what are you missing?" Glenndon rounded on him, arms crossed firmly across his chest while he inspected Jaylor.

"Not sure. Something flitting around the edges of my awareness, like a moth battering against a lighted window, then disappearing when I go to investigate."

"Know the feeling."

"Something about the iron flagpole."

"We'll figure it out once I complete my quest and have my staff. But there is more wrong with you than an uneasy feeling." The boy shoved his shoulder under Jaylor's arm and led—half carried—him toward the bed.

"I'm just a little tired. You should eat and rest before your quest tonight." He negotiated the two steps up to the bed.

Were they truly unstable or was that just his knees shaking? Then he gratefully sank into the soft mattress.

Stargods, he wished Brevelan was here to soothe him with her quiet songs and hearty broths. She made it so much easier to think through troubling problems.

"When did you sleep last?" Glenndon asked, too discerning for his years. "Or eat for that matter?"

"I . . . I don't quite remember. I'm not truly hungry, just empty."

"Your pulse is racing and unstable. Rest while I order food. Then you sleep. Then I bring in Maisy. She used to be a midwife, now she's a seamstress. What she is, and always has been, is your spy."

"You're getting too observant and used to princely authority," Jaylor muttered.

"Practicing for when you retire and I take over the University." Glenndon flashed a cheeky grin.

"Looking forward to that day. Do you think the palace kitchen can come up with something as homely as yampion pie?"

"They keep it on hand for me. Not as good as Mama's but the best thing for restoring a body after throwing a big spell."

"And . . . and since your mama isn't here to object, a chicken?"

"Of course. Perhaps some slices of wild boar as well?"

"Wake me when it comes. And don't let me sleep too long. I need to be ready . . ." He wasn't sure if he finished that sentence or not before sleep claimed him.

Can we fly? Valeria asked the dragon she shared this strange new body with.

(I have been with you since the beginning,) Lyman reminded her.

She winced mentally. He'd always been in the back of her mind, but she hadn't known he was there. Not really. Just sort of an uneasiness whenever she thought too hard or got too tired to sleep.

But slept she finally had, long and hard, until she awoke

in the strange library room underground. She remembered nothing of the hours that had passed since the . . .

(Transformation.)

I know you can read my mind since we are one mind now. But can we fly? She groomed her right front paw while she waited for a response. They had performed the task of finding that strange letter for Da and Glenndon. Lyman had needed her help sniffing it out. No one but Lillian expected anything more of them at the moment.

I have always longed to fly. I dream of it sometimes.

(I have not flown since . . . since I was little more than a dragonet. I do not know that I remember how.)

Oh, she sighed with disappointment.

(I too have often longed for the freedom of the skies.)

Can we try? Just a short flight to begin. We don't want to get too tired and be stranded far from the palace. And Lillian. Valeria wished mightily that Lillian could join them in this adventure.

(I know a place to launch into an updraft. That will help,) Lyman agreed.

Valeria allowed him command of the cat body, and they scampered up and around and along corridors until they found a door propped open with a much-folded lace-edged handkerchief covering the lock so it would not latch. For half a moment Valeria longed to stroke the fine linen and dainty lace.

Such luxuries belonged to a princess, not to the humble daughter of a magician who spent most of her days working in her mother's garden, getting her hands filthy and giving her nails ragged quicks.

(Our princess and her adventurous brother have made entry easier for Indigo, and now us,) Lyman said.

At last Valeria had an excuse to rub her whiskers against the soft cloth. She sniffed the handkerchief to see who had handled it last. *Lucjemm was with them.*

(That boy is everywhere the princess is!)

I do not like him. He smells of lies. Why does the king trust him with his daughter?

(As a very young man, many generations ago, I had a tutor who quoted a very old text. 'Keep you friends close, your enemies closer.')

Valeria had to think about that for a moment. *Know thy enemy. Da says that a lot in strategies class.*

(You are very young to be taking strategies. Isn't that class reserved for journeymen?)

Who said I was a student of strategies? Doesn't mean I haven't listened in.

(Then use your excellent brain to open this door and keep the lock block in place.)

Valeria had to study the problem. *I don't think there is a way.*

Lyman heaved a heavy sigh; their entire body rippled with the expulsion of air. *(Very well then. We shall have to return by a ground entrance or an open window.)*

Thinking together, they used extended claws to pull the door open just enough to insert an entire paw, and then squeeze their body through a narrow opening. The handkerchief fluttered downward onto their back. Valeria luxuriated in the way the silky fabric caressed their fur for a long moment before shaking it free so that it landed off to the side, away from foot traffic. She didn't want it to get any dirtier than necessary.

The long spiral staircase looked strangely familiar.

(I have been here before. Many centuries ago. You have not.)

In her own body, Valeria would have trudged up those endless stairs, one by one, her feet dragging heavily, her lungs laboring. Actually she never would have attempted the stairs, insisting Da or Glenndon carry her.

(That is why you never grew stronger. You never tried small steps, only big ones that exhausted you. So you never tried at all.)

A bit of guilt stung Valeria. *Everyone expected me to keep up, all the time. When I couldn't, they kept pushing harder until I had to insist on giving up before I got sick.* That didn't sound exactly right, but close enough.

(We can't fly if I can't trust you to keep going.)

Oh. But I do want to fly, even if only a short way.

(Short we shall keep it.)

I smell Indigo.

(He was here with the princess and her escorts. He marked the way for us, almost like he knew we would come.)

Dragons don't regard time like people. They let it flow forward and back. We plod along a straight line, ignoring all other possibilities.

(Who told you that?)

You did. In a dream. I dreamed of flying, she replied on a chuckle.

(I have been chained to human bodies for so long I forgot that. Now I have the chance to be a dragon again. If only for a few moments.) Lyman stopped beside a narrow door leading off a narrower landing. He stood on hind feet, placed paws on the wooden panels, and leaned all of their weight against the portal. A latch clicked and then the door popped outward, swinging easily.

Before it could swing shut again they leaped through and onto a flat roof that overlooked a rose garden two stories below. Palace towers rose around them like so many giant trees, stretching toward the sky. Some bore conical roofs, others open parapets with crenellated barriers.

Valeria gasped at how high they were, higher than she'd ever climbed in a tree. But her view of the city and the Bay was blocked by tall buildings and those towers.

Lyman lifted their head to sniff the breeze. Valeria smelled grass and plowed fields and the brackish river. The land smelled dry. Had they had any rain recently?

(We fly west,) Lyman said. Their whiskers twitched, helping them judge the strength and direction of the breeze. *(Warm, off the plains. We'll have a good updraft.)*

Shouldn't the air move inland from the Bay? she asked, puzzled by all the weather lessons Mama had taught her and Lillian.

Rather than answer, Lyman stretched their wings. The air caressed the sensitive flight feathers. Their feet didn't want to stay anchored, so they took five running steps toward the eaves, growing lighter, more buoyant with each stride until the updraft caught them just as they stepped off into . . .

Nothing.

The land fell away below them. Lyman found a path around a sand-colored tower with a red roof, then over the enclosed training arena where men bashed each other with blunted swords, and up over the palace wall.

Higher and higher he flew until the delta islands shrank to dull dots surrounded by the river sparkling in the afternoon sunlight.

Isn't this far enough? Valeria asked as the river bent to the north. Fields of bright green stretched below, on and on until they faded to dull brown at the horizon a long, long way away.

(Glory in the wonder of flight before your hesitation and fear takes control of your mind. Enjoy yourself. Let me take charge. This may be my last flight ever.)

I'll make sure we fly again before we transform back to my body.

(We may not have time. Time is a wonder, and a menace.) He paused for a long moment, flapping their wings when the updraft shifted. They rose up to catch another and glided onward.

I don't know, Lyman. We need to go back. Now.

(Just a few moments more, little one. Trust me.)

Valeria wasn't sure about that. This seemed too risky. She didn't want to collapse with fatigue so far from the palace and help. She looked for a good place to land where she could rest. A hilltop maybe to make launching into flight easier?

What's that? Valeria pointed toward an array of colored tents and banners spread out behind one of the rolling, rounded hills.

(The enemy.)

We have to go back!

(I can't. I've stretched our strength too far.) They dropped awkwardly, faster and faster, as the pull of the land overcame the wind's ability to hold them aloft.

I was afraid of this. I'm never going to trust you again.

They stumbled and rolled when they met the crisp meadow grasses.

Sharp pain jolted up their front paws to their shoulders and spine. Valeria sighed at the return of familiar aches. Lyman remained strangely silent.

Nothing hurt as long as she lay still. The tiniest movement sent spasms of sharp pain the length of her spine.

"Well, what do we have here? A bit of magic that must be

destroyed? Or a spawn of dragons that threatens my soldiers?" a young man of noble bearing sneered as he strode
from the encampment toward them. A thick black snake
draped about his neck, flicking its red, forked tongue at them,
glaring at them through beady red eyes. As it writhed to stay
in place, three pairs of leathery wings unfurled and refolded.

A bubble of magic littered with black and red sparkles
enclosed both the snake and the young man. No mundane
weapon could penetrate that shield to harm either of them.

"Yes, my lovely." The young man stroked the snake with
affection. "The magic in the cat's blood will feed you well.
We will grow stronger when you feast upon it."

We have to run. We have to warn the king!

(We can't move. Our hind legs aren't working right.)

CHAPTER 45

"WHERE'S VALERIA?" Glenndon asked Old Maisy after eating both his meal and Da's. Jaylor seemed asleep for the rest of day. He needed it.

The venerable seamstress sat in a pool of sunlight beneath the window of the family sitting room. Her needle flicked in and out of a frothy mint green material with lavender trim making nearly invisible stitches. Her chair rocked to the timing of a brisk dance tune, setting the pace and spacing of her needle.

"Went off with you. I daresay it's not my place to keep track of all the mortal souls that run in and out of the palace, appearing out of nowhere without warning. Constant interruptions to my sewing. I'll never finish this dress in time for court tonight, and your lovely sister Lily will have to be humiliated into wearing that plain homespun. A great shame it is. A lady like the Senior Magician's daughter not being able to hold her head up among her peers . . ."

"Maisy," Da interrupted with a thundering echo behind his voice that demanded attention. "Maisy, Valeria came ahead of us some time ago. We presumed she'd be here, with her twin, Lillian. Those two are never far apart. Didn't you leave any food for me, Glenndon?"

Glenndon shrugged out of habit and rang the servant's bell.

"And don't I know it, my lord. So alike and yet so different. Pretty and delicate, beautiful and full of life. Ain't neither one of them complete without the other. Midwifed them both and despaired at saving the little'un let alone her mother. Torn between my duty to both the babe and my lady. Figured the babe that survived and her older brothers needed their mam more'n you all needed a sickly baby without my precious Brevelan to take care of them. But miracle of miracles Old Lyman came to the rescue and took the decision away from me. He saved Val for us all. Special child she is. Beyond special . . ."

"Maisy, where are my sisters?" Glenndon cut through her patter.

"Well, young sir, Your Highness, or is that high and mighty . . ."

"Maisy!" he yelled, drawing on every trick his father had taught him.

She closed her mouth with an audible snap.

"Where are the twins?"

"Lady Lillian went off with Her Highness and her ladies; said something about Market Isle and eggs. Though why the Princess Royale should be shopping for eggs when there's ample kitchen staff to do it I don't know. Speaking of which, I told the scullery boy to bring a plate of eggs and meat and yampions when you rang the bell again. Should be here in just another minute or so."

Glenndon shook his head with fearful understanding. Linda had gone to seek out the importers of the Krakatrice eggs. "I have to go after Linda," Glenndon said. Instinctively he reached for his sister's mind and met a wall of cold fear.

"What about Valeria?" he asked Maisy again.

"I . . . I don't know," Maisy admitted reluctantly. Her needle paused in midstitch and a tear welled up in the corner of her eye. "I can't find her in my mind. Haven't been able to since she transformed into . . . into that thing." She gulped and returned to her task. She plied her needle in an uneasy rhythm that matched her rocking body and her heartbeat.

Glenndon reached out for the familiar pattern of Valeria, making an effort to define the search minus the aftershadow of Lillian's personality superimposed upon her twin.

Another cold wall of fear rose up and slammed him between the eyes. He recoiled, stumbling backward as if slapped.

"Where?" Maisy demanded.

"West and south. I can't get a firm location. She's too scared to let me find her."

"Scared to thoughtlessness or scared you will find her and come after her and endanger yourself?"

"Both."

"Glenndon, can you transport in, grab her, and get back here as fast as you can? I'm too weak and hungry to do it safely," Da asked, clearly shaken.

"Don't like that spell," Maisy clucked her tongue and rocked faster. "Tricky it is. And dangerous. But sometimes . . ."

"Linda?" Glenndon asked. "How much trouble is she in? Should I go after her first?" Glenndon paused a moment to clear his thoughts of Valeria's terror. Hard to do. Then Linda's aura rose up bright and shiny in his mind, reassuring him of her safety. Her concern was for Valeria and what she had learned.

"Linda is on her way home with much haste. She has bad news. Her ladies come more slowly with Lillian," he told Maisy. "Don't let her go anywhere else when she returns."

"Fine. I'll have Fred meet her and escort her home. You go get your other sister," Jaylor ordered, his voice rising to his customary roar as he grabbed a plate piled high with food from a boy in servant livery who barely had time to knock on the door before being dismissed.

"What are you waiting for, boy?" Maisy asked. Her chair rocked harder and faster. "Can't let my little Valeria get hurt 'cause you are too timid to go rescue her."

"Are we all your personal possessions?" he asked.

"No. You're all my special babies. Children of Brevelan and Jaylor. The royal ones too. All my special babies. Watched over every last one of you for the Circle I did. Now git afore I take a paddle to your backside."

"Yes, ma'am." A half chuckle helped him clear his mind and pinpoint the source of Valeria's fear.

A wide, grassy meadow, dry and turning brown for lack

of spring rain, rolling mounds with drooping trees on the crest. Battle Mound, where he and Fred had first arrived. Row upon row of tents and armored men. . . . Where were Father's spies? Hadn't they watched Valeria fall into their midst?

Or maybe they hadn't known what to do with a flying cat appearing in the sky.

Indigo, can you get me a little flaming diversion? He knew the purple-tipped dragon hadn't taken himself very far away. He just didn't know where his friend hid.

(I can try. Without the Tambootie my flames are weak.)

Anything you can give me will help. I just need their attention away from Valeria for ten heartbeats.

(That I can manage!)

Glenndon closed his eyes to clear his mind of everything but his memory of Battle Mound and the heart of Valeria's fear. The moment he had a firm image of her flywacket body cringing away from something . . . awful, he sent himself to her side, one heartbeat before he left the security of the palace walls.

He opened his eyes to the reality of a large black snake, with six leathery wings, coiled and ready to strike with bared fangs that dripped venom.

A mighty roar right over the top of Valeria made the snake look upward. It hissed at the dragon-shaped shadow that flew out of the blinding glare of the sun.

A ball of flame shot downward igniting the tents and sere grass.

Men yelled and ran, arms flailing in panic.

(Run, little one, run!) Indigo called to her.

Valeria yanked her mind free of the snake's hypnotic power.

Lyman! she screamed at her companion.

Silence. He was still enthralled by red eyes and flicking tongue.

"Valeria," Glenndon whispered.

She forced control of the cat body away from Lyman and swiveled her head to the left despite the sharp pains down and back up her spine. There! In the shadow of the only tree within the army camp, she caught a whiff of Glenndon.

Then smoke filled her nostrils and near blinded her.

A wisp of air across her whiskers told her that the snake's tongue flicked again in her direction, tasting the distance between them. The snake's need for blood overcame its natural fear of fire. Or did it welcome the spreading flames as more fuel for its growing hunger?

She saw a ripple of muscle along its entire length.

With every bit of effort she contained she stretched her wings and used her front legs to pull her out of the snake's reach.

Another push and she was in Glenndon's arms.

"Stargods! When did you get so heavy?" he muttered as he staggered.

She risked a look back. The snake firmed its coils, head swaying, tongue flicking.

Easier to close her eyes than risk immobility beneath its gaze again.

Lights sparkled around her. Time stopped. Bright coils of life enfolded her even through closed eyes. They reminded her of the awful snake. She wanted to look away, find safety in cool darkness.

(*Look, look carefully, my child,*) a feminine voice called to her. A soft, protective voice that loved her and wished only the best for her.

She opened her mind and looked at all the lives that touched her own: Lillian in soft, velvety lavender and green, Glenndon in rich royal rose gold, Da in a braid of bright red and blue, Mama's gold and rust and brown, Indigo in brilliant purple.

And herself.

Gentle violet shimmered around her.

(*You have found your own aura, little one. Now you are ready to become yourself.*)

What does that mean? I have always been myself.

(*Have you truly?*)

And then the world crashed around her as Glenndon crumpled to the plank flooring amid the stone walls and lush furniture of the palace.

Old Maisy caught her as she fell from her brother's arms. Valeria relished the security and love of the old woman for a moment, gathered strength and courage from her.

"Tells us what we need to know," Maisy crooned to her between phrases of an old lullaby.

The one you call Lucjemm. He leads the army that will march toward the city at dawn. The snake commands him.

"I know, I know, baby. But it is not yet time to reveal this to your Da or the king."

Who knew the old woman could be strong enough to squeeze the breath out of her?

If she bit and clawed her way free Maisy would drop her. She couldn't risk that. No more hurts. She'd had enough of hurting.

CHAPTER 46

"GIVE IT UP OLD MAN and get out of that body! Leave it to the little one so she can heal!" Old Maisy growled through clenched teeth.

"*S'murghit*, Maisy, what are you doing?" Linda shouted as she dashed from the corridor into the parlor. She wrapped her hands around the old woman's throat, pressing on her windpipe, just as she'd been taught by Fred to disable an attacker.

Old Maisy gagged and released her fierce grip on the flywacket. Glenndon dove to catch the heavy black cat. They both looked around dazed.

"What is the meaning of this?" Jaylor roared from the doorway, blocking everyone's exit. He looked tired and drawn but alert and very angry. There were no tunnel entrances from this suite. "Maisy, you have been loyal to me and mine since before Glenndon was born," Jaylor continued shouting. As if he didn't care who heard.

Linda kept her hands on the old woman's throat, but released her pressure on the vital airway. Suddenly, the seamstress who had been with the royal family for as long as she could remember deflated into a smaller woman, nearer P'pa's age than the bossy middle-aged one she'd projected. She smelled of an exotic, aromatic spice and towering woodlands. Where had the robust, older gabble-mouth who always smelled of fabric and dyes and fresh laundry blowing in the wind gone?

Maybe Linda should ask where she had come from.

"Maisy, I'm waiting for an explanation," Jaylor said, tapping his foot. His hands wove an intricate pattern and his fingertips began to glow.

"Valeria says there is a connection between Maisy and Lyman," Glenndon wheezed, still lying on his back with Valeria sprawled on his chest. The huge black cat spread her front legs to encircle his neck, like a child clinging to a trusted caregiver. Something about her hind end looked wrong, and one wing drooped half-unfurled.

"Well, Maisy?" Jaylor demanded. He nodded to Linda to release her prisoner.

Reluctantly, Linda lowered her hands and stepped away from the woman. She stared at her hands in fascinated horror, wondering if she really could have taken a life. She trained nearly every day to do just that with a sword.

The purpose of her training became terribly real.

She shuddered and pushed the self-defeating loop of thoughts aside. Glenndon and Valeria needed her. She had to help them.

Maisy glanced at Jaylor from beneath lowered eyes. Linda sensed that she weighed and assessed her story even as she opened her mouth to explain herself.

"Loved the old man I did when I were young, he masquerading as a journeyman magician in Lord Jemmarc's father's household, when he was just a minor landholder, subject to Lord Krej. Told me his history, Lyman did. Born a dragon, living out the centuries in different bodies. Helping, he said. Giving life to children who was dying." She paused for breath, uncharacteristically, but before anyone could interrupt the tale she continued.

"I were a serving girl with a bit of magic in me. Eyes and ears for Lord Jaylor when no one else trusted me. He was in and out of the household within days. Didn't know why then, still don't. But love him I did. Broke my heart he did." She paused, drawing in a deep, shuddering breath that set her entire body trembling. Then she steadied. Her body seemed to flash into old age with twisted, arthritic fingers. "When Lord Jemmarc's eye went a-roving, I had no reason to hold back and gave myself to him, seeing as Lyman didn't need me no more. Never truly did." She straightened and resumed her familiar stout figure. Who knew which illusion was true.

Linda felt deep in her gut that the ancient crone was the disguise, meant to gain sympathy for her frailty.

Cunning as a dragon, Glenndon echoed her thoughts. *She probably learned that trick from Lyman.*

Linda sensed that Glenndon shared his thoughts with Jaylor. The Senior Magician gave a half nod of agreement.

"What does loving an ancient magician who is really a purple-tipped dragon have to do with trying to strangle my daughter?" Jaylor asked.

Maisy's gaze wandered around the room, fixing everywhere but on the Senior Magician. Finally she allowed her eyes to linger on Glenndon and the flywacket.

Linda knelt beside them, one more layer of protection for poor Valeria.

"I knew he'd taken up residence in little Valeria's body. You'd recalled me to the clearing by then, to cure Glenndon's putrid sore throat. The dragons called me they did. Said I had to cure their special golden child. They couldn't and no one else quite knew how. Banished the fever I did but couldn't fix his scarred throat. Took our little Linda to do that. She's a good healer that one, needs training though. You didn't need me to watch Jemmarc, so I gave up my son to him. Mindblind he were as a babe. Not so sure about that now."

She's Lucjemm's mother? Linda shot to Glenndon.

An interesting wrinkle.

"I knew what was happening to little Valeria. Knew by the shadows beneath her eyes. Only knew it 'cause he'd told me his history. Shapechanger and trickster as well as flitting from body to body as he needed. Knew it in my soul as well as my mind." Maisy looked ready to shrink again. But this time defeat and disappointment weighed her down instead of illusion.

Linda ran her hand along Valeria's spine, trying to find the source of her awkward position.

"Can you take her into your lap?" Glenndon whispered, his voice cracked with a suppressed cough. "She's too heavy on my chest."

Linda shifted to sitting cross-legged on the floor, an

undignified position her mother would sorely reprimand her for. She didn't care.

Between the two of them, she and her brother levered the huge cat body into her lap, leaving the disposition of the royal seamstress to Jaylor.

Glenndon drew three huge breaths, restoring his lungs. Then he let his eyes cross as he breathed more normally, deeply, on a count of three, until his eyes glazed in the first stage of a trance. Then he ran his hands over the black fur, not quite touching. Long strands of fur rose to meet his palm.

"At first I thanked Lyman for saving our little girl." Maisy finally looked up into Jaylor's face, begging him to understand her dilemma. "But then little Valeria kinda woke up and fought him for control of her mind and body. Most times she succeeded, but it cost her. You know how frail she is. You know what it costs her to work any magic at all, and she does it for both herself and her twin . . ." She stopped abruptly at the revelation of that secret.

"So that's why . . ." Jaylor's face lit up with understanding. "But that doesn't explain why you tried to kill my daughter!" He stepped closer to the seamstress, eyeing the sharp scissors in her apron pocket.

"He's too stubborn, too greedy for life. Oh, no, not Master Magician Lyman. He won't let go of anything. Saved himself from death over a hundred times by stealing someone else's body. Justified it by saying there was always one more chore for him, one more up and coming magician what needed mentoring, one more anything, any excuse at all not to give up and let go of this life like any respectable human. But he ain't human. He's a dragon. Has a different sense of time and death, he says. Knows when the time will be right and it ain't come yet. And now he nearly got our girl killed because *he* wanted to fly again. Greedy old man."

She barely paused for breath before she started up again. Linda was still trying to catch up with everything she'd said.

Then she knew that the babble-mouth was the woman's weapon to keep people off balance, to control the situation and always come out atop her own agenda, whatever that was.

"Well, I decided he'd done enough harm. Time for him to

give up and let our little girl manage on her own." Old Maisy clamped her mouth shut and seemed determined never to open it again.

Not likely. Soon she'd find something else to control with an overlong spate of words.

"Linda, help me, I'm no healer," Glenndon croaked out. "You are. You've already worked one miracle on me, now I need you to do the same for my sister."

"What?" Jaylor demanded kneeling beside them. He placed his palms atop Glenndon's hands.

"Dislocated back hip from an unplanned landing. See, I told you Lyman was doing the child more harm than good," Maisy said. She should have said something before she tried to kill the flywacket.

"Can you pop it back in, son?" Jaylor asked, half a smile on his face.

"There is nothing funny about this. Can't you see she's in dire pain?" Anger burned through Linda's veins.

"Glenndon." Jaylor ignored her outburst. "Do you remember when you were five and tried to fly from the top of a Tambootie tree just like your dragon friend Indigo?"

"Barely," he ground out. His hands trembled with the effort of drawing pain out of Valeria and dispersing it through his own stronger body.

Linda's arms and back ached in sympathy. She wanted to lend her own strength to him by adding her hands atop Jaylor's. The effort of holding Valeria still, comforting her, and keeping her mind from closing down was too much. She sensed Lyman gleefully trying to take control. Linda couldn't let him.

Gathering vague memories and skills from Glenndon, she sent a mental probe to Valeria and helped her build a wall against invasion by the ancient dragon mind, and against the pain. Stone by stone, fitting this jagged edge into a gap, lining up smoother lines, making a barrier solid against the pain, against the wispy wiggles of Lyman, never letting him penetrate.

"Well, pop the joint back into place," Maisy said imperiously, as if they were all stupid and blind and selfishly ignorant.

"Hold her still, Linda?" Glenndon said, more a question than an order.

"Doing my best." She warded off another stabbing attack from Lyman to break through her wall.

(I'm only trying to help,) he insisted.

"No, the friggin' Tambootie you aren't," Maisy snarled. "Sit back and be quiet, like you're supposed to. When I get my hands on your rotten old mind, I'll give you enough pain to think about to keep you quiet for the rest of your unnatural life."

The attacks stopped. Linda reared back her head from the sudden release of pressure. But the sharp stabs of Valeria's damaged muscle, tendon, and bone increased. She reinforced the wall, numbing points here and there that burned unnaturally.

"Glenndon, place your hands firmly on the top of the leg bone," Jaylor instructed.

Glenndon looked at him in dismay.

"Feel the knob, right there." Jaylor guided their hands to the odd bump jutting out of Valeria's flank.

Glenndon nodded in apprehension. "I remember how much it hurt when Mama did this to me."

"Think harder about how much better it felt immediately afterward," Jaylor said. His eyes started to glaze over as he looked deeper into the flywacket, probing beneath fur and skin to muscle and bone.

Glenndon looked deep into Linda's eyes. "We can do this, sister. It's not a healing spell, just simple bone manipulation."

His reassurance flooded her with warmth and well-being. She did her best to pass it on to Valeria.

The flywacket squirmed in apprehension.

"Hold her *still*," Jaylor demanded.

Linda firmed her hold on body and mind.

Glenndon pushed. Jaylor pulled the hind leg.

Valeria screamed, something that sounded halfway between a cat and a dragon. The sound erupted from Linda's throat.

Pop! Grind!
Slither!
Slither?

The bone snapped back into place. Instant relief made Linda sag over Valeria's body. Her charge whimpered as a sharp ache took over and the stabbing pain evaporated.

"She'll be sore for a couple of days. She needs a real healer to get in there and warm the muscles into healing faster. Your Highness, Princess Linda, you can do it, little bits at a time, cain't have you wearing yourself out too quick. You ain't trained to do it. We cain't put poor Valeria's back half in a sling like you can with a dislocated shoulder. Though I believe rest and a hot posset will help her more'n anything," Maisy said. Her voice was suddenly deeper, the uneducated mangle of pronunciation dissipating. "I remember the time Nimbulan fought off an entire army with nothing but magic. He was chief Battlemage for a noble then. Don't remember his name. The fight near wore the man to a pulp, but he persevered. Needed six yampion pies and near a barrel of ale afore he could sleep, then sleep he did for three days . . ."

"Maisy?" Jaylor asked the old woman. He kept one hand on Valeria's hip, preventing her from moving it too soon. The other he raised, palm out, fingers curved, as if gathering information through his hand.

"Yes, my lord?" She looked to Jaylor, but her eyes didn't focus. Her voice sounded deeper, echoey with portent, as if coming from a vast distance of time and space, two voices entwined.

Empty, Valeria said weakly. *I feel so empty. And cold. I need Lillian. My twin will keep me warm. My twin will fill the empty half of me.*

Linda tightened her grip on the cat body, suddenly very afraid for all of them.

"Lyman's in Maisy's body," she whispered. "What do we do now?"

CHAPTER 47

"**B**REVELAN, I AM SO SORRY I didn't tell you this earlier," Jaylor said quietly into his scrying bowl. He scrubbed his face with weariness, anxious to find a bed, too worried about his daughters to sleep, concerned about Glenndon's solitary quest tonight.

"What's done is done. Bring her home. Now," Brevelan replied. "I need . . ."

"I know, dear heart. But I can't. Not tonight. If I tried a transport spell now, we'd lose both of us in the void. Forever."

"Glenndon can do it . . ."

"Glenndon is on his journeyman quest tonight. He'll need a staff come morning. I will be needed to lead the defense of our king and the city. Of our country." He sighed, hating to put his responsibilities before his family.

"Lillian?"

Jaylor nearly choked. "Um . . ."

"Don't 'Um' me, Jaylor." Brevelan looked near to tears.

"We have a slight problem with Lillian . . ."

"What aren't you telling me? How did you manage to damage both girls? I'm never letting you or any of my children outside the clearing . . ."

"Lillian is fine. She's only upset about Valeria's injuries. But . . . um . . ." No way to make this sound pretty. "Brevelan, please listen without panicking."

She glared at him through the glass, water, and candle

flame. He reached a finger to trace the curve of her cheek in the flickering image.

"Dear heart, Lillian has very little magical talent."

"But . . ."

"But Valeria has been bouncing spells off of Lillian so they look like Lillian threw them."

"So that's why Val is always so tired." Brevelan let a single tear slide down her cheek before dashing it away.

Jaylor ached with her.

"Did we push them too hard? Expecting them to be better and stronger than we are?" he asked her, as well as himself.

"Perhaps. When can you bring them home? I need to be with my girls."

"In a few days. We have a crisis brewing here. I'll need all the help I can get. I've already sent for Robb and three journeymen who already have their staffs."

"I'm coming with them."

"No, Brevelan. You have to stay there. Help Marcus. He's a strong leader, but he may need more if the malcontents see my absence as an opportunity to take over the University. Lukan is too young to do more than tangle things up. The little ones need you, dear heart," he pleaded with her anxiously.

"Keep my girls safe," Brevelan said on a whisper. Another tear escaped. "They are so young, and frail."

"I know. I know." He sent her a kiss and closed the summoning.

"And if we survive this I'll have to separate the girls and send them on their journey. It's time. But I hate forcing them apart," he told himself as he pushed his chair away from the table that held his bowl and candle.

Then he took a chair to sit beside the twins' cot in an alcove off of the younger princesses' bedchamber. If he couldn't sleep, he could rest and watch. Keep vigil over ailing Valeria and grieving Lillian.

Glenndon put his back into the oars. "Get your staff, son. You'll need your staff when we face the Krakatrice," Da had said. "The Krakatrice that holds Lucjemm enthralled."

He wanted to stay in the palace and prowl the towers up and down to make sure nothing went wrong. Make sure that Lucjemm stayed with his army and kept his pet snakes away from the royal family.

The current ran swift in the River Coronnan tonight. Low tide and a trickle of spring snowmelt made for an increased current running toward the Bay. He needed to go upriver to Sacred Isle. He had the muscle and the will to propel his little boat in the relentless but sluggish water.

The river felt thick, as if it carried too much silt.

The islands and temporary aits grew smaller, more isolated, as he progressed slowly toward his goal: a middle-sized island with multiple groves of tall trees and circular clearings. Legend claimed the Stargods had first come to Coronnan upon this island. The opening at the center marked the resting place of their cloud of fire.

It remained sacred many centuries later, isolated from the city without bridges of any kind, reserved for priests, those in need of private prayer and meditation, and magicians on quest.

Anything about the Stargods intrigued Glenndon now that he'd read that strange letter from Kimmer, Scribe of the South.

The river caught the nose of his boat and swung it off course. He cursed as he dragged his right-hand oar until his boat pointed in the right direction. No one ever said this most special ritual of any apprentice magician was supposed to be easy. He knew all that wood chopping at home and sword bashing in the training arena had to have some purpose.

He used his left-hand oar to steady his craft against a protruding snag, just barely visible in the growing twilight.

Silent and secret, Da says. Glenndon wanted to shout curses at the river, his oars, and the blisters growing on his palms. He'd have trouble wielding a sword for a week or more.

But if he earned a staff tonight, he might not need a sword.

Another half hour of hard rowing, and he finally beached the boat just as the last of the lingering light faded below the horizon. Glenndon paused and waited for his eyes to adjust. Brilliant stars against a black velvet sky and a low crescent moon gave him just enough light to pull the boat higher onto the thin grass above the tide line.

Now what? he asked the air.

A night bird chirruped at him from the top of a tree, one of many tall, taller, tallest trees that brushed the sky with waving tops. Which tree? He couldn't make out anything different, color, shape, or texture, among feathery branches.

I'm supposed to interpret signs sent by the Stargods. I guess that bird is calling to me. But where is he?

He could of course engage his FarSight to find the bird. Was he supposed to use magic on this quest?

He couldn't remember. Only to come alone, in secret, stay all night and wait for the dawn, when, if he was worthy, the Stargods should bless him with a staff.

How did his distant ancestors determine if he was worthy? He reminded himself that he was here to earn his staff so he could better help in the coming battle. He'd have to have both magic and a steel blade at his fingertips.

So, should he blatantly use his magic at every turn to get this over with and go back to the palace? Or should he save his talent and energy by using magic sparingly, judiciously, and only when he really needed it?

He'd come without provisions. No fire kit, no food, no blanket. Just himself. As dictated by tradition.

His stomach rumbled, protesting the long trip to the island and all the hard work of rowing the boat.

"No magic for a while." He knew better than to push his talents when his body was depleted. Da had made him do it once, two years ago, just to show him what it felt like. His knees had wobbled and he'd been sick with hunger. The first two bites of yampion pie had come back up again. Then he'd had to wait, lying with his head below his shoulders for quite a while until his stomach settled again, before he could keep a bit of broth down.

Call to me again, little bird. Help me find you, please, he said through a whistle that almost sounded like the bird.

The bird obliged with another, louder call.

The sound spread out and echoed, coming from every-where and nowhere.

Inland, Glenndon thought. He pulled the oars from the

locks and neatly stowed them in the bottom of the boat. Sand and dirt crunched beneath his feet. Maybe he'd better haul his only transportation a bit higher. Then he'd seek the elusive bird.

It called again, seeming to agree with him.

Chore finished, he walked slowly toward the line of small scrub trees. Thick as bramble bushes, he needed a staff or a stout machete to get through them. So he walked along them, deasil, brushing their leaves with his right hand. They seemed brittle. Too brittle for the wet spring months. He knew his home in the mountains got more rain than the valleys, but this was much too early in the year for the trees to feel like the last days of high summer.

More evidence of a disruption in weather patterns.

He stumbled along, cursing whenever he tripped over a protruding root or rock. At least it was dry enough to keep the moss clinging to those rocks from being slimy.

At last he felt a break in the shrub line. He patted leaves right and left to discover a distance about his body's width between them. On the other side of the head-height saplings the distances between things opened up. A little moonlight shone through the branches above his head. He'd found a clearing ringed on three sides by tall trees.

Not the middle of Sacred Grove. That opening at the center of the isle was supposed to be a perfect circle with a pond filling in the depression where the Stargods' cloud of fire had landed.

He kept to the outside perimeter of the open space until he judged he'd come halfway around. This should put him on a path leading inward.

The bird cheeped encouragement.

Using the same method of seeking space with hands and feet, he moved forward, nearly blind. He found another clearing shortly, then two more in rapid succession. Then just more trees for a long, long time. He felt as if he'd been walking all night. The bird had fallen silent, giving him no clues for direction.

Did he dare use a little talent to penetrate the murky darkness of the shadows beneath the dense tree canopy?

A faint glimmer akin to moonlight, but not, shone through the ground cover. He stopped and breathed.

The glimmer stayed where it was, not shifting as would moonlight.

Slowly he crouched down and felt the ground with his fingers and a tiny trickle of talent. He brushed something hard and smooth, like polished wood. Could it be? Had the Stargods given him a staff early so that he could return to the palace and help prepare for tomorrow?

Cautiously he stretched his fingers to grasp the cold, glowing stick. It warmed to his touch. Heart in his throat, he lifted it to eye level. Only about as long as his arm and too slender to use as a staff, he almost cast it aside.

Something in the back of his mind reminded him to never throw away a tool, no matter how unlikely.

He thrust the stick forward and used it to hold aside the brush and branches.

The stick worked admirably to ease his path. Several more sticks glowed through the underbrush. He made mental note of their location. But until he had enough light to examine them more completely, he would wait to seek them out.

Six more steps brought him into yet another clearing. He smelled water, not the ever-present saltiness of the Bay, or even the muddy river. This water was still, rank with decaying plant life as it shrank within its banks from the lack of rain.

At last, he shouted in his mind, feeling a bit awestruck that he'd actually found the central clearing before dawn. The moon rose above the treetops and glimmered down on him, robbing his stick of light. A bird flew across the crescent of light in benevolent symbol.

The end of his path was rough and rocky. Not a comfortable place to wait out the rest of the night. He edged to his left, keeping with the deasil design of his trek, using the stick to feel ahead of him.

Three steps. Then five more. The ground felt soft, like a freshly plowed field.

He stopped with one foot in the air. Freshly dug? No one was supposed to alter the land on this island in any way. Even the staff, if he got one, had to fall from a tree. He could not cut one.

He almost threw his stick back toward its original resting place, then kept it. It had lain directly in his path, inviting him to use it.

As he opened his ears and his mind, the ground beneath him crumbled. He slipped down, down, down, landing in a pool of rank water up to his chin.

CHAPTER 48

"TOOK YOU LONG ENOUGH TO GET HERE!"
Lucjemm protested. The splash of his quarry hitting
the bottom of the trap was most satisfactory. He listened to
Glenndon thrash about, cursing as fluently as any soldier.
How long before he tired and drowned?

"Ah, yes, my lovely, you think the pit we dug, with the
help of your mates, and filled with water from the pond is
deep enough. I am not so sure. My enemy who should have
been my friend is tall, taller than I."

"Lucjemm? Is that you? You aren't supposed to be here.
But I'm glad you are. Help me get out."

"Oh, no, my friend. That isn't allowed. You see, I have
studied magicians and their rituals for a long time. I know
about this supposedly sacred trial. You must do it alone."

"Alone on an *undisturbed* island. But it has been disturbed. Therefore the rules don't apply. Help me out and
we'll find out who has profaned . . ."

"Profaned!" Lucjemm protested. "Don't you know how
the Stargods profaned life on Kardia Hodos? That isn't even
the proper name of this world. But it works. Path of the
Heart. But whose heart?" Lucjemm's voice rose in volume
until it echoed against the ring of aromatic trees.

"Yes, my lovely. Your heart. You are the heart of this
world." He petted the weapon coiled about his neck.

The snake lifted her head and hissed, demanding the
blood of their enemy. *Before he drowns,* she insisted. She

needed living blood to grow and thrive so that she could join with her adoring mates.

"Soon, my lovely, soon you will truly be the matriarch of this world, mother of two dozen or more of your kind. Soon, soon, I will smooth the way for them to remove the excess water from the land," he crooned to her, momentarily forgetting the prey in the ditch while he exulted in his plans.

"Only when Coronnan is a desert will the dragons die and leave us free of their despoiling magic."

"You idiot!" Glenndon bellowed. "You say you hate magic, but that damned snake is a creature of magic, cousin to the dragons."

"Lies! Lies born of the dragons. Lies perverted by dragon magic," Lucjemm yelled back. "Water is the bane of my lovely and her kind. She cannot grow to her full potential with all of this water. Water captured by the dragons. While there is water, the dragons thrive. The time has come for the one to give way to the other. In removing the water, we will also remove the magicians and the magic, force them to flee to another part of the world, or die." He shouted his litany to the skies.

"I am an idiot. I thought you were my friend," Glenndon spat at him. "I trusted you. I looked the other way when you courted my *sister.* You have betrayed your king, your country . . ." he lowered his voice to a hiss that stabbed Lucjemm through his mind to his heart. "You have betrayed me, your friend."

"All magicians must die," Lucjemm said, repeating the words his pet spoke directly into his mind. Not magic speech, intimate speech. "My lovely says so. You are a magician first and my friend later, so you are the first to die. You betrayed me by having magic and using it. Magic must die too."

"Without magic or magicians, the dragons will fade away to dust," Glenndon muttered. He sounded like he was thinking aloud.

"They are the true enemy," Lucjemm confirmed. He liked Glenndon. Perhaps if he converted his friend to proper thinking he could save him.

The snake hissed a vehement negative. He sighed in disappointment. "My weapons and I shall hasten the demise of magic and magicians. Nearly all is in place now."

Glenndon thrashed and splashed about some more. Some of the filthy water drops touched his pet on her spread wings. She hissed in pain. Tiny burn holes ate at her skin.

"Now look what you've done! For that I should kill you right away. Most horribly. With fire. The opposite of water." He petted the snake, easing her agitation as well as his own.

"Die quickly, Magician. I shall console your sister in her grief. You see, you weren't ready for promotion to journeyman after all. And without you, the king has no heir. Only I can make order out of the chaos he leaves the kingdom in. Order. Dry order. That is the purpose of life."

"You are insane," Glenndon muttered. "Your pets have clouded your mind with lies. You lie just like them."

"We speak the truth. You and your kind have not matured enough to know the truth from lies."

"I could say the same about you!" Glenndon called. His words bore magic, trying to pierce the protective bubble his lovely granted him.

"I have no more need of you, Prince Glenndon." Lucjemm strolled away, stroking his lovely, whistling a sprightly tune that was certain to win the love of his princess. "She will love me when she has no brother to lead her astray. She will love me as my mother, Lady Lucinda, once loved my father. But he destroyed that. Destroyed her. And she did not love me enough to take me with her when she ran away to the magicians."

"I am afraid she must die along with the magicians for she did not love me enough."

Only my princess can truly love me enough.

Lyman is planning something, Valeria whispered to Lillian in the dark stretches of the night, after Da fell asleep in his chair. She shifted her cat body a little, stretching three of her legs. Her right hip was still sore, a sharp ache that traveled along her spine and made her wings pop in and out with each muscle spasm. She was tired, much in need of sleep. The queen's herbal tea helped a little, but did not allow her to overcome her spinning mind and grant her healing sleep.

"How do you know?" Lillian asked. She hummed a familiar tune as she stroked Valeria's back. Warmth and love spilled from her fingers and her song. The aches and pains eased but did not go away. Not yet.

Perhaps Lillian had found her true talent at last. She could be a healer even if she worked no other magic. Mama had been a healer long before she learned how to do other magic.

I learned a lot from Lyman since we transformed. I shared his mind even when he was not talking to me. He knows how to fix the flagpole and the Well of Life.

"We need to tell Da." Lillian swung her legs off the bed they shared in an alcove at the back of the suite occupied by the younger princesses.

A maid's room, the royal girls had informed them haughtily. A more luxurious and softer mattress than they shared at home, a lot more private, too. Though the entire palace was colder and draftier than their snug cabin.

Not yet, Valeria moaned.

"But . . . we have a responsibility."

We have to wait until morning. Lyman has to persuade Old Maisy of his plan first, whatever it is. He cannot act without a body to move him from here to there, or apply leverage to that flagpole.

"Do you think she really loved him long ago?"

I know he loved her.

"Where are they now?" Lillian asked. "We should talk to them."

We can't trust Lyman. He's so old he's lost his sense of . . . of morals. Da put Maisy somewhere in the palace with magical wards on the room. I think she needs some time alone with Lyman. Maisy needs time to remind him of what he should do, not just what he wants to do.

"You're probably right. We'll tell Da what you know first thing in the morning. Now we should get some sleep."

I hope I can sleep. Can you sing Mama's favorite lullaby?

Soothing words on a lilting three count filled the tiny room.

Valeria finally drifted off to sleep dreaming of flying, for real this time, not the half memory of her dragon-dream.

She woke with a start. All around her, silence enfolded the palace. She listened with her enhanced cat senses for sounds of life. Outside a soldier walked his weary patrol, coughing out dust. His boots scraped the stone parapet. Atop a turret a FarSeer blinked and blinked again, unsure if he truly saw movement along the river or not. Deep in the dungeons Old Maisy and Lyman shared angry thoughts.

Then far away and very weak she heard the plea that had awakened her: *Tell the king not to trust Lucjemm. Tell Linda not to trust him.* A long pause. *Tell Mama and Da that I love them.*

Glenndon! she screeched.

She had to help him. But what could she do, injured and crippled, unable to fly. Unable to walk.

She had to do something.

Maybe now was the time to wake Da.

Darville's body ached with fatigue from toes to crown. Yet he knew sleep would elude him once more.

He emptied his goblet of a last swallow, dregs mostly, but couldn't bring himself to spit out the bitter bits. The rough liquor had made him sleepy but had not countered the worry in his brain.

He scrubbed his face with his hands. Unable to banish his weariness, he rested his head in his palms, elbows propped firmly upon his desk—a huge piece of furniture that could be both sanctuary and prison. Tonight it felt like a dank cell deep in the dungeon, like the one where Jaylor had set guards and wards to watch Old Maisy and her unwelcome guest, Magician Lyman.

Fred had roused from his own fitful doze to sit beside his king, dutiful and responsible as ever. Darville had told him to sleep in the hall outside his office, or go back to bed. To be anywhere but here.

For once, the king needed very much to be alone.

Rather than allow his mind to spin through an endless loop of despair, he unrolled a map of the city, firmly anchoring each corner with an object from his desk. He focused on small details, banishing the muzziness in his head. A fanciful rendition of the palace with its towers and turrets surrounding the old keep, dotted with courtyards and gardens, sat in the middle of the map, even though the exact placement among the myriad of delta islands was slightly to the southeast of the middle. Smaller Ambassador Isle actually occupied that central place in reality. Still, the map was as accurate as his cartographers could make it.

Tediously he consulted a report listing each of the bridges his troops had inspected and either found sound or repaired. Most only needed a new dose of Amazon oil on the latches and hinges. A few needed rickety planks replaced. He'd ordered they remain unrepaired. The populace knew about the wear and tear. An invading army might not. He compared the list to the map and made check marks in appropriate places.

His people had been thorough. This city was their home, after all, and they had a vested interest in keeping rebellious lords from carrying their disagreement with the king to fighting in the streets.

Then he checked the faint tracery of gray lines indicating tunnels he and Jaylor knew about. Incomplete knowledge at best. He'd devoted years to exploring them as a teen. Jaylor had continued the job for him as a young man. Still they had not followed every branch or turning. Sometimes he wondered if the foundations of the city had been compromised with all that tunneling. He didn't dare think too hard about it. Apprehension would drive him to seek refuge elsewhere. Or in the cask of beta arrack.

He had nowhere else safe to take his family, except possibly the new University in the Southern Mountains—if Jaylor remained in charge after he broke the circle in the face of rebellion. By seeking refuge there, he'd effectively abdicate his throne and leave all the lords fighting to the death to fill the vacancy.

But the lords alone would not suffer in such a war. His people would suffer. They *were* suffering because he couldn't organize relief efforts for the drought that threatened many of the Provinces.

He turned his attention to the hills marked on the map and

the places where the FarSeers and his scouts had seen movement. Surrounded. He was surrounded by hostile lords and their armies.

The worst any king could imagine was about to happen.

When had he lost control? Long before he'd broken the Council of Provinces. Long before he'd given up hope of Mikka giving him a son.

"Darville?" Mikka asked sleepily from the inner doorway. "You should be in bed. You need rest," she added, moving gracefully and silently toward him.

"You are right. But too much troubles my mind."

"Let me brew you a cup of herbal tea. I can make a mild infusion that will relax you. More than the beta arrack you have become too fond of." She brushed a lock of hair away from his face where it had escaped his queue.

"You are the best thing that ever happened to me, Mikka. Have I told you lately how much I love you?"

"Only a few hours ago. But you can never say it too much or too often." She kissed his brow. "I love you too. And I fear for your health if you do not sleep."

"Then prepare your posset, my love. I'll welcome a few hours of rest. These maps and reports tell me nothing I don't already know."

"Dawn and a new spate of troubles are not far away. Come back to bed."

He let her take his hand and haul him to his feet. He wrapped an arm around her waist and took one step away from the desk.

"You needn't run away from me," an oily voice said from the interior doorway. Someone who could only have entered the private chambers of the royal family by the secret tunnel system.

The slight man, or tall woman, remained shadowed, little more substantial than a silhouette. Darville couldn't discern much from the voice. Husky, educated, malicious.

He pushed Mikka behind him and reached for his dagger. He'd replaced the useless ceremonial piece with a stout weapon balanced for stabbing, too heavy for accurate throwing. But he had a solid pewter inkwell and a sand canister. If only he could reach them . . .

Mikka slid the sander into his questing hand, anticipating his needs before he'd thought them through.

"Now, now, there's no need for weapons here. My lovely tells me her bite won't hurt much at all." Lucjemm emerged from the shadows stroking a writhing black snake coiled around his neck and down his forearm. It waved its wedge-head, tongue flicking in and out, tasting the air. A red gleam brightened its eyes. A shift of light clouded the edges of Darville's vision. He could no longer see the snake or Lucjemm clearly. But the doorway behind him, the colors in the carpet, the details of the tapestries snapped into focus.

Then Darville's stomach sank. The beast had six leathery wings. *Krakatrice.*

Behind him, Mikka gasped in fear as the snake slithered down the boy's arm, freeing itself of his neck.

He could see now that the beast was thicker than Lucjemm's upper arm—arms made strong with many hours of practice with broadsword and spear.

"The queen?" Lucjemm asked the snake, still petting it, seeming to relish the length of the creature. "You want the queen's blood. The king's is more valuable even if hers is more powerful with magic. You must satisfy yourself with the king. I promise you'll have magic from Jaylor, or one of his daughters."

"And I thought I could trust you. 'Twasn't your mother who made you feed the snakes. You did it willingly. Tell me, is your mother even still alive?" Darville taunted the boy, knowing full well she lived. "Or did you feed her to your pets?"

"Leave my mother out of this!" The boy screamed. "This has nothing to do with my mother, or my father. This is between you and me, and my lovely." He calmed instantly and petted the female Krakatrice once more, hand blurred within a strange distortion of light around him.

While the young man seemed preoccupied with soothing his loathsome pet, Darville threw the sander.

Lucjemm caught it neatly; his hand reached through the cloudiness and became clearly visible for those brief seconds. "Now that wasn't nice, Your Grace. Not nice at all."

The snake lurched, fangs dripping venom.

Darville dove beneath the desk, pushing Mikka ahead of him. He was fast, even with a half-befuddled head.

The snake was faster. His arm burned from elbow to wrist as star-spangled darkness pushed at his peripheral vision.

The alarm bell gonged. Once, pause, five short peals. An enemy army approached the first bridges of the city islands.

Heavy steps pounded along the main corridor. "Your Grace!" Jaylor yelled. "Darville!"

"Such an untimely interruption, Your Grace. Next time. We'll finish this next time." Lucjemm faded into the shadows of the interior room.

Darville heard the grind of a closing portal before Jaylor slammed his broad body into the wooden door of the office.

The alarm sounded again. Twice, pause, five short peals. The army had breached the first bridges from both sides of the mainland.

Then nothing. He sank deep into a burning blackness that ate at his arm and his soul.

CHAPTER 49

"**D**ON'T YOU DARE DIE on me!" Mikka demanded.
Darville clawed his way out of the darkness toward the light that was his Mikka. How could he ignore the woman who had stood by his side, borne his children, and loved him for half his life? She'd been his partner when he was a wolf and she a cat. She'd helped him survive many times since.

Once again he entrusted his life to her. *Stargods,* he wished he could move more than his eyelids. The words of love he wanted to say to her wouldn't move past the numbness in his lips.

He had to content himself with looking at her beloved face. Worry deepened the fine lines around her eyes and mouth. He needed to soothe them away with hands that wouldn't move.

"Jaylor, you have to save him," she implored.

Ah, yes, Jaylor had interrupted Lucjemm, probably saved Mikka's life, if not Darville's. If only he could move . . .

A difference in the quality of darkness pushing at his vision from the sides revealed a hulk kneeling at his side.

"Help me pull him out into the light," Jaylor said.

The darkness made sense now. Darville had dived beneath the desk to protect himself and Mikka. Mikka seemed to have escaped the lunging attack by the snake. As long as Mikka was safe . . .

"Send someone to follow that nasty young man," Mikka ordered. "Where were the guards? How did he get in here?"

"Tunnels," Darville said. He wasn't sure if he'd pushed the words out or not, he could barely hear his own voice over the roaring in his ears.

"I found Fred at the foot of the stairs, nursing a bump on his head," Jaylor said. He let his eyes cross as he sought information beyond this room. "I sent him to the kitchen for the fortified wine. He has a monster headache and fuzzy vision, but he'll recover." Jaylor added some instructions with a mental probe. "I sense him weaving toward your daughters' rooms to make sure they get to safety. He knows I will take care of you."

"We've got to get the poison out of him before it hits his heart," Mikka insisted. "No time to summon a healer."

"The boy is long gone by now. We'll not find him until he wants to be found," Jaylor added.

In the distance Darville heard the Temple bells. Two long gongs, a pause, then the five short taps. The enemy was stalled at the first bridge. How long before they raced ahead of the inwardly retreating populace?

Darkness closed in on him again.

"Poison in his heart?" Mikka's voice quavered in uncertainty.

Jaylor knew the same fear every time Brevelan went into labor.

Mikka raised her hands as if to cover her face and hide from this horrible threat. A mask of calm spread over her features. She felt for Darville's pulse and nodded in approval. "His heart still beats strong, though too rapidly. What do we need to do?"

"Bleed the poison out o' him," Maisy said, coming in from the main corridor. She too knelt at the king's side.

"How . . . ?" Jaylor shifted to interpose his body between the woman and his friend's body. The new angle gave him a better view of her aura. Her own pink and light blue dominated in soft, fluffy swirls. Black arrows, that once might have been dark purple, stabbed at her from within, trying to get out. She kept them tightly contained within her outermost layer of life energy. Not fluffy at all, an iron will controlled everything she did or said.

"Lyman invented the warding spells you placed on our cell door. He also invented ways around them," she said with a hint of a chuckle. "Now I needs a knife. A sharp one. And a bowl to hold the blood 'less you want 'is royalness staining this fine carpet." She fished scissors out of her apron pocket and slit Darville's sleeve to the shoulder.

"I never liked that shirt much," Mikka added. She might be trying to lighten the mood, but she sounded more vicious than nurturing. Jaylor imagined she was working up a good head of mad to carry her through the ordeal.

"It's the wrong shade of yellow. Go ahead and rip it up for bandages or whatever you need." A bit of a flippant laugh broke through at the end. Only a bit.

"Don't look like poison's hit his great vein yet. Lucky the snake bit in the fleshy upper forearm. Needs a bit to work through muscle to blood."

Jaylor nodded and handed Mikka his utility knife from his belt sheath, first whispering a cleansing spell and passing the blade through a candle flame.

"Save Mikka and the girls," Darville whispered. "Let me die if you have to. Save my family. See to the defense of the city."

The alarm bell interrupted him. Five quick peals. The enemy was on the move again. How? Where? Jaylor needed to be out there directing the defense of the city.

"Linda!" Darville tried to sit up.

Jaylor held him down while Mikka and Maisy wrestled his arm still. "Lucjemm wants Linda. She's his path to the throne. With her at his side he has a claim to legitimacy . . ."

"Then we will find a way to stop him," Jaylor reassured his friend. "First you must overcome this little setback. I will see to your daughter."

"Little setback? Seems to be more than that," Maisy said on a sniff. "Leave this to us, Lord Jaylor. We'll set the king back on the path to healing. You go do what you have to do.

Find Fred, if that perverted brat of mine hasn't killed him. Knew I should o' kept the boy rather than give him to his father to raise. But I loved the Lady Lucinda mightily and thought she'd raise my boy right. The dragons said you needed me more than the babe at that moment, and since I thought him mind-blind . . . well, I think I was premature in that assessment. Them snakes wouldn't attach to him if he had no magic at all. Only I didn't count on Jemmarc putting my lady aside with threats of stoning and burning. Now you go, Lord Jaylor. Get your girls and the princesses to safety."

Jaylor shifted from his crouch. His twin daughters were with the younger princesses. He had to warn them.

Surely the servants and ladies-in-waiting were rousing Josie and Manda. They'd round up the twins as well. That was their job.

Mikka put her fingers to Darville's pulse again, still worried and fearful. The lines in her face deepened with worry.

Jaylor took a deep breath to ground his talent, keep it from skittering off, looking to his daughters. The king's golden aura pulsed erratically. They hadn't a lot of time to get the poison out of him.

"The alarm bells will have alerted the household," Jaylor had to take a deep breath to keep from bolting to his children and transporting them back to the clearing and safety. "A guard will be here momentarily to check on you, Your Grace. I'll alert him to Lucjemm on the prowl."

"This'll hurt a bit," Old Maisy said. "An' you'll go weak. Jaylor, get him a bit of that fortified wine."

"He's had quite enough already," Mikka said dryly.

"Doubt he'll be able to swallow it yet, seein' as he can barely talk," Maisy continued as if the queen hadn't said a word. "He'll need it in a minute though. Gotta get his blood flowing good and proper once the poison's drained out. So fetch it, boy. And make sure it's the wine and not that fermented beet juice he prefers. That'll rob him of all the good bleeding does."

"No one has called me 'boy' in quite a long time," Jaylor said through an unnatural calm. "And if I remember cor-

rectly, you and I are close to the same age. You were one of
the first female journeymen I assigned to a noble household."

"And I were a good ten years older 'n you at the time."

"Which means we are contemporaries." He let his magic
sniff for the wine. Found a decanter and a fresh goblet in a
cupboard in the pantry behind a servant's alcove. He let his
magic swirl around and inside both, checking for tampering. Then he transported both to the desktop within easy
reach.

While they talked inanities, Mikka ripped the knife along
Darville's arm from near elbow to wrist, neatly avoiding any
of the major veins or arteries.

Darville inhaled sharply and bit his lip, drawing blood to
keep from screaming.

"Ah, now, that bite's going to hurt more and take longer
to heal than the snake's." Maisy clucked in disapproval.

Jaylor put both hands behind Darville's neck, absorbing
as much of the pain as he could. Flames seemed to climb
from palm to shoulder. The blood pouring out of Darville
burned both of their skins, wherever it touched.

He forced himself to take calm, measured breaths to counter Darville's ragged panting, which matched the alarm bells
in pitch and urgency. Second set of bridges breached.

"Breathe, my darling," Mikka instructed her husband in
her best queenly voice that demanded full attention upon her.
"Count the breaths. In one, two, three. Out with it on three.
Breathe. *Breathe, S'murghit.* I will not allow you to die. Do
you hear me, King Darville? You do not have permission to
die!"

Darville obeyed. Jaylor obeyed. Maisy obeyed. And finally Mikka obeyed her own orders. She kept up the breathing count, demanding, unrelenting. One, two, three.

Jaylor noted that the act of drawing in air and pushing it
out again became a little easier for both him and his friend.
They all followed Mikka's count. Then Darville took a
deeper breath to let his lungs find their own rhythm.

"Isn't that enough blood?" Jaylor asked. "It looks like an
awful lot." A lightness around the top of his skull made him
feel as if that was his own blood he watched pouring out of

Darville's arm. Still he maintained his sympathetic contact, sharing the pain, easing it where he could.

"Gotta get it all. Can't leave any poison in him or 'twill fester and grow and take over. Gotta get it all," Maisy replied.

For once she cut off her constant babble, cocking her head to listen to the bells. The enemy paused at the second bridge. Hopefully the populace had collapsed it before the army reached it. The river branch between islands was wide there with a swift current. Not easily swum, especially when encumbered with arms and armor.

Stargods, Glenndon was out there. Dawn approached. He should have his staff by now and be starting back to the palace, drained of magic, lacking food and water. He wouldn't have enough strength to do much but let his boat drift with the currents to the first island with a bridge, then walk back . . .

Glenndon hadn't been raised in the city. The codes rung by the bells meant nothing to him . . .

He had to go fetch his boy.

Darville's son and heir.

Jaylor's boy, *S'murghit!*

The alarm remained silent. No further progress by the enemy. Yet.

Lassitude spread from Darville to Jaylor. He just wanted to sleep. He was so very tired. Even his heart and lungs needed a break from the constant effort to keep moving . . .

"Not yet, you don't!" Mikka forced them both back into consciousness with a shake of Darville's shoulder and a stab of awareness into his mind. Jaylor shared her probe.

Darville and Jaylor opened their eyes, too afraid to disobey.

"That's it. Stay awake and breathe. That's all I ask of you is to keep breathing," Mikka coaxed.

"That's all for now," Maisy said. She sat back on her heels and surveyed the mess she'd made of Darville's arm.

"I need to . . . find Glenndon, make sure the girls are safe, root out Lucjemm from his hiding place . . ." Jaylor stammered. He slipped his hands from beneath Darville's neck and shook off his empathic sharing—something he'd learned from Brevelan but had to work at. It left him more drained than it would her.

"I'll get some clean cloth to bandage and bind," Mikka said, rocking up to her knees.

"I needs to stitch the edges together. Good thing I always carry my mending kit with me. Never know when a princess is gonna rip a hem or a lady needs a seam repaired on a too tight bodice. Oh, and Lord Jaylor, bring some'at big enough for a sling. He's not gonna want to hold up his arm on his own much. Needs a real healer he does. Guess that'll have to wait 'til those alarm bells don't have nothin' to ring alarms about no more."

"I know where the healers hid some of their potions and ointments before the Leaving," Jaylor said.

Mikka scooted into the bedroom. Jaylor forgot to listen to the old woman for nuggets of truth and wisdom in the spate of words like the tumble of a river full of snowmelt and spring rain. Darville winced every time she pricked his arm with fine, even stitches. She clucked every time he twitched away from the needle.

Jaylor forced himself to remember that the bells alerted the family. The girls would be safe. Glenndon was eighteen and a journeyman magician. Jaylor's priority at the moment was to get the king back on his feet and moved to safety.

Where was it safe in Coronnan City if Lucjemm moved at will among the tunnels and corridors?

Mikka came back, ripping white linen into even strips as she walked, starting each tear with a bite into the cloth.

Maisy knotted and snipped her thread. Then she laid a length of cloth along the knife wound and pressed hard against it.

Darville screamed again. But Mikka held his gaze with her own. "You'll be fine. A little weak for a few days, but undaunted," she reassured him. "We have to remember to make you drink. Lots of water but no liquor. Barely even wine."

The alarm bells started up again, sharp and urgent. Three long, three short. "Stargods! They've found a way past the second bridge!" Jaylor jumped to his feet, assessing what weapons he had on him, what he needed to gather from Glenndon's room.

His staff lay at his feet, where he'd placed it at Darville's first cry of alarm. Hours ago. Actually only a few minutes.

Darville tried to follow him. "Where's my sword and dagger? The Coraurlia . . . must wear it into battle."

Mikka pushed him back with a single finger, resting his head in her lap.

"I know. I know what drives you, what needs to be done. But you can't do it. Not yet. You've trained General Marcelle well. He and his men know what to do and will do it."

"Cold," he whispered. "I'm so cold. The people need to see their king . . . The Coraurlia will protect me."

"That glass crown will give you a headache, but I suppose it is necessary right now. This will help, my love." Mikka supported his head with one hand and pressed a cup to his lips.

Jaylor listened carefully at the door. Steady even footsteps down the staircases. Family and servants followed the evacuation plan. They'd gather in the old keep.

He took the time and concentration to let his heart reach out for Valeria and Lillian. They were safe.

He searched a bit further, widening his awareness. *Glenndon?* Nothing.

His heart stuttered in fear, then returned to a normal cadence. Glenndon lived. He knew that much. But did he fare well or face danger?

Darville rolled and thrashed trying to sit up. Mikka didn't have the strength to stop him, or help him.

"One more drink and we have to get you out of here, Your Grace," Jaylor said, returning to them.

"Go where?" Darville asked, slurring his words a bit from blood loss, fatigue, or wine. "Where are my girls? Glenndon? I need to see to their safety."

"They are safe." Jaylor hoped. He knew they lived. "You and I are going to the last place your enemies can get to. The place you need to be to direct the defense of the city." Jaylor got an arm beneath Darville's shoulders and steadied their balance before heaving him upright.

"If Lucjemm knows the tunnels, he can go anywhere in the city," Darville reminded them both.

Good, his mind was working again.

"Except the old University buildings. He can't get in there." Jaylor affirmed. "Only one entrance at each end to the long tunnel that runs between here and there, and both have traps for the unwary or untalented."

Darville frowned silently for a long moment. "You're right. And the University buildings are now a barracks for my troops. That is where I must be. Mikka, you stay here and direct the withdrawal of our family and retainers to the old keep. Set two guards at each tunnel entrance so Lucjemm can't escape. Warn them about the snake."

"The girls know what to do, Darville. Linda will direct everyone. I'm staying with you. Maisy will set the guards." Mikka folded a big square of cloth into a triangle, which Maisy fitted around his right arm.

Darville sighed in relief the moment the cloth took over supporting the arm.

"General Marcelle and Fred have spent the last three days weeding out any troops and officers who even considered siding with the lords. Fred? You said he'd been knocked unconscious?"

"He's up and moving. I sent him to the watch over our daughters," Jaylor said, checking his mental contact with the man.

Around them new sounds filtered through windows and along corridors and staircases.

"The palace prepares," Mikka said. "We need to get out of here before news of your injury spreads. Right now we do not need word of any weakness reaching our enemies. Our people do not need to know how vulnerable their king is. You must appear strong before them, bolster their courage and determination to defeat the invaders. Wear the crown." She placed, one hand flat upon his back, steadying his balance.

"Glenndon? The people need to see their prince . . ."

"He'll be here shortly after dawn," Jaylor reassured him. "We have only one enemy to contend with. Once Lucjemm and his snake are dealt with, the rebellion will collapse. I suspect the Krakatrice has directed most of his actions," Jaylor said. He grabbed Darville beneath his armpits and hauled him upright, also steadying him until he found his feet and knees, and made them work.

"Don't be so sure of that," Darville muttered. "Old grudges die a long and lingering death."

"So long as it isn't your death," Mikka said. "Or the death of Coronnan."

CHAPTER 50

L OUD NOISES penetrated Linda's dreams of giant snakes battling iridescent dragons.

Darkness outside tugged her eyelids closed again. She rolled over and buried her head in a nest of pillows and covers.

One long gong, five short peals.

The alarm bells.

Linda wrestled with the bedclothes that threatened to strangle her as she fought her way upward and outward. Bells. The invasion had begun. She needed to rouse her sisters, organize the ladies, get moving.

A sheet caught across her throat and threatened to choke off her air. She clawed at the annoying fabric.

The bells rang again. Two long, three short. Second bridge breached. Stargods, the enemy approached rapidly. Too rapidly.

Treachery. Lucjemm and his obsession with snakes.

S'murghit, she ached from her toes to her middle in regret. She *liked* Lucjemm. She'd found companionship with him that she missed with her ladies, her sisters, and even her brother.

And he'd kissed her with genuine fondness. She was sure of it.

A tear leaked out the corner of her eye. She could never trust him again. Even if he could come up with a rational explanation, she couldn't ever let him get close to court, her family, or her heart again.

She cast off the covers, finally, and swung her legs over the edge of the bed, seeking the portable steps with her toes. A stealthy hand slid across her mouth.

Startled, she bit down. Hard.

"*S'murghit,* Linda I need you to stay quiet, not alert the others," Lucjemm cursed. He hopped away from her, sucking on his fingers.

She could barely see him. Dawn had not yet sneaked around the edges of the window shutters.

A long shadow slithered from around his neck, down his arm. A wedge-shaped head nuzzled his fingers apart.

Was that a long, forked tongue licking away the blood she'd drawn?

She gagged, then clenched her mouth shut, stilling every muscle, every thought, waiting; afraid to capture the snake's attention. Her heart pounded loudly in her ears and her breathing remained sharp and shallow. Her blood tingled in her toes and fingertips, ready for . . .

"Hush, my princess," Lucjemm leaned over and whispered in her ear. The snake had disappeared. *Where?* She nearly panicked at the thought of it slithering beneath the covers, unseen, ready to bite . . .

Maybe she'd only imagined it. She hoped she'd only imagined it. Lucjemm's breath was warm and sweet, smelling of fresh fruit and flowers, not blood and carrion as she expected with the snake image so fresh in her mind.

"You are safe with me, my love. I have come to take you to safety."

Her rigidity must have told him she did not believe him.

"Trust me, my darling. Your father sent me. I will not allow anyone to hurt you." With that, he placed a gentle kiss on her cheek.

She wanted desperately to trust him.

"Come with me now, my love. We have things we must do to ensure the safety of the kingdom," he pleaded.

The alarm repeated.

Linda stilled again. This was an opportunity to find out his plans, to learn just how far he'd gone in his betrayal of the kingdom and the crown. Her ladies and the governess could tend to her sisters.

"I . . . I must dress," she whispered.

"Certainly, dearest. I shall turn my back to protect your modesty. Though soon we will have no secrets of mind or body between us."

He withdrew a few steps. She looked over her shoulder to make certain he had turned his back, then leaped out of the big bed on the opposite side from him. Hastily she dragged on undergarments and her trews beneath her nightrail. Strangely, he did keep his face averted from her. This gave her the courage to turn her back to him as she dragged off her sleeping garment and threw a masculine shirt and vest on. At the last minute she grabbed a leather jerkin with long sleeves. Scant armor against a determined attack, but more protection than just a shirt.

The horizon only hinted at sunrise. A chill breeze blew off the Bay. The days might grow exceedingly warm, but it was still early spring with cool nights. She could justify the extra clothing if he asked. While his back was still turned she secreted sharp throwing stars in each of her thigh pockets and small knives in the tops of her boots.

Fred had taught her to be prepared for attack from any quarter at any time. He'd given her these weapons for a purpose.

"Will Glenndon be coming?" she asked quietly as she stuffed her braid beneath a cap. Too much hair had escaped control; not enough cap. It would have to do.

"No. We do not need your brother for this." Lucjemm turned around and graced her with one of his charming smiles.

Her heart melted. Briefly. She reminded herself that she really couldn't trust him. But she needed to keep him smiling and willing to share his plans with her. Then she'd throw something sharp at his eyes and make a run for it and tell P'pa everything.

"Glenndon and I share everything. We're very close. I'd like him to come along." *You're only a thought away.*

Glenndon did not respond to her brief probe.

Brother? Where are you?

Still nothing. But she did catch a whiff of water rank with decaying plants.

Flusterbumps ran up her arms and down her spine.

"Now is not the time to cringe with cowardice," Lucjemm sneered at her. "Where is your famous royal courage, Princess Rosselinda?"

She firmed her spine and her chin, staring him straight in the eyes. "Ready and waiting for you to tell me your plan. I have a duty to my sisters and our retainers. I must make certain they are safe."

As if to punctuate her statement the alarm bells rang out again. Three long peals, a pause, then two short. Stargods, the enemy approached the third bridge already.

"They can fend for themselves!" he shouted. Then he calmed, instantly, as if his outburst had never been. "What I must show you cannot be told. It must be experienced." He grabbed her arm roughly and pulled her hastily out to the landing around the broad staircase that led downward toward P'pa's office and other public rooms. She glanced toward her parents' suite. No glimmer of light peeked beneath the doorway. The office and all of the other private rooms looked equally dark. Where were they? The alarm bells were tolling long and loud. Servitors and retainers ushered people down the stairs in an orderly mass. But there was no sign of her parents. Had they gone to the old keep already?

She was on her own.

I wish Glenndon were here.

(Courage,) Indigo's voice came to her unbidden. *(You are not alone in this. I cannot bring your brother to you yet. You must keep your mind open to me. You will not see me, but I will follow you. I will rescue you when the time is right. You may wish it sooner, but you have to be patient. Play this game to the end. All the way to the end.)*

The end of me?

No answer.

Glenndon's teeth chattered, his bones ached, and he could no longer feel his toes. His knees sagged and his head drooped in weariness. Water surged up his nose and down his throat. He coughed and gagged. The vile burning taste of regurgitated swamp burned the full length of his throat.

He spat and snorted to get rid of it.

Can't fall asleep. Have to keep moving.

Still blowing crud out his nose, he inched to his left, facing the walls of the pit, again. With fingers and knees and nearly numb feet he explored the edges for the sixth or eighth time, seeking something solid to grab hold of and leverage himself upward. *Fifteen feet across,* he figured. *The rim?* He pulled the glowing stick out of his belt and jumped extending it as high above him as possible. The tip brushed the rim sending clods of rank mud and grass raining on his head. He ducked and huddled close to the wall until debris stopped falling. He couldn't trust the crumbling dirt at the top even if he could jump high enough to reach it.

He pushed at the water, making it slosh a little. It lapped below his chin. It had receded three inches. At least. *Absorbed by the dirt? Hmm. How long before it lowers below my knees?*

He rested his back against the wall without danger of slipping down and drowning.

Linda! he summoned the most receptive mind he could think of. He caught only a foggy wall of sleep that his weak probe could not penetrate.

Da? Are you there? He found only a busy turmoil, anxiety and fear, barely an acknowledgment that they both lived.

Valeria! he called into the night with every bit of magic and love he could muster.

Something stirred at the back of his mind. His sister was still healing. All her strength and magic had to go into setting bone and muscle to rights again. *Val, just wake up and tell someone I'm in trouble. Please!*

He hoped he survived long enough for Da to realize this was more than just a failure of his journeyman test.

He looked up. Again. Anxious to find something, anything to get him out of here before his mind numbed and he drifted off to sleep and drowned.

The outline of tree branches appeared more clearly above him than the last time he'd looked. He could count the vibrant green of the new leaves that stretched over the pit. Fat leaves veined in pink.

As the light grew slowly around him, a shaft of low sunlight glimmered on a drop of oil on the pink tracery on an older leaf.

Tambootie! The tree of magic. The tree of life for the dragons. Of course the Tambootie grew on Sacred Isle. Where else would they grow unmolested by humans?

Please grant me sustenance, so that I may save this land from Lucjemm and his Krakatrice, your enemy as well as ours. Help me return to the city so that I may assist in restoring the Well of Life, he prayed to the Stargods, the dragons, to anyone who might be listening, prayed that this tree still held enough vitality to renew his talent and help him out of this pit.

Someone must have heard his pleas. A leaf as big as his palm drooped from a low branch. He took a tentative step toward the middle of the pool and swatted at it with the glowing wand. It dropped and drifted in a tightening spiral atop the murky water. He snagged it before it could sink in the whirlpool of its own making.

"Thank you!" Gently he licked the oil from the central vein. Instantly his mouth burst with exotic flavors, spicy, aromatic, gentle, and invigorating at the same time. Another drop on his tongue held bitterness, yet it cleared his mind.

He couldn't see any more oil droplets so he nibbled the tender tip of the leaf. His toes burned from the insult of frigid water trapped inside his boots.

He welcomed the pain as a sign of returning life and energy. He wanted to gobble the rest of the leaf. An old story or lesson heard in childhood warned him against too much too soon. One small bite at a time, chewing thoroughly and counting to sixty in between, he consumed the rest of the leaf.

His stomach awoke and growled angrily. Queasiness swamped his newly warmed body and mind. One deep breath, then two, and a third helped ground him. Another round of meditative breathing settled his stomach and eased his aching joints.

"Thank you," he repeated. Somewhat restored, he needed to find a way out.

A transportation spell was still beyond his strength and concentration. Tricky at the best of times, he didn't want to find himself inside out and trapped within a stone wall somewhere he didn't want to be.

Something like a dragon chuckle wiggled through his mind. Not a dragon.

The tree perhaps? He'd never known a tree to have a mind, but he wasn't beyond believing it could happen. Especially with a Tambootie.

Another laugh of agreement, soft, barely a whisper. Under normal conditions he'd not hear it, or understand it.

The tree snapped. The sound ricocheted loudly in the quiet just before dawn.

Glenndon started and clung to the wall of the pit, hands grasping for a weapon, anything. All he found was mud. Mud laced with rootlets.

Then a splash in the center of the pool sprayed his face. A long branch stripped of greenery and side shoots bobbed to the surface. The narrow end forked into two, each tine the length of his arm from wrist to elbow. The full length of the shaft appeared to be nearly twice his height.

"Is this my staff?" he asked hesitantly.

He caught a sense of agreement.

At dawn, if you are found worthy, the Stargods will grant you the gift of a fallen branch to use as a staff, Da had said.

Well, he had a fallen branch the right length and sturdiness. He hadn't cut it.

"Thank you, again," he said and clasped the staff in the middle. His fingers traced the whirling grain down the length. "Whirlpools broken by knots," he half-laughed. "I've never seen my magic before but that sounds like my pattern. Da's is a red and blue braid of light and energy. His staff also looks braided."

Another sense of agreement laced with impatience. He had a staff, now he needed to get out of the pit and get back to the palace to save the world from Lucjemm and his snakes.

(And the Well of Life. Save the Well of Life and the rest will sort itself out.)

"Who?" He looked around frantically for sign of the speaker. It sounded like a dragon. But not really a dragon. Something akin . . .

(We are all kin.) Dragons, Tambootie tree, ley lines, you. All kin. All connected.

The staff vibrated in his hand as if it had spoken. Not the staff, the mother of the staff, perhaps.

In the far distance he heard bells ringing in the city. What? Why?

Not once in his weeks in the city had he heard them ring except on rest day morning to call the people to temple.

This was not rest day.

Alarms. He remembered something about codes within the alarms, but no one had taught him the meaning of the long and short peals.

He had to get out of here; get back to the city; fight off invading armies, kill the Krakatrice and Lucjemm.

Ah, Lucjemm, why'd you have to turn out to be a traitor? I thought you were a friend when I needed a friend.

He frantically searched for a way out. Jabbing the wand into the pit wall to create a handhold just brought on a new onslaught of muck and the hole filled in as soon as he yanked the stick free.

What else could he do?

The tree! Low hanging branches. If he could just reach one sturdy enough to hold his weight. He sloshed and squelched his way to the center of the pool again. The water was down to his armpits. He jumped again with the glowing wand extended. Water dragged at his clothes, keeping him well below the lowest branch.

"*S'murghit!*" he yelled to anyone who might care.

He was alone.

Wand was too short, even if it did give him a bit of light to catch details.

An idea struck with a jolt akin to Lukan throwing him headfirst against a rock during a wrestling bout. With the wand in his right hand for light, he grabbed the thick end of his new staff and reached the tip upward. Up and up, standing on tiptoe, the tines of the forked end brushed the bottom of the lowest branch—a weak and spindly looking thing at that.

"Come here," he coaxed the tree. "Lower the branch, just a tiny bit. Just a little."

He stretched again. Maybe the staff cupped the branch.

"A little help here, please," he pleaded with the tree, the dragons, the land, the water, and the air.

The branch remained out of reach.

Glenndon closed his eyes, nearly giving into defeat. The chill water broke apart his mental fog.

What do I need here?

"I need the branch to drop lower. What will make that happen?" In his mind he saw a gentle breeze swishing through the upper canopy of branches.

Slowly, carefully, he grounded himself and steadied his breathing. With just a little magic, all he had left, he extended his awareness upward, making sure he maintained contact with all the elements. He had to search a bit to find Fire in the anger within his heart. Water and Land enfolded him. Wind eased past his mind, more concerned with getting from here to there than pausing to gossip.

"Come play with me," he whispered. "Come twist and twirl, and swoop and swirl. Come be my friend and tell me of the places you have been."

Air caressed his face. He reached out the wand to draw spirals for the wind to follow.

Tree rustled as the wind tossed its leaves about.

"Closer. Just a little closer." He stretched up again with the staff. The two tines tangled with a stout branch. He twisted it until leafy side shoots wrapped around and around his staff.

"Thank you, air. You may go play somewhere else now. I bid you good journey. Thank you, tree," he added the last for good measure.

The breeze died. The branch lifted.

Glenndon hung on for dear life. At last his feet dangled above the water. He swung his body back and forth, pumping his legs for a wider arc, greater momentum.

Just when he thought his shoulders would pop out of their joints and his body flagged, he let go at the farthest end of his pendulum and dropped onto solid ground.

The staff fell beside him, tines broken off to mere nubs, two more knots on the complex pattern of wood grain.

He still clutched the wand. Its glow faded as sunlight grew stronger. He examined it more closely, running his hands the length of it, feeling it tingle against his fingers, much as the oil from the Tambootie leaf had made his body hum with magic.

Not wood at all! You are made of bone. From the size of it, he didn't think it had come from a human. Not even a sledge steed.

Are you dragon bone?

(An arm bone of an ancient and revered ancestor,) Shayla said. *(This is where we come to die. Our bones glow with magic. Only a few humans are privileged enough to find one. Congratulations and welcome to my nimbus. Use the wand judiciously. The magic within is not infinite.)*

CHAPTER 51

VALERIA LISTENED TO THE ALARM bells. There was a pattern. She just couldn't figure it out. The long peals and the short. What did they mean?

She needed her human body and brain to figure it out.

She remembered the pain in her joints and muscles as she shifted from human to flywacket. Even with Lyman helping it hurt.

Now she was alone in her head. With Lillian so deeply asleep, she had only herself.

With a deep sigh of resignation she drew in huge lungfuls of air. Easier than before. One, two, three, she steadied her breathing until her mind freed from the constraints of a body. Slowly she visualized her legs stretching out, lengthening, ankles and knees popping into new positions.

Her hip still ached from the dislocation, but stretching it felt good, natural.

She moved upward, pushing her arms high over her head to bring her shoulders into new alignment. As she moved, her skin pulled black fur inward, leaving only a fine fair down on her body, a little thicker on her head. Her muzzle retreated into a nose and mouth, but her teeth . . . She left the incisors sharp while blunting the others.

Only her sharp, pointed ears remained. She thought about leaving them in place, just to scare people. I would be nice to have the augmented hearing of the cat. No, she'd better behave this time. The people in the palace wouldn't appreciate the joke.

Beside her, Lillian shifted uneasily in her sleep. Valeria nudged her with an elbow to push her to full wakefulness and awareness.

She had room in her head to be herself and only herself. And Lillian. She would always make room for her twin.

Valeria wondered if she missed the old man who had restored her life but drained her health.

No. But she'd probably miss his knowledge of all things magical and his affinity with the dragons.

(*You have your own affinity with the dragons, young Valeria. A name fitting for a purple-tip dragon who is also a flywacket.*)

Lyman's voice wasn't so far off after all. But she didn't need him at the moment. She needed to pay attention to those annoying bells. Behind her eyelids she built a wall, not a flimsy mud and stick wall, a solid thing of stone and mortar like the palace. Something sharp stabbed her eyes, reaching to the back of her skull. She winced but ignored it, building the wall even higher. The stab withdrew and took her headache with it.

Fists banging on doors matched the rhythm of the bells, stronger and louder than Lyman trying to beat down her inner defenses. The tramping of hasty feet up and down the staircases and out in the streets needed her attention. And Lillian's.

The bells rang again. A slightly different pattern. An alarm. A coded alarm!

"What's happening?" Lillian asked. Eyes still closed, she stretched and flopped onto her back.

"You healed me," she told Lillian. "But now we need to move, join the others. Something bad is happening in the city."

"I did? How'd I do that?"

"Think about it. But later. We need to get dressed and follow the people leaving the palace."

As if in answer to her questions, Lady Miri flung open the door to the bedchamber of the young princesses. "Up, up, everybody up. The rebels are invading. No time to dress. Manda, Josie, get up!"

Then the old seamstress, who seemed to be everywhere at once, the one who'd absorbed the spirit of the old man when he vacated Valeria's mind, dashed into the maid's alcove. "Lillian, Valeria, up on your feet now. I'm to see to your safety. And it's good to see you yourself again, Valeria," she whispered.

Hadn't Da put Maisy/Lyman in a prison with magical wards?

Valeria scanned the woman's aura. Something had changed from yesterday. The soft pink and blue looked frozen, unmoving with the pulse of her life. Jagged black lightning bolts couldn't penetrate her barriers.

Lyman was safely locked inside her. Maisy was strong enough to contain him. For now.

"Where are we going?" Lillian asked, rubbing her eyes free of sleep grit. She yawned, drawing in enough air to inflate her all the way down to her toes.

Valeria yawned too in instinctive reaction. She watched the old woman through half open eyes, feigning grogginess.

"You'll be safe with me, girls. Just come. Quickly. We haven't much time." She cocked her head listening to the newest round of bells. The pattern had shifted again.

"The enemy has crossed the third level of bridges," Maisy said. "Not long now. They'll be at the gates in moments. We have to run. Now."

Lillian bounced out of bed and flung a dress over her shift. She found clogs to protect her feet.

Valeria moved more slowly, still watching Maisy's aura to make sure the old man didn't escape.

In the outer room she heard Lady Miri and her companion Lady Chastet urging the princesses to greater speed as well, but more gently and respectfully than Old Maisy.

"Da . . ." Valeria began a protest.

"Your Da sent me. You're to come. Now."

Don't trust her, Lily. She thinks Da sent her, but Lyman could be lying to her.

Lillian nodded slightly in acknowledgment, then said "Come along, Val. I'll help you if your hip hurts too much. As long as we're together, we can handle anything."

Valeria limped heavily as she and her twin followed the old woman down a back staircase that spiraled through an outer wall and into an empty courtyard. *Let Maisy and Lyman think we are vulnerable. Surprise is our best weapon,* she told Lillian.

Before Valeria could figure out where they were in relation to the rest of palace Maisy wrapped her arms around both of them, holding tight enough to squeeze the breath from them.

"Hold on now," she said. "I won't hurt you."

The world went black then flashed bright with twining coils of life energy.

(You must become a flywacket again. The flying cat's strength and agility will be needed,) Shayla informed Val.

She could trust Shayla. Right now she didn't want to trust anyone, except Mama and Da and Lillian. And maybe Glenndon.

I need to be myself!

(You will be. But not yet. The king, the magicians, the dragons need you to be the flywacket a little longer,) Shayla insisted.

A nudge from Mama in the back of her mind only confused her more as she shrank back into her cat body.

"I have to rest," Darville moaned. His knees sagged as his head drooped. Whatever made him think he could leap to the defense of the city and dash into battle?

The Coraurlia weighed heavily on his brow and his heart.

He had to do it. He had to find strength hidden within himself. Deep inside his heart, not in the flask of fortified wine Mikka carried in her sash.

She wiggled to retrieve it. Her movements jostled his arm.

He suppressed a cry of pain.

"I'm so sorry. So, so sorry," she murmured repeatedly.

"I've had enough," Darville said firmly. For the first time in a long time, losing himself in drink and pushing his responsibilities aside, for a time did not sound appealing. He needed to keep moving, needed to get to the barracks. Then he could sit.

Jaylor, supporting from the left, anchored his staff and shifted his grip across Darville's back, steadying his balance. The glow ball on the tip of the staff faltered as he poured strength into his friend.

They were nearly of a height, but, thankfully, Jaylor had always been broader of shoulder and hip, with a barrel chest to support his heavy bones.

"We only have a little farther to go," Jaylor coaxed. "Once you stop, you won't want to get up again. Better to keep moving."

"You need food," Mikka said. She felt his face, neck, and hands with sensitive fingertips. "Cold and clammy with a rapid pulse. I don't like this. The only good thing is the lack of fever."

"Once we're in the old University buildings, I can summon a healer," Jaylor said. "But I can't do much of anything underground. I can't even talk to the dragons to find out what's going on up there." He urged them all forward again, pounding the braided wood of his staff against the stone floor with each step. The glow sprang back to life and flickered with the movement.

"Indigo has already called for a healer to meet you at the end of the tunnel," Glenndon said from a few feet away. A strong light haloed him, blurring his features. The only thing discernible about him was a new confidence in his posture and a staff in his hand—the source of the blindingly bright light.

"Glenndon, I am mighty glad to see you," Jaylor said on a long, relieved exhale.

"And I you. Indigo said I was needed belowground when I got back from Sacred Isle. There is chaos in the streets, people fighting each other to get to safety. I saw soldiers on foot moving toward the palace, still five levels out. But they are pushing aside or killing anyone who gets in their way. They are moving fast. And . . . and the river has slowed to a trickle, they don't need boats or bridges. I waded across at the last two crossings. I think the Krakatrice built a dam up-river, dirt and rocks and fallen trees, not permanent but enough to allow the troops to walk from island to island and only get their boots wet.

New chills ran up and down Darville's spine, not from poison or blood loss. From fear. How could he fight so formidable an enemy with only half strength?

"Every snake old Baamin and I killed was in the process of damming a river." Jaylor pounded his staff again. "It's their instinct to divert water away from the land, create a desert. As they did on the Big Continent centuries ago."

Silence as they took in that bit of information.

"Fire. We need fire, lots and lots of fire to defeat them. They seek to destroy Coronnan," Darville said. Anger made his steps firmer, steadier. "Lucjemm might think he's saving our land, but the snakes are lying to him, making him believe that what they want is best for everyone. We have to kill every last one of those monsters. With fire and sword."

"And magic, Father. We have magic. If they destroy the land, they destroy the dragons," Glenndon finished the thought for them. "I think I know what Lucjemm is planning, but I'll need help from anyone and everyone. Have Robb and his journeymen come?"

Jaylor shook his head. "I don't know where they are. And that worries me. Have you eaten, Glenndon?"

Glenndon nodded. "I found a meal hidden in my boat after I got out of the water-filled pit Lucjemm and his pet snakes dug."

"But you got your staff. That's the important thing," Darville said, remembering the night Jaylor had found his own tool. "But what's that glowing wand in your belt?"

Glenndon shrugged, like he had before he learned to speak.

"May I?" Jaylor asked, holding out his hand to examine the strange stick.

"It's dragon bone." Glenndon held out the white wand, letting them all see it but not touch it. "The island is littered with them. If you know how to look, and the dragons let you see them."

"Is that how you found us in this warren of tunnels?" Darville asked, urging them all forward toward the exit. He thought he heard an echo of the bells in the far distance. The tunnels muffled the sound. He needed to be out there, helping and directing.

"I found you by the stump of your staff, Da." Glenndon grinned hugely, thumping his own staff against the ground. The light flared again, revealing a short distance to solid stairs leading upward. Upward to the University cellars and nearly the end of this endless journey.

"Where's Linda?" Darville's thoughts flew beyond the immediate need to get to the barracks. Once the family was safe in the old keep, he expected her to come looking for him.

"She should be guarding her sisters," Mikka replied. "They know what to do. We've taught them well. I haven't sensed any fear from her."

"No, Mikka. Lucjemm is obsessed with her. We have to find our daughter." Darville lurched forward, stumbled, and nearly fell. "She may not fear him. She's bold to the point of recklessness."

"Wonder where she learned that," Mikka muttered in derision.

Darville ignored her words. "She thinks she can defend herself because she beat him at sword play. But the snake . . ." Darville surged forward. His body betrayed him and his knees folded. He'd lost a lot of blood.

Glenndon caught him. "Come along, Father. We'll find her together and stop Lucjemm and his plots, together."

Jaylor draped Darville's left arm about his shoulders, taking most of his weight. Glenndon propped him up on the other side. Mikka led the way, guided by the light glowing from the tips of two magicians' staffs. Darville's son and his best friend.

For a few moments life felt as if it had shifted into a natural and normal pattern after a long session of chaos.

Then the sound of the alarm bells filtered down the staircase. Four long, one sharp.

The enemy approached the gates of the palace.

CHAPTER 52

"I CAN FEEL THE LAND drying as the river slows," Lucjemm said on a thoughtful smile. "Only the Bay keeps moisture in the air. I can do nothing about the Bay. But the land responds to me and my lovely. The river obeys us and it deserts its old banks, seeking a new route to the ocean, far to the north."

Linda gagged, fought the burning bile in her throat. And turned a false smile back to him. She had to learn his plans. Information was more precious than gold. "Where are we going?" she asked sweetly, as if she believed his vile musings.

"The one place in Kardia Hodos where all power comes together. The one place where the armies will meet and the destiny of this land will be determined," he chortled.

"I don't like the sound of that." She stopped abruptly, digging in her heels at the center span of the bridge that led to University Isle. Her boots caught on an imperfection in the planks. It gave her an anchor to resist his tug on her arm.

A large group of people surged around them, like the receding river used to seek ways around the obstacle of the islands. Unlike the islands that welcomed the river on their banks, the people seemed to bounce off an invisible bubble surrounding herself and Lucjemm. No one touched her, and she . . . she tried to reach out and grab a large man to help anchor her but before her hand stretched more than a foot she encountered a burning wall as invisible as the air.

Linda bit her lip, fighting her fear and the lingering rawness across the back of her hand. What could cause the river, the lifeblood of Coronnan, to dry up?

"The rebels will meet your father's troops at the barracks. We will watch a new government rise from the ashes of the battle. Truth and right will win." Lucjemm renewed his grip on her with both hands.

"I will need a strong consort to rule this land. I prefer you, my princess, to Jaranda of SeLennica, a pale and wistful blonde. I adore your fabulous mane of hair."

Linda held back, digging in her heels. Lucjemm's depravity had grown just since leaving the palace. His eyes refused to focus on anything . . . except . . . perhaps the thoughts inserted into his mind by that hideous snake draped around his neck and shoulders.

"My lovely does not like the idea of me having any consort but her." Lucjemm removed one hand from Linda's arm to pet the snake's head.

Linda tried to wrench free, willing to risk the burning invisible wall, but he firmed his hold with the other hand, fingers digging into her upper arm until she was certain he'd leave bruises.

"My lovely has promised; she and I will rule together."

"Wrong," Linda sneered. "She lies to you. You are nothing but a tool to get her into position to rid the land of people and animals and . . . and anything green and lovely. She wants a sere desert with no life but her and her mates."

"No, no, no. I will rule with her as my tool, my weapon. This land belongs to me, and I choose the princess who will stand by my side. I decide. I am to be king."

His hands moved to her throat, squeezing until she had no words to counter him.

As darkness crowded the edges of her vision and stars burst before her eyes, she forced herself to nod in agreement.

The bells rang again. The rebel army approached the palace. Lucjemm cringed at the sharp noise. "Make it stop, Linda. Make it stop. It hurts our ears." He released her to slap his hands over his ears.

The bubble of burning energy receded with him.

A plan began to form in Linda's head. She had an idea.

The bells. There were bells in the old University tower. If the battle took place there, the clash of swords would swell the noise.

"We have to get inside the University walls. The bells won't sound so loudly in there," she coaxed. "But first we must get past those archers on the walls." She pointed toward the crenellated parapet.

A long line of men and women, over one hundred, stood in the openings. They all held longbows or crossbows. "The test to become a royal archer is to be able to shoot the eye out of a carrion crow at one hundred paces," she pointed out. "They have to recognize me or we will not get through the gate."

"I failed the archer's test," Lucjemm said wistfully. "My lovely tells me that if I let her guide my aim I can win any archery contest. I can't allow that. I will not use magic for myself. When I am king I will allow no magic in all of Coronnan."

"But your lovely is a creature of magic, a form of dragon," Linda said softly.

Lucjemm finally focused his eyes on her, then shifted his gaze back to the snake around his neck. "A dragon?" He touched the leathery wing membranes. "What is the right choice? Magic with dragons, magic without dragons? Magic? There must be no magic. Therefore I must dismiss my lovely. But I cannot . . ."

He grabbed his head in confusion. Then his eyes cleared and he grabbed Linda by the back of the neck, propelling her toward the gates.

"Those archers are loyal to my father," she said. "If I do not go willingly . . ."

"They will not shoot me while I have you," he snarled and yanked her off balance. "My lovely will protect me." As she stumbled forward he wrapped one arm around her waist, the other across her throat. His thumb pressed deeply against her airway. "Now you are too close for them to risk shooting."

"The dragons will protect me from you and your betrayal," she choked out. "You betrayed our friendship."

"You betrayed *me!* You accepted your magician brother into your household. He has taught you magic."

"Glenndon is bound to me by blood. As are the dragons." She had to defend Glenndon. She'd only go so far in placating this delusional madman.

"Are they bound to you? When I kill the king, will a dragon die?"

Linda squirmed under his hold.

"There is not enough Tambootie left to keep magic alive. The dragons no longer have enough power to protect themselves, let alone a mere princess. My pets have seen to that!"

With that, he marched them through the open gates of the barracks along with a throng of the populace seeking refuge from the approaching army.

He pushed her forward, cutting off more and more of her breath every time she resisted. He marched her directly toward the flagpole at the center of the courtyard. The stones beneath her feet vibrated with each step.

Half the archers turned inward, aiming for Lucjemm. One by one they shook their heads, unwilling to shoot their princess in order to kill him.

Linda doubted mere arrows, with or without flames, could penetrate the bubble the Krakatrice wound around them. She had to separate Lucjemm from his snake.

They stepped into the circle of paving stones surrounding the flagpole.

"Do you feel that, Linda? Do you feel the power beneath our feet? The stones confirm my right to rule over them. The only army that defends the center of the world is an old woman, a black cat, and the magician's young daughter."

Glenndon burst through the doors of the old University into the open courtyard. Dimly, he acknowledged that Da had designed the new University to match the old, smaller and wooden instead of stone, but with the same floor plan. He could find his way around the three-story central building and the lower cloister wings if he had to.

First he saw Old Maisy—presumably with Lyman joined to her mind—holding Lillian's hand while Valeria, still in flywacket form, stropped her ankles, growling and hissing at everything that moved.

Half-dressed city folk filled the courtyard, milling about in agitated circles. Men looked anxiously toward the archers along the outer wall. Some carried small caskets of valuables, others wore layer upon layer of fine clothing. Women looked anxiously for their children, or clutched favorite gowns or jewels to their chests. Children screamed in uncertainty. Or raced about in a new game of tag.

He heard a repeated refrain. "Bloody dragons; where are the bloody dragons."

Others shouted: "Kill the magicians. They caused this."

Only a few asked, "Where's the king? Where are the king's soldiers?"

A fistfight erupted between two teens with opposite questions. No one sought to quell their violence. Another fight broke out on the other side of the courtyard. This one spread to a dozen citizens. Men flinging fists, women slamming iron fry pans on unwary heads.

He tried to make sense of the chaos while Da found a bench near the main doorway for the king to rest upon. The archers along the wall looked anxiously at a young couple headed for the flagpole.

Lucjemm with a stranglehold around Linda's neck. No wonder the archers dared not fire.

The stone steps vibrated beneath his feet. His staff tingled against his palm with suppressed magic. The wand glowed, even in daylight.

"It is like a storm-tossed sea with waves breaking higher and higher but retreating farther and farther to build up momentum to break through the stones," he said quietly to Da, still keeping an eye on his sister and her unwanted escort.

He had to rescue her. Too many people were between him and her. He could blast Lucjemm in the back with a fireball, but the boy kept shifting and turning right and left, around and around, moving too quickly to aim and hope any weapon, magic or mundane, would strike him and not Linda.

Glenndon wanted to wipe away the moisture from the spray of those imaginary ocean waves. His ears roared with the ceaseless pounding, blocking out all other sensation. He forced his mind to retreat, as he would run from an approaching wave. He found something for his mind to cling to in the shaft of iron standing tall and deadly above the sea. "Only the pole is keeping the power from eating the stones away and spilling outward and upward."

How many would die if he and Da failed to contain the magical energy?

It had to be done to revive the dragon nimbus and the Tambootie. It had to be done to save Coronnan from the Krakatrice.

He had to get that iron pole out of the Well.

The milling populace stayed outside the circular brick pattern. He watched a young child, no more than four or five, younger than Sharl, step onto the outer ring of bricks. He screamed and hopped about as if burned. His mother scooped him up and retreated to a far corner behind a pillar on the left-hand cloister. A guard on the roof supported by that pillar peered over briefly to see if he was needed, then returned his attention to handing firepots up to the archers on the outer wall above him.

A roar outside the gate demanded attention. The army approached. All the archers but two turned back to face the enemy. They couldn't do anything at the moment to save their princess, but they could do their duty and defend the fortress.

Glenndon looked back at the flagpole. He and he alone had to finish that job before tackling the rebels. Until the Well was opened and restored, he could be of no help to the army. A layer of bricks close to the flagpole began to heave and undulate, ready to blast upward from their resting place. The snake around Lucjemm's neck and arm rippled in the same pattern.

Glenndon gritted his teeth at the way his former friend manhandled his sister. He wanted to rip out Lucjemm's throat.

"Da?" he called to Jaylor.

"I see, Glenndon."

"Linda!" Queen Mikka gasped.

King Darville growled something obscene and struggled to get to his feet. Da held him down with some effort.

She's scared, Glenndon whispered to Da. *But she's angry too, just waiting for the right moment to claw his eyes out.* He kept a part of his mind linked to hers, letting her know that he'd do everything he could to help her. But he had to break through the shimmering aura of power surrounding both her and Lucjemm.

"Touch your staff to mine," Da commanded Glenndon. "Ground it well before you join your magic to mine. We need dragon magic to combat land magic."

"I can't find enough dragon magic to join," Glenndon said under his breath. He cast about for the ephemeral presence in the air. Each probe of his mind and talent came up empty, as did the special place behind his heart where he stored the magic.

"*S'murghit,* neither can I," Da said.

The wand glowed brighter.

"There's magic in the dragon bone!"

Da smiled. "May I hold one end? You take the other. We should be able to join our magic through it."

Glenndon yanked the length of bone from his belt and grabbed the thick end, holding the slender tip out to Jaylor.

Da folded his fingers around the bone respectfully. *You are a strong telepath; link your mind to mine and follow everything I do, exactly as I do it. When I do it.*

Glenndon shifted his link from Linda to Da, alarmed and comforted that she refused to break contact with him while Lucjemm controlled her body. *You cannot help this time, sister.*

I can and I must. We must stop the Well from exploding before Lucjemm uses it to control the snakes. They are coming, relentlessly.

He can't use the power. He's mundane.

Don't bet on that. He feels the stones vibrating like a drumbeat at a festival dance. He's humming a tune that matches the rhythm. The song pounded through his head, competing with the waves of magic against the stones in a battle of loudness.

How can he do that?

I don't care how. Just do something before he does!

"You stop Maisy's brat by letting others take part of the burden," Lyman yelled, using Maisy's throat and mouth, piercing through the fog of magic and shouting and pounding waves of raw, untamable power.

"Leave my son alone!" Jemmarc screamed from the arched pedestrian gate. He drew his broadsword and charged forward. "My boy has done nothing wrong." He circled his blade above his head, threatening any who came close.

Glenndon knew his skills and his ruthlessness.

CHAPTER 53

"NOW, GIRLS!" MAISY/LYMAN YELLED, pushing Valeria and her sister toward the young man she'd seen in the army camp. The boy with the vicious black snake. Lucjemm.

Valeria braced her hind legs, spread her wings and leaped with all her strength. Her feathers caught air and glided her forward. Claws extended, she shredded the magic bubble around them, the magic inherent in her dragon-inspired body penetrating it easily. Viciously she raked the boy's face and clung to his neck. Sharp teeth found a vulnerable spot behind the snake's head. Savagely she bit down and held the creature immobile before it could react.

It screamed in her head, trying to break free. Valeria cringed away from the piercing noise, but her teeth held. The snake coils tightened about the boy's neck.

He screamed and fought both Valeria's claws and the snake.

Princess Linda wiggled free of his choking hold.

Lucjemm jumped and danced about, trying to free himself. He yelled until Valeria's ears hurt. That made her cling tighter.

Lillian grabbed the princess' collar and yanked her safely away, toward the main courtyard. They wavered unsteadily across stones heaving and roiling beneath their feet until they found momentary safety outside the circular pattern in the brick.

A circle of magic. A dome of power. Valeria understood these things. At the moment she didn't need to know more, only that she needed to drive this boy away from Maisy and Lyman.

And kill the snake. Her jaw ached, and the leathery snake-skin tasted strange. Her need for prey faded in the face of self-preservation. One drop of Krakatrice blood could kill her. *I don't truly have dragon blood in me to counter the toxins.*

She loosed her hold on both Lucjemm and the snake, dropping quickly to the ground out of strike range. The snake snapped open her six leathery wings and lunged toward her.

Valeria loosed her own wings and jumped, rising high above her enemies.

A small wedge-shaped stone shot upward inches from Maisy's feet, followed by a fountain of raw magical power. The mother of all ley lines. At the crest of its jet upward it burst into a rain of droplets that pocked the roiling but intact stones beneath.

Lucjemm stopped in mid-dance, one foot off the ground, as he stared gape-jawed at the sizzling rain of blue light. He backed up, toward the pole, instinctively, half-shielding his bleeding face from the burning drops of light sprouting upward from another break in the bricks.

The moment Lillian stepped free of the circle, Valeria flapped her wings and dove for the snake, driving it toward Lucjemm and the raw power erupting from the Kardia

Lucjemm bled and screamed curses she had never heard before. The snake slithered off, away from him and the burning power.

"You can't desert me!" Lucjemm yelled at the snake. "We fight this together."

The snake ignored him.

He followed the exodus outside the circle, gaze searching wildly until he found his father. A pitiful frown of vulnerability crossed his face. Jemmarc dropped his sword and reached out both arms to embrace his boy.

"Contain him!" Da shouted. A wall of magic sprang from the tip of his staff and of Glenndon's, encircling Lucjemm before he reached his father. The top of the dome reached a mere hand's breadth above his head. A stray drop of magic bounced off it and back onto the stones where it ate away at granite.

Lucjemm screamed more abuse as he pounded at the shimmering blue bubble barely wider than his spread arms. His hands were covered in his own blood. A sizzling sound and the smell of burning meat spread around the dome. He jerked back his hand, sucking at his wounds. Whimpering, he ducked into a tight crouch, burying his head between his knees.

Jemmarc tried slashing the dome with his sword. The metal blade softened and began a misshapen droop in the middle.

The crowd drew back from him, pressing against the walls. There were too many of them.

"Come to me, my lovely. The time has come. I need you!" Lucjemm cried, ignoring his father.

Valeria searched rapidly for sign of his "lovely." All she saw was something black writhing in the small gap between the closed gate and the solid ground.

Enough of an opening for a large snake to flatten itself and slither through. Lucjemm's pet rose up, greeting her mates, fluttering six leathery batwings; red eyes gleaming in bloodlust.

The mob screamed in abject terror, pressing back harder, nearly smothering or crushing those closest to the unyielding fortress walls.

Valeria flew higher on anxious feathered wings. She had to escape this ancient enemy, a creature out of legend. A creature known to devour young dragons.

She had to go to Lyman. He would know how to protect her. He would keep her safe.

"Stay back, child!" Maisy screamed from the base of the flagpole. "Stay back!" With her words she raised her hands and shot ten streams of blinding white light at the menacing iron flagpole.

The pole split with a great groan. Maisy backed away, maintaining a steady stream of magic cutting away at the lethal iron right where it sank between bricks into the Kardia—into the Well of Life. She stumbled on the uneven bricks and fell to her knees. Her magic faltered, withered, and died.

A new stream of mixed red, blue, and rose gold replaced

it. Da and Glenndon pointed their touching staffs at the pole. Together they set a glowing white wand atop their staffs. The colors intensified, flared, and compounded.

Valeria had to turn her head away from the blinding light. More screams from the mob pierced her ears. Were they more afraid of the magic or the Krakatrice?

The flagpole groaned again, tilted, and then succumbed to the pull of the Kardia. It fell to the ground, bounced and rolled, coming to rest across the bricks, nearly half of it on the paving outside the circle.

The ground rumbled and roared in triumph, shooting a thick stream of blue light upward.

Valeria held her breath, knowing what was to come when the raw power fell back to the ground. As all things must return to the land.

"Run free, Maisy. Lyman, help her run free!" Princess Rosselinda screamed aloud and into every receptive mind.

Valeria sensed the princess breaking free of her frozen position outside the brick circle, dashing to help the old woman.

Glenndon snagged her arm before she got two steps away. The bubble restraining Lucjemm wavered as Glenndon's concentration shifted.

(You must rely on yourself and your twin, now, Valeria. Remember to cap the Well, but do not seal it. A cap of clay when all the iron is removed. The Well must breathe,) Lyman told her, his voice a mere whisper of pain and . . . and resignation.

The magic fell, engulfing the old woman's body and the ancient dragon spirit in living blue flames that ate at everything within the circle and followed the iron pole to reach beyond to the crowd of people frozen in horror.

The snakes held their position, tongues flicking, eyes narrowed, assessing, waiting, coiled to strike.

Lucjemm's mind cleared. From his crouch he watched the Krakatrice retreat from the blue energy pooling beside the iron pole, like water seeking a path around an obstacle. Only this wasn't water, it was pure, raw magic.

The snake didn't like the scent of power that was stronger than she.

"But this is what we need!" he protested to her. "The Well is destroyed. Without the Well the dragons and the Tambootie will fail as well."

Her forked red tongue flicked in and out. She wanted the body of the old woman, wanted powerful blood, not ordinary people. The crowded mass of humanity was easy prey but not worth her bother.

"Take the two magicians. Surely their blood is more potent than the ancient ones," Lucjemm coaxed.

Only the princess will do, royal and magical. Leathery wings fluttered and the snake shifted direction. *Or you. Cousin to royalty by your father. A magician by your mother.*

Lucjemm cringed. "No! I have no magic. I hate magic. Magic is . . . evil! You told me so. You wouldn't lie to me."

The snake flicked her tongue at him in disdain, then shifted again toward Linda. His Linda. The more powerful blood.

"No. I have promised safety to *my* princess!"

The deep thud of a battering ram against the closed gate punctuated his words. The rebel army, advancing upon his orders. Orders to kill anything magical and/or royal.

Linda.

"Take the king and his queen if the magicians are not to your liking."

Six writhing male snakes followed in her wake, spreading out in an unstoppable phalanx. The biggest male bit and tossed aside a child that did not run away fast enough. Three men and two women met the same fate. Ordinary blood, not worthy of a Krakatrice.

Surprisingly, the archers did not shoot. They stood upon the wall as if frozen in time, arrows nocked but bowstrings not stretched. As did the king and his queen.

The magicians still fought with all of their magic and concentration to contain the stream of power shooting skyward.

The female snake undulated closer. Her entire body rippled with sleek strength and terrible beauty.

"*I* fed you with my own blood when no one else would. *I* cherished you, protected you when you were young and vulnerable! I order you to leave my princess alone."

Her tongue came closer to Linda. Linda did not see the new

menace ten feet from her. She looked only at the old woman by the flagpole, while she struggled to free herself from Glenndon's fierce grasp. The Krakatrice bared fangs dripping with poison. Each tooth longer than Lucjemm's hand.

"Glenndon, save Linda!" he screamed. "Archers, shoot the snake!"

Only the snake and her tongue moved. Time stopped for all but Lucjemm and his rebellious pet. She oozed ever closer. All else in the courtyard was frozen in time. Even the blue rain paused in its relentless fall back to the Kardia.

The thudding of the battering ram halted. A quick glance in that direction showed a long split down the middle of the right-hand panel. It sagged on broken hinges, but none of his army moved to step through the opening.

No one could save Linda but himself.

"I should have known that this creature of magic cannot tell the truth. Just like the dragons. Just like the magicians. Lies. All lies!" he wailed.

The blue rain broke free of the time thrall.

Jemmarc moved toward him, shouting and slashing with his sword any who got in his way. "I will save my son!"

Not fast enough. Jemmarc could not move through the crowd in time to save Linda. Only Lucjemm could penetrate the defensive bubble surrounding the snake. He was bound to the Krakatrice by magic and by blood. She could not keep him out.

He turned his mind inward, seeking strength and the will to do something, anything, to stop the Krakatrice. Something . . . powerful slid away from his mind. He sought again from a different angle, grabbed hold with his concentration, acknowledged it. Defined it and pulled it upward, up, up, and up further into his heart and his soul.

He raised his hands and pushed. The power faltered. He pulled up more. His body grew hot, his fingers burned and still he pushed, channeling the magical power beneath his feet and in the air toward the evil creature threatening his princess.

The Krakatrice jerked her head away from Linda and locked his gaze. He concentrated more power through his eyes, spearing the snake with burning blue light.

It shrieked in pain, splitting the air and his eardrums. He didn't care. He had to keep her from killing Linda. His Linda.

The smell of rancid burning flesh filled the courtyard. Raw pustules of red flesh and black blood split black skin and erupted along the length of the snake body. Her wings drooped and shriveled like parchment burning and curling in a candle flame. Her own poison consumed her from within.

Her consorts turned to flee. Lucjemm pulled them back with his mind, herding them into the blue rain. Each one slid into the circle and died, slowly, painfully.

Needfully.

He felt no satisfaction as flesh burned and black blood flamed. He did not triumph as their red eyes glazed in death, turned gray, withering into ash.

He had saved Linda.

"What did you do?" Senior Magician Jaylor shouted, shaking off the frozen time.

"How did you do that?" Glenndon added.

"Magic," Linda gasped. "You used magic. I saw the power rise in you through the Kardia. You are a magician born!"

Magic?

"I am as much a creature of magic as the Krakatrice and the dragons," he said flatly. The bitter taste of self-loathing in the back of his throat, and a knot in his stomach replaced his need to save Linda.

"I am what I hate. How can I hate myself and live. How can I . . . ?"

He closed down all his senses and thoughts. Slowly, his body crumpled, succumbing to the darkness. Seeking death. The sweet death that would allow him to atone for being a loathsome magician.

Linda was safe. That was all that mattered.

CHAPTER 54

"LUCJEMM!" LINDA BROKE FREE of Glenndon's grip and severed the connection of their minds. She dashed forward and knelt just outside the blue bubble of Lucjemm's prison. Jemmarc beat at the magic, uselessly, with both the flat and the edge of his great broadsword. Blue sparks traveled up the blade and died within the iron.

The reek of burning flesh made her gag. The snake smelled of burning blood and poison, truly evil. She wondered if the miasma flowing from the carcass was as deadly as the venom.

She held her breath as she reached through the bubble. It shredded beneath her fingers.

"He betrayed you, Linda. He betrayed all of us," Glenndon reminded her. He looked exhausted. His knees sagged and he clung to his twisted staff for support.

"My son is not a traitor!" Jemmarc continued his angry assault on the magic. Eventually the iron in his blade would shred the bubble. Not yet though.

"We have to cap the Well," Jaylor said, stiffly. His jaw clenched tight while he concentrated so fiercely on controlling the magic pouring forth from the Well "Now. Before it does more damage," he said, each word broken by a ragged breath.

And her parents came alert from . . . from whatever the snake had done to keep them frozen. P'pa pointed toward the people clinging to the walls, or kneeling over dead bodies. All of them screamed. Despair, grief, anger.

The twins, both human now, clung to each other, edging behind pillars, seeking safety in obscurity. The cloister roof sheltered them from the burning blue rain. The fountain slowed. The height of its explosion decreased to little more than waist high. But it pooled around the opening and spread.

Only she was left to care for her fallen enemy, who had been a friend and possible lover.

"Lucjemm?" she asked as she tentatively sought a pulse in his neck. "Luc!" she screamed when she couldn't find one.

"Don't touch my son!" Jemmarc said through gritted teeth. A bevy of soldiers wearing his livery fought their way through the broken gate.

The archers turned their attention outward, concentrating and shifting to mass over the gates, all of the gates at the front and far side of the quadrangle.

Linda wanted to shout at the defenders to spread out again. Jemmarc's sword penetrated the bubble, coming dangerously close to her head.

She ducked back, scuttling toward the scant protection Glenndon and Jaylor could grant her.

"Don't you dare defile my son. You killed him! You killed my boy!"

"I didn't . . ."

"Witch!"

"Witch? Witch! Kill the witch!" The army behind him and the crowd of city dwellers took up the accusation. Needing to expel their anger and fear by following the loudest voice. "She brought the snakes. She killed!"

"I watched you kill him with magic, Princess. You shall die a witch's death," Jemmarc proclaimed. "No member of the royal family may have or throw magic. You killed my son with magic." He raised his sword with both hands, poised to split her in two. His army surged forward, clogging in the narrow opening in the gate. Ruthlessly they tore at the iron-banded wooden gate. Arrows rained down on them, bouncing off helms and fine chain mail armor.

"Witch, witch, witch," the crowd chanted, pushing toward Linda and Jemmarc.

More arrows flew, inside and out.

The mob pressed backward once more. But the armed men marched forward.

Linda stood and backed away from Jemmarc's relentless stride toward her.

"I didn't. He killed himself!"

"Liar." Jemmarc's bark drowned out all other protests.

"Run, Linda. Run." Glenndon ordered. He pointed his staff at Jemmarc's chest. The white wand lost its glow and sank into dull, inert ivory, melding into the wooden staff. "Run. I can't hold him and the Well."

"Where?" Linda asked looking around frantically. The army spread out. Dozens of men and more pressing at the gates, big and small, on two sides of the wall. The crowd that had taken refuge from that army flowed forward, keeping up their ugly chant.

"Shoot him!" the king, called up to the archers. "Shoot them all! Save my daughter."

As one, the archers turned away from the army outside the gates and let their arrows fly before they'd finished the rotation.

The soldiers held up their shields so that they overlapped. They had to move closer together, giving her an avenue of escape. Maybe. They continued inching forward. The crowd pushed from behind them.

"Get high," Glenndon said. He twisted his staff sideways and circled it over his head preparing a field of magic between Linda and the mob. He drew up the power of the Well, so close, so helpful, so deadly.

Crackling flames shot out from both ends of his twirling staff. The white wand embedded in the wood glowed again, faintly. The army cringed backward. For a moment.

The sparkling air barely slowed Jemmarc down.

Linda knew that both Glenndon and his father had given everything to controlling the Well. A Well that was still uncapped and treacherous to both the land and the people.

"Climb, Linda. Get high. Indigo, we need you!" Glenndon commanded.

Jemmarc raised his sword and lunged for Linda.

P'pa threw her a sword. She grabbed it out of the air, awkwardly. With a weak grip she parried Jemmarc and fled to the far corner where the cloister met the University. A staircase spiraled upward.

She dashed, fumbling for a better grip.

Jemmarc took an arrow in the arm but kept running, his longer legs eating up the distance between them.

A loud boom announced the impact of a large boulder with the outside wall on the far side of the compound. Deep in her mind Linda knew the army had launched a catapult. Where? How?

The archers abandoned the attack on Jemmarc for the greater menace outside the walls.

She pulled in air and found the power of the land pounding against the stones beneath her feet. She pulled that in as well and fed it to her sword arm and her lungs.

Desperately she turned and parried another blow. Jemmarc countered and lunged again. She danced out of his reach. Taller, longer arms and legs, more experience. She knew he'd take her in a fair fight. He wasn't interested in fair right now.

Screams and shouts, the clash of metal swords, the whir of arrows passing through the air, all echoed across the half-mile-wide quadrangle.

She ignored them all. Upward. She had to climb high, and fast.

Above her she heard a dragon scream.

"Indigo!"

(Indigo here.)

"Princess Rosselinda," she gasped out her own respect for dragon rules. "Help me please."

"Climb, Linda," Glenndon reminded her, as much in her head as her ears.

She climbed, legs aching, lungs burning.

Another boulder struck the wall. Men screamed as the fortifications sagged.

She'd get no help from the archers.

Dimly she sensed her father struggling to his feet and his arms pointing and ordering people about. If he spoke, she didn't hear him.

Jemmarc continued his pursuit. "You killed my son!" He slashed his sword downward. Blinded by anger, he missed.

Linda kept moving up. Up the stairs. "I didn't. I . . . loved him." She glanced back to gauge the distance between them.

Blood dripped from Jemmarc's arm. He held his broadsword awkwardly in his off hand. Still he followed her, stepping onto the first riser. Grief twisted his face into an ugly mask. "You-killed-my-son!"

The walls around her shuddered all the way to the foundations. "Archers target the catapult!" her father called with all the power of a trained commander.

One step, three, a dozen. She rounded the last turn and burst onto the wide parapet.

No archers near. All at the front and far side shooting randomly at the army outside and the surging mob inside. If she ran to them, she'd only get in their way. Jemmarc would follow and interfere with the defense of the people. And the king.

(Up.)

She hoisted herself atop a crenellation. The overhang of the roof dipped to the end of her reach.

Climb, Linda. Climb higher, Glenndon called to her. His voice cut through the cacophony.

Climb, S'murghit. I will take care of the Well.

She closed her eyes and jumped. Her fingers closed on a gutter.

(A little higher,) Indigo coaxed.

She swung legs out and up, gaining momentum until she nearly split herself in two as she thrust a knee over the lip of the gutter. Slick tiles offered her no traction.

Her lungs burned. Tears streamed down her face.

Another crash of stone against stone. The far wall must be close to breaching.

Desperately she kicked backward with her dangling leg and connected with . . . something. A squish of rupturing flesh, the crunch of a broken bone.

The clasp of iron fingers on her ankle.

She kicked out again.

And suddenly she was free. Dragon claws snagged her leather jerkin and yanked her upward to safety.

She chanced a look backward and saw Jemmarc, three arrows sprouting from his armored chest and an archer aiming a firepot at his head.

The catapult ceased its thundering bash at the walls.

The mob and the rebel soldiers backed away from the archers. In ones and twos they slipped out of the gates, losing themselves in the leaderless army that even now retreated from the city.

But Jemmarc still stood; still slashed at where her feet had been.

As the dragon glided toward an open meadow beyond the city walls, beyond the army camp on the banks of the drying river, she watched drooping trees shiver and stretch, reaching for the sky once more. Indigo snatched a mouthful of revived leaves.

A dozen other dragons appeared in the sky. They too reached down for the essential nutrients in the leaves before flying off to toward the blockage in the river.

By the time Indigo landed in the meadow so that she could shift from his grip to riding on his back, she heard a roar and gush of water as the river surged through the opening dug by dragon claws.

(The land will thrive once more,) Indigo said with satisfaction.

"But will Coronnan? Or has it split forever?"

CHAPTER 55

GLENNDON STOOD TO THE RIGHT of his father's demi-throne in the Council Chamber. He held his Tambootie staff in his right hand, the base fully grounded on the stone floor. The white dragon bone had dulled but remained permanently embedded in the wood, as much a part of it as the spirals and knots of the grain. On the other side of the king, Da braced his own staff.

Behind them, Fred lurked. He had a bandage about his brow and scanned the room through eyes that dropped and winced at every shift of light. But he was there, trying desperately to atone for his absence when his king needed him most.

"Linda is safe?" King Darville asked quietly. Dark hollows ringed his eyes, and the flesh of his cheeks sagged. He wore the heavy Coraurlia, wincing at the headache it gave him. Still, he had recovered enough to command this meeting with the lords, less than a day after the battle, with only a short night of sleep.

A full dozen healers from the University had arrived as Linda soared away with Indigo. The red-robed magicians had restored nearly one hundred wounded citizens and soldiers to health, including their king and Lord Jemmarc.

No one knew where Master Robb and his journeymen had gone, only that they'd transported out of the New University an hour before the healers.

The ones the Krakatrice had killed were truly dead and gone.

Lucjemm survived, barely, not having awakened from his coma. No one knew if he would awaken, or if he'd have a sound mind should he open his eyes again. The healers took him back to the University for the constant care he'd need.

"The dragons assure me that Linda is safe with Brevelan and the children in the clearing," Da replied.

"Maigret is preparing to teach her proper spells and potions," Glenndon added, having more recent news directly from the exiled princess. His bond of blood and magic remained as strong as ever, even separated by a thousand miles.

A herald opened the door to the circular chamber and cleared his throat. Then, in his specially trained voice, he announced the entrance of the lords, giving their full names and titles as they passed him in order of precedence and seniority.

Andrall, first in line, was accompanied by his grandson, Master Mikkette, a curious boy of medium coloring and slim shoulders who looked around him with eyes wide and mouth closed.

Glenndon studied the boy eagerly, wondering how his cousin would fit in at the court as another potential heir.

Jemmarc entered last, stripped of seniority because of his son's leadership in the recent rebellion and his attack upon the Princess Royale. He wore iron restraints around his wrists, and two armed guards in the king's green livery accompanied him. His fate would be decided during the meeting.

A line of eleven anonymous magicians followed the lords. Glenndon knew them all, of course, but for now, they remained nameless. Each blue-robed man took a place, standing behind the chair of a lord. Some of the nobles glared at the additions to the Council. Others made warding gestures and hunched closer to the black glass table, putting as much distance between them and the magicians as they could.

"Your Grace, I protest the presence of magicians in our *private meeting*," Lord Laislac said, without preamble or permission.

"You have no say in the matter," Darville said firmly. "If this Council is to resume governing Coronnan, it will be done as it has always been done, with magician advisers beside each of us. I have recalled the Senior Magician to my side. He has appointed each of you a master magician based upon personality and seniority."

Glenndon noted that Samlan and his followers were noticeably absent. Their exile from the University was something that would have to be addressed, but not today.

The question of why Master Robb and his three journeymen had failed to come to Jaylor's aid was also under investigation by Master Marcus. He could find no trace of his longtime friend and the students.

"The question of your heir still must be settled," Jemmarc reminded them all.

"I have a son and a young cousin present," the king said curtly.

"But your son is a magician. Your cousin the child of a rogue witch and an idiot," Laislac snarled.

"My cousin is your grandson, sir," the king snarled. "You abandoned all governance of him when still an infant. To date he has shown no inclination to the . . . infirmities of either of his parents. In fact, I am told he has trained for the Temple and is better read than any of you."

"What of your son?" another lord asked.

"What of my son? He did more to save this kingdom from monsters and chaos than all of you combined."

"But the law says . . ."

"You ignored the laws regarding magician advisers. I chose to rewrite, and record, the laws regarding magicians within the royal family."

"Your Grace!" they all protested loudly.

"Enough!" Jaylor bellowed, pounding his staff.

The entire room vibrated with his anger and his power.

"I need to learn how to do that," Glenndon muttered, examining his own staff. That dragon bone was unique, special . . .

(The magic in the bone is limited. You used it all up in one grand gesture. Then you recharged it from the Well. That can happen only once. Use it sparingly.)

"You need to learn to listen and study the governance of this land," the king reminded Glenndon. "You need to become as much a part of this Council as you are a part of the University." Then he returned his attention to the lords. "Now as to the University of Magicians, you will have noted that they have resumed residence in the buildings granted them three hundred years ago by Nimbulan and King Quinnault. My troops have moved to the Old Keep within the palace grounds. Magic is not illegal in Coronnan. It never has been."

"We have not voted on that, Your Grace," Lord Andrall reminded him.

"Must we vote on a return to normal?" King Darville raised one eyebrow. "We will vote on new matters. Now we will discuss and vote on the matter of Jemmarc and his rebellion against the Dragon Crown. Then we will address my son's status as heir and the return of my daughter to court." He squeezed Glenndon's arm in reassurance. "I will not lose you, boy. Not now. Not ever."

"Same here," Jaylor muttered. "He's mine as much as he is yours."

Glenndon smiled, certain of his place in the world for the first time.

※

And so life and politics in Coronnan settle back into predictable patterns. Patterns I have longed to be a part of but have been barred from by Jaylor.

Soon the magicians and the lords will fall back into complacency.

They have forgotten the threat upon their border. They have forgotten that their wealth has left others in desperate poverty. They have forgotten how vulnerable they truly are.

That is when I shall attack. From without and from within. Their magic and their dragons are not enough to defeat the troops and the armada I control from the Big Continent to their east. I have captured Master Robb and his students. Diverted his transport spell with the simple insertion into his mind of a new destination, a port city with tall towers, similar to Coronnan City, but not the same.

Long did the Circle of Masters ignore my power and my

seniority. Soon they will learn the error of their ways. Soon they will bow to me and not the usurper Jaylor.

I have adopted the name the locals have given to my refuge. A name befitting me.

Monbastion.

Jaylor and the Circle think they have stripped me of power by the simple expedient of exile. They should have killed me.

I will not be so merciful.

Irene Radford's

THE DRAGON NIMBUS NOVELS
now available in three omnibus editions!

VOLUME ONE   978-0-7564-0451-2
    (The Glass Dragon, The Perfect Princess,
      & The Loneliest Magician)

VOLUME TWO   978-0-7564-0453-6
    (The Dragon's Touchstone &
      The Last Battlemage)

VOLUME THREE   978-0-7564-0468-0
    (The Renegade Dragon &
      The Wizard's Treasure)

and don't miss

THE STAR GODS

THE HIDDEN DRAGON   978-0-7564-0051-4
THE DRAGON CIRCLE   978-0-7564-0194-8
THE DRAGON'S REVENGE   978-0-7564-0317-1

"A mesmerizing storyteller." —*Romantic Times*

To Order Call: 1-800-788-6262

Irene Radford

The Pixie Chronicles

Dusty Carrick lived in the small town of Skene Falls, Oregon, her entire life. And, like many of the local children, she played with "imaginary" Pixie friends in Ten Acre Woods.

But the Pixies are not imaginary at all, and Ten Acre Woods is their home. Now, the woods are in danger, and if it falls, the Pixies too will die. Only Thistle Down, exiled from her tribe and trapped inside a mortal woman's body, can save her people-as long as she can convince Dusty Carrick to help her before it's too late.

THISTLE DOWN
978-0-7564-0670-7

CHICORY UP
978-0-7564-0724-7

"Enjoyable romantic urban fantasy." —*Alternative Worlds*

To Order Call: 1-800-788-6262
www.dawbooks.com

DAW 208

P.R. Frost

The Tess Noncoiré Adventures

HOUNDING THE MOON
978-0-7564-0425-3

MOON IN THE MIRROR
978-0-7564-0486-4

FAERY MOON
978-0-7564-0606-6

and new in paperback:

FOREST MOON RISING
978-0-7564-0710-0

To Order Call: 1-800-788-6262
www.dawbooks.com

DAW 70

Violette Malan

The Novels of Dhulyn and Parno:

"Believable characters and graceful storytelling."
—*Library Journal*

"Fantasy fans should brace themselves:
the world is about to discover Violette Malan."
—*The Barnes & Noble Review*

THE SLEEPING GOD
978-0-7564-0484-0

THE SOLDIER KING
978-0-7564-0569-4

THE STORM WITCH
978-0-7564-0574-8

and

PATH OF THE SUN
978-0-7564-0680-6

To Order Call: 1-800-788-6262
www.dawbooks.com

Fiona Patton

The Warriors of Estavia

"In this bold first of a new fantasy series... Court intrigues enrich the story, as do many made-up words that lend color. The smashing climax neatly sets up events for volume two." —*Publishers Weekly*

"The best aspect of this explosive series opener is Patton's take on relations between gods and men."
—*Booklist*

"Fresh and interesting...I look forward to the next."
—*Science Fiction Chronicle*

THE SILVER LAKE
978-0-7564-0366-9

THE GOLDEN TOWER
978-0-7564-0577-9

THE SHINING CITY
978-0-7564-0717-9

To Order Call: 1-800-788-6262
www.dawbooks.com

Once upon a time...

Cinderella, whose real name is Danielle
Whiteshore, did marry Prince Armand.
And their wedding was a dream come true.

But not long after the "happily ever after,"
Danielle is attacked by her stepsister Charlotte,
who suddenly has all sorts of magic to call upon.
And though Talia the martial arts master—
otherwise known as Sleeping Beauty—
comes to the rescue, Charlotte gets away.

That's when Danielle discovers a number of disturbing facts: Armand has been kidnapped; Danielle is
pregnant; and the Queen has her own Secret Service
that consists of Talia and Snow (White, of course).
Snow is an expert at mirror magic and heavy-duty
flirting. Can the princesses track down Armand and
rescue him from the clutches of some of
Fantasyland's most nefarious villains?

The Stepsister Scheme
by Jim C. Hines
978-0-7564-0532-8

"Do we look like we need to be rescued?"

DAW 130